ALSO BY C.E. HOLMES

Okoboji: Puppet Show of Memory

EXCAVATING OKOBOJI

To the Beat of the Waves

EXCAVATING OKOBOJI

To the Beat of the Waves

A Novel

C.E. Holmes

Iowa Master Book Breeders

2008

ISBN: 978-1-57579-380-1

Library of Congress Control Number: 2008928000

Cover painting: *The Swimmer,* Mike Koppert (1982)

All characters, with the splendid exception of the Fun Fouse Clown,
are fictitious examples of the author's spurious imagination
and should not – indeed, *may not* – be mistaken for any
person, be they living, deceased, or yet to be born.

Iowa Master Book Breeders
201 N. Garfield, Dell Rapids, SD 57022

Printed in the United States of America

PINE HILL PRESS
4000 West 57th Street
Sioux Falls, SD 57106

For Rynn

And to the memory of
Ruth Harper McKee

Whose friendship and encouragement,
beginning in the spring of 1982, in St. Paul,
sustained, inspired, and spurred on the author.

"You're going to miss me, you know"

And I do

So that when I stretched out my hand,
I caught hold of the Fille de Chambres

Laurence Sterne
"A Sentimental Journey
Through France and Italy,"
by Mr. Yorick

A note of some importance:

Parenthesis couched within the text, and indicating an Act and Scene (i.e. Act Four, Scene V) are referring to relevant spisodes in "Okoboji: Puppet Show of Memory" that may help to clarify or even elucidate the situation at hand in this novel, which may be considered a sequal to the earlier book.

– C.E.H.

TABLE OF CONTENTS

West Lake Okoboji

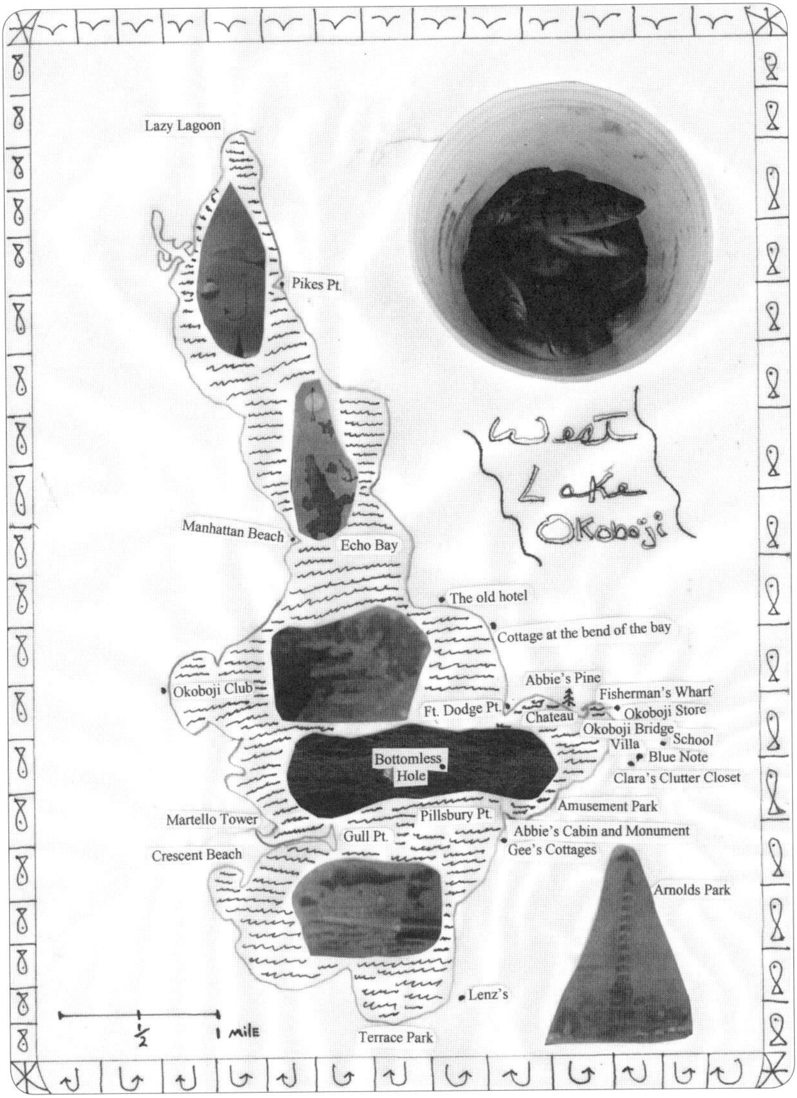

AMUSEMENT PARK

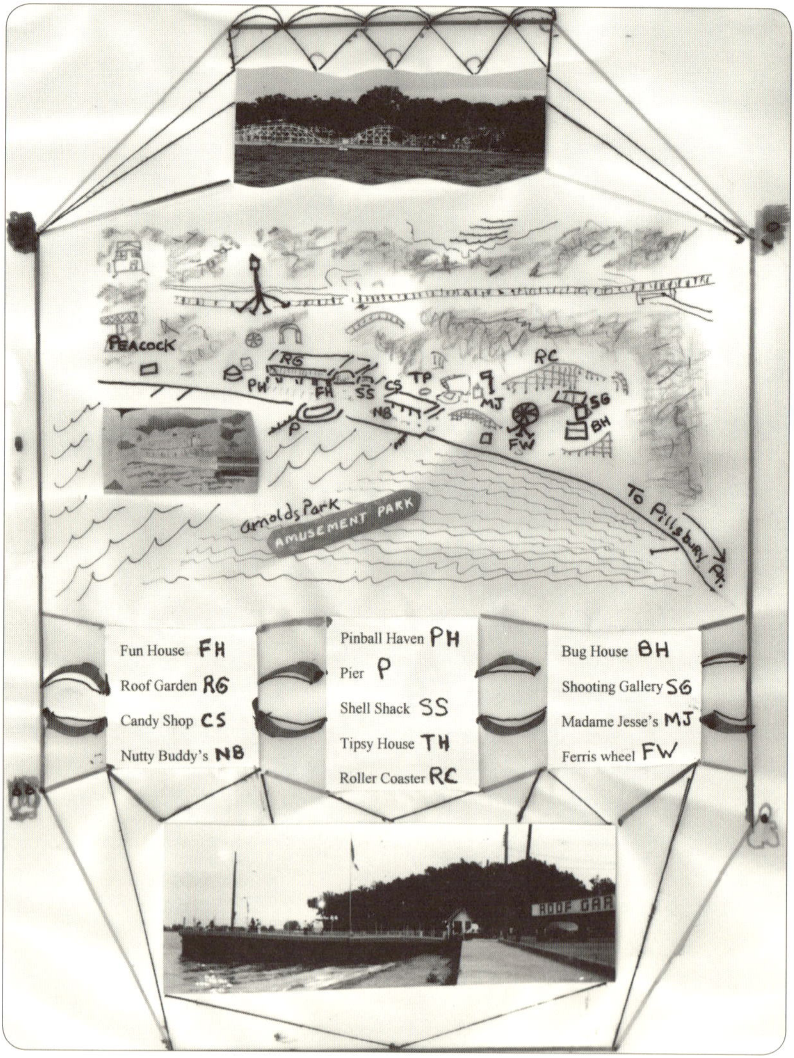

FOREWORD

If one of life's fervent desires is to achieve a *sweeping view,* Larue had wheeled himself into position to partake of a panorama which was second to none. He simply had to turn his head to marvel at the crumbling Depression-era bridge and the train-less trestle and Fisherman's Wharf and Smiths Bay and the amusement park - *the whole show!* - from his card table to the left of the door as you came out of the Okoboji Store.

He greeted everyone and sold souvenirs and leaned back in his wheelchair under a shady umbrella awning to wave at the cars and occasionally flash that famous sunny flying smile of his, unforgettable once it was beamed your way, together with his bright red baseball cap, scintillating orange t-shirt and high pitched valved voice. And who can forget the way that he reached for the items that made up his inventory, which had somehow discovered a route from their place of manufacture, however distant, to this strategically positioned souvenir laden card table guarding the straits of the Okobojis…and now his hands worked in unison to hover over his card table until one of them dropped down to pluck a postcard, a pen, a comb, a lighter, a battery - and hand it to you and receive your money, feeling the bills and coins, not for their authenticity, but as if to try and determine where they'd been, and why it took so long for them to reach their proper slot in the tray which anchored

The Inn Hotel on Beautiful Lake Okoboji, Iowa

the sports page folded so as to be able to easily consult the standings - *Yeah, those damn Yankees have increased their lead to eleven and a half games!* Larue exclaimed, returning your change, and at the same time shedding a whole new Iowa midsummer's sun and clouds light on the purchasing experience.

Postcards were Larue's hottest selling item, so he featured a vast array of the little three by five inch gravity defying compositions twirling about on rotating stands positioned at the far corners of his card table. They were magic mirrors! They were revolving reflections! They had been captured and printed by a local photographer nicknamed Sqintin' Vinton. They could be had for a nickel, and then a dime. They could be mailed for a penny, then two pennies, then three, then five. Whatever the price, they flooded the mailboxes and filled the mailbags, arriving and departing via the same route as the music, which is to say: *across the fields*.

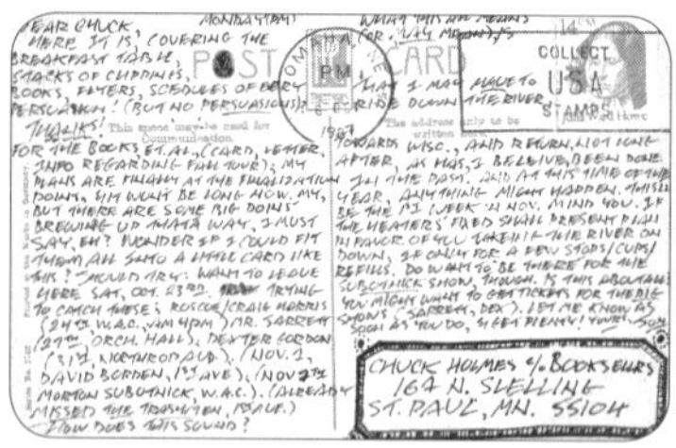

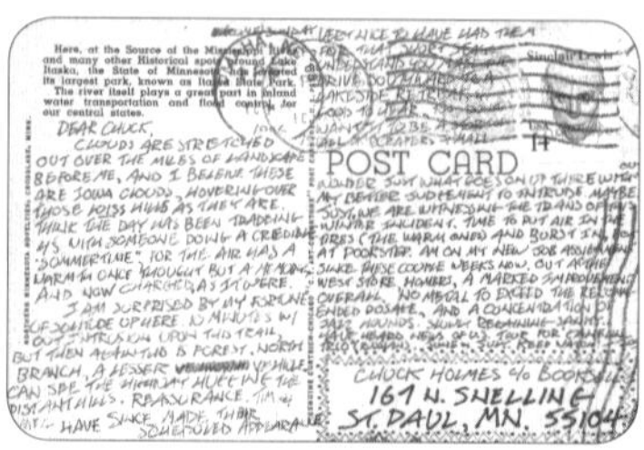

But hey! Maybe you missed the *Age of the Postcard*? Maybe you weren't even alive in the days when each carved and initialed wooden bench overlooking every dizzying lover's leap was occupied by *the one left behind*, who was so intent on distilling a tender thought (which must somehow fit in the space marked *Message*) for the one who had gone ahead, that the approaching thunderhead went unheaded until limbs and branches began to crack and crash. Correspondents were consumed with breezy salutations and fond farewells to the point where they completely forgot the great lesson of their correspondence teachers: *Conciseness! Students, conciseness!* It was distressing, to say the least, when precious tidings regularly overflowed their boundaries, especially given the effect of nib nosed pens on the looping handwriting of the day. But the later ball points were just as guilty in allowing a crabbed style of writing to sneak across the border, so that the side reserved for the stamp and address was always under assault.

Hand tinters, those curiously patient Bartleby-type technicians, were in high demand to heighten the colors of each scene, because the notoriety of a lake or a mountain or a city was based on the number of postcards it inspired, produced and dispersed. And then there were the collectors, who fought over and even tragically ripped rare postcards in half, like the one of the prairie when it was covered by an ocean, and the sky above the pink cliffs of Pipestone was thick with sea birds. We hesitate to mention the presence of spies (although this should please the conspiracy theorists out there). Among these spies were certain postal workers, who read other people's postcards and dispatched ones of their own, consisting of boiled slogans and simmering statements, unsigned of course, unless they'd succumbed to the use of an alias.

All this is to suggest that Larue and Vinton were both progenitors of the so-called *Postcard Era*. Larue would know the time frame, because he anchored the Okoboji Store. He was the one who kept it from flying away. Anybody coming into Okoboji from the south or leaving Okoboji from the north had to pass by Larue and receive his wave, which was a kind of blessing. After he left his post, the Okoboji Store became a victim, along with Fisherman's Wharf and the Fun House and the Roof Garden - to name just a few - of that propaganda called progress.

We decided to step back in time…to have a little talk with Larue… this man who used to know what everyone was up to…maybe he could help us find our missing puppet…

Now, when you say puppet, do you mean puppet as in a doll-like figure? Or are you speaking about a puppet as a marionette; a doll with strings, in other words; a lively doll, a doll with imagination, my favorite kind of doll. Or, more mysteriously, are you hinting at a pupa, a chrysalis, and the possibility of a butterfly? Now, I see all three pass by here all the time, heading both directions. Does this puppet you're looking for have a name?

He calls himself Carl.

Carl? Well, let's see, we've got at least three Carls around here. One of them owns a beer joint just up the street, you can see it from here, Carl's Place, where they smoke cigars and play cards day and night. And one is a champion trapshooter, shoots those little disks - what do they call them? - clay pigeons, blows them to pieces in the sky above the lake, and then they fall into the water and litter the lake bottom. And the other Carl I know of is a rather strange character, but he's also one of my best customers, because he collects postcards, he's passionate about postcards, he thinks anything that you want to say in life - or say well, that's how he puts it - any statement of love or hate or loss or regret should be able to fit on the left hand side of a postcard. Yeah, he's a character alright. He had some kind of boating accident on the Fourth of July, and now he goes by here on his bike.

Yeah yeah, that's him, that's who we're looking for.

That Carl? I just saw him! Let me think. Which way was he going? So many people go by here. Ten thousand cars crossed that bridge on the Fourth of July. It's hard to keep track of them all. But I remember Carl, because he was all wet. So if you just follow the drips...he had a newspaper rolled up in his back pocket, and he was headed south. He likes to eat breakfast in the amusement park. Check the little place between the roller rink and the cotton candy stand. You'll probably find him there.

We have no idea if you've had a chance to read *Okoboji: Puppet Show of Memory* - the little book with the watercolor of the prodigal sunbather on the cover. Maybe you read it, or part of it, but like a trip around the world, you got lost in all the time changes (which isn't going to happen this time, because we're going to hang around to guide you from scene to scene, so there shouldn't be too much confusion about where you are in the time scheme).

But just to tell you anyway: at the end of that book, Carl, who's in the water dog paddling for his life on the Fourth of July during the fireworks show, tells the Fortune Teller's daughter - as if she could hear him, much less save him - to meet him at Varna. That's Varna on the *Black Sea*! Notice how this *poseur* is forever dragging in the names of distant places and comparing them to Okoboji? We're here to tell you that Carl has about as much chance of getting to Varna as we have of making it back to New Orleans for the feast of St. Sebastien.

But life is amazing. There's so much to imagine. A good view is essential. You have arrived at the isthmus of the Okobojis. You are perfectly positioned.

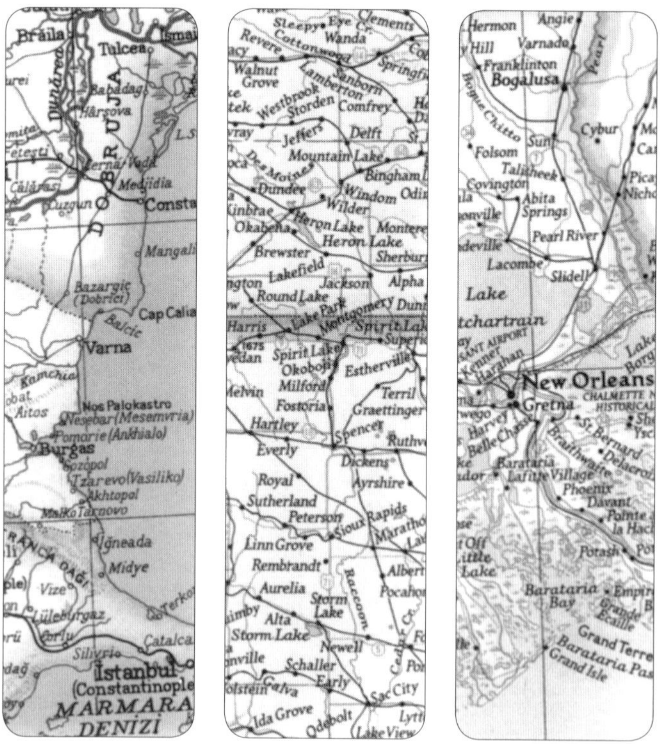

PART ONE

POSTCARDS

It was in the waning days of the Postcard Age - and, by coincidence, on the anniversary as well of the crash at twilight, out in the middle of Okoboji, of the Thriller and the Zipper – that the postcards began to arrive...

I.

A Cure For Instability

The indolent dream sleeper who'd floated through the wide open window on the waves of a night air bath to lay passively supine across an all but hairless chest had already drifted back to her kettle hole before the guy who ran the roller coaster could pound a single spike - there was never a shortage of wobbly ones, or the subsequent echoing forth across the lake to every corner of every bedroom - of sound through the heart of a man who would have rather been awakened by the birds or the cuckoo clock or the Skylingstad's three doxies.

His eyes opened to see spiders spinning their webs in the low beams of the bedroom ceiling, while the leafy branches scratched loose white paint from the cedar siding, and Mrs. Skylingstad shouted as if to make herself heard across a valley in the Alps: *Here Gretchen! Here Heidi! Here Honz!*

Immediately after the gratifying abdication of the contents of his abdomen, he shook the flakes out of the brightly colored box, and drank his coffee from a chipped teacup, and tripped over a throw rug on his way to jiggle the handle of the downstairs toilet which ran eternally. They were - box, plate, teacup, throw rug, toilet - like old friends that he'd invited, along with Claire, to share in his vacation.

But what is a vacation, and could his stay at Okoboji truthfully be called one, and - more to the point - did he even deserve one? For shouldn't he have earned this release from duty, and have broken a sweat and pocketed a paycheck and paid one's debts? Remember, if you will, those seventeen IOUs - those of you who read Volume One (Act Four, Scene I) - which were consolidated into one supra IOU, due on the day after Labor Day, as a result of the *Dixon Beach Accord,* signed late in the morning after that wild night when the delinquent ice had gone out.

And speaking of going out, Carl had taken to going out for an additional breakfast each morning, or nearly every morning, because of his close call at the end of the previous volume, which had convinced him of the necessity to enjoy life more. And since life, the starting over life of each new day, began at breakfast, he got up and had a bowl of cereal, and then immediately went out for an additional breakfast, having worked up a ravenous appetite during the night before, due to the visits of the nocturnal previously mentioned indolent dream sleeper, and in addition simply to immerse himself in the ways of a world that he was always desirous of belonging to, though at a delirious distance…

His day followed a remarkably strict routine for someone so unstructured, and, with the summer he lived for nearly half over, which leads the conspiracy theorists among us were led to wonder if his was not so much a vacation as an *intelligence gathering mission.* And yet he took few pictures, he made no phone calls, and he watched zero TV. Only a few scattered thoughts were recorded in his notebook. Granted, he carried postcards to the post office, but he didn't write them and he never mailed them.

He'd had his accident, and been saved by a Navy Seal, and come out of it with only a little lake water swallowed, not enough to drown a person. He'd lived on to read the story of his own rescue no page nine of the *Des Moines Register*, which at that time was still a great newspaper, although it was nearing the end of its greatness. He went on to get caught up in the other stories of the day, and in particular he always wanted to hear what Donald Kaul had to say, because he felt, as many early risers do, that a decent breakfast could not be properly digested without news and opinion, and so he set off first to fetch a daily from the machines outside the hotel down the beach. There was nothing the least bit haphazard concerning his choice of newspaper...

He sprinkled his bike ride with little hums, snatches of tunes such as...oh, you know the ones...they're the same old songs as in Volume One...

Out of all the possible and impossible breakfast spots around the lake, he almost always chose the oblong one in Arnolds Park, between the skating rink and the candy shop, because its slanted windows afforded the best view of the early morning amusement park. The stools were comfortable, and the coffee plentiful and strong, with a taste of chicory in it. And there was room to spread out a paper which an attentive waitress, if she were on her toes, could read upside down while waiting for the bacon to crispy fry. And the toast - the toast! - she indulged him in his love of rye toast that was buttered on both sides. And those packets of jelly were in abundance, she stacked them in a little leaning tower to the side of his plate, and quietly averted her eyes so that he could sneakily stock up on them, without being noticed, without being observed, abundant jellies, particularly raspberry, his berry of choice (*don't forget to water the raspberries*, he made a mental note). And as he jellied the brownest side he could watch, through the wrap around windows which leaned out at an angle, the amusement park yawn and stretch and come to life on a muggy late July morning.

To say that Carl knew the amusement park intimately is no exaggeration. It's the intense depth of his morbid interest in it that is more of a puzzle. Possibly for him - and here we can only speculate - it was a microcosm of the world at large, albeit a more interesting one. And at the same time it transcended the so-called real world to feed his imagination. There were infinite correspondences afloat in the old amusement park. For instance, this early morning scene he took in through the oblique windows was one of cleaning, sweeping, and getting ready for the new day - the identical skills he'd developed working for his grandmother as a child - how to vacuum and sweep and wipe - and which had stood him in such good stead in his professional life as a janitor in St. Paul. And the mirrors behind the pinball machines in the Pinball Haven that Jerry was spraying and wiping at the very moment that Carl put a piece of crispy slaughtered pig in to the bridgeless crownless corner of his mouth as he leaned over to peruse the fashion advertisements - these were the identical mirrors that his grandfather and father and Carl himself had spent hours in front of adjusting every wind blown hair, while his grandmother and mother and Patience had waited for their men at the top of the Roof Garden stairs, those tickets still in their hands. (Who should Jerry see sneaking up on him in the clear, for the time being, glass but Pesky Pete, no doubt to ask for a loan, the sponge, until pay day.)

It would have been only another in a long string of coincidences - and he was always on the lookout for them - which continually besieged Carl whenever he came over to Arnolds Park - no matter by boat or bike - if he had glanced up from his paper in time to see Sheri cleaning the same candy shop window which his grandfather had been standing in front of way back in the depth of the Depression, waiting to buy a caramel apple when he heard the scream and looked up (Act One, Scene III). But why was Sheri wiping so furiously, scrubbing so violently? Were those Depression era bugs still stuck on the windows after all these years, or was she being pursued by one of the characters in a novel that she could not put down; which so engrossed her that customers had to rap on the window - and thus smudge it, and thus dirty it, and hence all her furious cleaning - to break into the spell that had come over her once again?

While on the lake side of the candy shop there was the ever industrious Nutty Buddy, sweeping vertically from stem to stern the cobwebs that cohabited in the cracks of his shiny white wainscoting. He was neither a dreamer nor a pursuer, but an anticipator of weather, fair or foul, who never turned his back on a cloud, however light or scattered or lonely. They would never find each other today - the clouds - and so all of his doors were raised to send this signal to tourist and local alike: *It's the summer you've waited for, it's here, it's arrived, but it won't last forever!*

As Carl turned back to his newspaper to ponder further the violent political swings going on in the world, the waitress approached bearing more coffee, and he thought he could detect, in the graceful way she returned the steaming pot to its warming pad, without prejudice or anger at his refusal to have *one more cup* or even *one more half a cup*, a cure for the instability of the world, right there and at that instant, a few feet from the shore of Lake Okoboji, in the oblong restaurant between the skating rink and the candy shop.

The waitress spun the postcard display rack on the counter around - just set it spinning like it was a roulette wheel - it spun and swayed, creaking and swiveling like it was some amusement park ride, and *where it lands, that place you shall ride past,* so Carl waited for it to stop spinning...when it finally came to a standstill an old card of the Okoboji Store and Larue was facing him, looking him right in the eyes.

While at the same moment, in the post office at Okoboji, a frowning mail person slid a postcard into Carl's box. Although he paused to look at the picture, it is not known if he read the message...

Back in the amusement park, Jerry, taking a ten minute break, with his own ideas on the history of instability bumping around in the back of his head, said to no one in particular, when he tripped over a fresh crack in the concrete and spilled a few French fries: *Let it all fall down!* And then he said it again, this time with greater emphasis on the *down*, because he'd heard the rumors and taken them to heart. Ethel's French fries were salted to perfection, they were light and hot, and there was no residual grease. They would be the only loss, not this junk, thought Jerry, walking past the window of the Shell Shack, where the indomitable Mrs. Bird was dusting off her conch shells and rearranging her crab claw key chains. The junk people will buy, said Jerry to a reflection of himself peering in at a row of sand dollars and seahorses.

But then he saw Darla - Darla the ringmaster of the stunning seal show - a cyclopean seahorse hanging from her neck, doing figure eights around the blue poles which held up the Roof Garden. He marveled at how her reflected image had the strength to seize control of each pane of every window she passed. Why, she even turned the head of the Fun House Clown, and to such an extreme angle - for him - that he had a most terrible time returning it back over his sagging left shoulder.

By now it should be evident that people like Carl, who came back summer after summer to wander through an amusement park which was more and more deserted, did not actually walk past their reflections as they were, but as they had been. And these clean or dirty, clear or obscure reflections in glass were never cast back in a straight line, as people in any city are accustomed to seeing - no, they were always spinning uniquely counterclockwise in circles, once the line was crossed between everything outside the amusement park as *it wasn't*, and everything inside the amusement park, as *it was*.

"OK. Where do we go from here?"

"It's the same morning. Carl finishes his second breakfast in the amusement park, rides his bike back over to Okoboji, back across the bridge -"

"Does he wave to Larue?"

"Of course he waves to Larue! Everyone waves to Larue, and Larue waves to everyone."

"And then?"

"And then he goes to the post office, and opens his box, and takes out the postcard with the picture of Lake Louise on it."

"Lake Louise? I've always wanted to go to Lake Louise. They say that the water there -"

"One lake at a time, my friend. We're at Okoboji now. This next scene demands that we have an overview, so I want you to imagine that we're on top of a water tower –"

"I don't do water towers! I don't like heights!"

"I'm not asking you to climb a water tower. I'm only asking that you imagine that you have a view like you would if you happened to be on top of a water tower on Dixon Beach right at the curve of the bay."

"Where our story takes place…"

"Yes, where the majority of our story takes place. So, we're up on this mythical red-capped water tower, and we can see the Queen starting out from the amusement park, heading up the lake, and we can see all the boats and swimmers and sunbathers, but we're going to focus our attention on one boat - a rowboat - and on one person standing out on the end of a short dock, with a postcard in one hand and a pair of binoculars in the other."

"OK. I think I…I think I got it…"

"Then let's go!"

II.

Without Words

I read the message, glanced at the picture, jammed the postcard in my t-shirt pocket, forgot or neglected to mail Claire's letters and postcards, and pedaled to the cottage…without stopping…

Claire wasn't in her room…

She wasn't in my room…

I don't know why she would have been in my room…

Unless she was looking for money…

She wasn't reading in the bathtub…or in the kitchen either…although there was a book propped up against an empty cereal bowl…

She wasn't lounging in the chair of reflection on the front porch, scribbling notes to herself while swaddled in that colorful peacock bathrobe which she'd abducted from the closet in my grandmother's old room…nor was she out in the front yard, throwing a ball for the kids next door…

I grabbed the WWII Pacific Theater binoculars from the piano top and scanned the horizon, from Sunset Beach to Gull Point to Millers Bay.

Then I spotted her…

She wasn't too terribly far off the end of the dock, rowing for all she was worth toward the middle of the lake with the guy who ran the roller coaster.

I pushed open the front porch door and dashed across the front yard to the edge of the bank, dodging doxies and leaping over left behind toys.

First I tried to get her attention by alternately waving the postcard and the binoculars...

When that didn't work I scuttled down the steps and ran out to the end of the dock - one of the shortest docks on the lake that summer - to wave the postcard some more. But they were rowing with such intensity that they didn't appear to see me...at first...

MacJames was the first to notice, and after he'd nudged Claire, I had her attention at last. She didn't stop rowing though. No, if anything, she appeared to be straining at her oar so hard that she was half standing up.

Through the binoculars I saw her lips take on a quizzical shape. And then I heard her *What?* reverberating across the lake as if it'd been launched from a tuning fork.

I had what I considered an important message (a message of a private nature) to convey to Claire (and to Claire only), but how was I to accomplish this transfer across so much water and amid so many boats?

Because everyone knows that *words*, and specifically the meanings of words, dissolve over great distances, leaving the receiver grasping at mere leftover sounds.

But a song...maybe a song might reach her...

Hadn't my grandfather told me many times that the human voice in song is the greatest instrument in the world?

Notice how the singer is always out in front of the band, he pointed out to me once, when we were watching a show on TV called *The Shape of Jazz.*

A song, my grandfather defined, is simply a series of discrete sonic symbols. And because symbols as such appeal directly to the imagination, a symbolic song will carry across great distances of water, and even around the world, if it's a strong enough song, like *Summertime* or *A Woman is a Sometime Thing.*

Following his reasoning then, I had only to make my little tune come to life across a relatively short distance of Lake Okoboji. There was the danger that the symbol which Claire would deduce from my singing - if

I could come up with a song suitable to convey the essence of the message on the postcard - might not mean to her the thing that I'd intended it to mean.

She might have to wait until she was directly over the bottomless hole for my discreet communication to sink in to her subconscious.

So it was up to me to sing the song, and I stood alone out on the end of my little slivery stage, reviewing my abilities in a desultory fashion.

I had neither a powerful lower range nor a majestic upper range. In fact, I had no range at all. And yet I imagined myself singing with all the fervor and piety of a soloist in a choir in a cathedral.

I had no idea how my song would stand up against the other great songs which had swept across Okoboji. I knew that I was at a distinct disadvantage, because I had neither a shiny silver trumpet nor a twelve string Rickenbacker nor an electric violin to accompany me.

I envisaged that the roots of my song would be Middle Eastern, but performed in English with a Midwestern twang.

Maybe...maybe I should have some accompaniment after all, so as to not feel so all alone on my stage. Yes...a flute, a flute and an oboe, a clarinet and a bassoon. And a French horn, of course! But where was I to find a wind octet, and at such short notice? Okoboji has never been a gathering place for wind octets or sting quartets, or even piano trios, for that matter.

And what about the keen ear I would need, to say nothing of great breath control and the ability to float top notes and sustain strong low notes? Not to mention a *vivid dramatizing persona*...

I had only my peripatetic imagination.

But...if I waited much longer for a song to come to me, she was going to be out of listening range and I'd be left like a bird on a wire.

Open your mouth and just sing! I vociferated internally.

I had to make it *happen!* I had to sing it sensitive and swing it smooth...

Instead of a wind octet, what I really needed was a big band behind me. Yeah, five reeds, four trumpets, three trombones, a bass, a set of drums, and with myself at the glistening Steinway, snapping my fingers to the beat…waiting for Billie to appear from the wings…and walk out to the end of the dock and join me.

How she commanded time and swing! Her tonal variation. Her vibrato. Her reshaping of a melody line to make it her own. "*Fish are jumpin'*" for instance.

Fish were jumping! I thought I saw a big northern…or a walleye…

Sense the mood, I said to myself, so that she'll want to turn around…and come back…

Come back to restore our disharmonious landscape…

It just didn't seem like it would work…to sing a lyric like:

My soul rises
to your nut brown eyes
the way a lake sighs
toward the sky

Those flowery words had nothing at all to do with the simple and concise message on the postcard.

Ah, to hell with my soupy soul! I thought. Claire could care less about that part of my anatomy. She wanted her money back. That's what she was interested in.

But I was hung up on my voice: its lightness and brightness; its color and pitch and tone. It must display a transparent clarity, together with a rich feeling of gentile desire, if it was ever to have a chance of reaching her - and her alone - across that increasing - by - the - instant distance of water.

Because in the midst of all my analysis, Claire and MacJames hadn't stopped rowing for a second - on the contrary, they were rowing harder and harder, while sighting in on some landmark, no doubt, like Abbie's pine or a water tower, to carry them directly over the bottomless hole.

What I actually needed, I imagined, was a microphone, and a microphone stand, and a powerful PA system with a bank of amplifiers in back of me. And a rooster tail haircut, and a gravelly voice, and a rock and roll band with a horn section. And a catchy tune, and a refrain with a hook, and me holding that mike stand so that the base of it was straight up in the air, and I was surrounded by groupies, so that Claire couldn't even see me, just the base of the stand twirling around in the air. But she could hear my broadcast, it was coming through loud and clear, there was no mistake about what I was trying to get across...

Up on top of the bank, the Skylingstads - mother, son, and doxies - were waiting...just waiting for me to make a fool of myself.

Was it any wonder that Claire was rowing away from this scene as fast as she could? As if music, and music alone, could reconnect us.

Was I carrying this song thing too far?

It was only a postcard, after all...

I didn't care...

It was now or never.

I drew in a deep breath...I leaned forward, one foot in front of the other...legs straight, but not locked...firm buttocks, standing tall, elongating myself...a slight bow in my back...I threw my arms out, and I sang, as if I was Paul Robeson:

Your daddy's rich...and your momma's...

But the Queen...the Queen came out of nowhere to barge between us, and the strong flow of my voice - which was striving to reach the rear of the lake - drew back and faded into a gentile and disarming ebb...after the Queen had so rudely inserted herself between Claire and I.

The wind had been yanked out of my singing sails as well by two multidentate comments which had snuck under the curtain across the musical side of my brain. One, from my grandfather, had come to me in a dream:

Remember this Carl: when you feel like singing a song, sing it!

That encouraged me...but the other one...the other more damaging one - which had come from a night early in our stay at Okoboji, when I'd been singing along to *Salt Peanuts* on the record player, while at the same time typing Claire's work - came after she'd stamped downstairs to sneer at me in a biting tone: *What is there about your singing that makes me want to scream?*

And what is there about music I wondered, then as well as now, that appeals so directly to our emotions?

Both my grandfather *and* Claire should have heard the song I ended up singing to myself out there on the end of that little dock. The tone alone seemed pleasing enough to invite anyone on the lake or along the lake on that day or any day in the past or in the future - anyone who had the slightest desire to hear my private and personnel recital to *please ...please come in!* I wasn't singing just for Claire, or for myself, anymore. No, I had become by this time a *character in the music*, waiting for the long 'e' to come around again, so that I might stretch it out across the lake to her and him and all the rest of them. I was outdoors - I wasn't hemmed in by the concert hall - I was free to sing as softly and as quietly as I wanted, and without losing so much as a syllable. My voice mingled with the waves - the waves from the Queen, and all the other waves as well. Their inevitable splash - or crash, as the case may be - on the shore was the accompaniment that I'd been looking for.

There are people who never dance, but they imagine that if the chips were down and they had to dance, they could get up and dance, and dance beautifully. Or, they could hit the ball a mile - or throw the pass in the corner of the end zone - or make the speech that would leave the audience shaking their heads - or slay the dragon that was in the garden eating all the raspberries. For me the provocation was singing. Because I believed that for a singer to sing, all that was necessary was to be in love with *words*. And I loved words, especially their matchless peerless incantations. I carried sounds around with me like some people carry silver dollars. Wherever I went I heard them jingling in my mind. And like everyone, I had my favorites. *Patina*, for instance. That was one of my adored words. I saw the surface of the lake between Claire and I as a patina, and when the postcard that I'd been waving about all this time - as if it were a flag or a baton or a landing light - slipped from my fingers and fell into the lake, and the printer's ink blue of Lake Louise was formally introduced to Okoboji's truer blue, it faded - of course - in comparison.

It faded to the point of pure contradiction!

And then it blended together into a perfect patina that refused to sink, but, being at the mercy, as we all are, of the wind, that postcard was swept away in the direction of Claire.

It was then that I felt that I had somehow...reached her...

"That's enough of the ever present present. Let's go back in the past now."

"The beautiful relaxing yellowing crumbling peaceful past."

"To an earlier time, a summer morning around the dining room table, with the breeze off the lake lifting the curtains, and the sound of the waves lapping gently on the shore."

" And a search, already underway, a frantic search for a lost contact in the eye of the grandmother."

III.

Do You See It?

Opaque misty corner, with sleep leftover from the last century, and where no light is admitted from this one.

She raises the upper lid, you lower the lower lid. Eyeball to eyeball, her head to the light and leaning back against the dining room table, you bend over to conduct a search and rescue.

Do you see it in there anywhere?

There's no trip that can possibly compare to taking a trip around her eye after the lids have been lifted and all is revealed, every bloodshot vein, like the branches of a burr oak against the sunset.

Find it, will you please! It's got to be in there somewhere! Where oh where is Patience when we need her? Why did she have to let that baby next door roll down the bank, and then run away? I need those sharp eyes of hers right now to find my contact! Your eyes don't have that killer instinct. You're too passive Carl! You'll never succeed in business with eyes like yours.

You stare at any eye long enough, and you begin to see what that person saw through their eyes only. Not the word but the *picture*. So you see what she saw after she put down her Sackville-West and took her coffee out to work in the garden behind the root cellar at the edge of the field. And you see your father as a small boy, he's running up to her, crying, about a barn cat choking on a mouse in the barn, while a deer has snuck into the west end of the yard to nibble on green apples, and in the house a careless cleaning lady vacuums a penny, an ear ring, and a tiny whittled sword, while ignoring, *for pete's sake*, the dirty corner of a just-washed window pane, and a piece of dandelion fuzz attached to the curtain that the Siamese cats love to crawl up…

My contact can't have just disappeared!

You caught a glimpse of it once, it was drifting westerly over her vitreous humor. You took the pink suction cup, you were ready to snag it, the applause was about to ring from the rafters…and then…you lost sight of it again. Admit it: you could never have been an eye doctor or a dentist or any of those specialists who probe the inner sanctums, at times roughly, at times ruthlessly, for the purpose of extracting exorbitant sums of money.

The too delicate nature of the hand that shakes…

Then she blinked. And blinked again! Blinking furiously, as she had when the canopy of cottonwoods on the road to the farm had been cut down because their summer shade damaged the yield. Blinked as she'd blinked on the day after your grandfather had died, and she was driving alone for the first time in her life and the bright sun on the snow blinded her, peering through the steering wheel of her black Mercedes, caught yet again without her little dark glasses.

Could it be behind the cornea?

Through her eye you see her stand in the shade of the post office awning and watch your grandfather go into the small town tavern as a young man…but he's not like the others, he comes right out again, with not so much as a whiff of beery beer on his breath…and he's still a young man full of energy when he remerges from the dusky dank depths of the tavern…and together they start a business, and she is the force behind and the conductor of their business; her employees are working in the long stifling hot room above the hatchery - bookkeepers, accountants, secretaries - they're all working furiously in the heat, she's watching them work, the fans are blowing, the papers are anchored, the smell of the hatchery coming up from downstairs, you see it all take place in that one eye, her left eye.

Don't rub your eyes! she shouts across the front porch, when you're rubbing them because they itch after you've been swimming all afternoon.

And that's her, sitting on the top deck of the Queen in her smart little hat, as Captain Rolf brings it in to the Manhattan Beach Hotel. She stands up and leans over the rail to watch the boys make her fast to the dock. She's about to disembark and walk down the beach to Eagleharve, where there's to be a big party in two evenings time. She's dressed to the teeth, and with her gloved left hand she confirms that the pencil in her purse is indeed sharp. She'll mail her report of the festivities - from appetizers to entertainment - to the *Sioux City Journal* from the Inn, immediately upon disembarking.

What a life - *what a life she's had*, and you see it all go by - in faded colors and blurry edged shades of black and white, like a panoramic scenic movie - just by peering into that one eye to search for that one lost contact.

Carl! Don't read by that poor light! Do you want to strain your eyes? Let's change all the light bulbs. We'll put in stronger ones. Make a list please. But we'll have to wait until they go on sale, won't we? Because there's no need to pay full price if…

You see her watching the brown and white and yellow chicks hatching in the incubator machines in little towns all over the upper Midwest.

Then suddenly she's stretched out next to your grandfather on a deck chair, and looking out across the North Atlantic. She's writing postcards...postcard after postcard...they're on their way to the World Poultry Congress...where she'll count the medals on Goring's chest as he addresses the delegates...

Then she's encouraging your grandfather to obey the sign to speed up on the autobahn as they approach the fenced location of one of the camps.

Finally she's back home, giving one of her radio travel talks, praising German efficiency and cleanliness and the way that they're dealing with their Jewish problem.

Have you done your eye exercises? That's the only way that you'll strengthen your eyes. Do your eye exercises every day!

You see the bottles of pills on the dining room table, ready to go in a box for another trip to the lake. Pills for her eyes, pills for her blood pressure, pills for her insomnia. You see her slam into one side of the garage behind the cottage at the lake, and then she pushes in the clutch and lets the car roll backwards, to pop the clutch and shoot up the hill to slam the other side of the garage this time. Cigarettes burn in three different ashtrays on the front porch, while upstairs late at night the box of Kleenex on her bedside table turns into a torch because she stubs out her cigarette in it while reading the latest by Sackville-West.

I can't see anything but yellow!

If it wasn't so vacuous gelatinous you might suction it obliquely in the vicinity of the blue-green iris where she waits impatiently - I've been standing here forever! - for her bus, her ship, her train, her taxi - to take her to Isfahan, Cairo, Sophia, La Paz, Sioux City - because *I love to travel! I live to travel! Someday you'll have to travel! You'll see the world! A trip around the world is worth a college education...*

You see her sell your father's Chris Craft one fall…she takes it down to Zeke and says, I'll take whatever you give me for it…

The green of the stalks of my geraniums! Will I ever see such a green again?

Then out of the red of her eyes comes the red of a door on a barn in Lancashire. She has never seen such a red. *Let's paint our barn this red*, she says to your grandfather, who is uncomfortably holding a red rooster in his arms.

The blue green eye of a woman, an utterly fearless woman, who never learned to swim and yet has no fear, au contraire, she loves the water - lake water, river water, ocean water - normally the fields are her sea, except when she's at Okoboji…

But look! For heaven's sake! That's her, isn't it, jumping in the surf off Long Island and dancing at the Copacabana. Everything…everything is contained in the corner of an eye, and so I saw what she saw, once upon a time, first in the Midwest, the heart of the Midwest, that would be Iowa, and then…and then all around the world…

I'm seeing only blue!
Blue, blue…nothing but blue…

"Well, to think that a person could see all those days gone by in the simple search for a lost contact."

"Yes. Who would have thought it?"

"I'm never going to get contacts! If I need lenses, I'll get glasses."

"The contacts they make now are easier to get in and out. They're soft, for one thing."

"Let's keep going. Where are we off to next?"

"Gull Point, I believe. With Claire."

"Then we're back in the present. And it's summer. I always feel more comfortable in the present. The past makes me queasy, especially if it's poking around in intimate places, like an eye. Did you ever see that movie with the eye and the razor blade. By the Spanish director…what's his name. That's what I think of when I think of eyes up close. And it's not a pleasant image. But it is one that stays with you. Unlike most images."

"Can you picture Claire on Gull Point, with her books and notebooks and her cigarettes?"

"What's she up to?"

"You know. Reading and writing.

"She's a writer, right?"

"Right. But she can't write in the cottage anymore. She has to find some other place to write. And so she pins her hopes on Gull Point as a place where she can possibly feel free enough to write."

"She works with words, in other words. That's good. I like people who work. She's a slightly non-conformist type of worker, but still, she does work, and every day."

"But it does seem, don't you agree, that a change is in the air for Claire."

"You have that feeling? I do too."

"So this should be interesting, shouldn't it?"

"What are we waiting for?"

IV.

Flight to Gull

A schism running through the alabaster shelving in Claire's memory has left her leaflooped in her head and landlocked on her bed. A fusillade of past experiences crystallizes into foliated arrangements which have fractured her sense of futurity. She buries her eyes in her billowy pillows, and dreams dreams which are impossible to recall in the morning, save for the foghorns…

Did you hear the foghorns again last night, Carl?

Foghorns? At Okoboji?

I could not truthfully say that I'd heard so much as one solitary funereal foghorn. But I had felt the plates shifting - in the sink, of course - but also in the floor under my feet, and, most noticeably, in the low beamed ceiling below Claire's room. And while some shifted tectonically, others seemed content to merely rattle and tremble. All were unsettling though, and the surest evidence yet, as I sat on the living room couch looking at pictures of winter in *White Men Follow After*, that Claire was being bombarded unceasingly by an infinite number of unending distractions, some of which I list:

- her never ending rearrangement of her books and notes
- her ritualistic diminishing daily money count
- reams of magnetic cat hair that attached itself unrelentingly to her clothes and blankets
- irritating silence of her portable radio
- the barking of doxies, the shouts of boys
- lack of close female friends to confide in

- the absence of her entertaining musical friends
- intimidation by well known established pampered authors

All the differences separating the past and the present had been ground down in my grandmother's old room into a fine powdery dust: the soot of summers past. A flood of teary sparks was unleashed to bounce off the walls, and then collide and cool and fuse into what I called *Clairetites*, which hung down from the ceiling to give her room a cave-like feeling, and did nothing to sooth her recurring claustrophobia.

The magma of memory came bubbling up between her sheets to overwhelm her, dragging along in its wake the essence of life but also something more: an overwhelming burden of what had gone on before - in Lisbon, for instance, in 1754.

Dark black doubts flapped like hungry carnivorous crows on Claire's creative horizon. She was snared in the web of an unsympathetic epoch, restrained by the history of a room that she just happened to be living in, because I'd downed the stout and asked her, late in the evening of the previous St. Patrick's Day: *Will you go to Okoboji with me?* (Act One, Scene IV)

Day after day she sat propped up on her pillows, listening to wave upon wave scatter pebbles and wash away the carefully constructed sand fortifications built by the boys next door. The collage of notes arranged across her bed became nothing but a black and bottomless hole. She unearthed her journals from under her bed, sifting and digging through them until she found the talisman that she was looking for: the arrowhead, accompanied by her journal entry: *I was pierced by its translucence.*

It was then that she realized that it was *outside*, whatever it was that she needed to spur her on, it was *outside in nature*, waiting for her to uncover it and rinse it and hold it to the light.

On the lake map in the front porch she pins her hope for escape, despite its aggressive horseflies, on Gull Point. She makes arrangements with her second best rower (her best rower being busy running the roller coaster) to *Please row me straight across the lake and drop me off on Gull!*

She'll tolerate no detours - *not a one!* - on the way across. There will be no passing over, for instance, the bottomless hole...

The aluminum bow no sooner grates across the pebbly sand on the north side of Gull than she's over the edge with her bulging bag and shoving the boat back out into the lake. No goodbye, no adios, just a *See you at sunset!*

With her seahorse earrings and dress dripping wet, she's the very first one on the beach this Sunday. She anchors her bedspread to the sand with books. An intimate breeze ruffles their pages. It rustles the cottonwood leaves as well, which filter the light for her overstrained eyes. She can no more lay back and follow a branch to its tip than she can read a book to its last letter. Rather, she dips in and out of the branches and the books, skimming through them in search of an angle or a phrase or a simple sensation that will *touch her off,* as she puts it. Her toes go off on their own to feel the bumps under the bedspread, and her skin tingles as her dress dries, while her mind wades through thickets of words, looking for the ones with some life still left in them. She borrows ideas like they're sugar cubes, and they race off to bang around in her mind as if they're bumper cars. She's momentarily lifted by their buoyancy, while their suggestiveness stirs the humid air around her. And then...to cool off...she wades back in the lake...

Incongruous as she looks coming out of the water in her unusual bathing outfit (I've been observing her through the WWII binoculars as I lie at anchor and fish off Arrowhead Beach), which clings to her figure with a tenacious resolve right on the tip of the Gull Point, she immediately comes face to face with a few blank stares and a plethora of boat ropes all tied to trees or exposed tree roots, and which separate her from her bed spread on the beach. So she has to decide, right away, with each rope she comes to, whether to hike her long wet dress halfway up her thighs and go over it, or bend down and go under it and get everything sandy. Just to get back to her books on her bed spread!

Once she makes it back, dissatisfactions also begin to arise with the books she's brought along - books which, in spite of their beautiful spines and bindings, fail to yield, with rare exceptions, the corresponding expressive echo of what she thinks and feels about...about love for instance. When she'd been alone with them on the beach they'd been pleasant enough company, but now, amid the swaggering ski craft and blustering fume spewing boats, beached like the whales on old Cape Cod, no, now she needs something more.

So that at some point after she has landed at Gull, after she has read and swam and snacked and smoked, and climbed over and under all the ropes, she puts all the books back in her bag and takes off down the private beach on the south side of Gull Point in search of something... something else...

She picks shiny pebbles from the shallow water and watches their colors fade the second she twists their smoothness between her fingers. In her pocket they fall in with pieces of clam shell; she fills her dress pockets until sharp shells poke her thighs, while her fingers feel for the smoothest pebbles. Over and over in her hand she must examine, she must touch, she must feel, she must know which is *rock* and which is *shell* amongst all this jumble in her pockets. If there are any Indian rocks on the beach she cannot see or uncover or find them. But then it's hard to discover something if you're not alone, and she is not alone on the beach...

She cuts across the base of the point to the beach facing north, where a piece of driftwood which she tries to pick up is in fact a tree root attached to an old cottonwood. A chunk of chert under a *No Trespassing* sign briefly gives her hope that she might find another arrowhead. And she's often fooled by the common Sioux quartzite which resembles, in the blinding sun, pipestone...

Her dress is dry by the time she reaches the round stone look-out tower north of the lodge, where she climbs the wooden steps to overlook West Okoboji. It's a Martello Tower of her own imagination, and it handsomely frames her tiny figure and inserts it between the pages of a poetic longwinded bright blue book. Up there in that CCC tower she finally finds a permanent expression of love, carved in one of the dark round beams carted out from Oregon. She feels with the tips of fingers the initials dug out of the wood with a rusty jack-knife. She looks above and beyond and through me (I was fishing a hundred yards off the tower, in thick weeds where the walleye like to hide). Her sight is obviously set on a higher prize, something connected with Abbie's pine, which suggests a story for her, a way to proceed, a way to unite once again Inkpaduta and Abbie, for hadn't they walked past here on their way up the lake on the ice in the dead of winter, a bitter cold March, the two of them (there were others in their party, but she would concentrate on just those two) following he–who–makes–wind–as–he–walks.

She knew the way now; she had come to Gull Point to find her way forward, and she had come upon a path, where the oak meets the sky, signaling with its branches that the coast is clear, that she should take a chance, that it was alright for her to leave, that it was up to her to be where she felt most free, that she owed her nights to no one, that where the blue meets the blue, the bluey edge way out there…that's what she should try to focus on (she stares at it with eyes open wide).

As soon as she left the tower…that was my sign to reel in my line. I rowed straight east off Gull to fish some more and wait for sunset, as Claire walked along the beach and out to the tip of the point, like she was crossing a stage to get a degree, a Masters in *style* which had been bestowed upon her unexpectedly. (She always had that instinct for success about her. She had none of my appetite for failure…in catching a nice fish, for instance)

Back on her bedspread on the beach, she understands the warmth of words and the sound of the waves as the same thing. Then she starts to write, in a flying handwriting, under the cottonwoods bent back by the stiffening new breeze, which ought to have lessened as sunset approached. (But that's the present for you; it was already past to her) Long lost lines wing their way back to her, she repeats them in a chanting voice that doesn't seem as if it should belong to her. A boy and girl, wading after tiny minnows darting between the rocks on the tip of the point, interrupt their hum of a movie theme to listen for a moment to a voice on a beach now nearly deserted…

Deserted…she closes her eyes to hear the gulls…they've flown non-stop all the way from the Nubble…they've found her far inland…they keep her awake all night…they've carried the sound of the foghorn to her for a souvenir…a souvenir of the distant sea…

And as I row in to pick her up just before sunset, I notice, while trying to pretend not to notice, that she's smoking a cigarette while at the same time burying something under the large exposed root of a cottonwood near the tip of the point.

My bow light is working, but my stern light is out, so I'm rowing hard, hard as I possibly can, back across the middle for Dixon Beach. Six bluegill are flopping around in the stern. Claire sees me struggling against the breeze, she jumps up to sit beside me to help, all the way across the lake we row together, with boats that don't seem to see us until the last second, when they veer off and leave us with a view of the bottom of their underside, as it curves away, as it hurries off, as we row on toward the ever darkening dark.

"Whew! Things are always so intense when Claire's on stage!"

"I know what you mean. But at the same time, those scenes when she's front and center are very alive."

"It depends on your definition of 'alive', I guess."

"Let's not get into that. Instead, let's move on, shall we?"

"We've got to keep moving or we'll get stuck in some static state from which there's no escape."

"I think what you're saying is that the narrative must continue."

"But to where?"

"To the amusement park."

"Yes! To the Park! I love the Park! I love the people who work in the park. They seem very animated. Even the Fun House Clown."

"Do you ever wonder how the people who make the rides and amusements in the old run down park go round and around are coping with the unceasingly hot weather and the low pay and the non-existent benefits and the ever infrequent yet incessant and demanding tourists?"

" Well…now that you mention it, I guess that I do. I really do."

"Well then…let's find out!"

V.

To Collect a Debt

Jerry, on a break with Ethel's French fries in a greasy brown bag, was making his stern and purposeful way to the Shooting Gallery, in order to collect a debt in arrears from one Pesky 'past due' Pete.

But Pete, who'd just been paid, was on the alert, a high alert, with lookouts posted from the Ferris wheel to the Merry-go-Round. He'd even positioned (or imagined he'd positioned) a blue jay in a crow's nest on top of a cottonwood (their leaves being so musical in the breeze). So when he heard through the grapevine that Jerry was making the turn at the Tipsy House, Pete immediately pulled back from his forward position and merged with the thick spidery shadows behind the targets in the Shooting Gallery. But when Jerry picked up a rifle and started picking off the ducks in rapid succession, Pete (quick as a wink) snuck out the back door and became an illusion in a flak jacket which Jerry pursued through a convoluting labyrinth of amusements, such as the Mirror Maze and Laugh In The Dark, and then round behind Madame Jessie's, and up and down and through the Tipsy House. Until Jerry, his break being long over, and realizing that Gretchen would be burning with impatience at having to sit at the counter when there were so many other things

that needed doing, had to admit defeat and head back to the Pinball Haven.

But first, he thought, I'm stopping for a Nutty Buddy bar, why not, I won't get another break until dinner, you only live once unless you're a cat, and it looks like Nutty (leaning on the counter, chin in hands, listening intently to the weather report on the radio) could use some business.

Hi Nutty! One of your bars *please*. Say, have you seen Pete anywhere?

Hey Jerry! Beautiful day, isn't it? Did you see those clouds coming over from the Dakotas? Aren't they something? Textbook examples of cumulo-nimbus! Absolutely lovely! Aren't they? Let me get a big bar for you. No, I haven't seen Pete. Well…maybe I did see him earlier today. I can't remember. I really can't remember. This ongoing cloud show is just too much for me. I kind of lost track of what else I was supposed to be doing. I know I've got to make some more bars. Supposed to storm later on I just heard. Keep an eye on it, Jerry, keep an eye on it. Say, that Pete, he owes me some money, now that I think about it. I got it written down somewhere. No, he wrote me an IOU on the back of a postcard. That's what it is. An old postcard of the waterslide, when it used to be over there where the bath house used to be. You remember the old bath house, don't you Jerry? Wait! You used to work there, didn't you? Man, I'd forgotten all about that. That was a long time ago, wasn't it? A *long* time ago…Say, if you do see Pete, tell him he can pay me back *anytime* he wants. But the sooner the better. How's Gretchen treating you? Is she hard to work for? I don't think I could work for a gal like that. She's too bossy. Way too bossy! Here's your bar. Hey, don't worry about it. It's on me. Enjoy, Jerry, enjoy. Don't let Gretchen get you down. See you later Jerry.

Gretchen might not be so upset with my taking such a long time getting back if I stop to buy her a little candy, Jerry considered. And it looks like Sheri could use some business too. She's just reading. Look at those burns on her arms. Oh my god. Why doesn't she wear a long sleeved shirt when she stirs the candy? I've seen her reading even while she's stirring.I hate to interrupt her concentration. It's like trying to wake someone up when they're asleep. I just don't like to do it, but Gretchen loves candy, so…

What can I get for you Jerry?

How about…half a pound of walnut fudge.

Ok. Just made it today.

All those burns on her slender arms, Jerry sympathized. It would take a good lotion to sooth them. The tenderized directions on the side of the tube: *Apply with soft gauze day and night to the affected area.*

Jerry wanted to suggest to Sheri that in his first aide kit under the counter at the Pinball Haven he had a slightly used tube of…but instead, as he took the bag of candy, he asked, What 'cha readin'?

To The Lighthouse. Have you ever read it? It's wonderful.

What's it about?

It's about life really. It's about a trip that gets put off, and a beautiful woman who's a mother and who dies, and…and then her husband and a couple of their kids, years later, sail off for the lighthouse, and an artist paints a picture despite being told that women can't paint or write. Does that give you any idea? You should read it. It's not in the Arnolds Park library though. You'd have to get it…I don't know where you could get it around here…oh, maybe that bookstore in Spirit Lake. The Hill Avenue Bookstore. Check there, and if they don't have it, you can borrow my copy. I'm reading it again for the third or fourth time. Ok? Thanks Jerry. See you later.

Sure, Jerry ruminated, stopping to finish his dripping nutty buddy bar on the bench to the left of the entrance to the Fun House, maybe I'll read that some night, you know, instead of watching TV. Yeah, I'll stretch out on the couch and read *To The Lighthouse* and see if it's really about *life*, like Sheri says it is. I mean, this is life, isn't it: a girl in a swimsuit walking past with seaweed in her hair, and the Ferris wheel going around and around, and ice cream dripping on my jeans, and Gretchen probably ready to send out a search party for me. But I wouldn't mind tuning in to another kind of life too, especially a life beyond this amusement park.

And life as it's portrayed on TV, Jesus, that's no life at all, is it old clown? Jerry queried, looking up to address subliminally the Fun House Clown: What do you think about life and books and music? You never play any music any more, do ya? Why not? What made you stop? Maybe it's the same reason why I don't seem to want to go back to work? Is it? If you could talk, you'd tell me all, wouldn't you...

Is there any question why, starting at least by - and often before - the Fourth of July, the Fun House Clown began to long for winter every summer? After the first of August he sighed almost continuously...but only the children appeared to hear his sighs, and although they expressed, in their own silent way, a sympathy for him, as they would have for a lost puppy or a stray kitten, still, they couldn't quite understand, given his lofty position in his cage above the entrance to the Fun House, and the beautiful view which must have entranced him every time he turned his head, and his merry polka dots and glassy eyes and sleek white slippers, exactly what he was sighing about...

These children, park rats and innocent tourist kids alike, couldn't be expected to have any knowledge or remembrance of those inspirational *boogie-woogie* waves which had engulfed the Clown in the Twenties, when his piano and its bright red notes which lined the side were freshly painted and, being afraid to pound too hard on the keys and frighten the children, he'd raised his voice to such an elevated register that he could easily be heard from the roof of the Tipsy House and, on quiet clear nights, from as far away as the Bug House. But those long ago waves had long since ceased to reach him. It was as if Okoboji had receded like the Aral Sea. The untimely death, in 1937, of George Gershwin, meant that his favorite bluesy melodies began to abandon him in the Forties, and all through the dusty Fifties his tunes were so lost to improvisation (for he'd come under the sway of the percussive and immitigable Cecil Taylor) that he often forgot where he'd started, and had to stop. His floorboards no longer creaked under the weight of the music, and the scribbled requests which had once flooded his cage dried up and blew away and were burnt with the leaves. Then he became an easy prey to the prevailing musical currents, but only up to the point when the surf guitar took over.

No wonder the Clown's shoulders sunk deeper and deeper into his chest each summer, as he *longed* and as he *sighed.* It was not a pleasant view, and neither was the fact that no more masterpieces like *Summertime* were coming over the horizon. Someone had disconnected… someone had pulled the plug on…not that he believed in the ability of electricity to power music…not that he was about to plug in… or even dream of going electric…maybe it was the fault of those guys who worked in the amusement park…the ones who wanted to move him over by the fortune teller…some nasty person, at one inopportune time, had disengaged his *musical current…*

Nutty Buddy knew where to pin the blame for the Clown's sagging shoulders: it was all the fault of brutal weather patterns, and the terrible overbearing influence of winter, with its horrific absence of warmth and love and light. That was the reason that the Clown's shoulders sagged! *It was the weather!* stupid, not the music. Don't let 'em fool ya. Music is not and never will be a necessity, Nutty Buddy mused…but warmth is. And besides, anyone's shoulders would have sagged…

(Here his imaginings were interrupted by the Queen coming in, and the sight of long-legged Erica, bow rope in her hand, leaping through the air to land on the dock in a move that, had it taken place at Carnegie Hall, would have been acknowledged with applause and whistles and shouts of *Encore! Encore!*)

Business picked up a bit then, after a few of the passengers stepped off the ship and stopped for a Nutty Buddy bar, before continuing on to other amusements, or home for chores, or perhaps they worked the late shift, who knows? It was fifteen or twenty minutes before Nutty could return to dwell on the reasons for the sagging shoulders of the Fun House Clown…

Nutty Buddy, his own shoulders bent under the weight of those unfair accusations concerning the diminishing size of his Nutty Buddy bars, leaned on his elbows on the counter and listened and heard with his own ears Melvin Tornado predict a worse than average winter. He tried to visualize it, especially the clouds: long, low, and hazy, like thick sheep's wool. He pictured it alright, but he tried not to think about it, and especially not to feel it - no, not those long dark days to come, the overcast skies, the night air so cold that you could see every star.

Don't even mention the word *winter* when passing under the Fun House Clown. Stuck in his cage in that ungodly season, and hemmed in by three quarter inch, rough on both sides, sheets of knotty Canadian plywood, the Clown would be face to face with a silence of the unbearable variety, especially at night, when the only sound to ever interrupt it (until the advent of the dreadful snowmobile) was the frightening noise of the ice shifting.

And don't even intimate the vast variation in temperature between summer and winter, for hasn't everyone (fortunate or unfortunate as the case may be) who lives in this little corner of the world (the only corner which concerns us here) suffered in turn from frostbite and sunburn?

But it does keep the population down, that was one good thing, Nutty Buddy enthused. *And it keeps things cheap, until the time comes to pay the heating bill.* Nutty's shoulders sank a little more, just thinking about those hefty heating bills on his dining room table.

His windows shook…but it wasn't a quake…it was only a garbage truck dumping a dumpster somewhere near by. Seagulls in a shrill trill of excitement abandoned the pier, the points, and the spilled bags of popcorn to follow the garbage truck out to the country, where it would join more garbage trucked down from St. Paul, to mix together in a rotting delectable contaminating compost (its wafting aroma was later to be borne on the wind back over the amusement park).

Sheri suspends her caramel stirring/reading to turn down the fire and follow a finger pointing from beyond the glass, and to weigh a tray of maple walnut fudge. It was no longer for her a question of devouring every book in the Arnolds Park library. She had narrowed her search as the summer wore on; she would reread the one whose meaning drew her closest. The winter was meant for exploratory reading. There was no other time like it for concentration, and especially those endless winter nights were perfect for books, they were meant for books. She would read late into the night while smoke streamed out of the chimney and the streetlight lit up the snowbanks. She couldn't wait for the winter night, when it was warm under the covers, or she would make it warm, she would turn on her internal heater, and hold the book with one hand, while warming the other hand, only bringing it out from under the covers to turn the page…to turn another page…

Which brings us back by way of the fabled circle of life to the sight of Pesky Pete, that eternal borrower, and wanderer as well, formerly of the world, but now of the back streets, the dimly lit crooked little back streets of Arnolds Park. He's had some strong drink this evening, but now those hands that had gripped the bottle are in his pockets instead. He's a soul searcher in the hours before sunrise; seeking the sources of his ambivalence in his childhood, while lamenting lost love and wild weather and dodging tough unrelenting creditors. In the shadowy gaps between streetlights he stops to take a leak and reminisce autobiographically… looking through the wavering unshaven face in the puddle, he calls back an averted one from a shore leave in Hong Kong: swaddled in a red kimono with dragons across her chest; poking at an orange carp in a foggy glass tank. He shakes his head unbelievably. Can it be that he was once in Hong Kong and met the eyes of a dark haired woman who swished a stick at some colorful carp, that he might choose one for his dinner? This soldier of uncertainty has never realized how ill prepared he is, in the hours before dawn, for this or any other century…

So…at the end of the day…these amusement park characters are all passengers on an upper deck laden with pigment, applied in a brisk fashion with rough tools by a painter who obviously loves to move the paint around. Semicircular lines converge in the center of the deck, where the chronicler would naturally be sitting, pretending to read, but secretly gathering evidence for his paper-bed pages. Nothing at all appears harmonious about this crowd…that is until they're set out in relief against the lake. It must be the sunset cruise, because they're melding into shapes which coalesce with one another and with the colors and the clouds in the sky. Between them all there is, believe it or not, a bond. A single line connects them to each other, and to everything else in their landscape. Who's driving this ship is anyone's guess. Perhaps the captain is sleeping it off on cushions in the stern. Only one thing is certain: every turn of the propeller takes them farther and farther from their point of departure, which is where we wait, at the bend in the seawall, to watch them disembark (if they ever come back) so obviously changed, their very demeanor, even their way of walking.

"That sounds like fun. Why don't we go for a ride on the Queen?"

"We've got to ride this chapter to its conclusion."

"Where's it going to take us. Tell me!"

"Now it's a summer evening, rather late, and Carl, the devoted editor, is still typing Claire's fragments for her."

"But what's that noise I hear?"

"That's the buzz of mosquitoes against the screens."

"He's typing to that?"

"That and the music. He always has music on when he's typing."

"Is he, by any chance, typing what we're reading?"

"He writes it – types it – then goes out to live it."

VI.

The Path to Intimacy

Most of my fingers found most of the keys without even looking on those sticky nights when I continued to type in bare feet and frayed shorts to a stack of records spinning around in a corner of the wide open screen windowed front porch. My poor finger coordination (alluded to in Act One, Scene V) had been temporarily assuaged by a set of perfect or near perfect conditions which probably could not have been duplicated anywhere else in the world.

Patiently (for patience is one of the great attributes, and can only be acquired by exhibiting a commanding exalted dignified forbearance) I listened in the wave tossed lake air for a *touch-me-off phrase* and the concurrent matching rhythm from the record player, which together would set me sailing, or so I hoped…

At the hotel bar one night after typing, I observed myself exchanging confidences and making confessions and tossing out compliments with a troupe of actors from the summer theatre. First they'd invited me to join them at their table. Then they'd insisted that I fill my glass from their carafe. It turned out that they were celebrating the end of a weeklong ride on Tennessee's *Streetcar*. The curtain had finally fallen on the five o'clock rain of a New Orleans afternoon. I took another sip and tried to imagine a French Quarter evening, and the attendant distant tinkling of an out of tune upright piano. It was easier than typing - at twenty five wpm - for me. My imagination was faster than the speed of light under those circumstances, which were exemplary, as I've said.

A little basket of my raspberries - the first of the season - was on the table beside the nearly empty carafe, and the actor they called Blanche couldn't stop eating them. Her warm free arm (the one not reaching for the raspberries) was draped across one of my shoulders, and her lips and her fingers were stained a bright and succulent red.

It wasn't long, given the excitement of that little celebration in the hotel bar with its subtly enticing Polynesian theme, before I'd far exceeded my usual half carafe and was approaching, if not the same plane as the actors, where *everyone* is your friend, then a similar one, where everything was, if not quite rosy, a very juicy peach. They all became dear companions in the soft glow of the TV turned down low. But the character who always depended on the kindness of strangers - that character was the delicious one for me that evening. My arm had found its way around her waist. She laughed. And then she laughed again. *My real name's Lou*, she giggled. Her shoulders were the color of a *vin rose*, and she had freckles floating on the surface of her skin, which was warm while at the same time cool to the touch. One of her freckles looked like it was crawling. I'd never seen a freckle crawl. I looked closer.

That's not a freckle. That's a tick!

There's one on your shoulder, and another one crawling up your neck!

Hold still for a minute, and I'll get them for you.

It's like these ticks were glued to her. I wished I hadn't chewed off all my fingernails while I was typing. I trapped the ticks in a damp drink napkin, which I crunched and then flushed.

Back at the table, everyone was checking everyone else over for more ticks. I saw scratched legs and swelling bites and itchy bumps and cocklebURS attached to socks. We crossed a few fields to get to the bar, Lou said. We climbed over fences and got stabbed by barbed wire. She had the proof, she showed me the blood. I didn't have any bandages for her. I was no Doctor Destouches, but I had taken care of the ticks, so I was a hero of sorts, and somebody made a toast, and someone else seconded it, and we all drank.

You reach agreements and you arrive at understandings that are rare when you're sober. But most of it evaporates immediately as soon as the lights blaze on. Then all is revealed: the flushed faces; the empty carafes; the chairs on the tables. The sudden absence of music is disquieting too. All at once you're swept out the door and under a slur of stars, tripping along after the one with the playbook in her back pocket, who halts, reaches back, takes your hand and squeezes it, as if to say: *Follow me.*

Your legs lead you along, and it's as if you're gliding across the parking lot and up the hill and through the woods until you nearly tip over underneath the water tower. It's then you realize that you've been tilting and leaning - not gliding - all along. Lou, sweet Lou; she insists in a loud theatrical voice that we should *all climb it, all of us, all the way to the top-er-most of the pop-er-most, to the blinking red light!*

You're standing directly underneath the water tower, and along with the others you bend your head back to stare up at this outsized form which looks as if it's about to take off for far flung unknown regions of the universe…

You first Lou, somebody says.

But Lou doesn't stretch up for the first rung on the ladder…no, all she says is, *Hey, you got any more of those raspberries?*

So on we sail toward an island of lights, because the approaches to intimacy are as infinite as the crickets…

An incoming rip tide jerks and yanks and pulls us down a deer path through the long grass.

Watch out for that pale prickly purple moonlit flower atop that giant sticker bush! Weave carefully around it…

Gallantly drunkenly carefully, you place your tennis shoe between the two barbs on the bottom wire, and you hold it down hard on the ground while at the same time gripping the top wire between the barbs and propping it with your forearm so that she and the others can slip through without being stabbed.

Go ahead. Throw your t-shirt over a puddle, as if you're Sir Walter Rabelais…

Do you believe in the man in the moon? she shouts to you stumbling across the landing strip.

You look up at her man…to look for an answer…

The Tear slips out of her hip pocket and lands on a white stripe.

You pick it up and run toward her…

Those long blue running runaway runway lights…

If he's corn fed, you shout after her, but she's disappeared.

You come to a Hadrian's Wall of prairie dog hills. And then everything becomes suddenly manicured in the clipped nature of the wide open fairway. A family of raccoons is gathered about a tipped trash barrel under a tree which leans like a Pisan Tower. You plow on across the bunkers! You make a mess of the sand traps!

You find Lou sitting criss-cross on the green, a short putt for a birdie, still talking about the man in the moon: *Look how the clouds mask and unmask him. He belongs to me, he makes me laugh, he crawls inside my brain, he tickles me in my tummy, he'll drop any day now, I'll go into labor…*

A kiss to swallow every star before you pick her up and hoist her over another fine example of an Iowa four-pointed barb wire fence.

Then to set her down carefully and follow her, as if she's the first human, across a land bridge in the midst of a swampy slew. One wrong step, she says, and I'll sink from sight. I'll give birth out here like a turtle, for an audience of frogs, and bury my egg of the man in the moon in the quicksand.

Those hips of hers…they hypnotize…the playbook that's jammed in her back pocket, glowing like a distant star…a game of hearts in a field of corn…she stubs her toe on a stone…erotic fantascies trip over one another in their desire to keep up with her and her bleeding toenail…

But then…who startles who, crashing through the corn? It's either a herd of deer or a plethora of mosquitoes or a bevy of actors running toward the lights of their lair…

One of the actors: *I'm the one who played Stanley!* smokes and puffs in a director's chair beside the door of the residence cabin. Inside, a bare light bulb swings over a table littered with monologues and dialogues and catalogs and free newspapers and empty pizza boxes with crust and cheese attached. Clothes are strewn about, and towels dripping colors hang from nails and over chairs. To lean back against one is to feel the violets and the magentas soak through, while you do your best to ignore the posters of smiling celebrities, because the television and the radio and the telephone are all fighting for your attention, while over in the corner there's a tower of dirty dishes piled precariously in the sink.

There's a part of you that wants to dive in - even in your intoxicated state - and clean it all up, clean up the mess, wash all the dishes and clothes, throw away the garbage, arrange the plays and the scripts on the shelves in alphabetical order, paint the faces of the celebrities until they're unrecognizable...the janitor in you calculates how long it would all take...you figure you could have it done by sunrise, maybe, if they all go to bed pretty soon...but then, from across and under the table, she puts one of her feet in your lap, and just leaves it there, as if to nail you to your folding chair. And so you stay, anchored in the safe harbor of her painted toenails.

Nightgowns, bathrobes, and subdued conversations...One by one they all disappear to leave you with the last actor slumped in her chair ...relaxed, dreamy...her soft eyes framed by tiny eyebrows and celestial cheeks crinkled in a sly smile. You look past and over and around her, but you always come back to her sculptured nose.

She leans back in her chair and puts her other foot in your lap, so now they're both there, both bare, calluses on their soles. Sole of my soul! You study her toes carefully, as if they hold some secret. They seem like a very normal set of toes. If they were keys you could play them...if you knew how to play. You've always wanted to learn how to play. In the corner of her left big toe there's a line of dark dirt...

But she's telling you all about Duluth, and she's gotten out some pictures and postcards, and pushes stuff off the table to take you on a tour of all the sights. You see Lester Park and Park Point and Superior Street or Avenue and Engler Tower and Leif Erickson Park and lots of other places. There's no snow in any of the pictures. She doesn't want to talk about the winter. She lives in an apartment above a used bookstore called The Amazing Alonzo. She gets lost every time she goes in that bookstore, she says. She wants to work there someday. She gives you a red t-shirt with a picture of the lift bridge on it. It's too small, but you put it on anyway.

Tomorrow night, she says, looking out the window at the back of the theater, after the show, on my way to the bar, I'll stop to see if anything's hatched out there.

As she goes into the bathroom, she demures: See you on the sleeping porch.

You go back outside to go to the bathroom. You walk away from the cabin, out into the field, between the corn, just you and the deer, with the corn as your witness.

You were out in that field awhile - you don't know how long - until you calmed down – then you went back in.

Dark as a long tunnel on the large sleeping porch. All in their beds. Soft snoring punctuated by loud snoring. Which bed was Lou in? The moon comes out from behind a cloud to light the scene. You take a few tentative steps on tiptoe. In one of these sleeper's dreams you're destined to play a part it seems. Or so you most fervently hope. Wind shoots through the wide open windows. The moon comes out less and less often. You trip over a shoe and feel your moment slipping away from you because…you were too long out in the field…

You hold your breath and tiptoe on, wandering lost in a forest of dream sleepers.

She is here, somewhere in this room, sleeping or nearly asleep.

Lou, whisper, where are you?

Silence.

Then the moon illuminates a raised hand, fingers formed in a victory sign, or a peace sign, it doesn't matter, you tiptoe toward it, and slip into the tiny single bed. It's as if you've emigrated to the North Shore. The lift bridge goes up and stays up the whole night. The foghorn goes off at regular intervals as you swim out into the lake. All night you're swimming in Lake Superior, which has suddenly become deliciously warm, and you go down...down to the bottom...and back up to the top... you swim around the whole lake...never getting cold...not once...and among all the shipwrecks and sea wrack you find...you discover...you are washed over with...you know...happiness...

PART TWO

IMPROVISATIONS

"Imagine you're a butterfly!"

"I can't."

"You're a butterfly with a soaring overview. You have the gorgeous panorama available to a butterfly, with no stigmatisms, no glaucoma, and no cataracts."

"And no genetically engineered corporate corn?"

"There's nothing we can do about the corn. The corn is out of our hands."

"But if I'm a butterfly, that's all I see when I'm up there! Corn, corn, and more corn!"

"Forget about the corn, will you. I want you to focus in on a summer scene."

"As long as we don't have to clean…"

"But we do."

"Why?"

"Because the Seashores are coming!"

"Again? They're always coming."

"They're almost here this time."

"Then we're back in the past?"

"We are, with Patience looking on."

"I love Patience. I love her impetuous impatience."

"But she let the baby roll down the hill."

"Well, nobody's perfect. And besides, she didn't mean to. She was thinking about the dance, remember."

"Who's carrying the tune for this scene, anyway?"

"Carl, as a teenager."

"Shall we part the curtain?"

I.

Patterns

A cloudy pattern of motifs stored somewhere in your weather beaten memory hangs like a kite in the sky above Okoboji, patiently waiting to be reeled in and vacuumed over once again. Every fingernail, every muffin crumb, every tiny piece of string from kites long since stuck, ripped, and shredded in the treetops must be sucked up, because the professor is so terribly tall that he can see the dreamy dust on the top of a door jamb, while the professor's wife is of a shortness and a thickness that enables her to spot a little lentil pea under the piano's sostenuto pedal - which incidentally, since the Seashores should be arriving any day now - you should not forget to polish.

I polish the pedals, and I polish the floor, and I polish the door handles on all the doors. I polish every knife, fork, and spoon too. I polish and polish, while my grandmother enthuses:

...because, you see, the professor is that rare combination of scientist and artist, of musician and theoretician, of poet and inventor, who only quite recently has devised a machine to measure those tones which rise and fall beyond your ken...

...and if it's a calm day, your grandmother continues, *we'll take him on the Queen.*

But what if...what if it's windy?

(The wave maker wind: you're dependable friend in the fight against affectation and fabrication and ostentation)

If it's windy...if it turns out that the wind is a gusty and sustained one, then...then we'll just have to go visit Abbie's cabin again, because the professor, you must realize, living as he does in a country on a continent which venerates its history as his does, loves historical landmarks.

Rather than waste any more time reeling in a kite which is nearly out of sight...wouldn't it be much simpler to simply cut the string?

You run to the sewing cabinet. You grab the sewing scissors.

But wait!

Wait? For what?

Isn't that...isn't that you know who?

Who?

Patience!

Ah...Patience...

Sticky prickly try-my-patience Patience...here she comes again... floating...drifting...toward you on a summer morning unlike any other in its absolutely perfect flat calm still-life whimsicality. She's carrying a tune with her too, a clever tune attached to her perpetually evolving tale. Patience the indifferent next door housekeeper, at three times your hourly rate. Patience the frivolous and non-stop laughing nanny. Patience, your slightly older and much more experienced collaborator. The nearness of the two cottages and their wide open windows allows the two of you to coordinate your tasks to the peal and the seal of good housekeeping. If you're vacuuming, for instance, she tucks her polka dot dust cloth in her hip pocket and hits the switch on a brand new Electrolux. If she's washing the south-facing windows, you quickly warm the vinegar solution on the burner and meet her at a discreet upstairs north-facing window, rag bucket in hand.

With only a whisk brisk sly spirit of lake air between them
They washed those windows as if they were going to
Fall right through them and into each others arms

She doesn't see the world through foot square panes, eight to a window, like you do. She has the luxury of aiming her brilliant blue window cleaner at a vast expanse of glass, which she sprays and squirts until her tom-boy figure turns into a vague obscure outline. She can afford to wipe with a big sweeping strokes, using the endless rolls of platted paper towels at her disposal to reach the far corners. You pause for a moment at the beginning of her greatest stretch...just as her t-shirt is about to depart from her jeans.

It's not a race! you inform her by telepathy, but she always beats you anyway. In lieu of a victory lap around the room, she props her elbows on the windowsill and cups her chin in her hands and settles in to stare at you...shake her head at you...snicker at you and your rags and your pungent vinegar solution...

But the second that a song comes on the radio that you think she'd love, you give her the signal by tossing your wet rag out the window, and dashing to the radio to turn up the volume. If the song's a hit with her, she tries to thwack the snake-like rag in the grass with a wadded up bunch of paper towels. It's gets to be a mess at times, down in the no-man land between the two cottages. Both of you stand accused of neglecting the rest of your housework to concentrate on the windows on one side of the house. These windows take on a talismanic significance for you, and not only for the way that they frame her lithesome figure, but also for their ability to capture the emphatic essence of Patience.

But then she had to go and absentmindedly let the baby roll down the bank.

Her employers the lawyers will never invite her back to Okoboji again.

She had turned her back on the stroller, without setting the brake, to run and tell you something when you were up on the top rung of the ladder, sweeping the cobwebs out from under the eves.

Meet me at the top of the Roof Garden stairs...I'll be talking to Freeman!

It was while she was asking you if you'd heard of the band that was playing up there that evening - *of course you'd heard of them, because you were the one, remember, who threw your rag out the window and ran to turn up the volume when their song -which had climbed to number one - had come on the radio* - that those two little pink bare feet reached the concrete and set the stroller, whose brakes hadn't been locked, in motion and on a roll down the sloping sidewalk toward the stairs and the edge of the bank.

And there were *cries!* And there were *screams!* And there were *shouts!* And there were...

There was a nasty bleeding gash on that little forehead.

Patience was disdained, scorned, and suspended.

Patience was banished to her room above the garage in the rear.

Patience was to sneak off about an hour later, while they were still at the emergency room...

The lawyers, in her absence and thus unable to defend herself, labeled her arrogant and belligerent, irresponsible and capricious.

Well...she was a neglectful nanny at times, no argument there, but she was also a true goddess of housework. You dreamed - and you still dream - of a closer (indeed the closest) conspiracy with her. You're stretched out in one dream across your grandmother's carpet from Kurdistan, with your papers and pens and pillows, and you're writing *The History of Housework* together, working so closely that in the future it will be next to impossible for scholars to determine *who* wrote *what.*

In the end you have to admit that Patience mowed any former and most future schemers right out of your puppet show of memory when she cut a big **P** in the grass for you.

Patience might have flown the coop, but she still returns now and again to fly your kite. Watch her once more dancing in front of the lake map with a vacuum hose, and pointing to Fort Dodge Point with an attachment brush. Go on and meet her anew at the old oak, where the bent green ladder propels you both up to the first limb, and from there you explore every branch and peer behind each leaf and embrace the gnarls and burrs alike until the sunset catches you by surprise. And then as the band begins to tune up across the lake, she shouts: *I wanna go dancing!* But she has to tell you how she got her name first: *My mother had an extremely difficult time delivering me...* You don't want to go into the details, but she has to tell them to you anyway, from the twisting and twining cord to the blood and the screams and the… *You know, Carl, delivering a baby is like landing a jet…*

In those days leading up to the Seashore's visit, when you were under the sway of Patience, your grandmother looked at you more and more suspiciously.

Can I trust you, she asks, *to listen for the whistle?*

A high pitched whistle, the one you've been told to listen for, takes off from the kitchen. You run out to the backyard to tell your grandmother, who's left her wicker basket full of sheets under the clothes line to continue her argument with Mrs. Skylingstad concerning *your garage* which straddles *my property.* Unable to catch her attention, you run back to the kitchen and do what you've seen your grandmother do so many times: *hold the pressure cooker at arms length with hot pads and take it to the sink!* But you've forgotten to first turn on the cold water, and you arrive at a loaded sink with no place or space to rest a pressure cooker other than on a stack of china cups and saucers and plates. Billowing steam in the meantime has blinded you, and you let go of the pressure cooker to cover your eyes, crushing the dishes under the weight of the beef and potatoes and carrots and onions, just as your grandmother comes in from the backyard, and a Patience fueled lawnmower roars along the narrow walkway between cottages, shooting dust and pieces of paper towels and rags against and through the screen windows.

All this endless cleaning and dusting and polishing and straightening in preparation for a visit from the eminent music psychologist Doctor Carl Seashore and his wife. He is your grandfather's brother, and you were named after him with the hope, now abandoned, that you would have a career in music. The professor is so perceptive that he can spot a butterfly wing between the pages of *Pnin,* and his wife is so curious that she can open cabinets and drawers and bureaus using only her eyes. They are unaccustomed to dirt, living as they do in the exceptionally clean city of Zurich. At a great expense they are crossing the ocean because - although they are prone to seasickness - they abhor airplanes.

You have been instructed to not discuss your interest in baseball, or to play the radio, where a song by *that horrid character playing his frightful harmonica* may come on at any second without warning.

And you are - *and I mean this sincerely* - not to go *anywhere near the piano*, an admonition which you share with your grandfather, until that predetermined time arrives when you are to sit down and perform your Satie *sans* sheet music. But in the event Doctor Seashore consents to play the piano, and he plays a *very beautiful Stravinsky*, you have wiped every inch of the piano with a soft oily cloth. And you have polished the keys and shined the pedals and oiled the stool and arranged the sheet music, although he will need no music to perform *Petrouchka*, providing he consents to *treat us to it*. And you have feather dusted the beams in the ceiling and washed all the windows, not just the ones on the north side of the house. And...let's see...you've beaten the pillows and taken a broom to the cobwebs under the eves and evened the books and scrubbed the baseboards and changed all the light bulbs and...

And because the Seashores happen to come from the tidiest country in the world, you will forego your two o'clock swim and work straight through until five, keeping track of your time, for you will be paid by the hour at the end of the week. Doctor and Mrs. Seashore, as you will call them, are expected at *six*, when I will serve them martinis on the front porch. You may join us with your lemonade and grenadine, if you've cleaned up and changed clothes and brushed your hair and teeth and put on your polished shoes.

Doctor Seashore speaks slowly, you are forewarned, and his wife is hard of hearing. You are to remain silent and smiling slightly, unless you are spoken to. To answer a question from Doctor Seashore, use as few words as possible, choose them correctly, and pronounce them carefully, without an accent of any kind. You are to keep your own ideas about music strictly to yourself. Doctor Seashore is a scholar who doesn't like to waste time! His children and grandchildren are all successful, or well on their way to becoming successful. Ask to be excused before leaving the room. He'll no doubt want to see some historical sights. We must do everything we can to shield him from all but the most distant view of that run down amusement park which you find so enchanting. If it's a calm day, I know that he'd love to ride the Queen...

Once upon a time you were comfortably at home with the patterns in the carpet in the living room of the cottage on Dixon Beach. And you were perfectly alone and secure with and holding on tightly to all your kites in the air high above Lake Okoboji. But then the baby rolled down the sidewalk and disappeared over the edge of the bank, and in the rush to get her up to the emergency room, there was some blood that fell on the carpet. And Patience ran away, severing forever one of the kite strings with her incisors. And that night the wind - or was it the chipmunks? - sent Napoleon crashing to the floor once more. Whether or not the diminutive Corsican was a military genius - if there is such a thing as a *military genius* - is beyond the scope of this exposition on postcards and memory. Leave it to say that in the fragments of his shattered figurine-like life strewn across a rug from the other side of the world, you discovered that your future was not, after all, completely determined. But neither was it to be a totally random series of occurrences. At any moment you wished, in other words, you could insert your own pattern into the carpet of your dreams. And you could reel in your bright yellow Chinese dragon kite; or you could simply let it loose to find its own way around the world, that enchanting box kite from Zurn's souvenir stand in the amusement park, that your grandfather had surprised you with one day.

It was to be your own decision, your grandfather said. Whether you were to harmonize...or improvise...or devise some unique combination of the two.

"Am I to take it that we're like guides?"

"Most definitely. We are like wilderness guides who know the landscape by heart, and we're here to steer the reader through the swamp or maze or forest of narrative."

"But how do we know that they need guidance?"

"Because in Volume One they often complained of being lost."

"You mean the 'Puppet Show of Memory'?"

"Yes, they got lost in it, some of them, they didn't know where they were, the time period, I mean. They knew that they were probably at Okoboji, but beyond that, it was like they were stuck in Laugh in the Dark all the way through for many readers. So we're here to make it easier for them."

"You don't think that we'll confuse things even more?"

"Not if we stay on track. As long as we stay on track, everything - as McGuinn used to say - is gonna be alright."

"Ok! I'm inspired now! In school they told me that I'd never be a leader. If they could only see me now. I'm ready to lead on. Follow me boys! But where are we going?"

"We're back in the present, for want of a better word. We're with Claire and Carl once again and –"

"That compelling couple!"

"Don't be facetious, because it won't fit with the flavor of this next scene, which is very interesting from an historical point of view."

"I'm sorry. Where are they now?"

"They're sitting on the bank in front of the cottage, with their wine of course, and Claire is thinking out loud."

"That's what I like about Claire. She thinks out loud."
"And Carl is sitting cross-legged with his interior thoughts. . ."
"It's all inner with that sinner."
"And so, I believe we're ready to go."

II.

If For Some Reason

When I'm at Okoboji, Claire said, it's difficult to (hiccup) write and think only about Abbie and Inkpaduta and their brief time together at Okoboji. The subject wants a little (hiccup) distance…

Drinking wine sometimes gave her the hiccups, but this evening there were even more spaces than usual between her phrases. She swatted a mosquito, took another sip, and held her breath. As usual, we were sitting in the grass at the edge of the bank. At sunset she always appeared to become more reflective.

There's a certain advantage, she continued, having let her breath escape, to writing on location. You want to include as many of the local sights and smells as possible. But then not being at a place can call up such a desire of wanting to be there that there's more of a possibility that even less will be left out.

I was trying to find the right time to tell her about the latest postcard, but when Claire was thinking out loud about her work, I couldn't interrupt her and change the subject to something which had terrible implications for the completion of her project.

Quickly, in the brief space between hiccups, she asked me: *Have you ever longed for something or someone or someplace so badly that you actually found yourself transported to him or her or there or it?*

She didn't really expect or even care for a response from me. My ideas on the philosophy of longing would only have created a log jam in her river of rumination. And I was off on another tangent anyway, one more concerned with lakes and seas. There is only one Lake Okoboji, I was thinking, just as there is only one Black Sea and one Lake Superior and one Lake Herman and one…

I suffer, and have always suffered, from claustrophobia, she said. So to live at and think of and write only about Inkpaduta and Abbie at Okoboji…can you imagine how that could bring on a severe case of exhausting enclosure? I would feel more adventurous if I was, say, down on the Walker Percy's Mississippi Gulf Coast, leaning against a sturdy live oak that survived the hurricanes at Pass Christian, and looking out at the blurry outline of Ship Island, and writing *from there* about what it must have been like for Abbie to follow Inkpaduta across the ice on Okoboji.

Strollers were always out rolling at this rapturous time of the day, and just as one of them happened to pass by, Claire let loose with one of her infectious hiccups, which sloshed most of the wine out of her cup and on to my leg. But then the stroller pushing the stroller, as well as the baby in the stroller, echoed Claire's hiccup with hiccups of their own, which didn't quite seem to be sincere hiccups to me, but rather self-induced hiccups of the type to mimic and make fun of someone who had a severe case of the hiccups. Claire didn't seem to mind having been made fun of though - no, she just waved at the imitators, who were laughing as they rolled off, and handing me her cup, she said:

For some reason, this wine doesn't taste very good to me tonight. Here, can you finish mine? The next time you go over to the amusement park…think you could get me some fudge? Black walnut, or any kind really…

Locking her eyebrows on the two figures that were always looming in the foreground of her imagination, she stated unequivocally, as if standing in front of some omnipresent judge: I know I've told you before… that I'm not going to turn away from the task that I've taken on. I've got to keep following Inkpaduta and Abbie, at least until their paths diverge.

A few nights later she spoke to me of *certain unreliable narrators and their madding and inconsistent accounts* which she found so puzzling to decipher...and the many reasons why her work might have to remain, in the end, unfinished...*and the impossibility of, indeed even my fear of, ever finishing...*

I can follow both their stories, she said forcefully, speaking of her main characters, until the day, that fateful day really, when their paths suddenly diverge: May 31, 1857. After that, I can follow one, or I can follow the other, but I can't seem to be able to follow both of them at the same time. There are days that I just want to sit with Abbie and her son and his dog Old Man in their log cabin museum, listening to her telling her tale over and over - elaborating, fantasizing, hypothesizing - until she's too tired to tell it anymore, and so she plays a scratchy phonograph record of her account - once again: over and over and over. Her life, like all our lives, becomes one of constant repetition. A repetition of the rendition...But above all, I love the sound of the needle in the groove, and what's not said, what's never spoken of, what's left out of the account. That's what really interests me, and that's why I'm forcing myself to write their story, the story of Inkpadta and Abbie. And that's why, funny as it may seem, when you play your records late at night, I get inspired, but not by the music I hear - no, I try to shut that out, because it doesn't have anything to do with the story that I'm trying to tell. No, what really inspires me is when the record comes to an end, and all I can hear is the needle skipping in the groove, which for me perfectly matches the look on Abbie's face at the end of her life, when the story of her recorded life came to an end, and she just stood there in her long dress staring at her customers...and they stared back at her...

But then...then there are other days...days when all I want to do is follow Inkpaduta from the west bank of the James River all the way to the Little Big Horn. I want to see exactly what part he played in the defeat of Yellow Hair. Sometimes when I'm up in my room reading all these accounts I get so caught up in them that I feel like I'm riding with

Inkpaduta's son and Gall and the other Hunkpapas, and here comes Crazy Horse, and we're all galloping across the Greasey Grass looking for Yellow Hair. Because if we kill Yellow Hair then the battle is over, and all we have to do is drive an awl between the ears of Yellow Hair so that he can hear better in the next world than he did in this one...

And I'd like to know about Inkpaduta's last days in Canada, and whether or not he made it to the shore of Lake Louise. Because if he was never destined to look across Okoboji again, was he at least able to admire the reflections of the Rockies on the surface of Lake Louise? I've never been there, but from the accounts I've read, which I have to assume are accurate - although people do tend to exaggerate about the beauty of places - you for instance, Carl - I remember in St. Paul you telling me that Okoboji was one of the three blue water lakes in the world, or some ridiculous thing like that. Isn't every lake a blue water lake? But you were right, this is a pretty place, and there is something a little oceanic about it, which in turn lends credence to my Inkpaduta and Abbie story.

But why not write our history? Tell our story! That's what I wanted to suggest to Claire. Why not write in poetic detail about our thrilling late night walk across St. Paul on St. Patrick's Day, holding each other up on those crumbling steps down the bluff below Hill's house, and weaving past Harper McKee's bookshop with the faded reproduction of Maurice Utrillo in the window, that you insisted on pausing to admire, before continuing down West Seventh to the turn off for the High Bridge, where I said maybe we should turn around, it's getting late, we could get picked up for public intox, but you wanted to keep going, keep going, up the High Bridge, the old shaky wrought iron High Bridge with its wooden sidewalk, out to the exact middle on the down river side - you knew just where it was - that halfway point where all of the St. Paul lovers love to meet, and that's where you grabbed that silly green leprechaun hat off my head and kissed it goodbye and tossed it over the side, and both of us leaned over the railing like we were on the bow of an ocean liner watching it twirl and swirl its way down to the river, where it landed straight up!

Now, how could I know that?

There must have been a moon…you said the moon shines for you, meaning me…I'm paraphrasing, you said…it's from a famous soliloquy, you said…I looked into your eyes, I remember, and they appeared to say to me - in my state - they said: kiss me, so I did, we kissed on the High Bridge, put that into your book.

The old High Bridge remember, because people love a love story, the more offbeat the better. You better repeat the promises that we made to each other that night, drunken promises like:

We'll follow that hat to New Orleans someday, and drink coffee under the awnings of Cafe du Monde while we wait for that silly green hat to come floating by…

Drunken promises like that, which always evaporate in the bright light of day. But then we looked at the lights and talked about so many things while we waited for the sun to come up over Mounds Park, and that police car drove up and asked us if we were alright, and you said in a bubbly voice: *Never been better!* Why not write about that, or about our walks to the downtown St. Paul library, and how we picked catnip in the grass outside the county morgue, and sat over our beers in the Coney Island - events like those should be *preserved*, or so it seemed to me, although, at the same time, I had nothing against Inkpaduta and Abbie, beyond being slightly jealous of the hold they seemed to have over Claire…

But Claire kept talking, long after sunset, she theorized her way right through my little St. Patrick's Day reverie, worshiping instead at the little shrine of her own personal literary theory, so that while I was kissing her on the bridge, she was talking about some barrier - *A barrier that I have to break through!* A so-called *wall without windows* which kept her - *Which keeps me from being able to follow and write contrapuntally about the two distinct and separate life altering paths of Abbie and Inkpaduta...*

Then no more than a few nights later, on an evening of a summer which I had no desire - despite MacJames and Lou and the distance which had crept between Claire and I - to see end, and when my wine and her sun tea were gone, and the sun had departed, and the colors in the western sky had finally faded, and the clouds had been dismissed, and the darkness had waded in to shove aside the last light and obscure everything down to the alternating frown and bounce of her eyebrows...and the strollers (the ever present at all times of the day and night strollers) had returned home after a last gasp of the deeply satisfying fresh night air coming off the lake...and the boat noise had subsided and the humidity fallen and the crickets had lowered the volume on the tune they played on their legs...And as it was long past the time when Claire normally had climbed the stairs to her bedroom to return to those unreliable narrators, when all this time sitting right beside her on the bank was a man with a memory like a puppet show for pete's sake...and after I'd finally summoned the courage to show her the postcards of the falls of Sioux Falls and the cliffs at Pipestone, sent by my father with brief notes saying that he expected to be in Okoboji any day...that he was getting *closer and closer*...And after I'd assured her that she could stay at my grandmother's cottage for as long as she liked, and that she didn't have to move out of her room - although I hesitatingly made it clear to her that *some things might change*, given my father's interests, if not manias, for cooking and listening to music loudly, and reminiscing endlessly, and drinking wine, and especially French wine if he could get it, constantly - after I let her know again that she could stay at the Dixon Beach cottage f*or as long as you like*! - she then turned to me, still scratching the mosquito bites on her legs and arms and shoulders, some of which I could see were bleeding when she lit her cigarette, and asked, out of the blue and in a darkness so complete that I couldn't tell by the look on her face if she was serious or only joking...she turned to me and said in that musical little voice of hers, with its accent from some unknown distant faraway country...she said to me almost in a whisper, as if she was worried that the Skylingstads might hear...she said: If I am unable to continue with my story for some reason; if, for instance, I became incapacitated, as the insurance agents like to call it, after my characters get to the James River, because I know I'll get them as far as the James River...but anyway, would you take my story up along the lines of the general plan which I've carefully laid out across my bed, and bring it to some sort of conclusion, without exactly finishing it. In other words, what I'm trying to say is, please don't end it with the words: *The End,* or *Fini* either, for that matter. No finis please! Words like that are detestable to me!

After she went back in the house I fell back on my back in the grass and felt the creeping charlie crawling over me. Her light came on, and I listened to the lake, and I heard the waves passing through the dock posts on their way to the beach. So there was to be no finish, and there was to be no end. I could live with that, I imagined.

"Hold on, we're going back again."
"How far back this time?"
"All the way back to the early days."
"Those hazy crazy good old early days."
"Back to the beach at Arnolds Park."
"At the bend in the seawall?"

"You got it!"

"A hot day?"

"A very hot day. Sweltering in fact. Carl and his grandfather have escaped the Dixon Beach cottage, and the endless series of chores which continue even on a Sunday, because the Seashores are coming-"

"The Seashores are always coming!"

"They're in Chicago now, staying at the Drake for a few days, visiting the Art Institute and the Museum of Natural History, and taking in a few concerts, before they get back on the train for Omaha, where they'll transfer to a bus for –"

"Ok, ok, the Seashores are on their way, and Carl and his grandfather…"

"Carl and his grandfather have run away from all the jobs, they've taken the fishing boat to Arnolds Park in the afternoon, after most of the weekend tourists have started for home."

"Arnolds Park…on a summer Sunday…the sights and smells and sounds…Coming at them in one jumble of memory…"

III.
The World I Remember

Doesn't it seem like an ominous omen to you, Carl? (my grandfather theorized against the background of a storm-threatening cloud bank, after I'd returned the torn and dripping wet editorial pages to him, which had been ripped from his gentle fingers by an impudent breeze that had carried them off to land in a puddle under the roller coaster) *Because now…now you can see, can't you Carl, you can clearly see that the decomposing process has already begun before the opinions have had a chance to become…to become widely disseminated…*

My grandfather…he was always happiest after the tourists had left… and he wasn't bothered - not a bit, not at all - by the things that they'd left behind on the beach. It's better to leave *things* behind, he said, rather than people or pets.

He considered these abandoned forgotten objects to be simply misplaced artifacts which were waiting to be catalogued for a museum of our disposable culture that would no doubt be built one day on the edge of a disposable town in a disposable state in need of a tourist attraction.

Look over there! he pointed: a ripped life jacket wrapped in seaweed being tugged at by the waves at the edge of the water.

Look over here! he gestured: a broken pair of binoculars in an empty bucket of fried chicken.

I found half a sandy dog on a stick jammed in a crack in the seawall, but my grandfather looked at it contemptuously when I brought it to him

Under a dock: a child's bright red beach towel; under the towel: a dead fish, a bullhead that smelled.

But under a sandal on top of the seawall and right beside my grandfather was something precious, and almost holy to him: a *Des Moines Sunday Register,* which the wind, when it rose up again (for the wind had swung, in the space of an afternoon, from the west to the north, and was now aimed directly at the amusement park) would try to scatter, in all its multi-colored sections, throughout the amusement park all afternoon long.

As one would anticipate, the brightly colored funny pages blew off toward the Fun House, where the Fun House Clown was tinkling away at *A Woman is a Sometime Thing*, which my grandfather responded to by tapping his fingers and toes in time, as if he were the percussionist and the bassist, as he sat above me at the bend in the seawall.

I was the skinny sunburned bony shouldered kid with smeared Nutty Buddy chocolate on my chin, digging in the sand with the best friend I ever had that day - a girl who I'd never seen before and who I would never see again - a nameless little girl who, simply by coincidence, and because we were in Arnolds Park and not someplace else - was on the beach that hot day. Her shriek, which pierced me to my capillaries, reminded me of the cry of a seagull. I'd showed her where I thought I'd buried a tiny green plastic soldier - the one with *Phillip* scratched on its base - the Sunday before. I was certain I'd buried him right in front of the bend in the seawall…maybe it had been two weeks ago, or three…I couldn't remember really…

Phillip? Is that your name? she asked me.

No, my name is Carl.

Oh, she said. And then she shrieked again.

She always glanced in the direction of her parents, who were at the other end of the beach, at the conclusion of every shriek. And they lifted their heads and looked her way too, probably grateful of the distance between them.

My grandfather was watching us dig with a bemused wonder. He must have admired our energetic enthusiasm - the way we dug and dug, throwing sand this way and that. I knew that he also admired my nimbleness in jumping up and chasing down and stepping on the different sections of the paper as they happened to blow away whenever he got up and slipped on his sandals to pace along the seawall.

It's when I walk, he told me, it's when I'm up on my feet and moving around that my thoughts seem to come to me.

He stood up as if to depart for his favorite shade tree at the far end of the beach.

One particular phrase of his has stuck with me, down through all the years, whenever I think of my grandfather on the beach in front of the amusement park: *When we walk we talk seriously to ourselves.*

I can still see him in his wide brimmed Panama hat, standing up on the seawall with the sun over his shoulder, and me digging in the sand with my friend, and holding up for his approval the bottom of an old glass jar, the edges rounded from years of being in the lake and the sand, and shaped like it was the jaw of some long extinct prehistoric animal which had flourished during the time when Okoboji was part of a large inland ocean.

Maybe you'll turn out to be an archeologist, my grandfather said after he sat back down.

But then he must have felt another aphorism coming on, for he stood right up again, which meant that another section of the paper blew off, and I jumped up immediately to chase it down, finally stepping on it under the last hill of the roller coaster, just as the rattling cars passed

overhead, the greasy brakes grabbing for the greasy gears and inserting yet another wild strange noise into my ears. On my way back to my grandfather and my friend - who'd shrieked again in delight as she watched me run off - I discovered that it was the travel section that I'd stepped on, which that Sunday was featuring an article about a place very dear to my grandfather's travel-crazy heart:

Old Quebec!

He was ecstatic, holding the tattered section lovingly in his hands, while proceeding to tell me and my friend how he and my grandmother had ridden the train all the way across Canada - *The greatest country in the world!* - and stayed in petite Levis, a little town across the river Quebec Cité. And how every morning they rode the ferry across the St. Lawrence River to the old city, and they climbed the steep stairs and they walked the narrow streets and stood on the high bluff and looked to the far north, which made him feel, he emphasized, as *if we were standing at the very edge of the world.*

As we kept on digging for the green plastic soldier, he went on to say how he much preferred (*unlike your grandmother*) train travel to ship travel, because trains made stops, and you could get off, and you could look around, and best of all, you could buy a newspaper.

I read newspapers to feel less lonely, he said. When I read a good newspaper, of which there are fewer and fewer around, I feel connected, I find my place in the world, and I get ideas, ideas that I want to pursue and chase down, ideas for which I would need a big library, a library a thousand times the size of the Arnolds Park Public Library, to do my research in.

But I was always to remember - indeed *I was never to forget* - that when I read the news in a newspaper, I was to read it with one eye open and the other eye shut. *I'm speaking metaphorically, of course*, he said.

He was as nimble with words as I was in movement, I realized that day on the beach. Because his mind…his mind was like the flight of a butterfly, flitting here and there, from milkweed pod to sunflower.

But he wouldn't always be such a nearby inspiration - that realization hit me too that day, and hard enough to give me cause for pause… so that I put down my digging stick…until my friend tapped me on my shoulder with her stick and asked: *Why aren't you digging?*

It was a good question…I didn't have an answer that I wanted to share with her…I'd stopped because…because in the space of a year, I must have known intuitively, my grandfather would be dead…and I wanted this moment to last and last…I knew I'd have lots of friends to dig with in my life…I could see myself with my wife someday…we'd be digging in a garden by the river for the carrots and the potatoes…but once my grandfather was gone…it was hard to imagine a world without my grandfather there to guide me through it…pointing out the nonsense and the true sense…so that's why I'd stopped digging…I'd had a glimpse of a world without my grandfather…and it was ugly…and it was desolate…the newspapers would never mean to me what they had meant to him…the ability to decipher them, like the skill to make lace, would become a lost art…I had a glimpse of all this on the beach…and so I'd paused in my digging…but then, after my friend had challenged me… confronted me with her question, I started up again…

I dug and I dug and I dug. I attacked our hole at the bend in the seawall. The chert and sand and pebbles flew through the air. My grandfather looked up from his paper to remark that: *You're digging as if you're trying to uncover something buried in your past.*

He'd hit on something, this perceptive man. Because I was digging deeper - far deeper - than any plastic soldier could have sunk, and I *was* trying to uncover some truth about myself that afternoon…and I had this little friend with long red hair helping me, who was also curious about the past, family trees and time lines and genealogy - because she asked me: *Was Phillip the name of the toy soldier, or the boy's name who played with the soldier?* I confessed to her that I didn't know…I didn't know, but I thanked her anyway, without telling her so, for bringing me back to the present, and the search for the buried toy soldier, and not for an answer to a question that I had no hope of uncovering no matter how far down I dug. Some things are simply unknowable - and this is where I differed with my grandfather, who thought just the opposite…

So I dug on in the late afternoon sun with this little girl, and sometimes in our enthusiasm we were digging so close that our arms and elbows touched, and her curls tickled my cheeks and shoulders. We were in such close contact that it was almost like we were one person digging, and that in itself was thrilling. It made me dig that much harder. And whether a man and woman could work together, as a boy and girl seemed to be able to do, as well as other buried questions and unplanned separations and the possibility or impossibility of lasting relationships - I left such unknowns alone, I wasn't looking for symbolism in the sand anymore, I was only alive to the moment.

But my grandfather, watching the closeness with which I dug with my friend, suddenly stood up, on purpose as I can see now, so that another section of his precious paper that he was sitting on would blow off, and I would have to jump up and run off in pursuit of it, and my friend would shriek again in delight, shaking her curly red hair in the wind, just as the Queen came in, and a seagull flying overhead seemed to squawk unscripted at the whole scene, and the Queen tooted it's horn coming along side the dock and made my friend jump, as she'd been digging all this time with her back to the lake.

I never turned my back to the lake…I'd watched too many westerns on TV…too many episodes of *Have Gun Will Travel* and *Gunsmoke* …to ever turn my back on the lake…

But here…my grandfather had already begun giving his *dissertation on traps*…and I hadn't been listening, with all this digging…so I turned my attention to him, as did my friend...he had an audience of two instead of one...we both planted our diggers in the sand and paused to listen respectfully:

...because the news in newspapers is a trap too...the way it seeks to limit our horizons...rein them in...so that when things should appear limitless...and what people can do when they put their minds to it should appear boundless...newspapers and the news attempt to set limits...a newspaper trying to capture the news reminds me of your grandmother trying to catch her chipmunks in a trap. It's a lesson in futility. Chipmunks are simply too smart for mouse traps. She hides these traps in the fireplace, or in back of Napoleon on the mantle, or in behind her Gardner and Christie mysteries on the bookshelf. But in the morning - have you noticed? - those strategically placed traps are always empty, because you can't catch a chipmunk in a mouse trap, anymore than you can convince someone to vote their conscience on election day. Consciences are buried too deeply these days, just like that little toy soldier you're after. And chipmunks are too smart for mouse traps. And, by the way, people who set traps are already caught in a trap *themselves*, without even realizing it of course...

I don't know if it was my grandfather's insinuation about the soldier being buried to deep to ever be recovered, or his diatribe on the news, or his tirade about traps, but something appeared to have a discouraging effect on my little friend, who shrieked one last time before she wandered back down the beach to rejoin her family. My grandfather likewise got up to walk down the seawall, no doubt to replenish his thought reservoir. His rising up meant that another section of the paper blew off, this one being the weather page, and its forecast of the heat wave continuing for the near future...

When my grandfather returned, whether by coincidence or not, his mind was also on the weather, because he pronounced, even before sitting down, that *winter is the most essential season.*

My memories of winter, he continued, after letting his initial statement sink in, have risen to the top, and nearly supplanted my other

memories of other seasons…

Sitting beside him at the bend in the seawall, I tried to imagine winter in this intense beastly heat…

You can hear your thoughts in the winter, he said. And you can see them too, because they become crystallized. Suddenly they're something that you can grab a hold of. They're fragile, of course, as all thoughts are. But they're very clear. That's what I like about thoughts in the winter. *Their clarity!* They're so translucent that you can actually see all the way through them. You can see to the backside of your thought!

You must remember this, I remember telling myself at the time. Remember it all. Everything! This moment…this time…this day…

But winter seemed a long way off. I felt I needed something to remind me of winter, if I was to distinctly remember his thoughts on winter. So as soon as my grandfather left to cool off under the shade tree at the far end of the beach, I wandered under the roller coaster and into the amusement park, and the first tree that I came to, which happened to be an old cottonwood, I broke off a tiny little branch, and stripped it of its leaves, and took this bare branch of winter back with me to the beach and into the lake and underwater, where I pretended that it was a little divining rod that would help me find the toy soldier in the huge drifts of snow that would come one day, as predicted, to bury the seawall…

No snow though, and no soldier…even though I thought I knew exactly where I'd buried him. But I was never to stop digging anyway…I dug then, and continue to dig, up to this day…I dig through the sand of my imaginative desert…I imagine that toy soldier at the bend in the seawall, deep down in the dark sand, digging his way out with the butt of his rifle…inching his way back up to the surface. He should have been carrying a shovel instead of a gun. His weapon wasn't going to do him much good way down in that sand…

I think he'd be amazed by how much things had changed if he ever made it back up to the present day surface. He'd find that the amusement park, except for the restrooms, had been sanitized. He'd find the old bath house vanished, and the Merry-Go-Round disappeared too, because about the time that my grandfather died they auctioned off the hand-carved, hand-painted wooden horses, one by one, to the highest bidder …the lowest skidder…

Certain sections of the Sunday paper crept away like caterpillars that day…so slow that it was possible for Nutty Buddy to read *Ask Andy* as he and it inched past the Nutty Buddy Bar stand.

But then other pages seemed to sprout wings in the sudden gusts, and take to the skies like butterflies caught between burning forests and men with mescal on their breath waving machetes, and fields of poisonous genetically engineered corn…

I jumped up to chase after the business and market pages, but my grandfather put his hand on my shoulder and said *Let that section go Carl. Just let that one go on its merry way.*

I stood on the seawall and watched the wind wrap all the closing averages and futures prices around the braces, beams, and crosspieces of the roller coaster.

Notice how quickly, my grandfather said, his hand still on my shoulder, how quickly the numbers crumple and fade, and are in turn replaced by other numbers, which are even more deceiving and illusory.

You know Carl, you could pay a gang of painters overtime to brighten up this profit-hungry world we live in, but all they'd end up accomplishing in the end is painting the windows shut…

What a long hot afternoon it had been…I was feeling faint, standing there smelling the popcorn and the cotton candy, the French fries and the hot dogs, the hamburgers and the…

The day will come, Carl, when you find yourself being overcome by a strong musty smell, more powerful even than the smell of mothballs in the closet. It'll be the smell of the old days: your old days. I can still smell and taste and hear and feel and, yes, even see my old days, if I shut my eyes tight…I can see the steamboats lined up at the pier again, the Des Moines and the Sioux City and the Queen of course - they're all lined up in my mind, and their smokestacks are billowing, and Roy Rolf and Spotts and Jap Alexander are racing across the lake. And then later on your father joins the race in his shiny new Chris Craft Runabout that we bought for him and his brother. They race it across the lake, with girls in the front and girls in the back, spoiled to death before they went off to the war. And then everything changed! Everything! They came back different boys. They were heroes, but they were gamblers too, and smokers and drinkers and wife abusers and father failures. But they could dance all night! They tried to settle down, they built those ugly tract houses that litter the edges of every city and town, but they were still restless. And their kids…their kids grew up having to contend with all the indecencies that got passed down to them, which the newspapers, at best, only hinted at. The horrible smell of your grandmother's vinegar window-washing solution, for instance, which we came over here to escape from…remember?

It was drawing near the end of a long sweltering summer Sunday afternoon on the beach at the bend in the seawall in front of the amusement park. My long haired friend had deserted me long ago. Already I missed her. I tried to reassure myself that I'd see her again someday, while at the same time realizing that I probably never would. Or if I did happen to see a woman with red curly hair, cut short now for her job at the office, I probably wouldn't recognize her, or she me, with all the tricks that age plays with our outward appearance.

I was getting hungrier...and thirstier...by the minute...but my grandfather hadn't quite finished. He'd been threading the loops all afternoon, and now all he had to do was pull them together, and knot 'em, and then we could finally get in the boat and start for the cottage and sit down to the contents of my grandmother's pressure cooker...savory beef sauces with carrots and onions and celery...

It's almost as if this big red curtain that rises each morning and falls every evening is rising and falling on some puppet show of memory. Do you ever get that feeling Carl? While over in the wings, some disgruntled technician is playing with the lights, turning them off and on, on and off. And when we want to get close to something, to try and have a better look, to examine it more closely, then it's like we're suddenly strapped in a chair, and some omnipresent optometrist is shooting puffs of air in our eyes at point blank range.

My grandfather took off his dark glasses and rubbed his eyes. Then he took his hearing aide monitor out of his shirt pocket and adjusted the volume. These were his oft repeated preparations in anticipation of my response to a question he had poised to see what I had learned on this unique day: *If you had to write the obituary of that little toy soldier you lost, what would you say?*

I would say that he was brave and that he loved his country and that he wanted to fight for what is right. I would say that he believed in his cause, and that it's because of him that we're free, and that in the end...

People's ends, summations of their lives, that's what fascinates me, he said, interrupting me. Of course, much more is left out than what is included, because it's in the nature of newspapers to obscure more than they illuminate. But you can still get an inkling, simply by reading an obituary, of the marvelous things that people can accomplish, if they put their minds to it, over a lifetime…

Now, what am I trying to tell you? he asked me, as I was gathering together my towel and shovel and bucket. That the world I remember is not the world you'll remember. That you'll never see the steamboats line up, but you'll live to see something else line up. Because with people and places and things…they're always lining up, you know. And your teachers and leaders and ministers and masters always insist that you get in line, and once you're in line they demand that you stay in line and don't step out of line, don't dare step over the line! When this happens to you, what I want you to tell these line enforcers is –

Three toots from the Queen's horn obliterated forever this last bit of information…

There blows my grandfather's obituary…

He would have been terribly disappointed in it…he who was so fond of the obit page, the page that he always turned to first. It left out nearly everything that distinguished him, that elevated him, that made him who he was, my great teacher, the man whose voice was the most unique in the world. It was almost like some editor was trying to put him in line…

The Fun House Clown…he should have written my grandfather's obituary…because the greatest tribute ever paid to my grandfather was the one from the Fun House Clown…when he quit playing his cherished Gershwin…and everything else, for that matter…on the day that my grandfather died…

His fingers froze at the keyboard…

They remain frozen…

Frozen to this day…

"I don't think that I'll ever be able to read a newspaper in the same way again."

"They are rather unreliable, especially when it comes to the news."

"They certainly haven't covered this story very well."

"You mean our story?"

"I mean this never ending puppet show. They've ignored it!"

"Well…what did you expect?"

"Listen! Do you hear music?"

"Who is it?"

"It's that all-girl band that played up at the Roof, circa early Sixties."

"Don't tell me that we're finally going up to the Roof Garden! I've been waiting since page one to go up there."

"We're climbing the stairs…we're on our way…"

"Who are we following?"

"Gusty."

"Gusty?"

"Remember Gusty from Act Five, Scene V."

"Is that the guy who 'borrowed' the car?"

"It is, and he's back. This is a few years before the car episode."

"So he gets to go up to the Roof Garden to hear this all girl band in person?"

"Not exactly. He removes them from this racial slur, hangs out with them, shows them around the amusement park -"

"Don't tell me the whole scene!"

"I won't, I won't. I just want you to picture a red door on the lower floor of that cement block motel on the hill above where the bathhouse used to be. Imagine someone sitting there, just waiting for that door to open…"

IV.

Sounds of the Stairs

Three harmful shameful dirty words cursed and hurled out in the bright summer air by the crew cut driver of a shiny yellow Chevy scooping the amusement park loop. An expression of hate aimed like the sharp point of an arrow at three women standing in line at the candy shop.

The tallest, her hands shaking, drops her coin purse. The bills stay put but the coins roll out, each of them headed off in a different direction.

But then this *one kid* - out of all the kids who spend their summer days and nights roaming 'round the amusement park - Park Rats they're called - one kid out of this pack standing in the shade of Kennison's popcorn and cotton candy stand - one of the Rats that have been following the trio at a shy and respectful distance - one boy, the bravest boy, steps forward to scoop up the coins, among them a few silver dollars, while sending at the same time a message to the Chevy, a curt sign in the form of a elevated index finger.

Gusty, king of the Rats and all of thirteen, returns the purse to its owner, and receives her thanks, her smile, and, most importantly, her *autograph*. And not only her autograph, but autographs from the other two as well, on one piece of paper, which he swears to carry with him forever, crumpled in his pockets, shirts and shorts alike. He gets offers for it, but he refuses to trade for it, or to sell it at any price, because the trio whose flashing handwriting he is so in awe of (their signatures will dissolve like they were written in watercolor on a sheet of glass left out in the rain when, on the day before Labor Day, he gets pushed off the pier by Fritz or Robinson or Kendall or Pendlebury - one of those Rats shoves him in, and only Madame Jessie could have warned him ahead of time, but Gusty was too busy to seek counsel from her, he lived for the adventure like all the Rats, that's what they had in common, they scrounged for money under the roller coaster and the Loop-O-Plane, and they lived for the next thrill) is scheduled to sing that very evening up at the Roof Garden ballroom!

And why not - since he has their attention, since he's made friends with them, since they've become his good buddies - why not take them on a tour of the amusement park, and show them places they might overlook, like under the roller coaster, which is the best place to pick up a little spare change. Maybe introduce them to the Madame Jessie, if she's not staring into her crystal ball with a customer. And take them to meet the Zurns by all means, the eccentric family that runs the Skee Ball. And walk them through the tunnel, while the park train is in the station, and show them the paintings, which you get no more than a glance at if you're bumping along in the little cars. Then lead them through the Tipsy House in their high heels and their short shorts and their matching blouses and their sunglasses. Then take them for a ride on the water bikes, run by Gusty's friend Ray, who flips over his Bradbury paperback to watch Gusty paddling out toward Pillsbury Point with these three beautiful Black women from another world.

Eventually - after all the popcorn and the snow cones and the Nutty Buddy bars and the root beer - they have their show to get ready for, so the Gardner Cabin will have to wait, and although they could ride the Wild Mouse as many times as they want, because Phillip's sitting and grinning behind the controls, *save it, we'll save it for another day.*

Tomorrow maybe, the shortest one says, because we've got to get back to our motel room, do our hair, you know, tune these instruments, our voices need tuning.

Yeah, we've got to do some other things, you know, to get ready for our performance tonight.

Gusty escorts them through Kiddieland and around the old Merry-Go-Round and up the hill to their motel overlooking the lake, where he reluctantly parts company at the red door of room number four…

Are you comin'? Are you comin' to our show?

Hey! Thanks for showin' us around!

That same evening, Gusty doesn't show up for his job peeling potatoes for the incredibly popular waffle fries at the hamburger stand next to the old theater, which has been turned into a mildly scary ride called *Laugh In The Dark*. Mr. Maas, the owner - and the tough old school superintendent too - shakes his shiny bald head and shouts: *Where is that kid? Anybody here seen Gusty?*

All he would have had to do is take a short walk down the beach to the east - but Mr. Maas never takes short walks or long walks, no, he works all the time, because he doesn't trust any of his poorly paid school kids to man the register or take orders or flip hamburgers - so no, Mr. Maas on the beach, it couldn't have happened, he would never have taken a stroll along the seawall and looked up toward the motel, where he could have seen his errant employee, Gusty, sitting impatiently at a picnic table beside the bathhouse, tapping his toes while they're in there buttoning, and cracking his knuckles while they're behind the door of number 4 zipping, and etching faces and figures with a rusty nail on the flaked paint table top while they're busy putting on their faces. He's already noted the plethora of boats as they lace each other up, and he's watched Jerry at the bath house extract a long sliver out of Linda the Loud's left foot (he's a keen amusement park observer), and all these details will at some point come in handy when he begins to paint watercolors (after he gets out of the Army) of an amusement park where there are watercolors waiting to be painted everywhere…

Gusty is a less than patient Park Rat…

So even when he's forced to wait and be patient, it's still not possible for him to achieve forbearance and composure (if evidence is needed, please see Act Five, Scene V, or simply notice the mound of chewed fingernails under his picnic table). There's just no way he can cultivate patience with all the excitement in the air, because of what's going on behind the bolted red door of room number four.

So he waits...and he waits some more...just sitting there waiting, and turning around every few minutes to thread his poor eyesight through the burr oak branches to the motel on the hill with the big bold 4 on the door.

He's waiting...he's looking for a sign, any sign, for a curtain to part, for a face in the window, for a latch to lift, for a bolt to unbar...

The sun, in the early evening time, has belly flopped into the fields above the west side of the lake, and the reflections across the water, while in no way erasing the vision in Gusty's mind of the trio about to emerge in lieu of all that snapping and buttoning and lacing and tightening, has nevertheless hypnotized him to the point where he is only brought back to the present by the sound of the back-up band tuning up in the Roof Garden.

Now he knows, now he is sure, now he is positive that it is only a matter of minutes before the motel door opens and the trio emerges. transformed for their show.

In the entire history of pre and post contact Arnolds Park, is there a corresponding moment of joyful excitation which compares to the instant when the red door to room number four is finally flung open?

You had to have been there, sitting beside Gusty at the picnic table by the bath house, on the bench facing the motel on the hill, in a perfect position to see those six high heels - two yellow, two green, two red - step over the threshold and out of the room and hit the pock-marked sidewalk.

First to appear was the lead singer. She was followed by her harmonizers, each one dressed identically in every way visible to the naked eye (expect for their heels) down to their nail polish, which in turn mirrored the sunset, and Gusty's tendency to infatuate frenzy.

The back-up band, in the meantime, was milking every drop of accumulated tension it could out of this stately procession by laying down a rhythm which appeared to elevate and transport the trio effortlessly through the amusement park. Their current hit, after all, was riding high on top of the charts, and so were they, these three anti-thesis of the *still life*. Their refrain had already bounced up to Echo Bay and back by the time the trio passed Pinball Haven. Left in its wake was the bleating organ from the Merry-Go-Round. Swamped as well were the screams from the roller coaster. A tray of nuts fell to the floor of the Nutty Buddy stand. The candy man stopped stirring his caramel, and the Dog-On-A-Stick lady stabbed her hand - *ouch!* - instead of the hot dog. Pop was leaning out of his Shell Shack window, and the line in front of the Fun House stood at attention and watched the trio pass by, followed at a respectful distance by that familiar and somewhat pretentious Park Rat, Gusty, self appointed master of ceremonies.

At the base of the steps which will take them up to the Roof Garden, the trio pauses to catch their breath…and gird up for their ascent…their soaring up the steps…

And then, after the stairway is cleared of dance-goers, they begin their ascension…

Gusty remains at the bottom of the stairs - he hasn't found enough money underneath the roller coaster and the Loop-d-Loop and the Tilt-a-Whirl that day to allow him to order a *drag it through the garden* hamburger *and* buy a ticket.

The trio has not even noticed him following them, and now they've abandoned him at the bottom of the stairs.

With each high-heal step up the uneven stairs their distance from him increases.

Six finely tuned smooth muscled long legs of sound.

The melody rides side saddle on the brilliant tones which are teasingly revealed with each step heavenward.

A unique and perfect rhythm keeps them going, carrying them farther and farther away from rapt Gusty stuck at the ticket window with no cash.

Only an ostentatious magician would ever want them to reach the top of those stairs and disappear inside. Only a stone cold sober mathematician could remain sane enough to count off the actual steps, when each step reveals more and more secrets about the very nature of sound.

Halfway to the top they stop on the landing.

Half way to the top they stop and turn around to look back down.

At him!

At Gusty standing there ticket-less with his mouth open wide enough to catch a shoe fly.

Up until this evening he had only heard rhythm…

Now he had seen it - not with someone else's eyes - but with his eyes, and *his eyes only*. He'd seen their long smooth arms reaching out with flaming fingernails at their tips to grip the railing which he had gripped and would grip again, as soon as he had the money. He'd seen their tight skirts lift to expose knees capable of a graceful and effortless ascension. Where else could they have come but from out of the West, or the Isle of the Blessed, with legs like theirs, which were made for music, and music like theirs which was made for legs and voices and arms and hair waving wildly in front of the blasting rhythm-soaked band.

No two stairs alike in their unevenness, and no two steps alike in their irresistible accompaniment.

To the stage!

To their microphones!

To be escorted by Darlowe, in suit and tie, as the crowd parts.

Give 'em room! Make room for 'em!

Darlowe lowers the microphone to do the intro. His face beams, this is his scene, he's made it happen, he made the trip to LA, he brought this group back to Arnolds Park. And now here they are!

And without further ado! Ladies and gentlemen, may I introduce to you, from Los Angeles, California…

That their voices mixed and blended might join the instruments and reverberate together from the mirrored pillars to the revolving glass balls to the cobwebbed rafters to the walnut booths to the blouses and dresses and t-shirts and wavy hair…to finally escape, out the windows, pushed by the fans, passing the incoming cool night air, over the racist yellow Chevy and all the other cars still scooping their loops.

And Gusty, poor Gusty, left forlorn and abandoned at the foot of the stairs. But only 'til those three lovely soulful titillating live and in person voices find him again…

Over there!

See him?

He's sitting at the bend in the seawall, his head tilted to one side… the side toward the Roof Garden of course…so that his three new friends can sing directly into his ear…their voices so clear and close, coming at him in rippling caressing dancing waves that lap in to tickle his stirrup and tympanum…

"Say, I'm kind of worn out. Can we take a break?"

"No, not now. We've got a date to meet Carl and Lou at Fisherman's Wharf."

"I thought they tore that old place down."

"They did, but this takes place pre-bulldozer."

"I hope this scene is more restful. That last one kind of worked me up into a state."

"A lot of this one takes place in Carl's mind, while he's sitting in Fisherman's Wharf, drinking wine and waiting for Lou to show up."

"Fascinating! I hope he has a window table anyway, so we have something to look at, while we're waiting. I must be like that Gusty character, because I hate to wait. I really do."

"Well then, let's get thee to Fisherman's Wharf, while it's still standing on its shaky supports, so we can see who shows up, and who doesn't…"

V.
Once, at Fisherman's Wharf

I'd arranged to meet Lou on her night off from the theater…

Not at the hotel bar, but at Fisherman's Wharf…

And not just for drinks, but for drinks and dinner!

To meet someone for dinner is to partake in a ritual so steep in a stagey significance that it's a wonder every restaurant doesn't have a spire or dome or a minaret hanging over it.

To be certain that we'd have the table on the front porch in the corner closest to the bridge, I got there early.

At Okoboji it's not unusual, once you've crossed a threshold which is both venerable and matured, to be swept back immediately and forthwith into the past by faces which greet you and songs that serenade you and smells that stimulate you - proving that we are not, as the pipe puffing French philosopher insisted, insignificant little clumps of loose dust lint.

I took the *please seat yourself* sign to heart, and went straight for the table that I had in mind. I sat down by the window with my back to the bridge. The place was empty except for a couple with three small children.

I was peering through the tomato vines - some ripe, others green - and the leaves and vines of the other plants which ringed the restaurant on a narrow scaffolding (how did they water these plants, I wondered) at my rowboat tied to the dock down below, when the waitress appeared to hand me a menu. I tried to explain the situation to her as best I could, but listening to myself prattle nervously on, I could hear my tongue tripping over certain key words.

So...let me get this straight, she said impatiently. You've taken our best table, our most popular table, and our only table - without having to push tables together and completely rearrange the restaurant - which seats six comfortably. And you're waiting for an actor, a young actor from Duluth who played the part of Blanche in some play, and who may or may not show up, depending if she got your message. And possibly some of her fellow actors and actresses - you lump them all together as actors, which makes absolutely no difference to me, because I think of them only as customers - may or may not show up. And you've brought this Blanche character a little basket of high potency raspberries which you grew and just picked from your patch behind the whatever. And you want to sit at this table because this is the table where your father used to sit when he ran this restaurant way back when and nobody came because of the Italian sauces he insisted smothering everything with. Did I get all that straight?

Everything except the sauces. They were French, not Italian.

Can I get you anything to drink?

I'd like a bottle of your driest white wine.

With how many glasses?

A minimum of three please.

Three?

Three...

I'll be right back with that.

The click of her shoes against the creaky floorboards sounded slightly perturbed, but I didn't let that get to me - no - I just considered how we are constantly crossing paths in our lives with people - this waitress for instance - that we could swear we've run into at some misty time and place in the past.

I went back to my rowboat…back to watch it bumping up against the dock down below, as boat after boat went under the bridge, and wave after wave jiggled it, while a man in a wheelchair fished, casting into the wakes of boat after boat.

I saw myself helping Lou into my rowboat, and rowing her back to the cottage at sunset, and showing her around the cottage, and playing some records for her, and introducing her to Claire…

That last bit made me a little uncomfortable…trying to imagine introducing Lou to Claire…I put it on the shelf, and tried to return to the pleasant dining experience ahead of me…I mean of *us*, because she would come, I knew Lou would arrive out of breath…

Across the dining porch the two small boys were fidgeting in their chairs while their father was lost in his newspaper and their mother was feeding a baby in a highchair.

I used to fidget at every one of these tables…waiting for my father to finish up in the kitchen…

Would I ever be a father? I wondered.

I stared at those kids, and tried to put myself in the place of the man reading the newspaper…

But then one of the boys looked over at me, and so as not to appear to be staring, I turned my head to look out the window. I saw the man in the wheelchair jerk his pole and reel in his line as if he had something big on it…but it was only a clump of seaweed…

The waitress arrived with the bottle of wine. She carried on the quaint custom of the short pour, and waited for my nod of approval before filling my glass and jamming the bottle in a shiny little tub of ice cubes.

Enjoy, she said, although not hearing her clearly, I asked, Excuse me?

Enjoy! she repeated, and then once more, with force:

Enjoy!

The first sip of wine, mingling as it does with any leftover taste of toothpaste, only prepares our mouths and minds and stomachs for the rest of the glasses which we will drink that evening, if in fact we have been patient enough to wait until sunset before taking our first sip (although in the case of this party, it was still an hour or two before sunset).

For good luck, I went ahead and poured Lou a glass too, and then I leaned back in the chair to wait for her. It was a good thing to come early, I thought, if only to secure the best table. And to relax, of course. And to prepare to be confronted by her moon-like eyes, which would no doubt try to (intentionally or not) unnerve me from so narrow a radius.

I took another sip of my dry white un-nerving agent, and noticed that my fingers were already twitching and shaking, and how it took all of them acting in unison to grasp my glass as if it were a goblet.

I noticed too that the two boys had sneakily slipped away from their chairs, and were collecting sugar packets from the other tables, which they were silently opening and scattering on the floor whenever the waitress was out of the dining room. An older couple who'd come in not long after I had, and who were sitting at a table between this family and myself, were observing these boys - each of whom had long shoulder length hair - with an intent curiosity too.

In order that there should be no uncomfortable silences between Lou and I, once she was finally sitting across the table from me, I prepared - in my mind, as I waited for her - some stories to tell her. They had to be entertaining stories, stories that should make her laugh. I wanted to make her laugh because I loved the sound of her laugh. Her laugh was what had first attracted her to me. Her laugh was what I most loved about her. I never would have thought, until I heard Lou laugh, that you could actually fall in love with a laugh…

And to think that all that would separate us was a checkered tablecloth with three fake daises in a vase. And a salt shaker and a pepper shaker and a tray of sugar packets and a bottle of Tobasco. And the bottle of wine in the ice bucket. And our glasses.

Oh my god!

I took a sip…

In the theater, I reasoned, there is a discernible boundary - the edge of the stage - between the actors and the audience. That's the line which seemingly cannot be crossed or the spell is broken, the illusion dissolved. Art here - life there.

But at this table in this restaurant in front of this window, I can move the bottle over here…and shift the silverware over there…

Just by inviting this actor to dinner, I'm allowed to blur the line between life and art!

I get to play the puppet meister.

It becomes more like a game of chess, this dinner with my friend from Duluth, I thought, as I took another sip, while continuing to wait…

But the restaurant itself, isn't it a kind of stage also? Because the waitress who was joking with the cook in the kitchen assumed - with a quick shake of her head, I noticed - a completely different demeanor once she crossed the threshold into the dining area.

And that made me wonder which Lou I was waiting for. Was I waiting for the Lou that I heard laughing with her friends in the hotel bar? Or was I waiting for the Lou that I walked across the fields with? Maybe I was waiting for the Lou that had collapsed on the bed on the stage as Blanche. I loved that Lou too. I know for a fact that I was waiting for the Lou that had raised her arm like a sword in the midst of all the snoring sleepers on the sleeping porch.

Which one was the Lou who I was waiting for?

Maybe there was more than one Lou.

Are actors, due to the nature of their profession, made up of such a disparate conglomeration of personalities that they live in a parallel universe?

I took two sips while entertaining this last thought. Then I took a long look out the window…

How would she arrive? And from which direction would she come?

One if by land, and two if by sea…

I'd swiveled in my seat to survey the old bridge that Claire and I had walked out on right after we'd got off the bus in the spring. I was recalling Claire's remark about Okoboji reminding her of the ocean, and the jazzed excitement I got from her comparison then, and even now, months later, in this restaurant with all its family connections, when suddenly the illusory peace of the Fisherman's Wharf dining and drinking experience was shattered by a wild shriek from the little brother, who'd become a victim, when no one was looking, of a clever push from behind by his big brother. It was amusing to watch the father attempt to quickly fold his newspaper neatly to the place where he had left off…

Watching that father, I wondered if Lou would be interested in hearing about my father, and the two summers and one fateful winter that he spent running this restaurant? What I couldn't remember, because I was so young at the time, I could simply make up, with the aide of the wine. *He was responsible for the name of this restaurant,* I could hear myself telling Lou, because San Francisco at that time, before he'd been to Venice, was his favorite city in the world, and he thought it would be easy to pass on his love of the so-called city by the bay to the locals and tourists alike. But he was wrong.

Lou might find this California connection humorous because, like almost everyone, she wanted to feel the warm sun on her shoulders. I'd have to closely watch the rise and fall of her eyebrows in order to gauge her reaction to this or that story. Her shoulders too might provide a few clues. At times she seemed to almost speak with her bare shoulders…

Boy, it's funny (I could hear myself saying to Lou) that we're no sooner in a place that we practically used to live in and we're having conversations with people who are no longer around, while at the same time realizing that one day *we'll no longer be around.*

A never ending procession of cars crept across the bridge from both directions, while down below a non-stop pageant of boats went under the bridge, trailing their wakes back and forth between East and West Okoboji.

People never seem to be satisfied with where they are, and that goes double for the summertime. They've got to cross this bridge, or go under that bridge, to get to the next town…the next lake…

Odd how philosophic the wine made me feel. All that wisdom bottled up, waiting patiently to be released, that it may become a philosophical series of dry white considerations.

We drink one glass of wine, and immediately we turn into an historian like Braudel or Berlin.

We drink two glasses of wine, and suddenly we're Wittgenstein or Kierkegaard, investigating and trembling at the same time.

After the third glass, we look in the mirror behind the bar, or we see our reflection in the window glass, and damn if it isn't the reflection of a seer!

But after the fourth glass…the image in the glass…you can't quite get a fix on it…you begin to see through it…and then there's confusion that begins to creep in…

I took another sip anyway.

I'd lost track of how many glasses I'd had. A few I'd refilled before they were empty. But like the waitress, I'd definitely crossed the threshold, and thought that I'd come to an understanding about nearly everything…everything except for *Where's Lou?*

The restaurant in the meantime had filled up. It was bustling, crowded, and more waitresses had appeared out of nowhere. And then one of the boys nearly ran into a waitress carrying a tray piled with plates, and the family abruptly got up and left.

An actor, of course, is always busy, I thought, conjuring up a few excuses for Lou. They're constantly at the beck and call of flighty flaky theater people, after all. And their daily calendar has to be crowded with more appointments than they can ever hope to meet. That had to be the case with Lou, I imagined…

We're all prisoners of our professions, I realized at my window table. Providing, that is, that we have one! An actor is always acting, and a janitor is constantly cleaning, and a school teacher is forever teaching, and a cook automatically cooking. And a homeless person…they never give up looking for a home…or do they?

When this was his restaurant, I was going to tell Lou, my father was always stirring surreptitiously his serious sauces. He took over what had been a pancake house, and transformed it into a restaurant of delicate but delectable sauces over fish and poultry and imported wild game… but nearly all of his prospective potential customers streaming by on the highway refused to bite. He tried to bring San Francisco to Okoboji, but

Okoboji wasn't interested. *The world of Smith's Bay and the world of San Francisco Bay are worlds apart,* I could hear myself say to Lou, as if that wasn't obvious enough.

You know what Lou...we should start a restaurant...yeah, you and me Lou...you could be the waitress, and I could be the cook...we could specialize in something simple like...like...fish and chips...

I could almost hear Lou laughing out loud at this wild hair, drawing everyone's attention in the crowded restaurant to our table. Her infectious laugh, the first time she let it loose, would have everyone in the place looking our way, if not laughing along with her, within minutes after she arrived, providing I could come up with something funny for her to laugh at.

In the absence of the two little boys, and their baby brother or sister, there was a vacuum of liveliness in the restaurant which no other children, at this increasingly late hour, stepped in to fill. Children, not being the prisoners of any professions, are free, and that gets on the nerves of those who are the inmates, retired or not.

Oh listen to you, I could hear Lou say. Maybe it's time you switched to tea.

My father was free to travel though, I continued after emptying my glass, because when he sold this place at the end of that disastrous winter, he took off traveling, and he's never stopped traveling. I'm always getting postcards from all over the place: Vancouver, Victoria, but especially from Venice, his favorite city in the world now, because you can go everywhere and anywhere by water there. He must be following in the footsteps of the man who tried to bring the dream of Venice to Okoboji by building a series of canals and high arching bridges on the west side of the lake, just to give the tourists the illusion that they were in Venice.

Why this obsessive desire of trying to make this place someplace else? I could hear Lou ask. It was a legitimate question for a young actor to ponder. But then one of the old songs came on the jukebox, one of my father's many favorites, and the words of the chorus answered her question better than I ever could have:

I'm a fool…
to want you…

It is the restaurateur's duty, my father liked to say, to create a festive atmosphere.

Why don't you ever talk about your mother? I could hear Lou ask me.

And hard on the heels of that query, another one, equally tough:

How old are you? Tell me how old you really are?

If you look long enough into the eyes of the one who's absent, you'll see that she's holding open the door to her childhood in the port town up north. Her city is built on the side of a steep ridge, and from her earliest memories onward she is constantly going up and down a hill to get somewhere. She develops a love for hills and for climbing, the ascent as well as the descent, one foot in front of another, her legs very strong, every muscle quite firm. I couldn't help but notice them as she strode back and forth across the elevated stage in my mind, her hands on her hips, her head turned as if she saw me and was speaking to me, way off in the back row by the door.

Before I forgot, I wanted to tell Lou (there was still so much that I had to tell Lou) about the view that my father loved from this restaurant…from this very table, even though he couldn't see the sunset properly in the summer…he always hated missing the sunset when he was in the kitchen creating his sauces. He'd ask me to describe the sunset he was missing, and if my words weren't sharp enough or descriptive enough, he'd say: *Why don't you try that again, Carl?*

Another thing he used to insist on (and I don't know if I should tell you this, dear sweet enchanting moony Lou, except that, after all, you're not here yet, are you) is that he always found the operation of a restaurant, in all its intricacies, more interesting than most plays. And he said that the best way to see Okoboji was to take a boat out to…

What?

Are you ready to order now? the waitress asked, appearing out of nowhere to stand above me, pen poised over a notepad.

I've...ah...I'm still waiting and...

All these thoughts were like so many bees that had got out of the box, and I was running around trying to catch them with a net full of holes that I was waving around crazily in the air...when she suggested:

I recommend the Okoboji walleye, which is shipped in weekly from somewhere up in Canada I believe.

I felt a truck loaded to the gills with frozen walleye shake the bridge to its Depression era foundation; shake the shaky supports under Fisherman's Wharf; make waves in my wine glass, and shake the last drop of wine from the rim of Lou's glass, which I'll just finish...downing... drowning...this last little wave of...

Ten thousand nine hundred and forty nine cars crossed that bridge this past Fourth of July, I heard someone say at the next table.

That's an astounding number! I said to the waitress.

What?

The tiny little mole between Lou's shoulder blades that night in the field when she stopped to look up at the moon...

I had an affair with the moon, in which there was neither sin nor shame...

She had a prompter in the wings, he was her own age, he hailed from Warroad...or Baudette...

Have you made your decision sir?

Are you aware that...that Okoboji was once...once a gathering place for...for the tribes of the plains...

I'm sorry sir, but the kitchen is going to be closing and...

Would you care to join me at my table? I have plenty of room. Please try a raspberry. Have a glass of wine. I drink from two glasses. From two glasses I drink a wine that was previously unknown to wine drinkers. But both are empty now. All gone! My money too. Care to go for a boat ride?

I'll be right back with your check, she said.

"I'll bet old Carl had aftereffects after that one."

"Undoubtedly! But here he is again, in this next scene too."

"Experienced through the prism of a terrific hangover; while eating raspberries."

A 'catch me if you can' through the amusement park, carrying a postcard with a message."

"In pursuit of a fervent ride rider…"

"Anything resolved?"

"Not much. But at least we're hanging in the present."

"Are the rides spinning out of control yet?"

"Let's hope not. We don't want anyone to get hurt, do we?"

"No, no one's going to get hurt, with Nutty Buddy and Madame Jessie and Mac James running the show."

"Break time after this scene, right?"

"Correct. There's big changes in store from here on out."

"It's confusing, don't you think, all this jumping around in time. What's the purpose?"

"I don't know. Maybe he's trying to do the show from all sides."

"You think so? Something like that performance that we put on at the flea market in New Orleans one time."

"Where it was open on all sides?"

"Right. We had people sitting all around us. Remember?"

"So you think that's what he's trying to do here?"

"Possibly. But who can say for sure?"

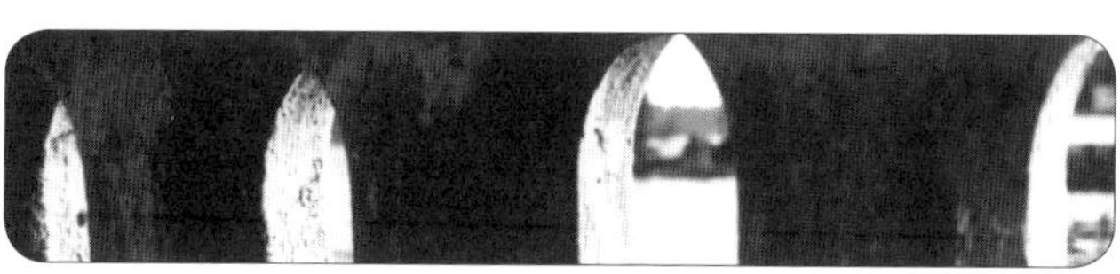

VI.

Weight of the Music

Nutty Buddy craved stability in everything except air masses. A developing weather system was the only change he could tolerate with enthusiasm. Madame Jessie's hazy crystal ball held no future for him…no, the only clues he required in regard to the world to come were in the clouds, as reflected by the polished glass windows of his Nutty Buddy stand across from the seawall.

In order that he might call a storm into play, when confronted by the blank monotony of a summer day, Nutty Buddy kept a reservoir of cumulo-nimbus waiting patiently in back of the western horizon, high above Lakota territory. A bright empty sky might be good for business, but it sowed a seed of anxiousness in Nutty Buddy's craw when he saw his customers sitting so complacently in the sand or on the seawall, chocolate smeared across their sunburned cheeks as ice cream slid down their sticks and into every crack and crevice.

Because what good was a sky that you couldn't even walk across, should the world become suddenly inverted and a few puffy clouds were required to serve as stepping stones? Let one cloud form - make it a *mammatocumulus* - and a multitude will follow, Nutty Buddy prophesized, imagining a sky dripping with pendulous globules hanging from the undersides of anvils, ready and willing to nurse the earth.

Lash Nutty Buddy to the mast of the Queen fleeing for safe harbor, that he might truly appreciate the brawn of a bolt of lightning. Or strap him to the biggest burr of the oldest oak, and let him witness first hand the approach of a wall of storm, and be drenched in the overdubs, and hear the sirens from every town around blaring shrill and faint…faint and shrill…

He was the only one among Okoboji tourist or local who had the ability to sympathize with an air so ionized that garbage cans were sent bouncing off like ping pong balls as the hard rain beat the grass to a mush and the hailstones united to smash every pane in their path. *Let the wind in to rearrange all the architecture!* he charged. Let it rip up the root and tear the leaves from the trees and drown all the mosquitoes while the world (as he understood it) was flipped topsy-turvy and swept into a corner of the universe by a big bristled push broom. Then we'll see if they sit on the seawall self-satisfied and contented, licking the drips and wiping their lips.

But there is, after all, always a space in the weather where the wind dies completely…a false final peace pause, as if to accommodate a shift in direction. The light…from the end of the battered pier you can see with your own eyes how it changes from a pale pink to a sticky green to a sickening yellow…as the seagulls instinctively have abandoned their posts…and bullhead and bluegill, and walleye and perch, and sheephead and northern, and carp and bass head out to hover over the bottomless hole…

Something's up, the world's disjointed, and here comes Carl again, with postcards and a hangover and a cottage cheese container full of fresh picked raspberries, tripping through the amusement park waving the postcards and handing out various varieties of fresh juicy raspberries to Jerry and Sheri and Pete and Nutty while he asks if…if they've seen her…

Seen who?

Claire!

The raspberries, along with the wine still circulating through Carl's head and body, have combined to create a Fun House series of mirrors in the imaginative lobe of his mind. In a convex mirror, for instance, he's brushing his teeth in his father's robe (Act Three, Scene IV). A good reason not to drink any more, being confronted again with this beast of a dragon on a robe which his father had given him, a souvenir from the war in the Pacific. (But then his father had taken it back when a stain of blood was discovered on the inside of the robe, down low. A permanent stain, which his father addressed by shouting: *Give me back my robe!*)

Next mirror please!

Here we have a concave mirror, with Carl dressed up in a suit and tie as a plate spokesman for a line of cracked plates. In the middle of the Fun House, between the slide and the barrel, standing in a beam of light from a high window, he's demonstrating how the intricately patterned English china plates can be heated in the oven over and over again until they crack. But not to worry, Carl assures the crowd, because they can be glued back together. And here he demonstrates the gluing process, and how noodles stick to the glue; all this amidst the noise in the Fun House, with the sugar bowl creaking and spinning, and the moving sidewalk and the hissing air blasters, and Carl eating raspberry after raspberry 'til his lips and the cracked plates are all stained red. And the last bit of light coming in to the Fun House from those windows high up on the edge of the ceiling. And Carl scraping his elbow on the slide, and picking up a nasty elbow burn in the Sugar Bowl, and bumping his head in the barrel, while just ahead of him the fortune teller's assistant dashes right through the barrel holding her little dog tightly to her chest…

With the postcard from Ocheyedan Mound in his hand, he thinks he's finally caught up to her, sitting in the last car of the roller coaster. But MacJames releases the brake just as he reaches the top step, out of breath, to see Claire shoot past him on the platform, her head tilted and her lips poised as if to say: *What*? He holds out the card to her, she reaches out

to grab it as she shoots past, but it slips from her fingers and falls under the track. She disappears down the slope…and the chain, which has been spinning in a loose rattle, grabs the car with a hook and jolt, and pulls her up toward the *Point of No Return*, a rattling clack-clack-clack counting the steps. The card remains stuck to the oil and the grease and the gum and the dust, so besmirched that even with a magnifying glass you would have a hard time making out how it had once pictured the so-called highest point in Iowa, at sixteen hundred and seventy feet above the level of the ancient vast inland sea, and from which you might still see on a clear day all the way to May City and Melvin and Allendorf… all this information and inspiration, insight and outlook, contained on a little postcard, in addition to carrying a message and holding a stamp and a date, with a fortune cookie fortune pasted vertically between address and correspondence, and a drawing of a head in a hat, and signed off with a carefree *Adios!*

The people who run these rides day after sweltering day…we pause for a paean to them…their eyes are spinning around and around in their heads…not much in the way of sweet rest for them…pulling the brakes and unlocking the cages and strapping everyone in and taking the tickets while bantering with customers and slapping mosquitoes and keeping a not-so-steady eye on all the girls and guys…hour after hour…this could only be in Arnolds Park…back then…way back when…a hot sticky night…everyone sweating…wiping their foreheads…

Carl carries the postcard of the Silver Lake fens in to the infinitely reflective confines of the Mirror Maze, in the vague hope she will recognize it, in the midst of all the multiple distortions, not as a lake, but as the unique place for plants and amphibians that it is. But though he spies her image reflected many times over, by the time he traces it back to the original, she was gone…had gone…is gone…leaving behind only a fragrance of insect repellent…

He spots her another time on the Ferris Wheel, halted in its revolution to take on more riders, during an interval when the wind, in the process of switching, leaves the leaves perfectly still. He watches her reach out from her gondola car halted at the top of the circle to grab a piece of cottonwood leaf…

Then there she is again, on the roof of the Tipsy House, staring off in the direction of Abbie's pine, as if to assure herself that it's still there. Elbows on the chipped-paint railing, her black cotton dress clinging to her figure in the humid night air, she bends her head in the heat to wipe her forehead on her sleeve, and wave to someone she's recognized down below…

And there she is once more, at the top of the front stairs to the Roof Garden this time, holding out her right hand to Freeman, to receive the florescent stamp of admittance, which she could have thoughtfully transferred onto Carl's hand, at the bottom of the steps, while it was still wet, so that he might see the show too. MacJames has directed her attention to the bottom of the stairs, where Carl is just about to shout up to her, in that dead zone between songs, the latest postcard message...and let them all hear it: the ticket seller, the people in line, the kids in their cars. Shout the short message up to her, over every footprint worn in the wood, under the innumerable fossilized cobwebs: *I'll be there on*...the card says he'll be here on...when without so much as a **two-three-four** the band kicks in and the wind blasts past him up the stairs so hard that Claire has to hold her hair from her eyes as she's blown inside along with all the rest of the ticket-holding crowd...

Hidden bursts of shameless pleasures backed up by finely betrayed bold breezes, each one from another time, as the floorboards creak and bend and crack under the weight of the music...

On the way to his aluminum rowboat Carl trips over a wine bottle on the beach, its cork protruding. The obligatory message inside is in fact a request scribbled on a torn drink joke napkin: *Will you please play 'Invitation'?*

Across the whole of the vast dark profound merging sky and lake there is nothing to be seen aloft or afloat other than a black buoy (Act Five, Scene III) curiously adrift...

Carl carries the request to the cage underneath the Roof Garden, where the Fun House Clown - he of the frozen fingers and the lapsed smile and the faded polka dots - is imprisoned in his prison of self. Carl looks at him closely...and for the first time, sees him intimately, the way his grandfather always used to look up and see him from his favorite bench in the amusement park (Act Two, Scene IV).

The Fun House Clown neither acknowledges nor refuses the request written on the napkin which Carl reaches up to slip in his cage. His glass eyes give no hold of emotion, as they would have had there been a child standing below him. He's seen it all already and, at this stage in his career, he's simply become preoccupied with listening for those rich triumphant echoes which come to him from his heyday, when he played with such abandon that he was constantly in danger of tipping, and of tippling too - he was always a great one for tipping and tippling, not to mention tripping - how his fingers had once tripped over each other in interpreting Gershwin - always Gershwin, *greatest of popular song writers*, he insists to anyone who will listen...

Faint tremulous echoes he plays (in his mind only), rising and falling melodies which serve to remind him of his place in the pantheon...and that keep him from falling backward off his stool, and safely...quietly... back into the past...

PART THREE

SONGS

"Ask anyone walking along Dixon Beach that day, and I'm sure they'd say –"

"Ask them what?"

"Ask them what it means to possess another person, and if it's even possible? Because possibly it's entirely impossible to truly possess another person. A girl, for instance. Or a woman, rather. I always confuse the two, don't you? I used to get weddings and funerals mixed up too."

"Until you finally got married yourself. And had children. And died."

"You're jumping way ahead!"

"I'd like to ask those sturdy people who wander along under the oak trees up and down Dixon Beach if they didn't think that it was a strange sight, an odd sight, a weird sight indeed, watching that woman in the long brown cotton skirt go rowing off with that guy in the Cyclone cap and that cat and all those boxes of books?

"How do you know all this? Have you been reading on ahead again?"

"I anticipated it. I could see it coming. I peeked in Madame Jessie's crystal ball, and I saw –"

"Don't tell me! You'll ruin the suspense!"

"There's a finely restored wooden rowboat, see, and it's packed with boxes of books, and they're aimed like a fluted arrowhead at Arnolds Park."

"Maybe she was never Carl's girl in the first place. Did you ever stop to consider that?"

"Hey! You know what? It'll play itself out, because this is a new act."

"I always fell hopeful when the curtain goes up on a new act. Don't you? What's the weather like?"

"Sunny. Some wind. A shifting breeze out of the south south-west, I believe."

"Any boats on the lake?"

"Are you kidding me? The lake is thick with boats. Like flies on a dead squirrel."

"And it's moving day."

"All those boxes and boxes of books! Imagine the weight of those sentences!"

"You think our story in one of those boxes?"

"What do you think?"

"Shall we find out?"

"Why not!"

I.

Sliver

Was it the turtle-like pace of their departure that got under your skin?

One oar at a time…draggin' through the water…

Fifty feet off the end of the dock, they swing around and row right back.

Claire hands you Gabo, and first he sinks his front claws in your writing arm before he buries his back claws in your stomach, and then he springs away and runs off as they row off and the doxies yelp and the waves break and you're left propped up against a dock post like a French Quarter voodoo doll with pins in his arm and a sword in his heart.

Claire switches to the starboard oar, and off they go pulling their oars hard through the water, leaving you behind to wonder if she'd ever been *yours* in the first place?

Your mind flies on…high above and ahead of the rowers…trying to snatch out of the humid air exactly what it means to possess another person…and if it's even possible…and that possibly…it is entirely…impossible…

Standing out on the end of that short dock, you're thinking that, while songs and novels and movies continue to portray love as making the world go round, it is in fact *unrequited love* that's the force behind the pull of the oars which has propelled this rowboat overstuffed with books to between seventy five and one hundred feet off the end of the dock…before they turn around *once again* and start back *once more* for the shortest dock on the lake, where you stand in a poor posture but at stiff attention to all these philosophical questions out on the end of…the far end of…at the edge of…

And here they come…again…

What could they possibly want now? you ask yourself, as the lovingly restored old wooden rowboat pulls up alongside the dock, and Claire stands up in the bow with a book in her hand.

I forgot…I forgot that I wanted to leave you this book.

She hands you *Snow of Despair.*

You remember this book: a picture of its cover is pasted in your memory from a night in her Mounds Park apartment in St. Paul…it had been on top of a stack of books on the end table beside her couch, and you had carelessly placed your empty wine glass inadvertently on its snowy cover, causing her to jump up and reprimand you and move your wine glass to a napkin on the coffee table.

You'll like this book. It takes place in St. Paul. The main character reminds me of you. He's a melancholy type who's prone to fits of overwhelming jealousy. You've got to read it. I think you'll recognize yourself. Except for the end, where he jumps off the High Bridge into the Mississippi. That's not you of course. That's not you at all!

And then they're rowing off once again, and you see, or think you see, her break off her stroke once to wave at you, causing you to consider anew how it's an uncommon sight to see your girl go rowing off etc. etc.

Like a song lodged in your mind you wrestle afresh with those age old questions of possession…

And of whether or not she ever really was your etc. etc.

And if it is even remotely *possible* to truly possess etc. etc.

But at the same time you see no use in discarding your memories of her clotheslessness on the Mounds Park sofa…or of the lightning that was to follow.

And to this day you still believe (though somewhat less passionately) in the myths that books and music beg you and induce you and trick you to believe in.

But the movies - with their close-ups and tracking shots, voice-overs and flash backs, touch ups and tricks - the movies have never fully recovered the appeal that they once had, which is a sad, because you used to enjoy them…sometimes…

As each dip of the oar divided Lake Okoboji up between *her half* and *your half*…

Odd, is it not, that what once had the power to draw you together, in the end only serves to separate you.

She has left behind a so-called *Snow of Despair*. You hold it in your left hand. The cover was a watercolor of the old High Bridge blanketed in snow. Within the pages of this book there supposedly resides a fictional persona who resembles you. You'll have to read it from cover to cover to find out if she is right. It will be something like an assignment.

And so she rows off…

And so you began to, alternately, read *Snow of Despair* and write of her rowing off…

Because she had also left behind for you an out-of-ink fountain pen rolled up in the sheets at the foot of her bed.

You didn't find the pen until you made the decision to move into her room.

You believe she left her pen behind *on purpose*.

Her room still holds her presence. It evokes her essence. It is pervaded by her scent and her spirit. It's a beautiful room to spend time in.

You sit in a chair by a window overlooking Lake Okoboji.

You decide to begin the story with MacJames, and his eloquent advice to you concerning the fine art of dock building.

It's the morning of her departure, then, and Claire has just left to go get another box of books, and to fill the uncomfortable silence between MacJames and yourself, both of you standing out there on the dock waiting for her, alternately looking at the lake and the clouds and the gulls and the other docks and the other boats and the swimmers and sun bathers and the people strolling by…finally you break the silence to question MacJames - knowing as you do that he's an expert dock builder - as to how you're doing on this dock that you've been trying to build and extend by yourself all summer long.

In its entirety, here is his reply, delivered in an annoyed tone, with his ridicule only slightly concealed:

See…if you get the first two posts in straight, then the rest of the dock… but hell, you didn't even get the first two posts in straight. They're crooked as shit man! I don't know what to tell you really. The best thing would probably be to just tear the whole thing out and start over. Start from scratch man, you know what I mean? It's a mess, man, I don't know, you'd be better off paying somebody to do it for you next time. Hey! Here she is!

Claire comes down the steps again, this time closely followed by Gabo, and as she passes off another box of books to MacJames, he says to her:

Ah girl, these are heaviest yet! How many more boxes ya got up there? Can't you leave some here? Look at my ship. See how low it's ridin'? Shit! If we hit a big wave your pages are gonna wrinkle in the spray. Leave some of them here why don't ya. In fact, leave the rest here. We'll come back for them. OK? Good idea. Great idea! Leave the rest here. What do you need all these books for anyway?

There's only one more box…

One more box. One more box! Where's it gonna go? Under the seat maybe. Maybe I can stuff it under there. Want me to get it? Hey, what's that cat think he's doin' in my boat? He's not coming, is he? He wouldn't like those big dogs that live over in Arnolds Park. He'd be better off staying on this side of the lake. I'll grab him. I can catch a cat! No problem.

He likes bluegill the best, you say to MacJames after Claire has left for the last box. *I poach it for him. Just make sure all the bones are out. He chokes easy, even on the little ones.*

You get a look from MacJames which seems to say: *What the hell are you talkin' about, man?* He's having a hard time trying to grab Gabo, who keeps darting just out of his reach, hiding behind one box of books after another.

To keep from laughing…you notice that Claire's move is taking place under a sky thick with puffs of perfectly spaced, brilliantly white, and constantly shifting clouds. People in the midst of moving though… they're always too occupied by their lifting and loading to notice anything as fleeting as a little cloud.

Why does she need all these books? MacJames refrains, without taking his eyes off Gabo, as the boat rocks from side to side, and the books packed spine to spine rock too, titles and authors alike, facing the same sun, the same clouds, the same light fingered wind which is just strong enough to raise the covers of the paperbacks…but not the hardbacks…

Like this one for instance.

He reaches down, picks a book off the top, a green one, studies its cover.

Dubliners! Fine if you're in Dublin. But we're here, not there. Maybe someday, but not now, not today.

Many of these books you remember…you remember helping her pack them in her Mounds Park apartment…and you remember carrying them up Des Moines Beach…and down Dixon Beach…you have a memory for book covers…particularly ones with snow on their covers.

Which of these should I bring? She'd almost begged your opinion, desperation in her voice at Mounds Park that evening. And you'd answered:

Bring them all! Bring every one! Because everything, even love - not unrequited, but consummate full throttle no holds barred love - had seemed possible on that stormy St. Paul night, when the blinking red light on top of Lindy's Tower had flashed so unreservedly that there was vertigo in your veins and amour in your arteries.

Here's the last box, Claire says. *Ouch!*

What's wrong babe? What'd ya do?

I got a sliver in my heel. A big one! Oh, it hurts. It hurts, it hurts!

Let me look at it, MacJames says, tossing Dubliners disdainfully in his rowboat.

Claire sits down on the dock, and MacJames bends over to examine her wounded heal in his hand, twisting it to face the sunlight.

Oh, be careful. That hurts too, the way you're bending my foot.

I'm just trying to get a good look at it. It's in there pretty deep, babe. What did I tell you about this rotten dock! And look, it's bleeding. It's bleeding like crazy. I'm afraid I may have to operate. Does what's-his-name have any tweezers?

Tweezers? Sure. I'll go get 'em.

You take the steps up from the dock two at a time and dash straight for the medicine cabinet, past neighbors out in their front yards feigning yard work while quietly watching the unfolding drama down on the dock. (By drama, you mean the rowboat, loaded to the gills with books, and the hide and seek game with the cat, and now an apparently serious sliver laceration).

From the looks on their faces, your neighbors appear to find it all a little amusing, in the same way that a parade with clowns and marching bands and jugglers can be amusing. The real estate agent has a smirk on his face, and he has to ask you, looking up from the lawnmower that he's filling with gas as you run past: *Is she going to be OK?*

You shake your head and keep on going because you're thinking about the sliver and what you'll need from the cabinet in addition to the tweezers. And you're also thinking about the ring…the ring on her finger…that you've just noticed…for the first time…

She's rough on rings…remembering the ring in the river (Act Two, Scene III), you think about warning MacJames, but as soon as you open the back door you realize…it's none of your business…

By the time that you finally get back down to the dock (because the first aid kit is not in the medicine cabinet, as you were certain it was, with the tooth powder and the lye soap, no, it was in the liquor cabinet, of all places, between the aged sherry and the venerable vermouth) you're just in time to see MacJames brace himself against one of your crooked dock posts and pull the nail-like sliver with his bare teeth from the heel of a woman who is flat on her back with one leg high in the air and one hand extended to shield, like she's Jack Johnson on the canvas in Havana, her lively eyes from the sun.

Special attention must be drawn here to the triumphal expression on the amateur surgeon's face as he clenches the terrible sliver between his incisors. It so impresses some passers by, and the little crowd on the bank, that they immediately break into cheers and claps, while the oldest of the boys next door shouts: *Way to go*! *Way to go!*

MacJames takes the sliver from between his teeth and holds it high in the air for all to see.

Do you want to save this for a souvenir? he asks Claire, and when she shakes her head in the negative he tosses it in the lake with a laugh, and then looks up at you as if to ask: *What've you got?*

You show him an old yellow bandage with a picture of Davy Crockett on it, and the even older jar of antibacterial ointment, which is caked around the edges and that slips from your fingers as you attempt to open it, landing on the dock and rolling right past Claire and off the dock and into the water without her making the least effort to grab it.

Oh god Carl, that reminds me of that time in St. Paul when we were sitting in the back of the bus with our groceries, and the bus stopped suddenly and…

She's laughing so hard that she has to pause…

...and that big squash - because you were going to make me your famous squash remember - fell out of the bag and rolled all the way to the front end of the bus and on out the door, hitting that guy in the foot who was just climbing on. And then...and then...

She's overcome by laughter now - laughter that's like a loud weeping - and which attracts the attention of even more neighbors up and down the beach, who come out to look busy in their front yards, as she tries to regain her composure, and MacJames, shaking his head, reaches out to take her hand and pull her up to a standing position. But she hasn't quite finished:

And then...and then...the squash got squashed when the bus driver ran over it, right in front of that publisher's office...what was his name? Thueson, I think. Remember Carl? It was all so perfect, like a little Welty story. Oh my god, I haven't laughed so hard since then...until now...Oh my god!

Yeah I don't think we need that old bandage, MacJames says to you. *Why don't you keep it for your collection.*

My collection of what?

I don't know. Your collection of old band-aids that maybe you should send to a band-aid museum, if at all possible, if you have the time, I don't know, c'mon babe, let's go, it'll take us forever to unload all these books!

Claire sticks her foot in the lake and swishes it around...and then she notices the cottagers in their front yards, and she's ready to go too... they're both in a big hurry:

We gotta go. Yeah, yeah, we gotta go!

I took your grandmother's robe, she says, looking at you slightly apologetically, staring right in your eyes, almost intimately, just to make sure that you understand the importance of this robe to her, and by extension, or so you surmise, the importance of your bringing her to Okoboji.

I hope you don't mind, she continues. I've just gotten so used to that robe, and I'm not even certain that I could write another word without it.

Oh sure. Sure, that's OK.

Then she leans close to me and whispers, *I'll be staying in the cabin - I mean cottage - the cottage called* ...but here, just as she names the cottage, your noisy neighbor starts his lawnmower, as if to personally deny you the name of the cottage in Arnolds Park where Claire will be staying, just in case you need to get in touch with her for some front page reason.

Hey, we're not taking this cat, are we? MacJames interjects impatiently.

Let's let the cat decide, shall we? Claire suggests. *If he stays in the boat, then he goes. But if he jumps out, then ...*

MacJames puts the last box of books in the boat, and grabs the cat and hands him to you, holding him out over the water as if pretending to drop him.

You take him, but Claire pulls him from your arms and climbs in the boat with him.

Untie us if you will please, Carl, thank you, Claire orders, steely voiced.

You do your best to try and untie his convoluted complicated roller coaster of a knot...until MacJames says:

Just yank on that loose end there and it'll come undone like a woman who's just spilled a goblet of red wine on her very best sparkling white party dress!

It comes off easy...one yank and it's unknotted and they're free. You shove them off with your bare foot.

Don't forget to feed him bluegill! I shout, as a way of saying goodbye.

They come and they go, don't they?

A voice out of the blue annunciates this trite phrase. It's a voice that you recognize, and one you've tried to shut out, so that you can listen to other more pleasing voices. It is the voice of the ever present real estate agent next door. You've failed to notice him standing on his dock. This *they*...is he referring to houses or lovers or books or cats? Maybe he's right...maybe he's not as flaky as you thought. Maybe there was something under that silly hat he always wears.

They come and they go…

Of course…like the flotsam…like the jetsam…

But they mostly go, he has to add, and then you realize that you were right the first time, that there's nothing under that hat but…flotsam and jetsam…and gossip and cliches…

You don't pay him any mind, no, you simply reel in your line of philosophical thoughts…boy, there wasn't one keeper on it, not even a string of seaweed. Hook empty, worm gone.

Your nut brown hair my dear Claire, and what's more, you swear that you will never lose her blue pen, that you will travel to the ends of the earth to get it refilled.

And so, one steamy morning shortly after Claire's departure, you ride your bike all the way up to Spirit Lake, where a man in a drug store named Steve helps you find the right ink refill. You'll forever feel indebted to this friendly guy for his aide in this affair.

You will use Claire's pen continuously…until in the late spring of the following year, when you're up in Duluth and scrambling over the rocks along the lake below Leif Ericson Park, and it slips out of your pocket somehow and falls between the cracks and…it's gone…it's gone…

But now…now you're afraid that the past and the present and the future have finally become jumbled beyond categorization, as you've always feared they would.

Because shouldn't Claire at least be allowed to row into the ether before you start sketching her fictional persona, while trying to smooth over the jagged edges of her criticisms concerning your piano playing, for instance, or your singing, or your inability to earn a living?

You can mute those harsh judgments once she's out of sight, and idealize instead the color of her hair and how the sun illuminates it and the wind lifts and shifts it about her shoulders…

MacJames has recommended that you tear down your dock and start over(!), but *no, never,* that would be like starting your life over, saying to yourself that all that has gone before was a waste, so **NO**, *not* until the ice is inching up the posts and has reached the crosspieces shall you consent to tear it down, you promise yourself, still gripping Claire's *Snow of Despair* in your left hand.

Nothing ever happens until you've written about it, does it? you ask yourself, unable to stifle yet another philosophical question as you start up the steps for the cottage, where later that evening you'll extract with your toes her blue pen buried in the sheets at the foot of her bed, which had been your grandmother's bed before it had become her bed and finally *your* bed.

Such is the history of a pen in a bed.

First you wrote: Here's a strange sight: watching your girl go rowing off etc. etc.

You tried to make this all take place in the present, but the past won't allow it, and the future doesn't believe in the past anymore…

It appears that they've become estranged…

It was at the top of the steps, with *Snow of Despair* tucked tightly under your perspiring armpit, that you heard the first burst of applause, followed by the opening chorus of *Jeep's Blues*…

"Well…that was thrilling!"
"Yeah, what a send off!"
"Think we'll ever see her again?"
"See who again?"

"Who do you think? Claire!"

"Oh sure. No doubt about it. She'll reappear. Doesn't everyone in this tale of woe?"

"But now. Look out, 'cause we're in for a sea change."

"We're in for a what? You're going to have to quit mumbling and speak louder!"

"It's the music! It's getting louder and louder!"

"Center stage is about to be commandeered by Carl's father, it appears."

"He's been waiting in the wings a long time, and now here he is!"

"So without further adieu…"

"We present to you…"

"Scene II!"

II.
Crescendo

Pry open the creaky lid and you discover that I was the kid who used his father's lap for a booster seat to grip the steering wheel so tight that my knuckles turned white as the bow came down hard to flatten shard upon shard of wave after wave that flew in my face but I wasn't in the least bit disgraced to get it again and again in the face 'cause my eyes were shut tight while the windshield rattled like some crazy Krupa drummer and my father the band leader held me with his left arm around my small shoulders to keep me from bouncing out and over and then down down deep down into the dreaded bottomless hole, while his right hand snuck up the steering wheel to inch the throttle faster and faster as the wind the *blaster* whipped our hair and my father's breath smelling like whiskey beer wine from all that time in the HiHo where the jukebox blew *Jeep's Blues* through my ears and lobes before the white-caps thumped the hardware and jolted and bumped and then dumped me once and for all time out of his lap and under the bow to hold on tight to his one hairy bare leg while he laughed and laughed and found it so funny and amusing to frighten and scare and give me a thrill that I'd never forget as he climbed up to sit on top of the seat of the Chris Craft Barrelback Runabout, wrapping his crooked clicking off-color long toenails around the steering wheel and swerving us portside so that the clear blue water poured in over the side and I was drowned in a sea of sound just as…

…a wild burst of applause poured forth from the front porch; and then, the killer: *Diminuendo and Crescendo in Blue*

I took the steps two at a time to the beat of the drummer who I believed at the time to be the one and only Cozy Cole, but who I later found out was Sam Woodyard urged on by Joe Jones.

At the top of the stairs I extricated Gabo from a low limb of a burr oak. Together in trepidation we approached the wide open windows.

The three doxies - Gretchen, Honz, Heidi - nipped and yelped at our paws and heels.

The diminuendos showed no sign of diminishing.

Gabo tried to get away. I held on to him tight.

He sunk his claws into my arm. I held on tight.

Up against the reflections in blue and green on the front porch windows, this blaring swinging dance music had segued into a thundering crescendo.

I nodded and bobbed, and then I peeked in the window…

At first I didn't see anybody. The front porch appeared to be vacant. But then I spotted him over in the corner, under the running blue Okoboji wall map. He was sitting on the edge of the chair of reflection, his head lowered under a wide brimmed straw hat, looking like a man who had just arrived and was catching his breath. His legs were crossed, and he was trying to hold the glass on the top of his knee steady, but the white wine in the glass sloshed and sloshed because his feet were carrying the same beat that he was listening to.

He listened with an intensity unknown to the casual listener.

His white shoes were tapping furiously, as if he, and not Sam, was the drummer at a live show in front of thousands of people with all kinds of boats in the background on a bay much like this one, that was filled, as this one was, with sporting craft of all shapes and sizes. If Claire had stuck around a few minutes longer she could have witnessed all this, the rapt attention that this man gave to the music, because as the sax solo went on he began to slap his legs with his free hand, and then he put his wine glass on the coffee table so that he could clap with both hands, and then finally he got up and started to dance, dance around wildly in circles, kicking up his legs, his movements perfectly matching the music. In my mind I saw thousands of spectators watching him, they'd made a big circle and he was in the center of it, losing himself.

As soon as I saw his face I knew who he was, but I didn't tap on the window or yell or shout, even though my heart was beating faster than Danny Richmond or Eddie Blackwell on the snare.

I was going to wait until the song was over…I wasn't about to shatter this mood he'd created, not for anything, so I waited in the wings, nodding my head and tapping my foot and slapping *Snow of Despair* against my hip, while still holding Gabo, who seemed more frightened of the music, the sheer volume of it, than he was of the doxies. I'd forgotten how long this song went on, chorus after chorus, each chorus wilder than the one before, the tension building up until it was almost unbearable, my father making me dizzy spinning around and around in circles, his white shoes a white blur. I thought about the guy on the sax, how his fingers and cheeks must have ached, but the crowd just kept egging him on, shouting and whistling. That's what a live recording has the power to do, make you think that you're part of it, that you're actually *there*…

Each chorus had to be the last, except it wasn't, they started in on another one, the soloist vying with the rest of the band, taking them on and knocking them down one by one…

When the song was finally over - and just in time too, because the situation appeared to be spinning out of control - my father collapsed back in to the chair of reflection and reached for his wine as the Duke shouted out from the scratchy recording:

Paul Gonsalves! just as I walked around and opened the door to the front porch and my father bounced up from his chair, spilling his white wine on his white pants and shouting *My god! Carl!* at the same instant that Duke again bellowed *Paul Gonsalves* above the cheering and clapping, so that I felt that I was Paul Gonsalves, and that I'd just finished playing twenty seven straight choruses and was walking across the stage to the cheers of the crowd to take Duke's hand in congratulation for a job well done. Except that it was my father who came right for me, and I held out my hand but he hugged me instead and kissed me four times, twice on each cheek. And then he gave me a few hard pats on my back, my shoulders, my arms, a bunch of pats, hard pats, not soft pats, hard solid impermeable pats.

Look at that cat! he shouted. He looks just like a cat that I used to have when I was a boy.

He gave Gabo a couple of strokes, saying *nice pussy cat, nice pussy cat!* And then he said, You look great Carl, you look great. There's youth Carl, and then there's middle age, and then there's you Carl, and you sir, look great! Although you are beginning to lose your hair on top. But you probably can't see it if you look in the mirror. Oh, I'm just joking, don't look so serious. You were always so serious. Too serious! And the house looks great too. Who's that woman going off in the boat with all the books? A friend of yours? Listen! As soon as I get settled, I want to have a party. A big party! A raucous rich delectable well-seasoned raconteur-filled shout-above-the-music kind of dinner party. I want you to invite all your friends to this party. Invite the woman with the books and the guy rowing the boat. Invite them all! We'll plan the whole thing out. Every little detail! OK? Great! Oh, it's something to be back at Okoboji. You can't imagine how fantastic it feels! I'll tell you, even when I was out in York Beach, closing my restaurant, I was thinking about Okoboji. Did you get all my postcards? I closed my restaurants in New Orleans and Bellingham too, and then I couldn't wait to get back here. *All because I had to see this view.* This view and you. You too Carl. So you knew I was coming? I knew you'd be here. Don't ask me how I knew. I just knew if it

James Booker at the Maple Leaf New Orleans, La.

was summer at Okoboji then there was a good chance that you'd be here. What are you reading? What's that book under you're arm? *Snow Of*... what? *Despair!* Jesus Christ Carl! For pete's sake, lighten up! I'm out of the restaurant business for good! Now we've got to celebrate!

I was taller than my father now...several inches taller...

His crooked teeth smiled at my crooked teeth, a big smile.

Well, come sit down. Come sit down. The house sure looks tremendous! To see these windows sparkling, it's almost as if your grandmother was still alive,. You keep it the way she kept it, except for the cat. No cats when she was around. Absolutely no cats! Ever! Remember? And a good hunting cat might have taken care of her chipmunk problem, don't you think? Are the chipmunks still camping in the chimney? God it's good to see you Carl! It's been a hell of a long time, hasn't it? You were short on supplies. It's lucky I brought some with me. We're going to have a hell of a dinner. I'm talking about a dinner party to end all dinner parties. I want you to invite every one of your friends. Have a glass of wine, why don't you? So you got my postcard from New Orleans, did you? Oh, it was hot down there. My god, you could hardly walk across the street. I had to have ice in my coffee, ice in my wine, ice wrapped in a wash cloth under the straw hat on top of my head. Don't ever go down to New Orleans in the summer. Wait 'til winter. So what shall we feature for our big dinner? Are the fish biting? Walleye would be excellent! Yes, fillet of walleye, marinated in one of my sauces. Well, don't just stand there! The wine's in the kitchen. You might have to open another bottle. *Too early?* What are you talking about? It's never too early. Look at all those boats on the lake! Do you believe it? A person could step from one to the other. And there's Gull Point. Remind me to tell you what happened on Gull Point one time. Your mother and I used to picnic on all the points - Manhatten, Pillsbury, Pikes, Omaha, Ft. Dodge - but Gull was always the best...

I had two glasses of wine, and then, after he asked me to find *Money Jungle* - which I found without too much trouble, my fingers skipping through the stacks of records leaning against the wall 'til I came upon it in its sleeve and jacket comfortably sandwiched between Davis and Evans - and I'd put it on for him, skipping the title track – *which is a good song but* – to set the needle down on the second song because *I'm in a hurry, I've come all this way to hear Fleurette Africaine* – before I went out into the backyard and took my swimming suit off the line.

It seemed empty back there, with none of Claire's dresses hanging in the sultry summer afternoon. The old cliche about how quickly time passes went through my mind. Her dresses had been so suggestive...once they'd had the power to stimulate my imagination just by hanging there on the line. But now...now they were gone, and probably for good, never to be pinned by those old clothes pins again. It was kind of sad but... there was nothing I could do about it...except maybe...go for a swim...

I walked down the beach to the public dock. I didn't wade in, I dove in. I dove in to some of the same water that I'd swum in as a child, and I went straight to the bottom. I dove into this kind of reverie where I imagined that I was still a kid with a line in space, an infinite line in an infinite space, trying to intersect with other infinitely interesting intersecting lines, but never getting any closer to them, or any farther either

- always remaining the same exact distance. It was frustrating, because I was under water after all, where parallel lines appear to have a chance of intersecting. But at the same time there was hope afloat, in the infinity that is underwater seaweedy fish thick Okoboji, that the laws of space would dissolve, and the trajectory of the lines be changed, so that in the end we could connect - meet up with each other somehow. It was an old reverie and a new reverie at the same time, and although it seemed highly unlikely that the lines would unite under water off the public beach at the of the bend of the bay in Okoboji, still I stayed down there for as long as I could, in the hope that I would find what I was looking for. Sometimes it's simply the search itself which seems to make such things worthwhile. And besides, those choruses, I just couldn't get all those choruses I'd heard on the front porch out of my head. They were reverberating away inside my brain…all twenty seven of them…at the same time …never to intersect in anything resembling a straight line…

"I think we're going to be swinging from here on out. What'd you think?"

"No doubt about it. The narrative has taken a left turn, and we appear to be headed for some extended solos."

"Maybe it wasn't such a bad thing that she boxed her books and went rowing off with MacJames."

"My feet can't seem to stop tapping!"

"As long as you tap in time, and take care to not let your strings get tangled, I don't see anything wrong with keeping a beat."

"Listen! I think Carl's father is about to start another story."

"He loves to reminisce, doesn't he? Even about cats!"

III.
Effortless Cast

This cat of yours…I can't get over…because it's just like…is it male or female? A boy…what's his name. Gabo? Nice Gabo…they like to be scratched (*reaches out with his right hand*) right here…under their chin …and right here, where his tail meets his…**Ouch!** (*withdraws hand quickly*) Easy Gabo, easy. Nice…he's just like a cat that we used to have on the farm …one of the barn cats…but they were all barn cats. Mother wouldn't let them in the house. Your grandmother hated cats! I don't know if you can remember how much she hated cats. But I used to sneak my favorite one into my bedroom at night, so that he could sleep with me. He was a cuddler, that cat. But anyway, one day (*pauses to take a sip of wine*)…one day Mother was working in her flower garden…this is one of my earliest memories…she had a huge garden between the barn and the house…behind the root cellar, facing south. When she wasn't working at the business in town or traveling, or speaking of her travels on the radio, or traveling for the business, we could always find her weeding (*grasps hands together as if yanking on a weed*) in her flower garden…in the warm months of course…Most of my memories are memories of summer…I wonder if it's the same for you Carl? (*pauses for a sip*) There was a little patch of woods in the middle of the fields…we called it "The Island"…we built forts on this island, which had a fresh spring on it…a spring (*takes white handkerchief from shirt pocket; wipes forehead and cheeks*) so we could stay cool…we used to drink water straight from that spring! (*takes a quick sip*) I bet it's not there anymore...I bet it's long gone...probably a soybean field by now... (*sips*) But I can remember Christmases too. The wreaths and the candles in the window, and Dad building roaring blazes (*hands thrust forward, fingers splayed*) in the fireplace, and my brother and I swimming one Christmas Day in the river or ditch or creek or whatever you want to call that trench a mile or so east of us. I can remember all that just like it was yesterday...(*long sip*)...and Mother in her wide brimmed straw hat (*as if adjusting the brim of a hat*) that she got in Mexico, taking care of her lilies and her gladiolus - her gladies, as she called them - out behind the root cellar. One day I'd been playing in the pump house when I heard a loud squeal (*makes a face*) coming from the barn...now that I think about it... it was more like a shriek than a squeal...Pigs squeal, but this sound was like no sound a pig ever made...unless it's the last sound they utter at the end of the chute...It was chilling (*shivers*), that sound...I can still hear it (*shakes head*), even to this day...(*sips, holds wine in cheeks before swallowing, grimly*) So I ran out to the barn, and I discovered my favorite cat up in the hay loft with something (*holds hand to mouth*) in its mouth. There was a skinny little tail dangling from its mouth, a mouse's tail obviously (*finger in air, draws a tail*), or maybe it was a rat's tail...who knows? The mouse or the little rat was shrieking from inside the cat's mouth, and it looked like the rat was going to choke on the cat (*takes a sip; shakes head before swallowing*)...wait, it's the other way around, isn't it? The cat was going to choke on the rat, that's how it was. I picked him up (*reaches out to pick up Gabo, who darts away*)...I can't remember his name now...I know it wasn't Gabo, but he looked a lot like Gabo, that black and white cubist face...I gathered the cat up in my arms (*folds arms to chest*), and climbed down the ladder with him - that was a trick! - and ran across the barnyard with him still in my arms, just tore across the yard to Mother lost (*motions as if parting branches in a thick forest*) in her geraniums, because I could see her hat (*points to the top of his head*), I couldn't see her...but I could see her hat...and then I saw her, she was down on her hands and knees (*yanking motion with both hands*), weeding. I shouted

Mommy! *Mommy*! *Help me! (throws both arms in air) What's his name has a mouse stuck in his throat!* I knew his name back then of course. And his name will come back to me. I know it will. (*pauses to take a long sip, nearly draining the glass*) I should have known better than to…I think it was the last time that I ever…that was a big mistake…calling her Mommy, I mean…(*empties glass*)…Mother turned her head to look up at me, and she shouted (*points finger accusatorily*)…she kept on yanking the weeds…It must have been windy, you know…the wind must have been rattling the corn stalks, and so she had to shout over the wind: *How many times do I have to tell you? Don't call me mommy! I want to be called Mother! Mother! Do you hear me? The next time you call me mommy I'm going to…* I can't remember what she threatened…maybe: *put you in bed without any supper!* or something like that. *Now what is it that you want*? Mother, I said, my cat has a mouse stuck in its throat and I don't know what to do. She'd gone back to working with her gladies or her lilies or her geraniums, pulling those weeds like that's all that mattered…because the only thing she said was…without even looking up from the water weed and the milk weed and the thistles…without even looking at me or the sick cat in my arms…all she could say was (*raises voice*): *I hate cats! You know I hate cats! Take him back out to the barn!* The cat was choking and gasping for air by this time, so I took him in back of the barn, and laid him down in the long grass by the silo, and ran back to the house to get my brother. But my brother (*leans back in chair*) was taking a bath, one of his long baths where he just sat in the tub and read his magazine from beginning to end. And I sat on the floor in the hall outside the bathroom door and waited for him to finish, because he was older, and he would know what to do…

(Sets glass down on low bamboo table. Stands up and paces length of front porch, stopping in front of window nearest the door to look out at the lake. Speaks as if he's reading a text that had been written for him on the surface of the water)

I'm done with the restaurant business, Carl. Finished with it. I've been a restaurateur all my life, but no more. No more restaurants! I've had it with trying to please other people. I closed (*brings hands together*) the one in the Fairhaven section of Bellingham, and I closed (*as if turning a key*) the one on the Short Sands in York Beach, and I closed (*handkerchief to cheeks*) my favorite one…the one off Esplanade by City Park in New Orleans. So that's it! I'm done with restaurants, believe me. (*gestures with right arm*) Look at that boat out there, will you. God they make them ugly now! Big pieces of molded floating fiberglass. They belong up on Lake Superior…or down on Lake Ponchatrain…but not on Okoboji. My god!

(Paces, left hand behind back, right hand holding wine glass, to the other end of the front porch, stopping in front of framed map of West Okoboji. Speaks as he studies the map)

I'll tell you Carl…it's always seemed that no matter where I was… (*waves hands in the air*) whether I was crossing San Francisco Bay (*turns head to left*) on the ferry to Sausalito…or maybe I was in a gondola passing under the bridge of signs in Venice…(*turns head to right*) it didn't make any difference where I was…because in a way I was still flying (*right hand at forty five degree angle: bumping over waves motion*) across Okoboji in my Chris Craft with your mother…or you…or the both of you together…(*laughs*)…she holding you, and me holding her, trying to keep the both of you from bouncing (*arms outstretched, hands extended, palms down*) out of the boat…and into the lake…which I always imagined, for some reason, as a miniature of the world (*hands cupped around wine glass as if grasping a small globe*), you might say…so that the canals across the lake in back of Crescent Beach became my own little Venice, and Fisherman's Wharf, when I had it, became my San Francisco…but then later on…when I came to visit the actual places (*takes a quick sip*)… I was almost always…disappointed…

(Sits back down, pours himself a another glass of wine, filling it to the edge of the rim, takes a sip, and continues)

Anyway, by the time my brother got dressed and combed his hair - he always took a long time combing his hair - and brushed his teeth and we went back out to the silo and I showed him where the cat was in the long grass...by that time, the cat was dead. The cat had died, with the little skinny rat's tail still twitching (*shakes head*)...still sticking out of his mouth. We buried him right where (*takes a big gulp of wine*)...right where he lay in the long grass...it seemed like as good a place as any...

Okoboji always makes me want to dredge up these old memories... something about this place...is it the air, you think?...or the water?... who knows?

Yes, that was a nice cat...a nice cat...and so is Gabo (*reaches out with his left hand to try to pet Gabo*)...nice pussy cat. Oh, let's hear a song, shall we? Take our minds off that sad story. A song and another glass of wine. I'm going to have one more. Would you like one, Carl? What have you got out here for music? How about *Swing Low Sweet Cadillac?* That might be appropriate. Please put that one on for me, will you Carl?

In the last of the sunlight I shuffled through the stacks of records propped up against the wall on the floor, until I found the one with the picture of Dizzy. He didn't want to hear *Night In Tunisia* or *Salt Peanuts* first - no, I had to put the needle down right on *Swing Low*...

Turn it up! he said.

I turned up the volume.

Turn it up a little more!

I turned it up some more.

Just a little bit higher!

It was after I'd turned it up just about as high as it would go that I left the front porch for the back porch, and grabbed my pole. In back of the garage, underneath my raspberries, as I heard *Commin' for to carry me home* blaring from the front porch, I unearthed a giant earthworm. On my way down to the lake I could see my father still standing on the front porch. There was no denying his rapt attention to music, and his inability to not respond, with arms and fingers, legs and toes, to a song that he so obviously loved, a song like *Swing Low*. I noticed that Mrs. Skylingstad was standing at her window and watching him too...

I planted that fat raspberry bed worm on my hook, and cast it out off the end of the dock. Just like that I had a bite. How he fought and struggled, battled and leaped! How he tried to hide in all those imaginary musical instruments tangled up in the seaweed down beneath the waves. His colors glittered and glistened in the dying light. The little guys next door came down to the dock in their pajamas to admire him:

Look at his bulging eyes!

He can't breathe!

Put him back in the water quick!

His was of a rare and foreign species. Okoboji was not his home water. H was splended...

But my lunker had swallowed the hook as well as the bait. It was deep inside of him. I yanked the line a few times...

You're hurting him. You're really hurting him!

I think I'll take him up to the house now, I said.

What you gonna do with him up there?

I'm going to get the hook out, and then have him for dinner.

You're gonna kill him then? C'mon, let's go tell our mom!

As I was carrying my catch up the steps to the cottage I was startled, not by Coltrane's take on *My Favorite Things*, but by the sight of what I took to be Claire standing at the window in her room, looking out at the sunset like she used to do. My eyes glazed over as I remembered how I used to invite her down for a glass of wine, and how she used to say *Be right there!* And then a few minutes later, there she was, sitting beside me on the edge of the bank, looking off in anticipation toward Ft. Dodge Point and the amusement park, bathing in the light on the water while I plunged into the iridescence of her hair, while at the same time trying to follow her conversation and fend off her pointed criticisms and appreciate her sense of humor and above all, her intelligence. And then finally, her smile...was it possible to simply miss a smile?

It wasn't Claire in the window, of course. It was only the willowy shape of a shadow from a tree in the path of the setting sun that I'd intentionally allowed to fool me. Those limbs had mimed her figure even to the point of the tilt of her head.

The fish on the line had finaly quit quivering…but not I…

"So…we're to assume that, in the midst of all that had happened to the cat and the fish, Carl is still thinking of Claire?"

"What about the poor mouse?"

"The mouse that the cat swallowed?"

"What other mouse could there be?"

"Did you believe that story?"

"When Carl's father was telling it I did."

"But now?"

"Now I'm not so sure."

"Let's keep going!"

"Onward!"

"Next we have a conception story?"

"You can't be serious!"

"Oh, but I am, I am."

IV.

To the Beat of the Waves

Standing at the same front porch window where Gabo, transfixed by a squirrel in the yard, arched his back and poked his front claws through the screen, he pointed dramatically across the lake with his right arm and index finger extended, and said:

I don't know if you know this but…you were conceived over there…

Where?

Laughing to himself, he said:

How could a person know where he or she was conceived…unless one of his parents just happened to tell him…but I'm sure your mother never told you. She never mentioned it, did she?

No.

No, of course not, why in the world would she tell you something like that at your age…I mean the age you were when you saw her for the last time. So now I get to tell you. You were conceived…over there…

He took a long sip of wine.

It's amazing Carl! Has this ever happened to you? You come back to a place, after being gone for a long time, and the spirits that inhabit it are waiting for you. Not only waiting, but they come out to meet you, even in this intense heat, when you'd think it'd be cooler for them to stay in the shadows…under a tree down by the lake.

But…exactly where…over there?

I was curious to discover the exact location.

Under a cottonwood on the tip of Gull Point. To the beat of the waves, my boy, to the slap and the lap and the beat of the waves! Do you ever get over there? I could probably show you the exact spot - if you were interested, that is. Are you interested, Carl? You look interested. You were reading that book you're always reading. What is it? Oh yes: *Snow of Despair*. But now I see that you've put it down and...say, let's have a song, shall we. I think I need a song to keep this story going. Let's hear...I want to hear...I'd like to hear *The Clothed Woman*. In order for me to continue with my story of your sandy conception, I must hear *The Clothed Woman*. One of my favorites! A compendium, if there ever was one, of piano stylings. Willie, Fats, JPJ: they're all in there, helping to cloth that woman. And Gull Point is one of my favorite points. I love it, and your mother certainly loved it. Hell, we loved each other out there on the tip of it. That long stretch of sand that gives you the illusion that you're out on an island. An island in the middle of the Middle West. That's the irony of it all. They didn't believe me when I was telling them about Okoboji in New Orleans. They thought I was putting them on, those people in that bar on Decateur Street...The Abbey...funny name for a bar...

I'll tell you Carl...when I'm at Okoboji, I'm not only here with the way things are, but at the same time, I'm here with the way things were. In other words, I'm in the historical Okoboji as well as the present day Okoboji. In fact, I'm probably more in the former than in the latter. Some of that air from the old days is still in this cottage, and that's what I'm after...all that old musty air.

Can't you find *The Clothed Woman?* What's the hold-up? We'll have to alphabetize those albums some day. One day when we don't have anything else to do. But it seems like we always have something to do, don't we Carl. It's impossible to run out of things to do at Okoboji. Especially at Okoboji!

Find it yet? Hurry! I'm going to forget what I was saying. My glass is empty. That's not a good sign either. I'm going out to the kitchen to refill it. I shall return Carl, just like MacArthur. We were swimming with the sharks out in the South Pacific and waiting for the call...the orders to *Begin the invasion!* Jesus! What a life I've had! But you Carl...from the look of things, you seem for the most part to have missed out on life. You should have joined the Navy right out of high school. Maybe it's not too late though…but they probably wouldn't take a man with hair on his shoulders and a ring in his ear. My god Carl, you'd have to be shorn and deringed. But at least you could see the world. You really could. Anyway, I'll be right back. I have to see a man about a…and I must not forget to grab a…grab a refill! Be right back…

It's strange, Carl, but when I drink at Okoboji I feel like I'm communicating with my mother and father…and my grandfather and grandmother…hell, it's like I'm talking to all these relatives that you see in the portraits on these walls!

Now…where were we? What were we talking about? I've completely forgotten! My god…

My conception.

That's right! How could I forget a subject like that? And the sea oats and the cottonwood leaves and the waves and the gulls and the fishermen in their boats casting and reeling, reeling and casting…and I don't know what else…all that was missing was the music, I guess. I'm so glad you found *The Clothed Woman!* Let's hear it again, shall we? Let's play that one again. At least one more time anyway. And turn up the volume a notch. I want to be able to hear every note. It's a short piece, isn't it? But what a piano player! The one and the only! (*lifts his glass in a toast*) The Duke!

Yes…I guess we made our own music on the day you were conceived. It was late afternoon, I think, and the sun, which had been going in and out of the clouds all afternoon, suddenly came out for good, and then nine months later, give or take a day, so did you, Carl. So did you! My god, what a deal. *What a deal that was!*

So that's why Gull is my favorite point, Carl, as if you couldn't have guessed. And really, if you want to get right down to it, it's the most beautiful place on the whole lake. It's *otherworldly,* if you know what I mean, especially on a quiet day in late summer or early fall. I could forget about the Spanish moss on the live oaks out by the Spanish Fort in New Orleans, I could forget about the ferry landing on Lummi Island, and the beach at Short Sands at York Beach…I could forget about them all if I was over on Gull Point on a day like the day when you were conceived…

Maybe not forget…forget is probably too strong a word…I can't seem to forget anything…but my longing for all these places could be assuaged, as they say…(*takes a deep sip*)

But hell…you can't be everywhere…unless you happen to be omnipresent…

If I could be anywhere, anywhere I wanted, I'd just as soon be on Gull Point…

Not on a day like today though, when there's so many boats out there that you could step from one to the other and never touch the water. No, it has to be the very end of summer, after all these people have gone home. Back to Des Moines, back to Omaha, back to Sioux City and Sioux Falls. When the lake is restored to itself, that's when you have to go over there. That's when your mother and I took the Chris Craft across the lake, and tied up at the dock in front of the lodge, and had a picnic in the shadow of the lake patrol tower…and then carved our initials on the top of the tower…under the roof…in the WPA logs hauled out from Oregon…they're probably still there, with all the other initials…

A friend of mine calls that tower her Martello Tower.

Her own little Martello Tower? Like they have in Ireland? That's interesting she would make that connection. What friend is this?

Her name is Claire.

Well, we have to be sure and invite County Claire to the party. We might have to have something similar to what your mother and I had that day on Gull Point…

And what was that?

Oh, it was a bouillabaisse, made with walleye. I hope to god that you can catch some fresh walleye for our party.

I can try…I can try to catch some walleye…usually I go for bluegill. Although I did catch a nice perch the other day.

Bluegill won't do for this party. It's got to be walleye. Too many bony bones in bluegill. But anyway…to return to my story…we had the picnic, and then we walked out to the tip of the point and went swimming on the south side, on the shallow side, where the water's so clear after it washes over the point, and there's nothing but sand. We went swimming right after we ate, we couldn't wait because it was so hot. We swam for a long time, and then we sat in the shallows holding each other. After we got out and dried off, we shared a bottle of wine on the beach, just the two of us, no one else around. Your mother wanted to play hide and seek. Hide and seek on the tip of Gull Point, can you imagine, in the days after the war. I'd just got back from playing hide and seek in the South Pacific…but there we were, on a beautiful day in late summer, with the waves lapping and slapping each other…

Here he paused, and seemed to listen again for those waves . . and hearing present day echoes hitting the beach below the cottage, he sipped a quick sip and went on:

I snuck up on your mother, I really scared her, she was expecting me to climb over a large dead cottonwood which must have fallen over not too long before, because all its leaves were still green, and just starting to turn yellow. I grabbed her from behind, and she screamed, and I saw a man in a fishing boat look over. We fell down laughing behind the dead tree…shielded from the fisherman by the trunk and all the leaves… shielded from the world…completely alone with each other. And she looked up at me…I still had her around the waist…she looked up at me with those gray green eyes…it was as if she had shouted *Kiss me*! *Kiss me now*! A woman says yes or no with her eyes. That look in her eyes was all that I needed to know…for the next hour or so. We were lost in each other over there…on Gull Point…

Here he took a long sip, but instead of swallowing his wine, he held it in his cheeks…for a long time…as the needle skipped monotheistically in the groove…

Refusing to swallow…until a seagull shrieked overhead…

And then he swallowed…

And then he said:

At least I think it was on Gull Point. It could have been Pikes or Ft. Dodge or Pillsbury or Manhattan or Omaha. It could have happened on any one of those points, because they're all lovely, they're all beautiful. But no, I'm almost certain that it happened on Gull…because in those days it seemed like we were always pulling the boat up on one of the points to have a picnic…

After the cuckoo cockatooed twice, I gave in with no resistance to my urge to go jump in the raspberry patch.

It was stifling and breezeless in back of the garage…and prickly… and so hot…it was just me and my…three dots…the past, present, and future gaps in my remembrance…all being caressed over…every pore at once as I floated on my back…my crooked toes sticking up above the vines and…spinning around and…bobbing over the leaves…the buoyancy of the berries keeping me afloat…gorging myself, lips stained red, eating the bugs too as I listened…to the cries of the crows in the trees high above me…

"I started to get homesick when he mentioned New Orleans and the Spanish Fort and the Spanish moss. When can we go home? I want to go back to where I was conceived."

"And where was that?"

"In the rear of a shotgun down Magazine."

"Really?"

"And you?"

"I'd rather not say. I'm not proud of it."

"C'mon. Tell me. I won't make fun."

"It was above a do-nut shop."

"Which one?"

"A funky place out by the lake. I don't think it survived the flood."

"Too bad."

"Well, what can you do? Anyway, that's enough concerning conceptions. Let's keep going if we want to get out of here."

"Before the snow flies."

"Too soon to think about snow. We've going to take in a pair of parallel stories next. On the one hand, we have more of Carl's father's picnic adventures on Okoboji, while at the same time we're going to hear Carl's remembrance of a day spent wandering with Claire in St. Paul.

"Carl's story being the interior one, correct?"

"That is correct."

"Enough said."

"Let's go!"

V.

Coincidental Solos

So I was the son who my father used like a landfill every afternoon and each evening, backing his truckload of memories up to the edge of my patient listening hole and dumping them all at once so that they all cascaded down to mix and compost with my own memories. His memories cum stories poured forth from every chair on the front porch, while holding his glass of wine so tight that his recollections turned in to pale little kites which floated off into the humidity hanging over the lake before he had a chance to reach out and reel them in. I watched him smile at a certain memory that just happened to be in the air, although he couldn't see at first exactly where it was leading to, and so his mind rattled over every bump and, shutting out the unpleasant ones, he held on to the good ones for all they were worth. Sometimes all it took was a song to recall them. *One song*. And then another song. And another. So that after a while there was no separation between memory and song, they were one and the same, they had fused. My father held them close to his heart, he showed me how to recall my own, as the wind off the lake ran up the bank to ruffle disdainfully our receding hairlines. There was the stale smell of spilled wine, as all these memories thumped our addled brains, and my suddenly energized father grabbed the memory wheel and spun it and we swerved portside and watched in fright and delight as this never ending puppet show of memories flooded in over the side:

…but then we used to picnic at all the points, your mother and I. We were always pulling the Chris Craft up on one point or another, just easing the bow across the sand so that it wouldn't float away on us. Even up as far as the Lazy Lagoon, I remember having a picnic there once, sitting under a cottonwood right where the canal meets the lake. The wind was blowing, the boats were going in and out, and your mother not missing the city for once, because she'd grown up on Lagoon, Lagoon Street in Minneapolis by Lake Calhoun. We had a bottle of wine, and some bread my grandmother had made, and your mother was sitting on a blanket with all of Okoboji behind her looking more beautiful by the second, she was just sitting there in a summer dress absentmindedly picking catnip…

(That catnip in front of the undertaker's office under Kellog in St. Paul…Claire said, Let's bring some home for Gabo, so I pulled up a whole plant, but she said, No - just pick the tops of each plant, they like the tops the best, I watched her pluck the tips off a dozen catnip plants, but then that hearse drove up and the back door swung open and the golden casket appeared just as the smell of the plastics factory was getting to us, so we took the steps up to Kellogg and risked our lives crossing the street to the library where we separated in front of the fiction section.)

…she always had a book in her hand, your Mother, she started and finished books on all the points, you name 'em, even Pike's, she finished Fitzgerald, I think, on the beach in front of that dangerous drop-off on the north side of the sand bar. She closed the book on Dick…what was his name? Dick and Nicole…you know who I mean don't you? For god's sake Carl, you've lived in St. Paul! Help me out! Dick…Dick Diver!… wandering around from town to town in Indiana maybe…or…no, it was upstate New York…anyway, she finished her book and I gave her my hand and pulled her up…we'd just lunched on a delicious noodle dish… from a Czech recipe…I haven't had that in years…what was it called?… I can't remember…but I remember her kissing me, as we were wading in…in front of that sign that said *Dangerous Dropoff* or *No Swimming* or something like that, she just pulled me closer and kissed me, kissed the living daylights out of me…those Minneapolis girls are like that, I don't know if you've had the luck to meet many of them, but they're… well, they know how to *portage* their love. Yeah, that day on Pike's I knew too...I finally realized that your mother was my girl, that she was really and truly my girl, that she was none other than my girl and no one else's...that she in fact belonged to me...that she was mine...

(After the library we went in the Czech Cafe, across the street to the east from the Landmark Center, and sat down in a booth under a big picture of Prague, and when the waitress came to the table I asked her, just to make conversation, if she knew Kafka, and she said No, are you him? *Claire got such a kick out of that, she laughed and laughed, she laughed so much that the other people in the place were staring at us, but she kept asking me,* Are you Kafka, Carl? Are you Kafka? *Finally I said, No, I'm not Kafka, he's much taller than I am, and he walks in a loping kind of walk with his head to one side, and no, I said, for the last time, after the waitress had brought out our soups and sandwiches on a tray,* I am not Franz Kafka, *but Claire kept laughing, there were tears on her cheeks, she was wiping her eyes and tapping her little thin black Chinese dance slippers under the table. I'd never seen her in such an aroused state of amusement, to the point of being consumed by laughter - except possibly when the squash rolled off the bus - and in fact she only quit laughing when she got the hic-ups, and had to beg me, in a note scrawled on a napkin, to order her a bottle of Czech pilsner.)*

...and then we took our bottles, we took our flasks, across the lake to the Okoboji Club, the beautiful old Floate Mansion, with the drowsy distinguised doorman, and the waiters, the columns, the stairs. And that walk-in bar downstairs where we danced to the jukebox, tunes like... like what you're got on right now Carl, my god, turn it up a bit, will you please! And the beautiful bar upstairs, and the dining room with its excellent food, and that gorgeous view of the lake, and the big umbrellas over the tables out on the lawn. But oh, that drive back across the lake, navigating our way out of Miller's Bay at night in low water, the line of rocks and weeds, Jesus Christ, I hit the throttle full speed coming out of there for the middle of the lake, with your mother shouting *Slow Down*! and

We should have stayed upstairs! I knew what she was talking about, those comfortable rooms with the beds turned down and the Swiss chocolate on the pillow and the rose in the vase on the bedside table, but we had to keep going, go tell Murial, because I'd asked your mother to marry me on Omaha Point - or was it Manhattan? - the point where she found the arrowhead anyway - so I had to go tell Murial, and we were flying across Okoboji in the fastest boat on the lake. If Micky Landen had been trying to catch me he wouldn't have had a chance…I would have left him in my wake…you better believe it!

(From the Czech Cafe it was only a few skips down St. Peter to the Coney Island, which was always quiet in the late afternoon. Definitely a step back in time, going in to that place, cigar smoke from the 1930's, hard-backed booths, no cushions on the seats. But the beer was ok, it came in a bottle, ice cold. Claire always ordered a glass of water too, and as soon as the bartender went in the next room she slipped up to the front windows and watered those plants that were dying of thirst, plants like the plants in that Grant Wood painting, Woman With Plant. A crusty time warp crept over us, sitting by ourselves in the Coney Island. We forgot what time period we were residing in. My grandfather would have loved it. We both had to go to work later on, so the timelessness of the situation had a great appeal for us. Claire asked for a couple of quarters to play the jukebox, but after she got up to go drop them in the slot, she stood up on the seat of the empty booth behind ours, and looking down at me, she said, I hope after we're finished with this boyfriend-girlfriend stuff that we can be just friends, because I'd like to stay friends with you, I really would, I'd like to see what you look like when you're an old man, I mean you're already kind of an old man, but I'd like to see what you look like when you're really old and you have to walk with a cane. Then she went to play the jukebox, and I listened closely to the words of the first song that she played - Nature Boy - because I knew King Cole's vocals were aimed straight at me.)

…because yeah, we were in a big hurry…we had to go see Murial to tell her the news…Murial at the Peacock…she was so funny!…people like her hardly exist anymore - what an entertainer! - my god, the way she threw her head back and belted out *Bye Bye Blackbird!* Oh Carl, you should have seen her…I wish I could remember just one of her jokes… she had a joke for every occasion…so when your mother and I told her the news, she let loose with a dozen or more marriage jokes, non-stop. And I mean non-stop, they were flowing out of her.

(Claire had to be at work at McCarthy's, we just had time to hurry up the Hill past the Cathedral to Frosts for a quick Irish to perk us up. Tommy the bartender told us a few good political jokes. I laughed. Claire seemed preoccupied. Then Tommy left to go downstairs and get some wine. It was quiet at the bar, just the two of us. I put my arm around Claire, but she brushed it away and got out of her chair to pick up a dime on the floor. Then she left without saying goodbye. I stayed on for a while. I didn't have to be at work until ten.)

…and then Murial ordered set-ups for everybody in the place. There was a band in the Peacock from Chicago, a black band, because Murial's bar was one of the few places where they could drink, in those days, between Minneapolis and Omaha. One of those guys got up to play the piano, and everybody stood up at their tables to toast us, and Murial got up on the bar to do her fan dance. You see Carl, this woman knew how to create a festive atmosphere. But life was different then, it really was. Life was much livelier. I feel sorry for you, not being able to experience what your mother and I saw and heard and felt back then. It seems dead here now, with no Peacock and no Okoboji Club and no Inn Ballroom hanging out over the lake. Where the hell do people go these days, and what the hell do they do? It's beyond me, it really is, *it's beyond me!* People now don't know how to let loose! They have no idea how to dance to a jukebox! Can you believe it? Maybe they can't dance because there's no dance tunes on the damn jukebox! Maybe that's it! Who knows, Carl? Who knows? It's too depressing to even think about. Man, I've got to hear something to cheer me up. Quick! How about…how about *Fly Me To The Moon!* Franks's version. Not Tony's. And not Steve's. Frank's and Frank's only. The occasion begs for Frank. My god! And turn it up. And my glass is empty. We're going downhill, Carl. We got to turn this damn boat around and head for the Roof Garden. We've got to blow the roof off of the damn place! You know what I'm talking about? Do you know what I mean?

(Frost's started to fill up later on. I had to move a few times to make room for this group and that group. Pretty soon I was sandwiched in at the waitress station at the end of the bar. I was listening to the music, lost in thought as they say…just lost in thought. I was trying to picture Claire and myself at Okoboji. It was rather hard to imagine because…Claire was a city girl. The city seemed a cold place to me. The Cathedral was cold too. And so were the buses that ran up and down Selby. Detached onlookers filled every window. Frosts was warm, but it was a false warmth. I left Frosts finally, and walked down Western to the overlook, where I sat on a bench and gazed at the NSP smokestack and the High Bridge and Cherokee Heights and the stars and the moon, if there was one that night.)

"I think I finally figured out what's going on here."

"Pray thee tell."

"Other people probably figured it out a long time ago."

"Figured out what?"

"The trick?"

"The sleight of hand trick behind this book."

"Which is?"

"Reading this book is like looking in the wrong end of a telescope."

"You really think so?"

"I'm sure of it. The past is being telescoped on to the present. It's the old time trick of: What tense are we in?"

"Knowing that, will we enjoy it more?"

"That I can't tell you. But we may have to read it more than once."

"I don't read books more than once. Once is enough for any book."

"But you listen to songs over and over. And you watch movies again and again. And you insist on visiting the Delgado Museum to see Degas and Gauguin one more time."

"Don't talk about New Orleans! I'm already homesick enough as it is!"

"Ok. Let's move on. The last act in the scene. I mean the last scene in the act. Are you ready. I've got a feeling that there's going to be some fireworks."

"I can handle it."

VI.
Rise and Collapse

The summer appeared to reach its zenith at one precise moment in early August, as my father, teetering on the edge his chair of reflection with a full glass of wine in his left hand, raised his right arm high in the air, and then brought it down hard, to perfectly coincide, not only with Max Roach's drum stick hitting the snare drum on some hard bop tune, but also with the sudden gun blast which announced the start of the sailboat races.

From that lofty apex he sat back and turned his head to the lake and proceeded to take it all in: the sun on the water; the tones of the saxophones; the color in the clouds; the rhythm in the base lines; the noisy boats darting across the lake like bloated water bugs; the breeze which swept in the wide open windows, and of course the glass of wine which he raised to his chapped lips. He was still dressed in white, though not the bright white of the day he'd arrived, but an off-white, as if the never ending bombardment of reflections had caused his white to gradually fade toward a grey.

Something was amusing though, because he was smiling, and smiling so intensely that I had to smile along with him, sitting across the porch from him, watching him smile at I had no idea what. Neither one of us had said anything, funny or not, for a long time. Was it the little figurine of Napoleon on the bamboo table, and its close proximity to the old picture book of Paris, that he somehow found humorous? But then when I took his World War Two binoculars down from the top of the piano and went to stand at the window, he stopped smiling and immediately asked:

Do you see her anywhere out there?

It was the way he said *her*, dragging out the r with a slight slur, that made me wonder who he meant by *her*?

I found *who* I was looking for pretty easy. Their rowboat was the only boat out there that wasn't moving…they were floating over the bottomless hole…

Boats were flying past them, shooting off in every direction, as they sat together on the middle seat watching the sunset. The waves jostled them…turning their backs to the colors - but with a few quick strokes of an oar, they spun around and laid the oar back down and poured something into a cup that they passed back and forth between them.

When the Queen passed fairly close, she blew her horn and sent out waves which appeared to rock a bit of their drink over the edge.

I hope she has her life jacket on, my father said. She never used to wear a life jacket, and that's why she drowned, or so they say.

I don't see a life jacket on her.

Then she's going to drown again, my father said.

She can't drown for the first time before she finishes her book.

The one she's reading, or the one she's writing?

The one she's living.

She's a reader and a writer?

Both!

Neither!

What difference could it possibly make? She's going to drown, and that's that. She did drown. They never found the body…until it washed up on Gull Point. But that was a long time ago. You weren't very old…

Feeling an obvious need to change the subject, he said: Carl, don't you think it's time to play Chet now?

Which one?

Which one? You know as well as I do which one!

I found the one that I thought he was alluding to, wiped it off with my t-shirt, blew the dust off the needle, and let it roll.

Turn up the volume! The voice…I want it to drown out everything… and I mean everything…

It was a frail halting sinewy voice that I increased the volume on. It was a man's voice, but it carried the emotion and the sensitivity of a woman. It was a voice that could reach a person no matter how far away they were. In a world thick and overwhelmed with voices there was not another voice like it anywhere else in the world. It was a voice meant for the ear and the ear alone. It gave me a shiver that I couldn't shake, and for days afterwards it followed me around. It was the voice and the words that I was looking for, I realized, when I was trying to sing out that message to Claire…across the water…

My father took a long sip…he was clearly relishing the voice, and lost in it too. The voice had suddenly superseded the sunset for him.

It's not every morning that you wake up in a strange bed.

One morning I woke up on the edge of Claire's old bed.

That same day I took up residence in a new room.

On the first night after I'd moved into Claire's old room, and probably under the influence of my grandmother, who was always so interested in gainful employment, and whose bed and room this had been long before it was Claire's, I dreamed that I was back in a city very similar to St. Paul, working in a used record store on a side street shaded by a long row of maples. The door to the store had a string of little bells dangling from the handle, and whenever the door opened the bells jingled and leaves blew in across the floor. Then it must have been the fall time! My job was to classify each record and put it in the appropriate bin. Pretty students with long eyelashes under their bangs praised my classifications, while the serious collectors who were always looking over my shoulder criticized them. But I was happy because I got paid every day in cash, and my pockets were always bulging with wads of bills. Then one day the bells jingled, and the potential customer who came in with the leaves was wearing the mask of Chopin as he was painted by Delacroix. He asked me where we kept the *Reflective Music*. I noticed, as I led him to the Reflective bin by the window, that he neither spoke with a St. Paul accent nor walked with a St. Paul walk. I'd resumed my classifying when the manager put on a record which was the very antonym of reflective. The man in the mask came up to me and said, *I can't stand this music.* He lifted a corner of his disguise, and I could see that it was my father, who I hadn't seen in years. I'm leaving, he said. Wait for me, I told him. Outside there were banks of leaves so high that it was impossible to see over them…

I was halfway between the front porch and the bathroom, my arms full of toilet bowl cleaner, along with the brushes and rags and disinfectants (this was no cleaning dream), when my father called me back out to the front porch, in order to ladle out additional instruction on how to determine if a Yorkshire pudding has in fact risen.

Open the oven door very slowly, he said, as if you're sneaking up on a butterfly on a milkweed pod.

All afternoon long he'd been playing different renditions of *All or Nothing at All*, narrowing his favorites down until there were only two contenders left: Sinatra and Coltrane. For some reason the tune reminded me of Lou the actress, so that in the kitchen, when I should have been sneaking up on the pudding by tiptoeing across the floor to the oven, instead I was daydreaming that I was following Lou, who I knew was in rehearsal for the last play of the season, across the fields. I was thinking about her playbook, and the way it stuck out of her back pocket and undulated to the movement of her hips. And because I became completely caught up in this daydream of her - her nimble mind, her playbook hips - these had become my instructions now - so that when I came to open the oven door, I opened it with the same enthusiasm that I'd watched her open her oven, that night in the actor's cabin, to check on the pizzas: jerking the door and letting it fall flat, bending over at the hips, keeping her legs perfectly straight, the playbook within an inch of falling from her pocket, grabbing a hot pad and laughing in the face of the heat against her face. But I was not looking in on a pizza which had just started to burn, but on a Yorkshire pudding that had risen to a golden brown and then collapsed upon itself and was…in ruins…

But if something has risen once, might it not rise again, and even higher next time, if given half a chance, if left alone, if fussed over, even prayed, chanted, or meditated over? It would simply mean spending a lot of time in the kitchen…

Back on the front porch once again, I told my father about the beautiful rise, but I didn't see any need to mention the unfortunate and unnecessary fall, as I poured him a full glass of white burgundy. He seemed happy at the news, almost carefree…

While you were out in the kitchen, he said, the sun set and the clouds turned a color which I've never seen anywhere else in the world. I don't believe there is even a name for the color those clouds turned. But now it's gone…I was going to yell for you, but I didn't want to frighten you or the pudding. But that color reminded me of paprika. Now if we just sprinkled a little paprika over a Yorkshire pudding which has baked to just the right color of brown crust, you would have a good idea of what the clouds looked like. I forgot to bring paprika, but I'm sure they would have it at the Okoboji Store…they carried it when I had Fisherman's Wharf, because I used to risk my life crossing the highway in the summer for that and other spices. Would you mind riding your bike down to pick up some. It's all we need for a perfect pudding…

The Okoboji store…I started to try and explain…*the Okoboji Store*… it was a year or two after Crandall's came down…these things always happen in the fall, after all the tourists leave…Crandall's…Crandall's kind of started a chain reaction…that continues to this day…

Disbelievingly he looked at me, as if I'd torn down the old building myself. He gasped, then brought the glass to his lips and gulped a deep draught. I could see that he was gathering together all the indignities that he had suffered in his life, and bringing them to the forefront of his consciousness, due to the disappearance of this one particular building. He was about to make a statement. Someone was going to have to pay the price. I braced myself, as he set his wineglass on the glass top of the bamboo table, between *One Hundred Views of Paris* and *White Men Follow After*, and then walked over to stand, possibly symbolically, beside the portrait of the old Civil War general who'd taken part in the siege of Vicksburg.

Is it possible, he began, *that such a historic building, which figured in nearly every early photograph of the lakes…the Okoboji Store, the swing bridge, the isthmus…is it possible that such a building, standing as it did at the crossroads of Okobojian civilization, could have been torn down without you, coming from a family of brave war heroes and fire fighters and business people and restaurateurs and artists and journalists and philosophers and world travelers, doing one thing to try and save it? Maybe you were too busy pursuing some girl, or you had to go swimming, or you were out in back of the garage lost in your raspberry patch. Your were just too otherwise occupied, whatever it was that you were doing, you were too busy to submit the one lousy nomination that it would have taken to place the Okoboji Store on the National Register of Historic Places, which probably would have saved it from demolition. One single lonely solitary good for nothing nomination…*

His eyes had narrowed to a tiny slit, almost to the point where I would have said that they were closed, if he hadn't turned his head ever so slowly in the direction of where the last remnant of reflection had dissolved, not so very long ago…

PART FOUR

FROM THE TOP OF THE TIPSY

"It was a late summer morning."

"No, it was a late summer evening."

"The sun was rising."

"You're mistaken. The sun was setting."

"The sky was blue but tinged with red."

"Do you need glasses? The sky was red but dappled in blue."

"Someone was strumming on a guitar."

"I beg your pardon. That was a piano, and they were tinkling on it"

"A tree stood still to salute the morning."

"That tree you're talking about was all in motion."

"Its leaves were beginning to curl on the edges, for a hint of fall was in the air."

"But no more than a hint, and only where the underside of the leaves were losing their green and turning brown in the sun."

(together): "Brown, brown, turning brown in the sun…"

"One thing that I think we can agree on - shifting tenses - is that the amusement park is waking up."

"You can see it in the eyes of the people who work there."

"Who's that long haired gangly kid squirting the sidewalks with a hose?"

"I have no idea. Never saw him before."

"Me either. But I think I could watch him spray his water all day, making little rainbows here and there in the air."

"It's such a relief to be out of that claustrophobic cottage and back in the amusement park."

"Because while Carl has been listening to endless stories of conceptions and deceptions and receptions-"

"Punctuated by jazz tunes at ear splitting volumes-"

"An economic displacement drama has been brewing across the lake, in the vicinity of Pinball Haven."

"I can't wait to go there!"

"What are we waiting for?"

I.
Cross Words

Newly hired, impudent, long haired kid with a high pressure silver handled hundred footer hissing squirting rattler in his hands, hosing the cracked sidewalks, spraying the cobwebbed walls, aiming point blank at *the mess* : sticky cotton candy paper tube roll jammed in the cracks with a Nutty Buddy sharp as *hell* little pointed stick stuck sticky bits of chocolate covered peanuts, *won't come loose*, still attached, his high pressure spray aimed squarely at…until *finally* off it shoots and slithers away down the sidewalk while this lanky lean kid in jeans shouts *Damn*! as he aims his hose at the sky and shoots high…just to see the rainbows…a plethora of thirsty rainbows waterfalling…

Only thing was, he got Jerry wet, unintentionally or not, a few drops landing like soft summer rain on his checkered rayon shoulders…

It felt kinda good…but still he had to yell:

Hey! Watch where you're squirtn' that thang!

Grey haired Ester of the always aching back bent over rearranging in the multi-tiered Shell Shack display window, busy always so busy never stops constantly rearranging Lake Okoboji souvenir trinkets, looks up in alarm at Jerry's stern admonition.

Since Jerry last sailed past the tom-tom key chain has lost its place of front and center prominence to the comb and mirror set in the attractive leather case, with *Lake Okoboji* emblazoned on the front, and tiny teepees and moccasins stamped in the leather. It's an easy to display-sell-carry-ship-send-give away-kind of souvenir, and one that if the winds are favorable might last a lifetime or get lost in the attic or end up in a museum or, in a pique, an unfortunate spur of the moment love related tantrum, get tossed overboard from the Queen.

Jerry, hurrying past on his way to work, droplets in his hair, crosswords sticking out of his back pocket, is accosted by Ester on the sidewalk in front of the Shell Shack:

Tell me Jerry, tell me: How does it look?

What Ester? How does what look?

My new display, what d'you think, ya knucklehead, my new display that I've been working on rearranging all this long humid morning! How does it look to you?

Jerry pauses, looks through the glass, sees his reflection, brushes the damp stray wisps of hair from his forehead with his free hand, sees the comb, the mirror, the tom-tom, the tee-pee, the seahorse, the sand dollar, the whoopee cushion, and says, immediately and forthwith to his philosophic inner self: *Junk! The junk people will buy! And read! And listen to! And look at! And collect!*

Fine Ester. You know, it really looks fantastic! Great job! You could have been a…you should have been a…one of those…what do you call them? Interior decorator! You could have made a lot of money.

Thanks Jerry. Oh look! Your lunch is leaking…

Drip drip drip through the double strength brown paper, dripping on his jeans, hell, it might have collapsed all over the soaking wet sidewalk underneath the Roof Garden leading to Pinball Haven, had he not grabbed it immediately with both hands from the bottom.

Jerry let me…let me give you another bag. A stronger bag!

New bag…keep going…onward…toward Pinball Haven, his destination this warm sultry summer morning.

Hurry quickly past Ethel, another interminable conversationalist, who's up on a ladder, and at her age, sweeping possibly a bit too brusquely the dust and the cobwebs from the Fun House Clown's faded red polka dots.

Be careful, Ethel. You don't want to fall. We're all uninsured here remember.

I'm not going to fall. But I'm not going to let the spiders do our dear clown in either, Jerry. It just wouldn't be right.

Why don't you take him down south with you this winter? Let him warm his fingers in the Gulf of Mexico, and by next summer he might be ready to play again.

If there even is another summer! Don't tell me you haven't heard? This might be it for us, Jerry. We could all be out of a job the next time Memorial Day rolls around.

How many summers have you been selling tickets and sweepin' cobwebs?

And oiling the barrel and greasing the slide? Too many, way too many! You'll never catch up with me, Jerry.

Then it was the sight of Sheri stabbing a box full of Yakima red delicious with pointed little sticks, and dipping and twirling them in the caramel with her long deft ringless fingers, then cooling them side by side on wax paper over a multitudinous marble slab, that was enough to awaken in Jerry the desire to purchase one - right there on the spot - and bite into it while it was still *warm*, going down deep with his good teeth from the strong side, to get a taste of the *whole* apple for once, a simple but tremulous taste to remember when it was pitch black at five in four months time, and the cold nipped at any foolish bit of exposed skin, and held him hostage in front of the natural gas fire, rotating himself like a dog on a stick to keep from getting burned.

A bad omen: that the roll-up doors to Pinball Haven should be raised before Jerry had gripped the handle and lifted all five to the ceiling? Ask Madame Jessie, but later, later, because here's the Gretch…

New machine, Gretchen?

Yeah Jerry, a brand new machine. Get a hammer and help me get it out of this crate.

What kind is it?

It's called a change machine. We'll name him Jerry Junior if it's a boy, or Geraldine if it's a girl. What's your replacement gonna be, Jerry? A boy or a girl?

If you gave birth to it, Gretchen, then you should know. Who's the father? Ralph or Bernie?

Bernie's up north drying out. You know that! Ralph ok'ed it. Listen Jerry, if you're not gonna help me, grab a broom! We're still gonna pay youse to sweep.

Tell the machine to grab the broom. Tell it to clean the glass too, and kick out motorcycle gangs like the one that was banging on *Auto Race* last night.

Why get confrontational, Jerry? The machine isn't confrontational. It gives out the correct change, it won't short us, and it doesn't dispense advice or opinions or philosophy or history, like you feel it's your duty to do. And it doesn't take messages or do crosswords or take lunch breaks. And if anyone has a problem, they can read the sign:

IF YOU NEED ASISTENCE OR A ROOT BEER
GO TO SKEE BALL

Patience dashed in out of breath, dressed concurrently for the beach and the ballroom:

Jerry! If you see Carl, tell him I'll meet him on the tracks at sunset. OK? Don't forget! The railroad tracks by the raspberry patch. At sunset remember. Promise you won't forget!

She ran out before Jerry had a chance to say... *Wait!*

See what I mean, Jerry? What good does that do us? How much money do we make for you to tell some Carl character to meet what's her name to go get run over together by the train while they're suckin' down beers up on the tracks by the raspberry patch? It doesn't *make* any sense or *mean* any cents for any of us in the hierarchy here. We're interested in dollars in this operation Jerry. Not in any of this other crap. Do you read me Jerry? Do you know where I'm coming from?

Patience was her name, and the train you're talking about quit runnin' through here a *long* time ago, Gretchen.

What a weird name. Imagine a mother naming her child Patience! Whatever turns ya on I guess. And I could give a damn when the train quit runnin! Just tack up that sign above the counter, and then go get me the other tool box. You know where it is. Hurry!

I can't hang up a sign that has a misspelling, Gretchen. You know me better than that.

Jesus, Jerry, you're makin' things difficult. Just go get me that other damn tool box.

You're going to have to train your new machine to fetch things for you, Gretchen.

You want us to pay youse to sweep? I'm telling you, go get the tool box!

In the little room behind the counter Jerry saw the *other* tool box, the tools in it damp and rusting from Katie Sage's little black two piece, hanging on a nail above, trying to dry from the day before.

He felt it. He felt the soft cloth.

He saw Katie in her two-piece, bare feet, crooked toes, wet frizzy hair dripping all over his crosswords, showing him a sliver in her foot, picked up off the pier.

He'd come in the back room to get something…but what was it?

Then he saw it: the thing that he'd come to get: his radio, yeah, his black transistor radio.

He grabbed it, and nabbed his lunch from the counter, leaving behind a tiny pool of chili broth for Gretchen to…*lick up!*

And then he was gone. Just like that…

(*I left Mom! Just like that! I walked out the door! Or under the door.*)

And he didn't look back, not once, not even when Gretchen slugged in anger the rear of her new machine with her one claw hammer, like so:

Bamm!

No, he kept going, going on, not looking back, not once, not ever.

Now he was hurrying under the roller coaster (the ghost coaster had just re-arrived; his heart was pounding like crazy to the squeal of the brakes).

Now he was trying to stroll nonchalantly past *Ring the Bell* (for lack of muscular types, it had hardly rung all summer).

Now he was tripping in front of *Guess Your Weight* (the guesser was out to lunch; waistlines were expanding).

The amusement park seemed to be falling to pieces all around him.

Let it!

Let it, just let it, let it all fall:

down
down
down
down
down

He waved to Madame Jessie, industriously polishing her crystal ball with her soft red cloth from the near shore of the dim Black Sea. (His wave wasn't returned, because when she was polishing - and Jerry was quite cognizant of this fact - Madame J was oblivious to all progressions, whether ascending or descending, as well as to parameters of sound: that is to say: pitch, timbre, loudness, and duration. Nor did she pay any attention to clouds or newspapers or the seal lady or the Human Torch or even Jerry, doyen of the amusement park, so recently laid off. She polished and she polished, until what remained of any reflection in her crystal gazing ball was absolutely anonymous. She will continue to polish, to the amazement of her flirtatious assistant, long past the time when all the future events she has predicted have been set in motion, including Jerry's position being taken by something as inhuman as a change machine. Because nothing must be left to coincidence if a potential customer is to catch a glimpse of his or her life beyond the horizon. You think a crystal ball is only a simple single futurity predictor? she asked her assistant as Jerry hurtled on toward his future. *It contains multitudes!*

Now Jerry was walking on air in the vicinity of the Loop-O-Plane. (It can now be stated unequivocally that he was feeling *free baby freeeeeeeee...*)

What a day! he overheard someone say. *Best day of the summer so far.*

I wouldn't go that far, Jerry said to himself, swallowing the lump in his throat and flying on auto pilot past Pesky (ducking behind the shooters) Pete.

Around the Bug House, under the coaster, and across the street to the Indian path that will take him out to the point, where Jerry will reach his maximum cruising altitude...

Before he knows it, he's touched down on the tip of Pillsbury Point.

How did I get out here?

Not in years...have I been out here!

There's the old smooth stone WPA bench, overrun with weeds.

A fitting parable for our time.

Eleanor and FDR: we need you now more than ever.

You stuck up for us!

Oh shoots...just sit in the grass and look out...

Up and down the lake...

Old Indian hangout for Inkpaduta and the boys.

Did I do the right thing walking away from my job like that?

Am I going to regret it tonight? Tomorrow?

Should I go back and make up to Gretch?

No! Absolutely not!

Imagine a shining sword rising up out of the lake, somewhere in the vicinity of the mythical black buoy. Swim out and grab it, swim in and give it to her.

Here Gretch, go scalp yourself!

Then give me back my sword, dear sweet greedy Gretch.

If she were screaming for help off the pointed rock where all those girls drowned, I'd laugh and wave.

Save yourself girl!

Her scowling (*Go get me the tool box!*) face in those wispy clouds above the west side of the lake.

Take her away clouds, carry her over to Wisconsin, drop her in a string cheese factory.

His shaking hand on the transistor radio dial: turning it on and running through the frequencies, searching for a song to drive from his mind that ugly confrontation with…

He finds one: it's the Pelvis singing about the rain in Kentucky, from the summer of…the same summer that Phillip fell through the roof of the bathhouse while peeking in at Linda…Linda the Loud…

Whenever somebody played *For Your Love* on the jukebox…Linda… she'd jump up on the counter and dance…and I'd be sliding damp root beers down the wet counter…between her legs…

But that was a long time ago…

And now?

Now that I have successfully achieved my freedom, should I eat my lunch early?

Or should I at least wait until the siren goes off?

(His baloney sandwich in the saggy bag had been contaminated with chili juice).

Spicy chili in hot August? My god Mom! Why?

Horsefly! Out-a-here!

Jerry finishes his sandwich just as the siren goes off. He opens up his book of crosswords, and thumbs absent mindedly through them, his blunt pencil at the ready. Sharpen it at home later.

My syrupy sugary peaches?

Save 'em for later.

Okay. Here we go:

23 Across: Local color

What am I going to do for money? My paycheck! I forgot to pick up my paycheck. Get it later, after Gretchen and Ralph go do their thing.

16 Down: Holy place

There was nothing I could do about it, Mom. I can find another job!

17 Across: Arab port once British

Because she's having an affair with Ralph, all of a sudden, she's my manager, half my age, telling me what…

7 Across: Privatization

That's easy. The Ft. Lauderdaleization of Arnolds Park and Okoboji. Private: bench, dock, water, sidewalk, tree, bush, air, cloud, seagull, thoughts, history…everything private private private…

22 Down: Peep hole

Patience, you surprised me, coming out of the past like that. You left that message for Carl a long time ago…the summer of…But Gretchen heard you too! I'm confused…Where are you now, Patience? I wish I knew where you are now? I love it when the past comes back like that, just reappears out of nowhere, intrudes on the present to leave an old message from the past. That only happens in Arnolds Park, by the way. *Only in Arnolds Park!* In no other place does that happen. That's why I live here, that's why we all live here: Ester, Ethel, Sheri, Nutty, Pesky, Madame Jessie. You've got to have what it takes. You have to possess the ability to live in the past in the present. Lucky Carl, meeting you on the tracks like that, in your lovely outfit…your other suit, the little red one, is still hanging where you left it on the nail in the back room, right beside Katie Sage's black one…probably doesn't even fit you anymore. Gretchen wanted to use it for a rag one day, but I said *Don't touch that! That is not a rag!* What it reminds me of is those…it reminds me of the old bath house days. I carried it over from there, to hang it on the nail in the little back room behind the counter. Because I thought you were coming back, dear Patience. But you never came back. And Carl, he never knew what happened to you either. But I never…I wasn't about to use your little red suit for a rag. No way Jose!

34 Across: Tyranny of the workplace

Finish the crossword, start for home. Forget about the paycheck until tomorrow. One of Sheri's caramel apples might taste good…just enough change for one I think…

6 Down: Another word for freedom

Stomach hurts…ants…can't concentrate…

Out on the tip of Pillsbury Point it was as if Jerry - after he'd filled in the remaining squares - the ones having to do with how many were saved, and how many drowned - and had stood up, stiff jointed and sore backed, to face a breeze that had just come up - it was all movement that he was surrounded by now - everything was in motion, and the world… the world was consumed by change - creation was ongoing - he was helping to create it - that was his job now - he didn't need Bernie or Ralph or Gretchen to tell him what to do anymore - he was free - free to take his place in the bow of a Cunard-like Liner, steering north…up beyond Atwell and Manhattan, that would be the wide open ocean…somewhere up there the ship would turn southward…

So…he was finally sailing away from his job at the amusement park… sailing off toward another adventure…ready to land in another port…assume another identity…sample the local cuisine…sit back and observe, in the shade of a fragrant flowering tree, the customs, the history, the way of life in this new place where he'd just happened to…land…

"Hey, can we get on that ship with him, 'cause he looks like he's going somewhere…maybe even down to New Orleans!"

"I believe…I can't be sure, but I believe that ship that he was on was a metaphorical one."

"You think so. Well, metaphorical or not, I still wouldn't mind being on it."

"You want to leave just when things are starting to get exciting?"

"You stay behind and tell me about it. Write me a letter. Send it general delivery to the Magazine Street station."

"But Patience is about to come back on stage."

"Oh. Well…that's different. That might be something worth sticking around for."

"Even if she takes us back in the past?"

"I can handle the past if Patience is present."

"It's the evening of her defection, the evening of the day after the baby rolled down the bank in her stroller, and Patience has run away, and Carl, after visiting with his grandmother on the front porch, listening to her stories of her trips across the North Atlantic to Paris, Carl has jumped in his little aluminum boat for a voyage to Arnolds Park, and has gotten the word from Jerry to meet Patience up on the tracks. So that's where we are: back in the past and up on the tracks."

"Say, you set the scene very nicely. I feel like I know exactly where I am for once. I feel like I can just sit back and enjoy this one, 'cause Patience has a stage presence, you know, kinda like Carl's father."

"Hey, we gotta go. Patience is comin' down the tracks right now!"

II.
Kiss My Cobweb

All the jumbled sounds and lights from the amusement park rose up and ran down the tracks to where I sat between the raspberries and the sumac, waiting a little impatiently for the ex-nanny who had run away from her nanny job after the baby had rolled all the way down the bank, and who was now sleeping, as I was to later find out, on an undisclosed couch in an enclosed porch belonging to a kind older Jewish woman.

She was always late, she was never early. I sat on the tracks. I waited, I smelled, I listened to the warm-up band.

And then - then I heard a - *ping!* - followed quickly by a - *ding!* A freckled stone had kinked another stone and bounced - *tink!* - against an iron rail (releasing that encrusted geological sound that all railroad stones seem to carry inside them) before landing a few inches from my tennis shoe. I looked up and saw Patience walking down the tracks toward me, rather languorously, exaggerating the slink of her hips, a girl acting like a woman and pulling it off. She had the ability to bend those rails right before my eyes. *Watch out!* my grandmother had warned me, but her voice was snuffed out by this bold apparition in a short light white cotton dress walking toward me in the last vestiges of a brilliant sunset, as if she was stepping right out of A wider-than-the-world screen movie, sandals first, and getting closer and closer to me with every step, a six-pack dangling dangerously in her left hand.

She came up and sat down beside me. And put her arm around me and gave me a tongue kiss, the bold little ex-nanny. I wasn't ready for her tongue, not like that, not on the tracks. But I didn't run away, I just got red in the face and slightly embarrassed and over excited, all at the same time. But it was almost dark, that was lucky...I could hide in the dark...

Hey! she said (my head was still *spinning*). On my way across the amusement park to leave a message for you with Jerry, I stopped to watch these long-haired guys unloading their equipment in back of the Roof Garden. It was so hard to tell who was in the band and who was just along for the ride. That was one strange bunch of people climbing off that bus with California plates. Everything about them was strange, Carl. The way they looked and talked and laughed and walked. And the women were just as strange as the men, in their wild clothes and hair. I didn't know who to ask for autographs, so I just asked them all. They were probably the oddest bunch of people ever to land in Arnolds Park. They thought everything was funny. They couldn't stop laughing and giggling. I'd love to go with them Carl. I'd love to get on the bus with them and go out to the ocean. We've got to go see them play tonight if it's the last thing we do this summer.

I don't have any money. Do you have any money?

No...I had some, but I gave it to this lady I'm staying with. But it doesn't matter 'cause I know a way that we can get in for free. This guy Phillip who runs the Wild Mouse, he showed me how to go up the fire escape. Yeah, we can sneak in, but we'll have to be extra careful because they already caught me trying to sneak in on the Fourth of July, and they said if they caught me doing it again it would be...that would be it for me. So we've got to wait 'til it's completely dark and the band starts before we try it.

As we drank it got darker and darker, and the lights from the Ferris wheel got brighter and brighter, and I regained my composure, and the beer made me braver, and we could hear the band tuning their instruments.

Have you heard their song on the radio? Patience asked me.

I had…I'd been vacuuming, and that chiming guitar sound…I let go of the vacuum and ran to the radio…I heard it later on another station…

I snuck a good look at Patience. She had little earrings on, seahorse earrings. Her hair was long and not so spiky. She was trading in her tomboy look. She looked like she was more interested in dancing than climbing trees these days. I thought of how beat-up her knees used to look up in the burr oak on Ft. Dodge Point. I think she'd been shaving her legs… and under her arms too. I saw the Ferris wheel spinning around in the reflection of her lively eyes. She was using make-up too. First it felt weird to have her tongue in my mouth. But then it felt pleasurable. A multitude of feelings on those tracks that night…

I think their song is number one, she said. I don't want to miss it. Let's go!

We flutter up like sodden hummingbirds from our rocky thrones on the iron rails above the amusement park.

On our way down the poison ivy bank and across the parking lot, she lays out the strategy: after the band kicks in, Gary the guard, he'll get distracted, and that's when we open the bottom door and smash through the wall of cobwebs and sneak up the stairs…Ok?

Everything but the cobwebs sounds cool to me. Ferocious mosquitoes have arrived with the twilight, biting us left and right, Patience on her neck, me on my knees. All of a sudden, Patience loses her patience. She's in a big hurry now, thinking that the band might open with their hit song. I'm walking a little wobbly, but Patience is navigating like a clipper ship in full sail through the parking lot and around all the cars, the shiny cars with people in them playin' their radios and kissing and drinking and…I'm trailing along behind her…in her wake…

For some reason I feel like I'm trying to keep up with Inkpaduta. Yeah, all of her leadership qualities are now in full bloom, and she's flip-flopped the gender roles to boot, so now it's like I'm little Abbie, and this impatient Inkpaduta has kidnapped me and we're threading the dust and making our way for the sound and the light to meet these long-haired sons of the pioneers who play electric guitars instead of banjos these days…

We join the crowd and get swept along, and Patience…

Hello Patience…

Where are you Patience?

She'd had a hold of my hand…just a second ago…

Ah, there she is…waitin' for me at Pinball Haven, elbows on the counter, trying to talk to Jerry…who's busy…pouring root beer…

Some of the crowd is going up the Roof's back steps, and a whole lot of them are going up the front steps, but I'm following Patience because she knows another way we're gonna hear this band without having to stand in line and buy a ticket.

I'm hangin' with her on the blue poles between Pinball Haven and the Karmelkorn stand. She points up to the fire escape that drops down only in emergencies. There's our way up, she says. But first the coast must be absolutely clear. When it is, you jump on top of a pinball machine, like so. Then you grab a rafter and swing one leg over it, and then the other. And then you pull yourself up and disappear right away in the shadows…and the cobwebs…

After we do it, Patience whispers: Let's catch our breath! Anybody see us?

People milling around right under us…if we wanted to we could reach down and part their hair with a fine tooth comb on a stick. You feel like you want to get someone's attention down below just to see the look on their face when they look up.

A couple stops to kiss.

Kiss me, kiss my cobweb.

It's fun to watch people from above, how they turn suddenly and follow each other, a random pattern of heads of hair. One guy stops to comb his hair in front of a window.

There's Hair, Patience says. You know Hair?

No, I don't know Hair.

You don't hang around here enough. If you did, then you'd know Hair. Because everybody that hangs around the amusement park knows Hair. Hair's always stopping to look in a mirror or a window to comb his hair. Just watch.

That's exactly what Hair does. He slips around behind *Auto Race* and starts combing his hair to the accompaniment of his reflection in a finely polished mirror…

Army wanders into the picture…we could lift his policeman's hat right off his head.

But then here comes tall dark unshaven ominous Bernie, weaving along. Just the sight of him - *oooh!* - makes us shrink back in the shadows, because if he sees us, if he catches us he'll drag us back to his office and - *nooo*!

He stops to talk to Army…right underneath us…

Bernie's blasted, Patience whispers. Look at him wobble. Hey, there's Jimmy R. I'd know that hat anywhere. What a guy! He's so cool! And a pool shark too…

Jimmy sits down on the bench below and to the left of the Fun House Clown. My grandfather's favorite bench. He doesn't seem to be in a hurry to get up to the Roof Garden, or anywhere else…He's just watchin' the people. It's not a bad occupation…it seems to fit him perfectly…he has the look of a sage…

Patience motions: Follow me. We walk a tightrope along the rafters, stepping over frayed electrical connections to make our way to the fire escape ramp. A few short steps up and we're at the fire escape exit, our secret entrance to the Roof Garden.

Let's just wait here until the band starts…

We wait…I'm trembling…not with fear, with excitement, the floor's creaking above us, everyone's talking, there's a smell of old cigarettes…

And then:

Ladies and Gentlemen! It is my pleasure…

That's Darlowe. He introducing them! C'mon!

Patience pushes the door open a crack to look for Gary, but there's no sign of him in the screaming crowd pushed back to the top of the fire escape exit. Now we're catchin' another view of everybody, from their shoes up, they're all shakin' because the first few electric twelve string guitar chords are overpowering us all, like being swept away in the blast of a jet taking off. Patience knew that they were gonna start with their hit. The song has words, but you can't hear 'em, they're completely drowned out by the guitars and tambourine and smashing crashing cymbals.

I creep up the stairs behind Patience. We pause at the top step, then take a few steps in, and we're just about to blend in when somebody taps us each hard on the back of the shoulder.

Gary spins us both around. He's waving a nightstick in our noses. *I knew I'd find you!* he shouts in Patience's face. He's got the cuffs out, but then someone slams into him, and he turns around to see who did it. We're gone, split up into the crowd. He'll never catch us together now. I head for stage left, plowing my way through shoulders and elbows until I'm right under the bass player, who looks expressionless under his hair, only his fingers flying. It's so crowded that we're all cells of one body: when he moves she moves and so on and on, ripples of movement. One song ends, we scream the same scream, another begins. Broken guitar strings cascade out of every guitar neck. I'm jammed in among the people from the bus, there's no mistaking their frantic dance style, they're as much of a show as the band.

Patience is on stage right, I wave, she doesn't see me, she's too busy looking up adoringly at the twelve string player with the funny glasses.

The glass balls and mirrored posts reflect light and refract sound. I get as good as lost in the music…you have to work yourself up into a state…it's easy with those chiming guitar bell chords pouring in through every sweaty pore that we've kept open all summer long for just such an occasion…every sensation is invited to *please come in*…let them all come in!…and they keep coming in and they never stop coming in until the band takes a break, and the crowd en masse heads for the breezy windows…

A very good thing that there was such a breeze…it helps to dry the sweat from…

A girl shouts in my ear but I can't hear her because my ears are ring ring ringing. Her lips are moving, her green eyes sparkling like little stars…*Sweetheart!* She rubs her nose…all those eyes, all those noses…the way they detach themselves from their faces to bounce against the glass in a thousand little glances off the revolving mirrored balls…

From the front windows of the Roof Garden you can see that the lake is as tilted as everything else in Arnolds Park. The water flip flops right in front of your sweaty face. The bottom comes to the top, and the top falls to the bottom…as Patience runs up to me and asks *Which one's Roger and which one's Jim?* And then disappears again…

You sit down with a bunch of people that you don't even know. You cross your legs and listen in on their conversation while you wait for the band to start up once more…

I only know how to dance to the slow ones…

This ballroom seems a little bit haunted…

Look at that seagull with the pie crust in its mouth!

Is that weird or what?

Cut it out! You're freakin' me out!

Hey! If we're gonna dance then let's dance right up front under the microphones and in front of the speakers so we can feel the vibrations!

(He hopes they never stop playin'
while she wishes it might never end
and they all want it to go on forever and ever)

But if we're not gonna dance then let's go sit back in one of the booths, you know, take in the high view, lean out the windows.

A touch of cool in the air...

I'm not sayin' Miles was there...

but the Turtles played twice

and Louis and the Count and the Beau Brummels

and half of the Beach Boys plus both of the Everlys and all of the Yardbirds and...June and Johnny and the original Byrds minus Jay of the Americans but including Sam the Sham jive dancin' with his Pharaohettes while Roscoe and his Little Green Men waited over in the wings...

White Wing! Where are you?

The sound carries and the tones are set free. Seagulls drop the pie crusts and pick up popcorn on the pier and glide off...

It's Showtime! Part Three...

Oh no, here come the horns...

It's the fabulous...

It is indeed a great pleasure to introduce...

All the big halls...

Where Buddy and the Bopper went down...they did a show...in a field in the snow...I think...

But hey if we're not going to dance let's have a drink and watch the dancers in the revolving...

We can dance the next slow...

I know the piano player by the way...he promised to play a *Summer Sequence*. Maybe he'll even...*Clothe a Woman...*

We missed a perfect chance to dance on that last song...a slow blues, a sax solo. Did you get the name?

Did you say you're from South Dakota?

She wouldn't dance. Then she left with somebody else.

Stay out of trouble, and avoid bumping into those blue poles on your way out...to the point...

Let's head out to Pillsbury...

Walk sideways as far as…

Call off the rescue mission, I'm gonna make it…

Those twinkle twinkle lights across the lake? You know they're islands, don't you?

As yet unnamed, as yet untamed, little islands…

That's some kind of strange seagull pigeon bird flying divine and diving, white wings flashing in the night, taking it further and farther out, over the park, across the lake, into the bedrooms of the sleepers…

You mean your mom and dad across the lake? They're not sleeping! They're waiting for you to come home dear! They're getting rather impatient.

Ladies and Gentlemen! Please welcome: Sun Ra!

Spaceless and placeless…a commodious compendium…

Just shut up, will you! You're talkin' nonsense!

A flowing commotion of tones…

"I feel kinda dizzy…after all that…"

"So that's what it was like, being up at the Roof Garden?"

"Yeah, we should'a been there, don't you think?"

"We were otherwise occupied."

"We were down in New Orleans."

"Listening to Lee Dorsey and Ernie K Doe and Longhair and Booker and Dr. John and Earl Turbinton and Charles Neville and…"

"But at least we know now what it was like to sneak up to the Roof Garden."

"With a girl like Patience to serve as a guide."

"I wish we could just follow her around for awhile."
"She takes a lot more chances than Carl."
"So…where are we off to next?"
"Back to the cottage. Carl's father has somethin' cookin' for us."
"Is he going to take us…back into the past?"
"He's taking us out on a tour, I think."
"On a tour? I love tours, especially if they're guided."

III.

Out of Balzac

This time - after spending most of the afternoon picking, eating, and swimming raspberries (and recuperating on the beach to the beat of the waves) - I approached the record player with a confidence unbeknownst to those fearful of staining their fingers red or filling their ear canals with Lake Okoboji…

My confident steady right index finger cradled the needle directly above the third cut on the second side, while my set of left hand fingers were poised to increase the volume once the needle made contact with the vinyl.

It was what we used to call a slow-dance type of tune. A ballad…

My father enthusiastically praised my selection:

Fantastic choice Carl!

He took a sip, executed a swallow, then questioned:

What kind of sauce can we use to compliment a boney bluegill? Let's consult *Diat's Sauces*, shall we? If anyone knows, it'll be old Diat. I just wish the walleye were biting instead of the bluegill. We'll have to serve a thick crusty bread, or our guests will be choking at the table, little bluegill bones stuck in their throats.

(Directly behind his head hear the sputtering buzz of a horsefly being squished against the screen by two white paws belonging to a cat that was always there, despite having a furry presence which was often taken for granted, but that could never be denied.)

He went on:

The walleyes are no doubt out in the deep water far off the end of your dismally short dock. But there's no point in extending the dock anymore, is there? You've done enough damage as it is with that dock down there. And summer's almost over. My god! Another summer nearly gone by...do you believe it?

He suddenly got up and grabbed the binoculars from the windowsill, as if to try and survey the last rays of summer before they escaped. I watched him take in all the motion on Okoboji without once blinking... through the chipped and scratched Pacific Theatre glasses which had seen Okinawa being blown to bits and his card playing buddies lying on the beach with blood coming out of their ears...

And now...

Now he was surveying a lake so bottled up with boats that if you were out there among them you could theoretically get bounced and battered from one to another... and never...once...ever...get your feet wet...

They're looking in every direction but the one they're going, he said, still peering through his binoculars.

The world, as he imagined it would be after the war - the war that he and all the others had left their farms and towns and cities to go off and fight in - was not the world he saw through his binoculars. He put them back on the windowsill, beside the cat who had trapped the horsefly...or deerfly...

At least...at least, he said, looking at the record spinning on the record player...at least you can hear music better at Okoboji. The tones seem to...unite with the air here, instead of quarreling with it...

Later that evening, inspired perhaps by the poached bluegill with soubise sauce (a trial run for the upcoming party), my father seemed full of energy and very lively. He asked me to follow him from room to room, and so we traveled from the front porch to the living room to the dining room and into the kitchen, looking at the portraits and landscapes and still lifes, while he lectured:

Your great grandmother painted pictures like you pick raspberries. By the way...your raspberries...they are delicious. But while you might overlook a big red ripe one under a leaf close to the ground, she never missed a thing, walking up and down the lake paths, carrying her box of paints and her canvas.

As he paused over Napoleon, whose broken arm was hanging on by a thread of old glue, I thought: here comes another anecdote which has miraculously survived by holding on to a piece of flotsom floating around in his mind...

...because in those days your great grandmother, as you can see in this sailboat painting of hers, was intensely interested in *blue.* And she passed on this intensity to me...and to you...

Old stories, I reflected, as I noticed the cat following us from room to room, are like a good sauce complimenting the main course...

And look at this one...now, it's obvious, isn't it, that it's the Queen coming around Ft. Dodge Point...but there's a whole other story behind this painting...look closely at the bow...do you see the woman in the red hat? That's your grandmother! Now, I wonder if she ever told you about a trip she took on the Queen...in the late teens, I believe. She'd boarded

Home from the Race

ship at Manhattan Beach, after doing a story about a man who had lost a very expensive pocket watch (Act Four, Scene VI). The boat was filled to overflowing. On the lower deck she sat in back of a group of Native Americans who were *dressed to the teeth*, as she used to say. She gathered from their conversation - she was a master eavesdropper - that they were on their way to see Abbie Gardner. They had gifts for Abbie which they were passing around amongst themselves, and your grandmother, in her boldness, asked if she might see them too. Just imagine this short woman in her Parisian hat approaching a group of tall elegantly dressed men out in the middle of Okoboji, and asking to see a Pipestone pipe which one of them had evidently made especially for Abbie. After talking with these men awhile, she decided to go up to the upper deck to get more air. It was a terribly hot day, she said, and she'd been fanning herself furiously, but to no avail. On the top deck she sat next to a man who was making notes in a little book. He wore a round Spanish style hat, with a loop under his chin, and was obviously not from anywhere nearby. His first name was Ricardo or Fernando, something like that. His last name…escapes me… He was having some trouble with his pen, and he'd asked to borrow your grandmother's, which she was very proud of, and which he admired so profusely that she gave it to him. I wonder if it was a pencil, and not a pen? She discovered that he was a travel writer and a poet from Lisbon, who was touring the country, and they exchanged notes and ideas about a variety of things, while at the same time watching with great interest five jaunty extraverts who were part of a band that was to play at The Inn that evening. Your grandmother had seen their picture in the paper she reported for. She'd come up to the top deck not only to get some air, as she put it, but to use her opera glasses to see if she could see your grandfather out on the lake anywhere…anchored off one of the points…fishing…

He paused to take another sip…

Gabo was on the floor between us, looking up intently at him.

How could my father possibly remember all these events, which he related as if he'd been there, when in fact they'd taken place before he was even born?

He must have noticed my consternation, because he said, pointing to a portrait of my grandfather and grandmother:

She told me this story so many times that I can tell it as if I was there. They were such vivid storytellers, your grandmother and grandfather. They made the past come alive! Movies and TV shows are pale in comparison. Anyway…where was I?

My grandmother was looking for my grandfather…she thought he must be fishing off one of the points.

Oh right, right. But he wasn't fishing. He'd walked up to the Inn to check his mail. And then…so then he was sitting in one of the rocking chairs on the long front porch when the Queen came in right on schedule. And he saw your grandmother on the top deck, the smokestack soot wafting above her, surrounded by a cast of characters *right out of Balzac*, as your grandfather put it. He hurried down to the dock to say hello to her. Those jagged old oaks were flaying and flagging…I hope they're *still there!* What a breeze there was that day! The waves on the beach had turned up a big clam shell, and a kid had jumped down off the dock to pick it up and show it to his family. Your grandmother smiled - because she was a *traveler* who loved to *travel* - and waved and yelled down from the top deck that she was going on to Arnolds Park after all, that a story at the Gardner Cabin had come up, but that she'd be home by supper. Then the Queen blew its' whistle and backed out - the smoke poured out of the stacks - the men in the band on the top deck took out their instruments and played a bit of New Orleans music. That's what they called it back then. The Queen steamed down Dixon Beach on its way past Ft. Dodge Point and on across the bay to Arnolds Park…

So that's the story behind that painting, he said, as I followed him barefoot across the large living room rug from Kurdistan, with the cat following me, in a continuation of our voyage out to the blurry edges of the past…

In the dining room he paused to refill his glass, before we proceeded on to a still life with flowers.

But he was still thinking of the painting of the Queen…

Your grandmother told your grandfather - after she came home that evening - that she felt as if she'd been on an ocean voyage, sitting on the deck of a liner going across the Atlantic, because of all the different kinds of passengers she'd sat beside and talked to and listened to. And your grandfather…your grandfather said that he'd had the same feeling too, as he'd returned to his rocking chair on the long porch, and watched the Queen pull away from the Inn, and the child with the clam shell skipping it and then diving for it…and the clouds above the old oaks - he was always a great one for clouds - together with the waves on the beach and the waning music of the band and the sound of the Queen's engine and the sight of all the sailboats and rowboats on Okoboji. He'd had the feeling - just as I have always had the same feeling - and maybe you have too, Carl - that this place was and is so unique, that it could not be duplicated, that it was unlike any other place in the world…until the people arrived with the money to invest…to try and make it like every where else…

We were still standing in front of the painting of the flowers…we hadn't moved…he was staring at the flowers…I was staring at him…the cat was on the floor, looking up expectantly at the both of us…he wanted some of the bluegill…without the soubise sauce…

I was looking at him looking at the painting, with the same intentness that he listened to music, and I asked myself, in the impasse: How can a remembered life be so impossibly rich? And how can it be so full of memories that the past almost seems like it's in the future. It was something that Claire and I had never shared. It's what had separated us, out in the middle of the Okoboji Bridge (Act Three, Scene I) on the day we'd arrived. The bridge had failed to connect us. Claire hadn't wanted to draw on her past to live in the present, while I was just the opposite. Claire paid no attention to these sometimes sentimental backward glimpses,

but if you could have seen my father then, looking at this painting as if he'd inhabited it, as if he'd lived among those flowers, as if he'd breathed their fragrance and rubbed the pollen on his cheeks and felt the breeze that bent the stems and furled the sail and curled the wave and lifted the curtains even now. Claire wouldn't have agreed with this philosophy of life. She'd seen the flowers and she'd seen the sails, but they were nothing more to her than flowers and sails, and anyway, she was someplace else now. She was across the lake, she was in a little cabin, she was oblivious to this moment…this moment that was much more than a moment to me…this story that was *more* than a story…

Claire had her own stories. But Claire was gone. And Claire wasn't coming back.

Goodbye Claire!

The doxies next door broke out in wild barking. They had a squirrel up in a tree, and three pairs of front legs were on the bark, scratching and howling.

The world is full of peerless and unparalleled places, my father said, though less and less so. And *this place* is *definitely* one of them. The air and sounds and sights are unlike anywhere else. It's funny…but wherever I've traveled since I left here, I've always compared it to Okoboji. It's never mattered if I was on my way to Okoboji, or on my way from Okoboji. I've always taken Okoboji with me…I've taken those old oaks that hang over the lake in front of the hotel with me…I worry about those trees for some reason. They're too much like me. One day we'll all fall in the lake. I suppose. I hope they're still there. Are they in good shape? Have you sat in their shade lately?

Did she ever write an article about that particular trip across Okoboji?

What? Who? Oh, your grandmother? No, she never reported on it. And do you know why? She found it too fantastic to report about. No one would have believed it. *Leave the fantastic for literature,* she always said.

Somehow we'd ended up where we'd started: back on the front porch. It seemed as if we'd been around the world. My father settled back in his chair of reflection. The paddle was still in the corner, sticking up above his head, as if to remind me…as if to say: No swirling eddies escaped those eyes, no clash of tribes or subtle evasions…

But what about the collisions? I wanted to ask…those terrible collisions, both imagined and real…the most famous one being the crash at twilight, in the summer of 1927, of the Thriller and the Zipper, piloted by those improvident captains, one Yarnes and the other Alexander. The paddle in the corner was both a witness to and souvenir of that tragedy. Did my great grandmother paint tragedies? Did my grandmother and grandfather talk about them?

I put on *Around the World* because my father asked me to…and I left it at that…as Frank's voice filled every corner of every room in the cottage…and Gabo got his bluegill…and then went outside…and sent those doxies packing.

"I not sure that I understand the point behind that last little episode."

"Scene, you mean. Well, maybe there wasn't one. I don't know. Maybe it's best to not ask too many questions. What's the story behind the story? Who can say for sure? The answer is probably in the song selection."

"Does it ever seem to you that we're back in New Orleans watching a Fellini or Godard or Bergman movie at the Prytania Street Theatre?"

"A little bit maybe. But I think we're more entertaining."

"You don't think that they'll think that we're trying to take over the show, do you?"

"I've heard rumors that we already have. That people are really relishing our comments, asides, and pictures, and skipping over everything else."

"So we're only here to provide comic relief? Why can't people ever take puppets seriously?"

"It's just a rumor, remember. Hey, are you ready to climb that water tower yet?"

"No! I'm not! Unless we can take the girl who's sitting on the seawall."

"Well, like it or not, that's where we're going. Up, up, and up."

"To the toppermost of the poppermost."

"I'll follow you."

"No, you first!"

"One rung at a time, remember."

"Yeah, one rusty rung at a time."

IV.

Higher

There was a deserted fall-like cast to the theater grounds...all the actresses and actors, the lighting technicians and stagehands, directors and carpenters, costumers and prompters, appeared to have abandoned the theatrical arena. I sat at the picnic table closest to the cornfield, eating the raspberries that I'd carried across the fields to help break the ice, while I contemplated a world without drama. It was difficult to imagine, given the emotional fragility of my species in the face of so much uncertainty. I ate a raspberry...*we're all going to die*...and then another...*summer is almost over*...I couldn't seem to stop eating them...*she's leaving soon*...once I'd started...*maybe she's already gone*...one by one...*I didn't even get to say goodbye*...I only ate one at a time...

I might have eaten them all, but for a door which swng climactically open, revealing a pensive actor who refused my offer of a raspberry before disappearing around a corner of the building.

Then Lou came out.

I'd never seen her looking so...ethereal...

As she approached the picnic table, I casually put the lid on the container.

Remember the first time that you brought me raspberries? she asked, sitting down beside me.

I'll never forget the first time that I brought you the raspberries, I said. It was at the hotel bar, and you had a tick on your shoulder, which I thought was a –

Did you bring me more raspberries this time? she interrupted, eyeballing the cottage cheese container on the picnic table by the cornfield.

These are the last of the raspberries, I said, handing her the half empty cottage cheese container.

She ate all the rest of them very quickly, and then she drank the juice and turned the container upside down on the picnic table. Her fingers, lips, and teeth were all stained a ravenous red by then, and little red raspberry beads were hanging on tiny hairs at the corners of her mouth.

I sat staring at the last of the raspberries…until she said:

What're you lookin' at?

Then she got up and invited me inside the deserted barracks.

Carlos, she said. Do you mind if I call you Carlos? Carl is too drab, but Carlos rolls off the tongue. *Carlos Carlos Carlos.* Would you help me close my suitcase?

I sat on her suitcase while she poked the socks and tops and bras back in with a butter knife.

Carlos, she asked, Can you help me clean the oven?

I sprayed a cloud of hydrogaseous florocarbon foamy cleaner into the oven and stood back until it had settled and soaked into the remains of a thousand pizzas left to bake until burned, the crust on the rack with no cookie sheet to catch the cheese. I scraped and scraped and scraped some more.

Carlos! She yelled from the bedroom. Can you hold up this box spring for me while I put the slats back on the frame?

I liked the way she called me Carlos, dragging out the s 'til it hissed.

It's like she'd bestowed a new identity on me…

Carlos, there's one thing that I've wanted to do with you all summer. Would you do it with me now, on my last day?

For we may never meet again, she sang, as I scraped in the oven.

Because it will be the great regret of my life if we don't do it at least once before I leave. And Carlos, I'm leaving in a few hours, so we've just got time. Let me tell you Carlos…not to do it would tarnish my fall, t'would miss-color my winter, perhaps even sully my spring…Do you think I'm a poet? If this acting trip doesn't work out, do you think I have a chance at poetry, if I write like I talk? Know what I'm talkin' about, Señor Carlos?

I knew very well how the stars and the moon affected her, but I still said neither yes nor no…I just kept scraping, on my hands and knees, the blackened inside of that rusty oven…while listening to her singing as she scurried about…straightening up the place…preparing for her final exit…

Within the hour I was to discover that you cannot possibly think that you know another person unless you've climbed behind them up a steep metal ladder to the top of a water tower.

Of all the rungs, the first rung is the most difficult.

Its distance from the ground alone makes it out of reach for all but the most enthusiastic of the unauthorized.

And after that first rung? It's one white knuckled rung at a time…

You try to summon a Human Torch-like bravery to carry you up toward the red capped peak…it pulls you closer and closer…it's like the long lost lighthouse of your night dreams…

You are attempting to achieve an *overview*…

For once, just once, you want to see…the whole story…

As you come up out of the trees, you climb forthwith into a layer of blessed forgetfulness, where you lose track of the number of rungs, and your place in the netherworld down below, while in your mind you hear a song you've never heard before, and your past is gradually and blissfully washed away, as you're forced to balance on the threshold of the moment.

While you climb, she glides, pushing up through layer after layer on her way to the spheres. The raspberries are working their magic in this elevated atmosphere, so that you don't notice the rust on the rungs which covers your hands, because you are another now, and it's on this newly exposed otherness that the mosquitoes and deerflies and horseflies nip.

She's far enough above you that you might've turned back except for the fact that when you dare to look down all you see are the elongated chipped paint steel legs of the water tower. But when you hazard to look up: there are her legs, her short-shorts-summit-surmounting all conquering legs, far more attractive than a water-towers, and it's those legs that you climb toward, reassuring yourself that you can climb as high as you want and no one will ever discover you or her unless they happen to... glance in the direction of Nirvana...

Peace be upon you who grippeth the right rung tightly! You're on you're way to finding out what these orbs that separate us are composed of. Nothing less than the death of your old self will take you on to the next rung. Throw it overboard then, along with all your stale words, like so much ballast, get rid of it, leave it behind, watch it tumble away...

Then you reach out across the ether in a frightening grasp for an outstretched hand...because you've come to the final rungs which arch out to reach the platform. You gave her the raspberries so she would have the strength to pull and swing you up on the see-through metal platform. She has the grip of a lover who won't ever let go.

She yanks you up into this nest in heaven so that you might see:

Look at the view from up here, Carlos!

Foolish or not, we were fools for that view...

A soft curtain of stillness settled...over all the other water towers... from all the other towns around...the trees outlined the shape of the lakes...the wind shook the leaves way below us...in the dying light we saw the flash of a seagull's wing...while from the legs of ten thousand crickets, a sonata...before a plane came in for a landing...

There's nothing like this in Duluth! she shouted.

Heart to heart you hold on to each other high above the earth, lashed together by the raspberries and the fragrance in her hair...

But then we discovered that we weren't the first to climb this local Everest. Someone had been there before us, a libertine named Norman the Morman, and this *N* the *M* had written his name, and those of his loves, in a variety of colors, boldly and brightly on the side of the water-tower. The second he found a new love, he climbed to the top to cross out the name of his old love and write in the name of his new one, so that all along the top of the water tower there were names dashed in and out:

Shiela > Vicky > Susan > Jane > Sherri > Joanne > Anna > Kari > Keri > June > Autumn > Ellen > Suzanne > Joni > Joan…

Reading all the names of these lovers and ex-lovers, we fell into a kind of trance, such as one might have after chanting a word over and over. So that Lou, who had never looked lovelier than at this height, set as she was against a backdrop of fertile Iowa air, acres and acres of it for as far as we could see, had to grab hold of me again, and in a hurry, just as I had to clutch on to her. We made haste to embrace, confronted with this evidence of the fleetingness of relationships. We pecked to the wooing and the cooing of some pigeons that had followed us, and who were watching us. We smooched because the sun had almost set, and we would be that much closer to the stars, which had begun to appear between the clouds. We caressed to a depth which nearly dissolved the occasion. Kiss a person on top of a water-tower, then you'll know what they're made of. And what they taste like…

The axioms and aphorisms that we bathed in that night! All your life you climb and climb to get to a place where they're as thick as flies.

Lou produced a green marker out of nowhere, and she's the one who wrote, in a large flourish, our names on top of the water tower…

And then she threw that marker overboard…

We watched it tumble head over heels out of view…

The color of the clouds…a soothing magenta…which affected us deeply…made us want to hold on to each other that much tighter…because, after all, we didn't want to fall…the pigeons cooed on and on…the crickets never let up…

What did you put in those raspberries? Lou wondered.

It'd been a great crop…a great year…but now…they were gone…so many raspberries that…I was seeing things…like the Manhattan Beach Hotel…back where it belonged, hanging out over the tip of Manhattan Point...and the Okoboji Store, and Vern and Coila's, they were all back where they belonged...and I was hearing things too, when I closed my eyes...the soundtrack of my father's life came up to me, live and in concert and very clear from the front porch of the cottage...*Fly Me to the Moon* and *My Funny Valentine* and *Summertime* and *Willow Weep for Me* and all the rest of those greatest hits...

Opening my eyes, I saw the moon coming up above Lou's soft round left shoulder.

She turned to see what I was starring at, but pivoting about she inched within a half inch of the edge, before I siezed her arm and pulled her back...from oblivion...

All she could say was: *That would be like wanting the moon in my hand!*

That was the kabosh for me...

J'taime Lou...I carved it in the sky...

The crickets and the birds...but between us, we hadn't said a word for a long time, until Lou blurted: This Norman the Morman guy, either he must have been a sailor...or he must get up pretty early to accomplish all he appears to accomplish.

It was her theatrical imagination at work, trying to imagine this Midwestern Casanova.

And he always stays up late, I suggested.

But how in the world does he do it?

We were script writing now...on top of the water tower:

Look in his hammock in mid-afternoon of a summer daydream.

Only to be awakened by:

Jesus Gods Norman! Will you sleep all day?

He's dreaming he's dancing to get to know all these women.

A triple stemmed long legged one of a kind dancer.

A lover, a thief, and his normal Norman self.

Multiple Normans for all to fall, once and for all, in love with.

What attracts Vicky repels Shiela, and vice versa.

Tell me the story of the King and his Queens!

Her infectious laugh…the one you picked out from all the other laughs (Act Six, Scene IV) at the hotel bar. An actor who knows how to make herself be heard in Emmetsburg…her climbing legs dangling over the edge…let her voice do the projecting…and realize that you will never be able to look at the water tower again without falling for her… again…

Hey! I shouted out to the endless darkness surrounding the stars of lights: How are we gonna get down from here?

Shall we take the quick way?

"She was just joking, wasn't she? You don't think that they really…"
"Now I feel dizzier than dizzy. No more heights!"
"That was a long way up."
"And a long way down."
"Did Lou catch her ride to Duluth?"
"I don't know."
"Despite the height…that was good."
"I agree."
"It was passionate, wasn't it?"
"Quite."
"Let's read it again!"
"We can't."
"Why not?"
"We've got to keep going, if we want to go home."
"Yeah…well…what's next, then?"
"Next…next, we're going for a boat ride."
"A boat ride…who's driving?"
"Carl's father."

"Oh no. He drives fast. He's always racing somebody. Thinks that he has to have the fastest boat on the lake."

"Then we better hold on tight, don't you think?"

"I'm going to do more than hold on tight. This time I'm going to wear a life jacket."

"So you won't sink?"

"So I'll float. Cause there's a lot of bad drivers out on that lake. A lot of people not lookin' where they're goin"

"If it looks like we're goin' down, I'm going to hold on to you."

"Then we'll both sink, I'm afraid."

"If we both sink, then neither one of us will make it back to New Orleans."

"To hang with the Spanish moss."

"Out at the Spanish Fort."

V.

This is the Song!

...when something bit me on the heal of my foot! I didn't know what the hell it was. Except that it had teeth as sharp as razors. I was bleeding like crazy off the bow of the ship, way out in the middle of South Pacific. I screamed, and they got me back up on deck, and the doc bandaged me up right away, and then they carried me to my bunk and brought me my mail. And that's when I found out that my friend George had died. My best friend that I grew up with here. We did everything at Okoboji together, George and I. We swam, we raced our boats, my Chris Craft against his Century, we dated the singing swinging Swingle sisters, we did everything together, and then I opened my mail in my bunk with my heel still stinging like hell, and I find out that he's been killed. And later that night, when the lights were out and I could hear everybody snoring, I cried and cried in my bunk. I just cried and cried for all that was lost because George was gone for good. Can you understand how I felt, Carl? Do you know what I'm trying to get at here? You chose not to serve your country, so you've never had to suffer the hell of having your best friend die like I did. How can you think you've lived if you've never seen your best friends die right in front of your face! What have you ever done? Mop office hallways and bar room floors in St. Paul? That's not living! That's not life!

Here he pauses to take a sip. He swishes the wine around in his mouth like he's at the dentist. Then he swallows. A slight tone of regret tempers his bitterness. He continues:

Ah...maybe it doesn't matter. Maybe none of it matters. Maybe I'm just fooling myself. Maybe ever yone of us is just fooling each other...and our own disillusioned selves...

He shakes his head in bewilderment, takes another sip, and gazes out on the lake.

Look at all those people out there. Do they remind you of a certain farm animal? They're driving their boats with wool over their eyes. They don't know where they're going. They're just going. They follow each other like sheep, back and forth under the bridge. I used to watch them when I had Fisherman's Wharf. They drive like sheep and they vote like lambs. I know that you're not supposed to say anything bad about them, but I'll tell you right now, we live in a nation of rams and ewes and lambs and sheep. I wish I could be more subtle, but today I'm afraid I can't.

A noisy boat pulling a skier blasts past just off the end of the docks. He takes a sip before pressing on with his tirade:

I shouldn't call them sheep. I'm being too harsh. It would be more polite to say that they're *sheep-like*, wouldn't it? They just don't appear to have any idea where it is that they're off to in their noisy boats. I guess that's what bugs me so much. Whereas I…I always knew exactly where I was going when I was out on the lake. Before the war *and* after the war, I knew where I was going and I went there. I might have raced somebody on my way there…George or…Mickey Landen…but I was still on my way *somewhere*, and not just *anywhere*. And my Chris Craft barrelback runabout made such a musical noise where ever I went. Not a droning noisy noise like all those boats out there!

Here he suddenly leaps to his feet with his glass nearly empty and sweeps his arm toward the lake as if to encompass the entire horizon and all that is contained therein. He follows this dramatic gesture with a gulp that drains the remaining contents of the long stemmed wine glass, before he sits unsteadily back down and makes a request in a slightly slurred but still commanding and somewhat demanding voice:

Let's here a song, shall we? Your choice, Carl! But choose a good one. Something that will pick us up, you know. Give us a lift, like we're on the coaster, and about to go past the Point Of No Return. Can you remember the first time that I took you on the coaster? You were so scared you were shaking! Oh my god! It was funny. It was *hilarious!* Maybe it's a

good thing after all…that you never went in the military. Anyway, play a song that'll take me back up to the Roof Garden, will you please.

(This is a direct order from the upper deck of his ship, on patrol out in the South Pacific. I'm down on the lower deck, but if I blow it, I'll be demoted below deck, to the galley or the latrine, for double duty. So I take my time. I take my sweet time…the silence itself is heartening. I could use some of the enthusiasm that always seems to come to me whenever I step out onto a bridge. I immediately try to find the middle of a bridge. There are several ways to try and determine the exact middle, because that's where the strength is. But now I must find exactly the right song. And as I rifle back and forth through the stack of LPs leaning against the bamboo table, my bare knees rubbing against the rattan rug, I feel, understandably, a strong sense of having been here before, walking back and forth across the bridge of jazz, trying to find the exact middle.)

Having trouble? That's ok. Take your time. Take your time. The problem, after all, is to find the right distance, is it not? The right distance between the song and the listener. The right distance between the performer and the table or the seat in the hall or the ballroom. The right distance between two lovers. The right distance from Okoboji. What is too close, and where is too far from Okoboji? Questions like this can confound a man. Just keep your mind on the objective, Carl. We are looking for the ideal song to carry us back up to the Roof Garden. Because the war is over! The war is *finally* over, and I made it home, and my brother made it home. George didn't make it home. George is buried on an island in the South Pacific. But my brother and I are in our Chris Craft, and we've got it full throttle aimed right at the double O's of the Roof Garden. The girls are in the back. They're all dressed up and holding on to their hats. We've just picked them up at the Okoboji Club. The old Flote Mansion. We're flying across the lake. We've raced everyone, and beaten everyone, except for our friend up in Echo Bay. I don't mean picked them up as in: *We picked these girls up*. We had dates with them. They were sisters, two sisters from Minneapolis. My brother's driving. Why, I don't know. But he's driving across the middle when for some reason and without any warning he kills the engine over the so-called bottomless hole. To give everyone a thrill I suppose. Now the wake created by the stern digging into the water is actually higher than the stern itself. So when my brother cuts it so suddenly, it looks as if the wake is going to collapse upon us like a tidal wave, and swamp us over the bottomless hole, which would have ruined the whole evening. I can't speak for my brother - your uncle - whom I haven't spoken to for many years, by the way, but my entire life up to this point, including my tour of duty in the South Pacific, has been a careful preparation for this one of a kind full speed approach to this particular ballroom on this particular lake with this one particular girl. And those blue and red poles holding it up are getting closer and closer. And the red shingled roof, and the larger than life letters which spell out its name, and the long row of windows framed by shutters, and the musical angle of the whole thing. My god Carl, you should have seen it! But of course it's still there. They've torn down a lot of things, but they haven't torn down the Roof Garden yet. Or have they? Listen Carl, if they ever tear down the Roof Garden, don't tell me. Promise me that you won't tell me. Promise me this one thing, Carl.

I finally find the record, and remove the album from its jacket and sleeve. I look up at him, leaning toward me from his chair of reflection.

I promise, I say.

Then, as I put on the record, I ask him:

But the wave? What happened with the wave?

Oh yes, the wave. Well the girls…they shrieked…and then…

Thunk…a…thunk…a…

Listen! The record's skipping…

I nudge the needle gently ahead.

This is the song! my father shouted instantaneously. This song is the one! See, from out of the audience the band leader would select the man who in his opinion was the best dancer of the evening…and that man would be handed the baton, with great fanfare…and with much applause…to direct the band for one song…and that night the song was… *the song that you picked out!* Artie's little tune! The song that's playing right now. My god, Carl, what a great choice, what a *tremendous* choice! Turn it up just a little bit, will you please. Oh god, I was conducting the band, they were paying this song, and the piano player, her dress strap kept slipping down her shoulder. She'd push it back up, but she was playing with such intensity that before long it would fall back down again. Most of my attention was directed at her…her and her bothersome dress strap. My god, I can't hear this song without thinking of that dress strap. And now it's over. Let's play it again Carl. One more time…

I start it from the beginning, staying at the stereo to nudge the needle over the skip.

So after I gave the baton back to the bandleader, we were sitting in a booth by the window…one of those knotty pine booths that looked out over the lake…we could see all the people sitting on the seawall…fanning themselves and each other…and the boats on the lake, of course…and the seagulls…and the pigeons…there is no other spot on this entire lake where you can see how unlike this place is from any where else…than from a knotty pine window booth facing the lake up at the Roof Garden…Your uncle left to dance with my date, who'd been going on and on about the pigeons in the Plaza San Marco…she'd never been there…she'd just seen a film, I think…so there I was, sitting across from my brother's date…and our eyes met…surrounded as we were by all the smoke and music…and the talk and the beauty and humidity…when our eyes… they met…I'd never met any eyes like that…sitting across the table from each other…our eyes met before our hands met…the table was all wet… somebody had spilled their drink…our eyes met before our legs met… the floor under the table was crunchy with popcorn and peanut shells… we got lost in each other's eyes…across the table of a window booth…a knotty pine window booth…up at the Roof Garden Ballroom…that was just the first time I got lost looking in your mother's eyes…only the first time…

The record ends…my father pauses…takes a long sip…looks out on the lake…blinks his eyes in disbelief at all the boats…it is nearly sunset… he seems about to continue…he takes another sip…he crosses his legs… and turns toward me:

You know, I'm worried…I'm worried about our sauce that's been simmering since I started my story…I hope you left the burner on as low as it would go…you must be getting to know my stories by heart…well, you're a good listener…one of the best there is…but there's one thing that I don't want you to ever forget…one thing, and one thing only… but I think that you should go out and check the sauce first…and while you're out there, see if the bread has risen…I want it to rise to twice the size it was after you kneaded it the last time…so…whisk the sauce… and lift the cloth gently to look at the bread…and that should…oh, you may as well bring another bottle of wine out too…don't worry about a corkscrew…I've got one right here…And then…as soon as you come back…I want you to promise me…promise me that you'll never forget… but we'll get into that…as soon as you…come back…

"I felt like I was there, didn't you?"

"Out in that boat and up at that ballroom."

"The South Pacific! Lake Okoboji!"

"Literature can take you anywhere."

"This then is literature?"

"It must be, to create a wave like the one that almost swamped them."

"Could you hear the music?"

"Every note. I can still hear it."

"Maybe we're in over our heads."

"We can't bale out until the Park dies."

"And when does the Park die?"

"The Park is due to die…next!"

"I don't like to be confronted with death. I used to have a black cat. He was beautiful, and handsome, with a personality all his own. But one day I found him dead in the garage. After that, I hated death, and what it does to people and animals."

"This is just an amusement park, so it's not too sad."

"Good. That's good. I'm glad it's not too sad."

VI.

The Park Dies

Balancing a towering a stack of summers on your head on the closing day of summer, you grip the railing and pull yourself up to the crooked peak of the Tipsy House. The colors of the walls inside are the fabric of space, and what was fuzzy becomes continuous, and what's continuous is made of sticky gooey threads. You lean out over the peak to see the farm girls standing in line at Mrs. Kennison's popcorn stand. They've labored all summer long, in the fields and barns, the gardens and sheds, and so as a reward she generously fills their bags to overflowing, and the popcorn spills out on their way to the pier, leaving a crowd of bickering seagulls to follow along in their wake (the farm girls appreciate and even applaud a noisy entourage). The dregs at the bottom of the bags are offered to the farm boys, who refuse (they're sick of corn, any kind of corn) with a shake of their sunburned hatless crew-cut heads. Their luck in fishing or in love is showing no sign of improvement. But they have the fall to look forward to…

I watched the old park die from the top of the Tipsy…

An omniscient veterinarian with a needle the size of the Washington Monument administered the euthanasia in close proximity to the back of the Bug House. To hear him tell it (and he was something of a raconteur) it was all really quite *painless*.

And except for the short last gasp of a breath, it was a beautiful death.

In the time it took for the drug to take affect, here's what happened (I was in attendance, I saw the whole thing, standing on the crooked peak and leaning out over the railing):

Water sprayed over the seawall
Massive waves bounced back into the lake
Oak leaves showed their brown underside
The coming cool clashed with the waning warm...

And then...the wind shifted suddenly to the northwest, and swung the creaking Nutty Buddy sign violently during the identical interval when Nutty Buddy was on the phone with Melvin Tornado, predicting an *early fall* and an even *earlier winter*–

Tornado interrupted to ask:

What in the world is that sound I hear?

Nutty Buddy listened...

His doors facing the lake were only half raised to keep out the gale.

That's the sound of the wind! he told Tornado.

That's more than the wind, Tornado begged to differ, unless it's the wind moving something.

Nutty Buddy listened again...his squeaky stools were empty of customers...

A flock of seagulls, he informed the weatherman, is following a trail of popcorn. That must be the noise you hear!

Sounds more like a sign creaking to me. You got any signs creaking in the wind up there? Give me your wind speed!

Gusting up to thirty!

Any white caps?

Lot's of 'em!

Can you explain that clack clack clacking?

Easily! That's the flag pole at the foot of the pier...

Hard earned money shoved deep in their pockets - a rich vein high on their thighs - impossible to extract without pickaxes for fingernails - the farm girls stand in line on the last day of summer to buy caramel apples. Sheri watches them orbiting from one farm boy to another, hopping from foot to foot, jostling, rotating, tanned and with every pore wide open, desperate (in an unassuming way) to cram the whole of their summer pleasures into one day, and exuding so much energy that they begin to appear to her not as a few farm girls standing in line, but as a plethora of farm girls impatiently waiting for their caramel apples. So she turns up the heat on the copper cauldron, and stirs the caramel hard and fast, gripping the ladle and swinging her hips with such enthusiasm that the farm girls pause in their nervous twittering to stand as one and watch her…until she snaps the ladle handle, and suffers a splinter in the palm of her left hand, as she stares into the bubbling brown hole which has swallowed the splintered spoon. It's the stuff that light operas are made of…

The summer heat, once so obtrusive, has departed with the holiday tourists, and the few left behind shiver collectively as they walk under the turning leaves of the Labor Day trees.

Madame Jessie shivers along with them, but not because of any dearth of degrees. She's been peering into her crystal ball, of her own accord, and what she sees she cannot believe: there's a crowd gathering on the end of the pier. She throws the red cloth from Romney over her ball, and dismisses her assistant with brief instructions and a wave of her hand: *Go investigate!*

The assistant gathers up her little dog, and walks quickly, purposefully, taking long strides down the seawall, her colorful brilliant dress sprinkled by the waves and blowing in the wind, while her eyes stay fixed on the bluey edge way out there, where the sea finally meets the sky…

...while back in her parlor, Madame Jessie draws the floor to ceiling curtain of her prediction performance space for the last time, signaling *the end* of something more than the summer.

Say, Nutty Buddy says on the phone (once again) to Tornado, could you pass on to your listeners that my nutty buddy bars are now *half price!*

The only one in the amusement park who isn't thrown off balance by this chilling blast of low interest loan progress hovering just over the horizon is the Fun House Clown, who goes on pleasantly dreaming his musical series of dreams...fantasies in which his concerts are standing room only in acoustically perfect halls with wild applause echoing throughout his cerebellum, while his complete catalogue of recordings is in print in every format and available in record stores on tree lined streets in cities attuned to music...as rave reviews come to him in wave after wave, and keep him from falling backwards...far away from his piano...safely into the past...just out of reach of his keys...

And Jerry, who never comes down to the amusement park anymore...who walks his dog on the other end of town...but whose absence is felt...whose presence is missed...by none more so than the farm girls, who counted on him as their intermediary, to relay their messages to the farm boys. Jerry was the one who used to give away free root beer after five on the last day of summer...and who set the juke box on automatic replay...on the last day...he's still there in spirit...passing out the free foamy stuff...

MacJames on the coaster platform takes up some of the slack - he gives a free ride to anyone who can tell him how to get back to Jackson on the aft of a crisp twenty. A woman in the front seat knows the answer to that one, and a few more. She rides repeatedly, nibbling on a cheese sandwich, leading the chorus of screams, her hair straight out behind her...

storing up for future reference minute detailed descriptions...while gathering her narratives from the stories unfolding around her...she's thrown caution and passion to the wind...for the meantime...she'll stand up past the point of no return...hand on her heart...

Bulldozers camouflaged in the corn east of Upper Gar...

Seagulls apprehensive at the end of the pier, their ranks in disarray, deserters flying away...

Farm girls bolting from the Mirror Maze, where they've just seen themselves - No! - *old* - No! - *aged*...Quickly they rent, with the last of their money, scuba diving equipment.

In front of where the bath house used to be they grease the grooves of their keels and squeeze into their wetsuits. They hoist their tanks and slip into their flippers and brush the hair away from their goggles and adjust their lucky rocks around their necks. Flamboyantly they wave goodbye - even from the top of the Tipsy it's possible to see them waving without binoculars - *Goodbye!* - goodbye to summer, all arms and hands waving. Who knows what is going through their heads? Whether or not they're frightened by their reflections? Soon all you can see are the heads of the farm girls. After those heads disappear there's nothing left but a little flock of ripples, where there should have been waves, on the surface of the lake.

The last dancer dances to the last song up at the Roof Garden...the song, for the record, is *Black and Blue*...it carries, just as the sun sets, across the water to the Black Buoy (Act Five, Scene III) off Pillsbury Point, and wakes up its sole occupant, who once again believes in the power of pitch...tone...timbre...

The last drinker quickly becomes the last swimmer after she says 'bye to Butch, throws some cash on the bar (including a huge tip), and runs out the front door of the HiHo, sprinting down the seawall to the pier, discarding articles of clothing in her wake - here a sock - there a bra - while never missing a beat 'til she comes to the naked unraveling end of the pier (the Empress has slammed it head on several times that year) and takes one flying feet-first final leap...over everyone gathered out there: farm boys and girls, prodigal sunbathers, seagulls...screaming *San Gregorio!*

Splash!

Her first deep breath takes her down to a trembly freedom measured in seconds, cheeks puffed out like Dizzy's, until she gets nipped on the left nipple by a bold bluegill and quickly returns to crash through the reflecting curtain of water. She swims for the pier using a variety of strokes: slow crawl, sidestroke, backfloat, backstroke, Australian crawl - then out of breath she grabs the splintery beam and holds on, pulling herself up, scraping her stomach 'til it bleeds...

The last ride left spinning is the Ferris wheel...going round and round with no one on it...until Pesky Pete, from his post at the shooting gallery (which he refuses to retreat from) begins to shoot out the lights on it...first the red ones (colors carry a great significance for him)...then the greens (colors signify symbols to him)...at long last the blues (colors demand action from him)...finally the yellows (he can't stomach passivity)...until the amusement park as we knew it is shot into darkness...

PART FIVE

ALL THAT FALL

"Hey! I smell something burning!"

"Me too!"

"Wonder what it is?"

"A ballroom perchance…or a pile of leaves…because it is the fall, after all."

"Remember down in New Orleans, when Fred on the other side of the double shotgun was always burnin' them beans?"

"Oo yeah. That was a terrible smell. This doesn't smell as bad as that."

"No, but some food kind of thing is burning. Think we should call a first responder? I know a pretty one…she lives over by the monument, I think…"

"Naw, 'cause look, Carl's wakin' up. He'll take care of it."

"The needle's skippin' in the groove."

"He'll take care of that too."

"And what about the money that he owes Claire?"

"I don't know…did he find enough under the Loop-o-Plane to pay her off?"

"Not hardly!"

"Things have a way of working out…hopefully…and anyway, it's a new act…the last but one!"

"Then what'd ya say we raise the curtain on it?"

"On the count of…"

I.

Day After Labor Day

The soup was still simmering and the lake still shimmering on the day *after* Labor Day.

When I came downstairs on the morning of the day after Labor Day, I found the soup still seething warmly on the stove. I stirred it once. I stirred it twice. A crust as hard as ice had formed on the bottom of the pan. It seemed like a bad sign.

On the ever-climactic day after Labor Day, the sun off the lake glimmered intermittently between clouds, while the soup, which should have been shut off the night before, percolated undisturbed by spoon or spatula.

A thick crust had hardened on the bottom of the soup pot on the day after Labor Day, and no amount of stirring, clockwise and counterclockwise, could loosen it. I relocated the pan to a cold burner, before turning my half-awake attention to a sauce pan in a similar state, and the twin loaves of bread that had risen and collapsed sometime in the night, while my father sat dreaming, as I was to find out later, of a little restaurant in San Francisco, and of swimming in the bay, as if he were a member of the Polar Bear Club.

I was just about to peek in the striped red envelope - on the day after Labor Day - to scan the **bold amount** of the overdue, final notice, imminent shut-off, pay-it-or-else, *this is your last chance* electric bill, propped between dishes in the dish drainer, when my ears caught the rousing sound of geese flying over, which sent me dashing out the back door to look up beyond the tree tops just in time to see a clump of acorns coming down at me from a high branch.

On the melancholy day after Labor Day morning, my father continued his snooze in the chair of the past, with the boat-less lake draped beyond his drooped head (as I framed it through the wide open French doors between the front porch and the living room) appearing to serve as a flat calm fluffy pillow for him, while the record needle skipped needlessly endlessly rhythmically in it's groove at the far end of the second side of *Sketches Of Spain.*

I lifted the needle arm from the record and returned it to its rest.

And then I gave Gabo in the windowsill a hard and a soft pet.

Napoleon, I noticed, had lost his head and his arm again.

Claire had left *The Sailor from Gibraltar* at anchor in the bookcase amongst all my grandmother's mysteries. I propped it open on the breakfast table in the kitchen, but after reading just the first page alone, I knew that I had to take a trip too, buy a ticket and go somewhere, with that little bit of money that I'd found under the Loop-o-Plane in the amusement park the night before.

The money that I owed Claire was due on this day too.

I thought about telegraphing her…to ask for an extension…

But instead I went upstairs to put a few things together.

I was just going away for a few days.

I left a note on the record player to that effect.

Goodbye! I'll be back soon!

I filled Gabo's bowl with dry food, and gave him some fresh Okoboji tap water (the water bill was due too). And for the first time in a long time, I put some fresh sand from the beach in his litter box.

I pulled the door quietly shut until I felt the latch catch. I lifted my hand stealthily from the handle.

I went as quietly as possible across the yard toward the bank and the beach…crunching a few acorns…snapping one or two twigs…

There were no doxies about.

The neighbors to the north had already left…gone back to Des Moines…

Down on the beach, I threw my bag in the boat and shoved off.

I didn't take a break from rowing until I reached Ft. Dodge Point.

The bright little wild red rose hips all along the shore…they would have made a healthy and delicious tea…but there was no point in stopping to gather them now…

I saw the bent green ladder leaning against the tree…

The tree where Patience…

Where was Patience? What was her life like now?

What was Patience doing on the day after Labor Day, twenty seven years after the summer when the baby, who had just returned to Des Moines with her family, had rolled down the bank, and Patience had had to run away?

On the tip of the point there was a rabbit sitting perfectly frozen. Inside, I bet, his heart was thumping…like mine…

When I was a kid, I thought back, I used to have a fort, right where that rabbit was. I'd controlled all of the boat traffic in and out of Smith's

Bay from my fort. In the winter I manned it too. I built little fires, and kept my driftwood guns always cocked and loaded.

It seemed that fall had arrived...in the space of only a few hours...

A new season...they always take some getting used to...at first...

I wanted to stay and see it in...

But I wanted to run away too...

I didn't know what I wanted to do...

I propped my feet against the back seat and rowed as hard as I could for the Chateau...

Because I knew...

I knew what time the bus was due to come through, so I was standing there waiting for it - without a watch on - just north of the bridge on the east side of the highway, right in front of where the Okoboji Store used to be.

I had this funny feeling that Larue was watching me...even calling out to me in his unmistakable voice:

Where in the world are you off to, Carl?

He was waving one of Vinton's sky blue postcards at me, trying to get my attention as I was looking for the bus.

You can't leave yet. It's not the right time!

His sunny flying smile, his baseball cap, his postcards and his knick knacks spread out across his card table, perched right at the fulcrum of the two lakes.

I heard the bus, and then I saw it, steamrolling across the grade, picking up speed to climb the hill. I grabbed my bag and waved my free arm until I knew the driver had seen me, because he hit the brakes hard and pulled over in the dust and the ruts along the side of the road.

The door swung open and - *Holy Nabokov!* - it was the same driver that had dropped Claire and I off across the road (Act Three, Scene I) in the spring.

He bounced down the stairs, took off his driver's cap, ran his fingers through his hair, and asked enthusiastically:

What's happening here? What's going on? Are the fish biting?

He looked around, took in a deep gulp of air, put his cap back on, lit a cigarette, scratched his ear, and commented offhandedly:

You know, September is without a doubt the most beautiful month at Lake Okoboji. I see all the seasons along my route, and I have to say that September at Okoboji can't be beat for beauty. Is that your boat down there? Nice little fishing boat! Are the perch biting? They always get hungry right after Labor Day. Have to wait for all the tourists to leave, I guess. Your boat could use a little trolling motor, but you've got oars there, so what the hell, you're set. Boy, I'd love to go fishing right now. Where are your poles? Got any stinky bait? Where's that cat, anyway? I suppose she's got it. Where is *she*, by the way? I hope you've been feeding them both some fish. Fish is good for their coats, they say. I've still got cat hair floating around my bus you know. Cat hair is weightless. Oh, what a day! So...where are you goin'?

Duluth.

Duluth? You're all going up to Duluth? Now?

No. Not all of us. Just me.

Just you? To Duluth...

The driver shook his head and took a deep drag from his cigarette, holding it in his lungs for a few seconds before releasing it in brief bursts through his nostrils.

Listen to my bus...I mean the way it's idling...roughly idling...have to have them check it out up in the Cities...

After another inhale, followed by the obligatory exhale...

And then: Well, Duluth is certainly...Duluth is colorful this time of year too. The leaves are already turning up there, I suppose. And you've got your big lake, and you've got your lift bridge and your ships going in and out. But one thing you won't have up there is the woman you brought down here. Now I hope you don't mind my asking, but: *Where is she? What's happened to her?*

She moved to a cabin…a little cabin in Arnolds Park. It's by the monument, I think. You know the monument I mean?

She must have taken up with somebody else then?

Yeah…she's got another guy…he runs the roller coaster.

Well, that's too bad, but still, you know, that stuff happens. It happens all the time. It's happened to me. Believe me, it has happened to me, and more than once! After I got divorced - because I was gone all the time, see - I fell in love with this waitress. She worked in Fairmont, at a truck stop. But she went off with a truck driver, a truck driver who was already married to somebody else. She must have wanted to see some country…see it really bad! And there was nothing I could do about it. I can't count the number of times that it's happened to me. I try not to fall in love with waitresses anymore. But that's hard, in my line of work, not to fall in love with waitresses. There's just something about the way that they pour the coffee, you know…

Another puff and release, before he continued:

Yeah, if you ask me…I think you *owe* it to *her* to stay *here*. Because you never know how long it will last, you know. I mean, her and this roller coaster fella, it might not go on forever. That roller coaster is shut down for the season now. Correct? His appeal to her might fade rather quickly as this new season takes hold. You know what I mean? You know what I'm talkin' about? So…you never know, do you? You just never know what could happen. *Stay tuned folks!* That kind of thing. Say, tell me: what was in those bags and boxes of hers? I lifted them off the bus. Remember? They were heavy! Heavy as hell! They had to be either full of rocks or full of books. Books or rocks, one or the other. Writers and geologists, they're both diggers and excavators. But then aren't we all? Aren't we all, brother? Amen! But which was it? What is she?

Books…she's a writer…

See! I knew it. She's a poet. I could tell by her eyes. Her *exquisite* eyes. She seemed somewhat preoccupied that day that I dropped you all off here. Probably composing a few convoluted sentences. You can't desert her now, buddy. She's on the cusp of her season of creativity. She's a creature of autumn. One look in those eyes will tell you that. She's gonna blossom this autumn, and you don't want to miss it. You've got to be here for that, man!

He threw his cigarette down, rubbed it out with the toe of his boot, lit another one, and continued:

I got a full bus as it is. Not right at the moment, but a big group is getting on in Sleepy Eye. They're going up to the baseball game. The Yanks are in town. Catfish is on the mound. You don't want to go to Duluth anyway. They put in that new highway along the lake up there, and it split those splendid rose gardens of Leif Ericson Park right in half. Yeah, there's nothing like a new highway to ruin a place. I mean *kill its character!* I hope it never happens here. Yeah, you better go find her before they build a new highway. Take her out in that boat of yours. Let her read, let her write, let her do what she likes. A woman like that isn't writing for you and me. She's writing for posterity, for pete's sake. Catch some fish for them while you're out there! I bet she'd love a big walleye, broiled in a wine sauce, with sprigs of parsley sprinkled on top.

She doesn't eat fish. She's a vegetarian.

You're kidden' me? You're puttin' me on? Well…to each his own. That's what my grandmother used to say. *To each his own.*

My grandmother used to say the same thing.

Grandparents know how things go, you know. No question about that! Hey, take my word for it. You don't want to go to Duluth. They used to do mean things to people up there. I don't think they do it anymore but…hell, they did the same thing at Ft. Snelling. And Mankato! Right in lovely downtown Mankato. They quit doin' that up there, but it's a stain, you know what I mean, a deep bloody red stain on their Scandinavian psych. Maybe that's why they try to be so polite. Who knows? Yeah, you just don't look like someone who's ready to leave Okoboji. Hell, if it's drama you're lookin' for, there's more drama here than in any theater on Hennepin or Washington Avenue. Your friend will know where to find it. She'll show you where the drama is. You just find the fish. For the cat! For you and the cat. You're not a vegetarian are you? I didn't think so…

He unhooked a cuff link, pulled his uniform sleeve back, and glanced at his watch.

And now I've gone and fallen behind schedule. Again! So I gotta go. And you gotta stay. I can make up my time, and you can make it up with her. You were gonna leave behind a *boat, a cat, and a girl?* Man, I can't believe it. You weren't thinkin' straight when you woke up this morning, were youse? I'm glad I caught ya. I'm glad I stopped ya! That would have been a very foolish move. You would have regretted it. You could leave behind one of those three - the fur ball easily - but not all three. Well, keep the cat hair off of her. Do try. That stuff gets in your eyes, and then how are you supposed to see the beauty that surrounds you…and I mean envelops you…at Okoboji? But there, I'm getting poetic. I wish I had time to go fishing in your boat. But I don't. I gotta go. Say, you were the one who was telling me about mountains under the ground, weren't you? (Act Two, Scene V) I've been thinking about that, and I've got a few questions for you, but they're gonna have to wait 'til next time. There's always a next time, my friend. World without end, you know. Just listen to how rough my bus is idling…

He threw his cigarette down and stamped it out, with his heel this time.

Yeah, I can still hear the lilt in your friend's voice. She's still your friend, isn't she? You parted amicably, didn't you? You don't owe her any money, do you? I can do without that cat though. I like dogs…say, listen, that reminds me. You could do me a favor. A big favor! I've got something to keep you company 'til she comes back. Something that I found in Omaha…

So…this bus driver…all of a sudden he's opening up the middle baggage door and reaching in for something…and then he's handing me a little carrying case with holes, and I can hear and feel something shifting about inside it. He says: It's just something that was given to me in Omaha, and that I was going to take to the shelter in Minneapolis…but now I realize that Okoboji would be a much better home…for it…

Then he jumps on the first step of his bus and turns to me and waves grandiosely, as if he's a President about to take his last helicopter ride...

And then he's slamming the door and grinding the gears and lumbering out on to the highway and shifting into second and third before I can think to say:

Hey! Wait! I don't really need a...

Larue's not there anymore either. He's abandoned me too. But I turn toward where Larue was, where he used to be, there on the edge of the bank, on the outside corner of the store, under his awning, wearing his baseball cap, all that stuff spread out on his card table. I turn to Larue, who used to anchor down that rare and exalted spot on this earth...

I appeal to the blessed and fond memory of Larue, on this day after Labor Day.

And I say:

Larue, I don't want this animal. This dog, I mean.

Because looking in through the holes in the case, I could see a brown dog, with a white spot on his or her chest.

I don't need a little dog, I try to tell Larue.

And Larue...he just looks at me across all the years...all those winters and summers that have blown and drifted between us...looks at me like he used to look at everyone else back then: with true compassion, and with complete understanding. They were more than just words to him. He'd put those concepts into practice, until he *was understanding,* and he *was compassion.* He looked at me with these twin towers of belief that sustained him through his hardships. He looked at me, and that soaring shining smile of his came across his face. From north to south and from east to west, his wide smile took over his whole face. And then to top it all off, he waved. Waved me away. Waved as if to say: *Hey! Get on with your day!*

Or was it: *Get on with your dog!*

Day or dog...it didn't really matter...they each had some relevance to the situation at hand...

"So now there's a dog in the picture?"

"We're never going get out of here!"

"Dogs need lots of attention."

"Let's give him a chance. Maybe a dog was what he needed all along."

"Follow that scent!"

"Did you see how we almost lost Carl? The sneak!"

"He was going to get on a bus for Duluth."

"Without even telling us!"

"And leave us in the lurch!"

"The bus driver brought him back in line."

"We owe that guy a favor."

"But now we have a dog."

"Yeah, now we have a dog."

"To protect and defend."

"To love and to hold."

"A dog…a dog might help to keep Carl more focused. Did you happen to notice how at the beginning of the last scene, he seemed to have trouble getting going?"

"He was definitely repeating himself."

"More than usual."

"Unless it was only a literary effect?"

"We gotta go! He's taking the dog to meet his father. This should be good!"

II.

Sailor From Okoboji

I had to take my new companion home to meet my father…who was just waking up…right where I'd left him…in the chair of the past…

What's this? A dog? What kind of dog? Come here pup…

The doxies were on the front doorstep, scratching the door and barking their three heads off. I shut the door tightly to muffle the noise.

He looks like a mixture. Part setter, part…

In other words, you don't know what kind of a dog he is. I can see he's a combo. Here, let me pet him.

Gabo raised his back and hissed from the windowsill. My father lifted his head from the pillow and shielded his eyes from the sun as he reached out to rub his long nose.

What a good dog! Who does he belong to? You? Oh! Well…he looks like fun. I'm sure that the cat will enjoy his company. Say Carl, could you find *Solea* for me, and turn it up loud enough to drown out that barking. I was just having the most interesting dream. I was listening to *Solea* on the jukebox in a little corner bar and restaurant in San Francisco, across from Washington Park…and I was telling another guy at the bar that I was going to open a restaurant exactly like it in Okoboji…right down to the last detail…even the writing on the bathroom walls…it would feel like San Francisco, and taste like it too…I would transpose San Francisco to Okoboji, so that when you were at Okoboji and sitting in Fisherman's Wharf waiting for your entree, you'd think you were in San Francisco. And when you looked out across the Smith's Bay, instead of seeing the Queen, you'd see big ships, ocean ships, capable of carrying you wherever it was…that you wanted to go…just like that. And my restaurant would be capable of serving you whatever it was that you wanted to eat…crawfish etouffée, clams linguine…you name it! Just like that…But then this guy at the bar says that it had already been done, and that it had failed, the people hadn't gone for it, the restaurant had failed miserably. *But at least you gave it a try, didn't you?* he said. God, I wish I could dream like that every night. I feel completely refreshed, like I just went for a swim in San Francisco Bay…down in front of the cable car turn around…with all the rest of the polar bears…

I looked for *Solea* everywhere, until I realized that *sketches of Spain* was were on the turntable. I put the needle to the groove, and stuffed my going away note in my pocket.

But then:

From that distinct trumpet in that singular song played at that specific volume a concise message of timelessness suddenly seemed to reveal itself to him, so that he had to ask, knowing full well that I'd have no answer:

What is it about music, Carl…

He paused to take a sip of last night's wine before completing his question…

…that affects us so profoundly?

Later that same morning, and possibly under the influence of Kenny Drew's *Fall*, he commented:

It's almost a little chilly, isn't it? Maybe you should gather some wood, Carl, and build a fire in the fireplace. The chipmunks won't like it, but that's ok.

Early in the afternoon, I grew restless again:

I'm going to row across the lake to get some dog food. Is there anything else that we need from the store?

Well…this big dinner that we're going to have for all your friends…we've got to start making preparations for it…so what do you say…we put together…a list…

Just as I was about to go out the door:

What a noisy dog this is! It loves to listen to itself lament. Does he or she…oh…she's a he, isn't she? Does *he* have a *name?*

Ginsberg sat on his hind legs on the bow, but after a few face fulls of waves as we came around Ft. Dodge Point, he retreated to beneath the bow.

We had the lake almost all to ourselves…Pillsbury was empty. There wasn't a soul on the benches, high or low, stone or peeling green slat. Quiet on the Indian path too…

I didn't want to run into Claire…owing her all that money, due today…I'd signed the accord, and agreed to pay…I wondered if she wasn't hiding in wait for me behind the leaves of that crab apple tree on the point, her books and papers spread out across the roots and the rocks… or maybe she was up on top of the point, hidden by the thick red sumac, her legs crossed, smoking a cigarette, talking with MacJames…

Ginsberg and I followed the shore until we reached the beach in front of the amusement park. I pulled the boat up on the sand at bend in the seawall.

Was it that same day…or another one just like it?

It was one of those beautiful early fall days, with the gulls swooping and swiping…and with the flag on the pier standing stiffly at attention and aiming straight south, as if to point the direction that the gulls should go. Nutty Buddy had already flipped his calendar ahead to next May and migrated to far-a-way Milford. The leaves had begun to turn on Ft. Dodge and Pillsbury, while acorns rained on asphalt shingles all around town, to gather on the ground like marbles. And the squirrels - the ones that hadn't been run over - were busy burying some of those acorns in little mounds - at the same time that I was digging absent-minded holes in the sand in front of the seawall, with Ginsberg beside me, digging holes too.

But then I leaned back…to rest my back against the pocked concrete, although not at the favored bend in the seawall, because Sheri had already beat me to that spot. We'd seen each other, and waved to each other, and continued on with our reading. From the distance between us, a stones throw or so, I couldn't tell what she was reading, nor she me, if she was in the least curious. (For some reason I always find it interesting to see what people are reading. The Atlantic beaches, especially those on the coast of Maine, are in the summer great places to discover exactly what people are reading.) I was still wrapped up in *The Sailor from Gibralter*. Ginsberg had dug a hole big enough to nest in, and we were both eating apples from the tree round behind where Muriel's Peacock used to be.

It was peaceful…and quiet…with only a few boats on the lake. Ginsberg was watching the seagulls from his hole, as I set down the *Sailor* and picked up *Snow of Despair*. I could only read, at any one time, small sections of this claustrophobic novel…a few pages at most. They were always so gloomy: the weather and the main character. The snow fell heavily upon his shoulders, and he never had any money, this Paul person who lived in a room with one window which faced an alley. It was right across the alley from where F. Scott Fitzgerald had written *This Side of Paradise*, so it was an historically significant alley. I knew this neighborhood well, but that did nothing to relieve the incipient doom. He didn't have any money because he didn't have a job, and he didn't have a job because he was - or thought he was - a writer. But the writer was the character from across the alley…the one who'd lived in the brownstone and hung up his pages with clothes pins and stopped traffic on Summit after he learned that Scribners was publishing his *Paradise*. The rear of the brownstone wasn't nearly as handsome as the front, with it's little bronze historical plaque hanging above the door…

That's what *I* was reading, uneasily and uncomfortably and quite willing to be distracted by birds or squirrels or *a coincidence* - and because

I was in a place where coincidences were *the norm* - those same two Park people who had been arguing over the Fun House Clown, and what to do with him (Act Four, Scene VI), in the spring, were now trying to determine his future once again. They'd abducted him from of his cage above the entrance to the Fun House, and they were stuffim him into a coffin like crate filled with styrofoam peanuts. I had act as if not to be watching this kidnapping. I had to pretend that I was so immersed in my *Snow of Despair* that I didn't notice what was happening to the Fun House Clown, in broad daylight, right in front of the Fun House. This muse of my grandfathers was about to be shipped off somewhere...

At the same time that all of this was going on - my reading, and the crating up of the Fun House Clown - a man pulled up in his truck and walked out to the end of the Hi Ho dock with a hammer and a crowbar and a rusty nail puller, and proceeded to start to take it out. As soon as the prying and ripping began, Sheri got up and left. I noticed that the dock man was struggling with a bad limp that made it hard for him to carry the lumber to the shore. Then he happened to look over at me - after Sheri waved goodbye, Ginsberg and I had moved to the bend in the seawall - and he yelled, in a rough tough mumble jumble:

Hey! You want a job?

It was like *a challenge,* his question.

I looked at Ginsberg. He was going to need a steady supply of dog food. And I pictured on the utility bills that I kept in the dish drainer. And then there was the money that I still owed Claire. She could probably use it, she must be running low. I didn't have to count the small amount of cash that I had in my pocket, the money that my father had given me to buy some wine and a few other things at the store. I looked out at this worse for wear dock man standing near the end of the Hi Ho dock, rubbing his hip, nail puller in his hand. I jumped up and shouted out to him:

Yeah! Sure! Why not! I'll help you take your dock out!

I tied Ginsberg to a roller coaster post in the shade, and walked out to the end of the dock. He was pounding his nail puller into the plank, and yanking rusty nails out, one after another, and then throwing them in the lake right where people swam in the summer. I took away the planks and posts, the braces and cross pieces, and stacked them on the shore. It got hot - I was sweating - I threw my t-shirt in my boat - Ginsberg was chewing on something underneath the coaster - I took him a bowl full of lake water, and went back to work.

It felt odd to be employed again. I got paid in cash at the end of every day, *'cause I don't like to fool around with the paperwork*, he said. He carried a billfold in his back pocket that was bulging with bills. I'd never seen so much money in one wallet. We didn't talk much, and the days all kaleidoscoped into one long day of hauling dock lumber to the beach. But suddenly I had money to pay the electric bill, to pay the water bill, and to go to the store. My wallet would never feel bloated, but there was some cash in it, nearly enough to pay Claire back. It was hard work, I was sore, my arms ached. I rowed home every evening at sunset. I could always hear the jazz wafting over Dixon Beach...

Just as it was something of a tradition that the amusement park docks were taken out in the first few days after Labor Day, wind permitting, by hard nosed dock workers who were paid *by the plank*, it was also a tradition that the day after Labor Day saw the sheets of three quarter inch thick plywood being nailed over the windows of the shops and restaurants and amusements, all in a nail pounding effort to keep the winter out. But because it'd been the last summer for one side of the old amusement park, now it was the last fall, and rather than nailing plywood, the shops and amusements under the Roof Garden were being emptied.

While I was carrying the planks and posts and crosspieces back to the shore to stack in a *neat* pile, I had the perfect vantage point to watch exactly what was going on, which was nothing short of the total dismantling of the Roof Garden side of the amusement park. I witnessed the odd sight of all the mirrors from the Fun House piled in a heap outside, and all the incongruous and outrageous reflections that entailed, including myself, carrying the heavy lumber. And there were all the shells from the Shell Shack being sorted in boxes in front of the shop. In back of the Fun House I noticed, when I took a break, that the Sugar Bowl and the Barrel were being loaded on trucks. I took special note of the crate that held the Fun House Clown being carried into the Merry-Go-Inn. Everything, in fact, had been pried from its familiar surroundings, given a number, and arranged on the sidewalk under the long awning beneath the Roof Garden. Bumper cars all in a row, numbers taped to their steering wheels. Revolving glass balls from the Roof Garden, and the walnut booths, and the inlaid agate urinal - everything had been reduced to a number.

I kept a camera aimed at on all this dismantling while I was helping take out the Hi Ho dock, and all the other docks in front of the amusement park. I was working hard, carrying those water-logged posts, stacking that lumber, getting slivers, sweating - but at the same time I was watching the amusement park being deconstructed in preparation for an auction. And while I was laboring - harder than I'd labored in years - at the same time I was pausing now and again to document the scene, which irritated the dock man no end. I'd bought a used Canon T50 at Clara's Clutter Closet, and I was imagining myself a photographer now: a Steiglitz, or an Atget. If I saw a choice composition, I had to stop and capture. Over and over Art trumped labor. But I don't think the dock man understood or agreed with this never ending picture taking...

It seemed predetermined - given this head butting of history butting heads with what is so inanely called progress - that my grandfather's voice should come back to me - not faintly - but loud and clear. It happened while I was toting an algae-laced brace, one that had been soaking up the lake all summer, to the stack on the shore. I just happened to look down the beach toward my grandfather's favorite shade tree by the curve of the roller coaster - the one that he used to go and stand under when the heat became unbearable - and suddenly it was that hot summer day again, and those two kids were digging in the sand for the buried soldier. And there was a man, as conscientious a man as ever walked along the seawall at Arnolds Park, standing under an old cottonwood, sacred tree to the original inhabitants, in a handsome wide brimmed Panama hat purchased along another seawall, this one in Havana. *Where once had stood a grove of trees*, he said in his musical way of speaking. It was my grandfather, of course, and he was saying that someday, *mark my words*, someone will find a reason to have this big tree shading me taken down. They'll want to widen the road and put in curb and gutter, so this tree of course will have to go. They won't be imaginative enough to figure out a way to accommodate the tree, as they have on St. Charles Avenue in New Orleans, with those huge live oaks, and their roots which buckle the sidewalks...

My grandfather's voice was gaining in strength, his indignation was always in tune with his volume. I was trying to do my job, carrying the slivery lumber, keeping up with my silent and sullen boss pulling the nails, but my grandfather's voice was demanding more and more of my attention:

All these people who've worked in the amusement park day after day, summer after summer - and here I remembered listening to him inquire into their lives with a real, not a feigned, interest - their old familiar comfortable dusty cobwebbed horizon is about to be bulldozed as a result of a few stories buried deep in the market pages of a once great but now nearly worthless newspaper. All the developers have to do is open their wallets and let these poor people get a peek at the big bills. But you know, don't you Carl, that in the end they're just going to get nickled and dimed to death, and live the life of a servant, up in the attic or down in the basement, where the servants always live. The developers defile the landscape with their ugly buildings, ruining it for the rest of us. They step on us for the buck, and they rob us

of our appreciation of architecture. They knock down our historic buildings with no more thought, no more regret than if they were knocking over a stack of dominoes or a house of cards. The developers, if the town councils and zoning commissions don't stand up to them, will spoil our landscape to the point where we'll neither recognize it or feel at home in it or sleep comfortably in it...

I don't know...maybe I'd paused one too many times...between taking pictures of what was happening to the amusement park, and listening to the shade of my grandfather under the shade tree at the far end of the roller coaster...because they *were* taking that tree down, as my grandfather had predicted. I must have stopped to watch it fall into the lake. I was glad in a way that my grandfather wasn't here to see it hit the water. Maybe I'd lowered my head in mourning, I don't know, after I'd dropped the plank I'd been carrying on the pile of lumber. *Stack it neatly!* he'd shouted.

We were down to the last dock left in front of the amusement park, and this guy I'd been working for said that he had some more docks around the lake that he *might* want me to help him with. But then just as we were finishing up this last one, he must have had a change of heart. Was it my picture taking, or my listening to my long gone grandfather? I think it had more to do with him wanting to let me go, as his hip had

seemed to be feeling better. But he know how to let me go, other than by getting mad and accusing me of not working hard enough. He was a man of few words, who must have worked hard all his life, but who obviously had trouble expressing himself succinctly. We'd hardly exchanged ten words the whole time that I'd been working for him. But he didn't have to throw the nail puller at me. It tumbled toward me tomahawk style through the fall air. I ducked, and it glanced off the dock and fell in the deep water. A big row ensued concerning who was going to dive in and retrieve the sunken tool - the only one he had with him, evidently.

This intense drama (foretold by the bus driver) was being played out with only my dog for an audience - unless those amusement park guys had been watching (but I don't think they were) - on an otherwise very peaceful day - unless you happened to be in the wind (which we were, the wind was blowing right in). And just as the cook has to yell at the dishwasher about the egg-caked frying pan, and the waitress finds it necessary to scream at the cook when there's mold on the lemon wedge, and the bartender will castigate the waitress over the spilled martini, and the hostess will dress down the bartender about his over generous pours, and the manager will criticize the young hostess about her dowdy dress, the dispute between this guy that I *just happened* to be working for and myself about who should jump in to get the nail puller - an essential tool to take out a dock, and one that I knew I'd need to take out mine with - was one that would have to resolve itself in my absence. Because I could never have continued working for a person who would throw a nail puller at an employee, just as I could never have worked or eaten in a restaurant where everyone shouted at one another. And now that I had some money again, enough money at least to pay Claire back, and to pay the water and electric, and to buy a few groceries, including dog food, I didn't need to work for an abusive nail pull thrower anymore. And so I left, just got in my rowboat with Ginsberg and rowed off…

But I'd marked the spot where the nail puller had hit the water…positioned it in my mind, and later that same evening, after dark and when no one was around, I went back and dived in and swept the bottom until I finally found it. And while I was there, I snuck in the Merry-Go-Inn, and found the crate where the Fun House Clown lay buried in the styrofoam peanuts. It was lying across the bar where the scantily clad dancers had once pranced. But revolving bar was now still…everything in the amusement was eerily still…

I hoisted the clown out of his box, and tossed him over my shoulder. A trail of peanuts was all that was left in the wake of our way to the beach. But there he was, propped up in my boat, rowing across the lake after dark, a worried look on his face. And who could blame him, for he'd been through a lot, poor clown.

I took him in to the cottage on Dixon Beach, and propped him up in the chair of the future, where he looked and seemed almost comfortable. And in the days and weeks that followed he heard a great deal of good music, and his frown gradually turned to a smile, especially when I set him up at the upright and invited him to improvise, which he did, hurting his fingers at the keys with no hesistation…only abandon…

"Are these so-called scenes getting longer, or is it just me?"
"As the days shorten, the scenes lengthen."
"Maybe it's the camera…"
"Or the dog…"
"Or the clown…"
"I bet it is the clown. He thinks he has to entertain the clown."
"And so now he goes on and on."
"At least he was working…"
"Until he lost his job…"
"Was it because of the camera?"
"He'll find another…"
"He lost his camera?"
"Job! He'll find another job!"

"What makes you so sure?"

"I read ahead."

"Again?"

"I couldn't help it."

"Why…couldn't you help it?"

"Because the narrative seems to be picking up steam."

"So is the lake."

"What do you mean?"

"The lake is starting to steam. Just look!"

"You're right. Things are becoming obscene…I mean: obscure."

"Obscurer and obscurer."

"That's the way it should be. Don't you agree?"

"No. I don't agree. I like clarity myself."

"Well then, you, of all puppets, should like this next bit."

"And why is that?"

"Because Carl traverses Arnolds Park, when it's enveloped in a haze created by smoking piles of leaves, to find a couple who are very clear about what they're doing. And he also comes upon a familiar young women who is able to work no matter what the distraction."

"There's always another surprise at Lake O, isn't there, and just around the corner too."

III.
ALONE AND IN PAIRS

To some, we are surrounded by destruction, while to others its architecture that envelops us, while to still others its nature we're immersed in while we're alive, and even after we die. On the steps of the massacre monument, which, after much lobbying, Abbie had finally had erected in 1895, I found an ideal place to follow the progress of these various theories, as I felt the cool of the Minnesota granite seep through my virgin wool jacket. The wrecking ball is cool too, I philosophized, and smooth and round besides. But what possible comfort can it carry in its contagious and unalterable swing toward an old cabin? Must everything come to its end as a target? Are we born simply to become targets?

I aimed my zoom lens at a little cabin across the street…on the other side of the conical lake stone grave marker…the sign above the door read: *Pleasant View.*

Down in the amusement park, where my aluminum rowboat was pulled up at the bend in the seawall, it was anything but a pleasant view. The Park seemed to be coming apart, and so I aimed my camera at the seams, if only to document some of the destruction. On a scale of architectural tragedies from around the world, it might have come in low, but when you added up what had gone on there: on the dance floor of the Roof Garden, in the Sugar Bowl, in the Fun House, high in the sky with the Human Torch, out on the end of the pier with the prodigal sunbather, the shops and cafés, the fortune teller and the games of chance - all that life and all those experiences - then it became a tragedy of epic proportions, and in the wake of an all pervading and overwhelming melancholy, I had to turn away, I had to seek alleviation for my quivering undulating palpitations, and so I fled the scene (to return another day), taking my camera and my dog, pursued by memories and ghosts and the droning monotone of an auctioneer's amplified voice, *to plunge*, head first and eyes wet but wide open, deeper into Arnolds Park than I had ever been before...

I climbed over glacial till smooth stone walls, I skirted leaning rock pillars, I came upon a fountain with baby alligators warming in the fall sun, I crossed a mound of green plastic toy soldiers all arranged for battle, I saw a man digging a big hole in his front yard, I waved to a woman with white hair whose arms were full of Siamese cats. Each narrow back street which I walked down seemed to have at its end a smoking smudge pot around which there was always a dog or two or three, lying together and licking the sleep out of each other's eyes. Dogs seemed to roam freely through this veritable maze of eccentricity, but I kept mine on a rope, a short rope.

I was trying to reach the center of the maze, because I knew that's where Claire was - sitting at a table or lying on a bed, writing her life away while the leaves were falling...and waiting for me to pay her back. I knew I'd have a good story to tell her as I counted out the bills...a story with all its parts and components intact this time...a story that she could sink all her beautiful, perfectly formed little white teeth into...a story where she could finally put to good use that St. Paul Irish temper of hers. I just had to find her first, but the few people I stopped, to ask if they'd seen her, just looked at me askance and askew before they moved on.

I knew that the cabin she was in had to be one with a view that would inspire her. But the ones bordering the amusement park looked like they were about to lose their views and be torn down, because the beds and sofas and rocking chairs were piled out front, and a yellow bulldozer was in position off the front steps, like a hungry dog over a carcass.

Oh, what was the name of her cabin?

Somebody help me!

She'd told me the day she left, the day she'd gotten the terrible sliver in her foot. Skylingstad had started his noisy mower just as she'd said:

I'm staying at...

It would come back to me...it would come back...I just had to walk around Arnolds Park, reading all the names on all the cabins, until I recognized it. I knew it wasn't the pea green KWITYERBELLYAIKEN or KWITYERKICKEN. And I knew it wasn't the red trimmed RENO or the bright yellow SACRAMENTO.

I saw a cabin...an old cabin...possibly one of the original cabins...it was wrapped in plastic...had Cristo been in town without anyone knowing?

I felt like I could use some help, a little guidance, some inspiration from somewhere, but my invertible reticence made it impossible for me to approach the man in the Stetson raking leaves by the monument. Time was running out, the money in my wallet wouldn't be there much longer, there was just time to chant:

Inkpaduta! Where are you when I really need you?

They say that *progress,* which always looks much louder than it really is, happens between the time you go off on a boat ride to document some destruction while trying to find a person who has disappeared from your life altogether…and when you come home once again, after the picture taking and the searching.

But the thing is: I could hear it: a droning remote controlled roadside progress bomb honing in on Arnolds Park, aiming leave a deep crater and not much else. A few people would get rich out of it, while the rest of the crowd would get by on credit…expensive, high interest credit…

Claire! Where are you? I finally found a story for you…

Inkpaduta! They're serving pancakes in the Gardner Cabin, and you're invited?

Abbie! Remember the Reverend Prescott who stole your cabin? His ancestors have evidently come back to cause more trouble…

Isn't it odd how in times of need we appeal to historical characters, as if they can somehow step out of the past - the golden age that we'd thought we'd left behind - and into our present predicaments, to save us from ourselves and each other.

Then there was the peerless character perched on the front step of his cabin by the roller coaster. *Zoom's the name*, he said, shaking my hand with a firm grip. He said he'd been ordered to vacate, that they were going to *knock it down*, that it was all a *conspiracy*, and that he would have to go back to San Fransico. As he happened to be holding a handsome walking stick, I asked him if he was planning to walk all the way out to *ol' Frisco*. **Don't call it Frisco!** he blurted vehemently. But then, instantly calmer, he said: *Of course I am*. Because who can trust mass transit? I told him to watch out for the hairpin curve just south of Spencer. He seemed to know which curve I was taking about. In case

you don't know it, he said, that curve is a conspiracy too. He said that he'd worked at the skee ball in the Park, but now that was all finished for him too. *They always paid me in cash,* he said. *Hell, I haven't had a paycheck since '69,* he boasted. He seemed resigned to the fact that his cabin was on the hit list, and that he would have to start off for the *city by the bay.* He insisted on showing me exactly where his cabin was attached to the roller coaster. He said that as soon as they demolished his cabin, the roller coaster would probably collapse too. *But that's not my problem,* he said. He had his walking stick, and he had a comfortable pair of sandals, and a watch as well to keep track of time. There was something nobel - possibly even heroic - in his demeanor and bearing. In a weird way he reminded me of one of our Founding Fathers. But which one I'm not sure. I wished him well. He said it was all a conspiracy. I agreed, if only to comfort him. He stood up as if to depart. *God speed, Zoom,* I said. I had never wished anyone god speed before. That innocuous little phrase seemed to float in the leaf burning fall air as he headed west. *Watch out for the big lake!* I shouted after him. Without pausing or looking back, he yelled that it was all a ____!

As I continued my descent into the heart of Arnolds Park - and sometimes I wondered if I wasn't just going around in circles - the flavor of the air turned chary. Long piles of burning leaves lined both sides of the street. I saw thc rakers leaning rakishly on their rakes, smoking cigarettes, obscured by clouds of grey smoke. I got as close as I dared, and peered at them through stinging eyes to see if there was any one among them who might possibly know where Claire was. Squirrels scolded me from the trees, while the fires crackled and acorns exploded. Every winding street led to another meandering street which ended in a lake. This town was an island inhabited mainly by squirrels who were active beyond the imagination of anyone who has not been in Arnolds Park in the fall.

I didn't want to think about it too much but...from my seat on the steps of the monument, I could hear a bulldozer crunching an old cabin, and no doubt any nature that happened to get in the way, over by the amusement park. To my left and across the street, where the cattle were slaughtered for Inkpaduta's victory party, a flock of cabins stripped of their rocking chairs was about to get a taste of the big black wrecking ball.

How was it possible to feel any affection for an old cabin, its paint fading and peeling, the shadows of the trees and the wrecking ball laid out against it? Because...well...maybe something of great importance had taken place in it...and sitting with my idle thoughts against the monument, I came up with a few possibilities, which I could never imagine having happened in a big house on the lake. That green cabin over there...the one that was attached to the roller coaster...a child was conceived in it who went on to become...who studied and grew and traveled and went on and on to become...become a concert pianist, or a jazz pianist...an interpreter of Stravinsky, or a devotee of Monk. But there's no historical designation or plaque, so of course no one will ever know, and besides...

A bulldozer across the street to my right was poised to crunch the brown and yellow cabins occupying the ground where Inkpaduta pitched his teepee. The old cabins, in their simplicity, invited you to come in, their screen doors swinging in the wind. It's as if Thoreau himself stood in the entrance, feeling sociable for once. It's easy to imagine the interior, and it's here that you might still have an original thought, sitting at a wobbly table, drinking tea from a chipped cup. A girl with hair the color of an oak leaf in fall spent all summer in the smallest cabin once...the best summer of her life, I imagine...because she was free to she swim,

swim as much as she liked, and maybe she worked on the Queen; she read, of course; and once: once she threw a frisbee that *looped* the monument.

The cabins in back of the stone teepee, known as Gee's Cottages, were also being taken down, but in an unusual way. With a childlike attention to detail, an older couple was tearing down these cabins board by board. I approached the couple finally…to see if they knew anything about a woman named Claire, but they thought I was asking them if they needed any help. I knew I could learn something about disassembling, and about patience, by working with them day after day. I didn't have to fill out an application. They hired me on the spot.

In those tearing down days, I felt a real affection for this couple right away. They didn't throw nail pullers at each other, or hammers or crowbars either. They pulled each nail, straightened it with their hammers, and threw the nails - *chink!* - into a bucket. The boards were stacked in piles according to length, and bundled while still liftable, and put in the back of a yellow pickup. Everything was saved except for the shingles, which were too beaten to be salvaged. It's as if they were going to reassemble these cabins in a museum of turn-of-the-last-century vacation cabins, of which these were beautiful examples, with their wrap around screened-in porches and hooks for hanging dripping wet swimming suits.

The couple were working on all ten cabins at once - they'd work on one for awhile, and then go on to another. Once the outer walls were removed, the inner ones were exposed, so that the inside came outside. Day after day I rowed across the lake and came to work to do my part in altering the landscape of Arnolds Park. But this couple, whose names were

Helen and Leo, taught me how to do it in a reverential and homopolar way. I watched them exhibit the greatest patience with these old cabins, as well as with each other. They took frequent coffee breaks, and were always ready to stop and talk with anyone walking by. The retired history teacher, on his way to his bench on Pillsbury Point, often stopped by to chat and laugh about this or that...

And so it came to pass that in one of these cabins, as I worked on taking it down - the one called *Pleasant View* - where Abbie had once lived (according to Leo) when it had been over beside the log cabin - I was astonished to finally find Claire. She was sitting at a table, writing against a backdrop of faded yellow wallpaper. A small red clothbound book was propped open by the salt and pepper shakers to a poem entitled *Correspondences.* It seemed like such a coincidence for her to be reading a poem called *Correspondences.* I shook my head in disbelief, and pried off a corner of the roof sheeting. She was wearing the thickest of her thick sweaters, and a knitted stocking cap pulled down over her ears. She seemed oblivious to the walls coming down around her. Helen and Leo and I worked even more carefully so as not to disturb her.

> CORRESPONDENCES
>
> NATURE is a temple where living pillars
> Let sometimes emerge confused words ;
> Man comes there over forests of symbols
> Which watch him with intimate eyes.
>
> Like those deep echoes that meet from afar
> In a dark and profound harmony,
> As vast as night and clarity,
> So perfumes, colours, tones answer each other.
>
> There are perfumes fresh as children's flesh,
> Soft as oboes, green as meadows,
> And others, tainted, rich, triumphant,
>
> Possessing the diffusion of infinite things,
> Like amber, musk, incense and aromatic resin,
> Chanting the ecstasies of spirit and senses.

On one of our breaks, I explained to Leo, after Helen had left to get more coffee, that when Claire was deep in concentration she could not be distracted by anything or anyone. But how did I know this? he asked. I would have referred them to *Okoboji: Puppet Show of Memory*, but it had yet to be *written*, much less *published.* So I gave him what became a lengthy explanation of my meeting Claire, and my inviting her to Okoboji, and all the books she took, and her work and my typing, and even the money that I owed her…it became such a long story that it completely devoured our break-time, and our lunch time as well. Helen had to go home to make *more* coffee to get us going again…

When we finally went back to work, I noticed that on the table where Claire's book was propped there was a vase of flowers which had lost their colors. The leaves had fallen on her bed, her table, and the chest of drawers where her pages lay buried. How happy she looked! How free of any personal history she was, except what directly concerned her. She'd gained a little weight, her face looked fuller. She laughed at something she read, the screen door slammed in the wind, the leaky gas stove smelled, but she was oblivious to it all, and in her own world, as we all are when we work. Being in Claire's world meant that she was surrounded by all her books, as well as the notes for *her* book, which were tacked on the wall and fluttering in the wind that we were letting in with all our dismantling, fluttering like so many white capped waves rolling down West Lake from north to south. And all the while she was cutting and taping, making outlines and charts, and hanging chapters with clothes pins from an improvised clothesline…

We were winking at each other from up on our ladders - Helen and Leo and I - trying to work quietly so as not to disturb Claire…who resembled nothing so much as a soloist in a small group…she was the flute…she was the cello… concentrating and interpreting…despite our hammers and crowbars.

At one point, after she got up from the table and walked across the room to lie down on the bed - which was quite squeaky - and put her hands on her stomach, I heard Helen whisper to Leo: *I believe that girl is pregnant.*

We took all the other cottages down, and hauled all the nails and boards away, before we came back to finish off *Pleasant View.*

There was no sign anywhere of MacJames. He must have been pulling out docks.

One picture was tacked on the wall, and when the time came to take down that wall and that picture, I removed it without ripping it. It was a picture of a man with his hand just inside his coat or jacket. He was staring straight at the camera. On the hand holding the cigar, Claire had written his initials. C. B. He was *the one* evidently...certainly not a publisher...obviously a poet...a poet for all eternity?...without a doubt her guiding light...you could see it in his eyes...his sharp piercing gull's eyes...she'd made a little alter to him, with a candle and incense. There were curled oak leaves on her floor, covering the old rug.

It was enough...it was more than enough...to observe such beauty and dedication...from such a short distance...

Whatever Claire writes about, it will be *authentic*, I thought, pulling out a stubborn square nail.

I knew now that Arnolds Park deserved its reputation as a haven for eccentrics...but I also had to admit that our world doesn't suffer eccentrics like it used to...and what's going to happen when all the eccentrics have been driven away...north or south of the border...because eccentricity means authenticity...and money can't buy it...once it was a way of life which was sought after...children were encouraged to *be themselves.*

Because you see they'll have no place to stay, once all the old cabins are torn down. This is the last home in the last town for eccentrics. And

I was helping to tear it down. Leo and Helen and I - we were aware of this, but we kept on working because, as they always say, *we had a job to do*...they paid me in cash...and the money I owed Claire...I left it in an envelope under her pillow...when she left one time to go for a walk...

Alone and in pairs, singly and in droves, leaves fell and birds left. Geese emerged from the steam over the lake to honk franticly above the quivering crooked abandoned branches. In one dream I followed them down to an island of live oaks and pecan trees covered in Spanish moss. A burning nightmare woke me up, and I looked out the window and saw steam over the lake, enveloping everything, even the moon. I understood why the birds had left their homes and nests. The weather was changing...

You cannot know what it was like to have stayed in one of these cabins unless you have taken part in it being taken apart piece by piece. Neither can you know the importance of an invisible stud on a dormant thought until you have seen one both exposed and removed. The season mixed with the destruction were the catalyst for these philosophical thoughts which seemingly followed the steam skyward.

During one of my breaks, when Helen and Leo had to go off somewhere, I walked across the street to the monument and traced my fingers over the engraved names of those who had lost their lives, and of those who had come to bury them. All were listed on the monument I leaned against, listening with my eyes closed. It felt good to simply listen for the link between the past and the present. They can and did coexist in a single listening moment, and so I listened for that *moment* on those fall days, listening with my eyes closed, that the moment I heard might carry me kicking and screaming into the future. I listened and listened…above and beyond the sound of the bulldozers and the wrecking balls…until they finally quit for the day…and I heard a mother's voice say in a pleasant sort of way: *Dinnertime! Dinnertime!* to her three little children who were playing on the monument grounds. I stood up and realized that I was hungry too…hungry for a lot of things…and I started walking toward the smell of the meatloaf and the baked potatoes and the green beans…

But then I heard the sound of a piano…a jazz piano…

It was time to start rowing…

"Interesting how he found Claire again."

"Interesting maybe, though hardly believable."

"But don't you think, after coming this far, that anything seems possible in Arnolds Park?"

"They're tearing down the cottage that you happen to be living inside of, and you don't even notice? C'mon!"

"Her powers of concentration are truly remarkable."

"Is Carl paying you off, now that he has some money again?"

"He finally paid Claire back."

"Is he going to pay our way back to New Orleans?"

"I wouldn't count on it. We'll probably have to hitchhike."

"I'd rather float down the river than hitchhike…I think…"

"It would take a lot longer by water."

"Let's ask the historian what he thinks."

"What historian?"

"The retired high school history teacher historian who's sitting on the tip of Pillsbury Point on one of those old peeling green slatted benches smoking cigarette after cigarette. Let's ask him."

"Good idea! But don't you think we'd frighten him?"

"We do seem to have that affect on people, don't we?"

"Maybe we should just subtly invade his unconscious, so that he's considering our question as if in a dream…"

"Or in a haze of nicotine…"

"There you go!"

"But what was it that we wanted to know?"

"One if by land, or two if by sea."

IV.

Canoe on the Bottom

In the fall, the lake and the town and the people who lived along it all year round were restored once more to themselves. Whether observed from the bridge or the Chateau, Ft. Dodge Point or Pillsbury Point, the beach in front of the amusement park or the old cottage at the bend of the bay on Dixon Beach, a certain peacefulness, illusionary or not, had settled over the lakes area. A few of the sadly depleted eccentric characters - almost everyone thought that they'd left for to Canada - came out of hiding. And the retired high school history professor resumed his walks to the point

It's old, see, so it's given in gradually, the canoe at the bottom of the lake, to the muck and the seaweed and the crawdads surrounding it.

He said it was a great story that nobody knew or would ever know. He said that the people who went down with the canoe were condemned to silence, and that it sat upright in the deepest part of the lake, close to the bottomless hole, still somewhat preserved in the mud and the muck, like some birch bark Titanic.

He considered the bench on Pillsbury Point his bench. He let other people sit on it during the summer, but on the day after Labor Day, it became his bench again. He loved to smoke a cigarette or two at sunset, on a fall evening…no matter what the season was, his wife wouldn't let him smoke in the house.

I would often meet him out there, after my day's work helping Leo and Helen dismantle Gee's Cottages. I liked to sit on the bench at sunset beside the retired high school history teacher, and every once in a while run my hand over my left front workpants pocket, just to feel the cash

in it...because they always paid me daily in cash...unless, that is, it happened to be raining...

Just because the pioneers didn't find any canoes left behind when they first came here, they determined that their predecessors hadn't used canoes or any kind of boats here. And to support this theory, they made up silly stories of lake gods who got angry and liked to drown Indians foolish enough to go out on the lake. What ingeniousness! What posturing! Tell me, what is the opposite of *imaginative thinking?*

Unimaginative thinking?

Exactly! Proceed to the head of the class. Just like their offspring, and the offspring of the offspring of those offspring, the pioneers suffered from unimaginative thinking. You know, you remind me of one of my old students, he said.

I don't think he ever heard much of what I said.

And that's because he was a supreme monologist, as teachers often are.

Retirement doesn't suit me, he said.

I said that it didn't suit me either, that I was happy to be working for Helen and Leo, even if it was tearing down the old cabins.

I don't think he heard me.

He said that the most imaginative, and therefore the most intelligent person among the staff in the school where he'd taught - Arnolds Park High School - had been the janitor. He said that the janitor - Hugo - should have been the superintendent, and that the superintendent -Mr. Maas - should have been the janitor. After he went on to list the various attributes of the janitor and the superintendent, it all made sense to me.

But he didn't stop there. He went on to say that janitors are usually the most intelligent beings in the building - *any building* - whatever building they happen to be janitoring in. And that things would run more smoothly if the janitors could exchange positions with the people at the top. This was all music to my ears. And like I said, it made perfect sense to me

It made sense to me, and it confirmed a sneaking suspicion of mine - one that I'd had since childhood - that the power pyramid was topsy-turvy. I told him I'd been a janitor in St. Paul. I asked him if he knew where the Hamm Building was. He said he'd never heard of the Hamm Building. I told him it was downtown, and left it at that. I didn't say anything about any Irish bars or Czech cafes or Coney Islands of the mind, because the retired high school history professor had suddenly returned to his canoe story:

Look at the old photographs all you want to! You'll see the crowds in the park under the oaks, the ladies dressed, the men hated, the children swimming, with rowboat after rowboat pulled up on the beach, and steamboats in the background, tied to the pier, their smokestacks blatantly belching thick black smoke. But you won't see *one* of the twenty-nine Indian dugout canoes that were pulled up on the beach in front of where, one day in the distant future, the bath house would be…

How do you know all this?

Imaginative history…like the memoirs of U.S. Grant, only less bulky. It's all up here, he said, pointing to his head. Then he lit another cigarette. And he continued:

There were twenty nine dugout canoes, and one birch bark canoe, that were pulled up on the beach. Don't ask me how the birch bark canoe got there. Birch is rare in this part of the prairie. It was just there, I know it was, because I can see it in my mind, as clear as any photograph, clearer in fact, pulled up so beautifully on the beach, a work of art if there ever was one, for all to admire. I mean the swimmers, the paddlers, the fly swatters, the storytellers. They revered its lightness, its ability to float above the waves a feather thickness away from death by drowning. They adored its swiftness, and idolized its economy of line. Its materials were simple, but its structure was quite complex, a brilliant fusion of technology and art. Everyone realized that the canoe on the beach before them was either the key to the heart of Okoboji, or a one way ticket to the bottomless hole. It took great skill and strength to paddle one into the wind. But just imagine the spiritual thrill of riding in a birch bark canoe across Okoboji on a summer's day when there was a complete absence of machine noise.

He paused to take a drag…he was always pausing…always dragging…he was a little like Edward R. Murrow in that way.

Because you see, Carl, we're all of us history makers. That's what I used to tell my students. At least the ones who were listening, the ones who weren't talking or secretly listening to music. Each one of us makes history in our own way. This is nothing new. Have I ever told you…you remind me of one of my old students. But I could never talk to any of my students about the birch bark canoe at Okoboji. One time I started to, but I stopped myself when I looked in their faces and realized that the movies and the TV had stolen a high, a very high percentage of their imagination…yes, it's going to be a beautiful sunset tonight, isn't it? So peaceful with all the boats off the lake…I like to think that for every cigarette that I smoke out here, there's a former student of mine afloat in the world who hopefully remembers my lecture on the uselessness of Ulysses S. Grant as a president. I'll tell you what I told them: We must always reevaluate our histories *and* our historians.

The deep and passionate tone of his voice…in his unrelenting earnestness, there was a certain resemblance to a certain grandfather. The silent spaces when he looks out on the lake, either for a confirmation, or a way to go on, much as my grandfather had depended on the Fun House Clown. His lectures, he said, were punctuated by his throat clearing and his hacking coughs, along with fervent appeals to his students to forego smoking. How much money they could save if they didn't smoke! Enough to buy a new car. A Cadillac. Or a Ford. How he cupped his chin in his hands, between cigarettes, and stroked his ever present whisker growth with his fingers, before he went on:

Arnolds Park is a town of puzzling occurrences and amazing coincidences. How else can you explain why a truck full of Florida oranges bound for Canada would suddenly capsize - to avoid hitting a family of raccoons - on its way through Arnolds Park, and flood the town with oranges. I was like everybody else in town. I stood on the side of the road and shook my head at the sight of all those oranges rolling toward the lake. I picked one up and peeled it right there. I wasn't the only one eating oranges that day…history teachers are like everyone else, in that way…we shake our heads at the old trees being cut down for no apparent reason other than someone somewhere has decided that they've outlived their useful life. And you have historical buildings purposely being set on fire for a fire drill. That's exactly what's going to happen to the Roof Garden in a few days. Smell the smoke and weep. My students, my former students scattered across the world, they tell themselves: *Oh, don't worry, I'll remember everything!* But in fact they remember very little, only fragments, a tiny fraction of what I taught them about history. When they come back every few years to see the elderly aging family that they abandoned to go seek their fortune, why, they shake their heads like any other tourist at the conical stone marker; at the plethora of acorns; at the smudge pots; even at the pointed rock! No, I'm telling you Carl, they remember next to nothing! Only the air perhaps…and the feel of the water possibly…

Here he had to pause to light another cigarette, after first stubbing out his old one and throwing it underneath his seat. Between the slats I could see that there was quite a collection of stubbed out cigarettes under that bench. I made a mental note to come back with a garbage bag and pick them up someday, before the first snow.

Back to my canoe story, the retired high school history professor said. My canoe story which takes place in the pre-contact days. The vast majority of my students think history only happened here after the arrival of the Europeans and their descendents. As if all that took place here before was the product of some Dark Ages. What do we know about their homes, their gardens, their abundant hunting harvests? The desperately cold winters and excruciatingly hot summers that they suffered through? Imagine all the handsome babies and children and women and men that spent their time on earth here, in this spot. And it all has yet to be chronicled. We can only imagine it. But we don't want to turn the lights out on it. No, we've got to illuminate it! Have you ever been in an art museum, Carl, and noticed how in the African rooms, for instance, the curator has felt it necessary to dim the lights and create an atmosphere for the pieces on display. They don't dim the lights for Picasso, do they? Or Duchamp! Can you see them dimming the lights on his R. Mutt urinal, just to create an atmosphere? But what am I getting at? What was my point? I've lost it…

You were talking about the history here that happened before the first settlers, with special emphasis on a birch bark canoe.

What a good listener you are! I would have liked to have had you for a student. I could have gone on teaching for a few more years if I'd been fortunate enough to have a few more students like you. Who taught you to listen so well? You must have had some training. May I think of you as…my last student?

It was nearly sunset. I would have to row across the lake in the twilight. My boat was pulled up on the beach at the amusement park. I saw myself out there…rowing after dark…the only one on the lake…

My question to you, Carl, is: why did the people in my mythical birch bark canoe - and remember that the first white historians said that, because no boats were ever found here, the Indians didn't use boats - what rational! - but what made my canoe people ignore the approaching storm and shove off in a foolish and finally fatal attempt to cross the lake, to reach what we now call Gull Point? For a paddler, then as now, is only as good as the nicks on his paddle, just as a story, any story, only survives thanks to its embellishments and garnishments. The people who rode in that canoe, rode it down to the bottom, near the so-called bottomless hole of Okoboji, those people in that canoe were the supreme storytellers. Their bubbles rose to the surface and popped. The others, the ones who were left behind on the shore, right where we sit, here and down on the beach at the amusement park, the ones left behind, the ones still alive, they mourned, they shook their heads, day after day they walked the shore, hoping the waves would cast up their dead. This lake has always swallowed people, and will continue to swallow people as long as there are people brave or foolish enough to go out on it in a storm. Although these big ugly boats they have now-a-days have taken away a lot of the - what? - mystery, you might call it? I don't know. I better get home. My wife is making burritos. I think I've had my little vision of history. For today anyway…but maybe…maybe I'll see you here tomorrow?

On my row across the lake, long past sunset, I felt how filled with stories my head was, filled to bursting, because in addition to the retired history teacher's stories, and my eyewitness accounts of the gradual dismantling of the amusement park, which I was documenting with the help of my Canon T50, I don't think I've mentioned all the stories that Helen and Leo had been telling me as we were taking down Gee's Cottages, funny stories that came back to me as I rowed across the lake in the dark, hurrying to reach Ft. Dodge Pt. so that I could sneak along the shore safely, and not have to worry about being run over by some errant speedboat left over from the summer. Then I heard the music coming from the cottage again…this time it was Mingus…*Fables of Faubus…* echoing up and down the beach…

"A canoe at the bottom of the lake?"
"I don't believe that either."
"And he was a history teacher!"
"He still substitutes now and then."
"He didn't answer our question…"
"Who cares…what's next?"
"I'm cold."
"Me too."
"Let's go over and dangle by the fire."
(They move closer to the fireplace)
"This dock lumber puts out a good heat, doesn't it?"
"Where's Carl?"
"Out gathering flammables."
"While his father snoozes on the couch before the fire."
"And then gets up to play records."
"Music is everything to some people."
"I don't quite understand it."
"Me either."
"Where's the clown?"
"Over there…in the chair of the past…"
"What's he doing?"
Daydreaming…listening…who knows?"
"Throw on some more wood!"
"Was that last piece from a post or a plank?"
You can't tell?
Treated? Or untreated?
We're in for a treat?
You think so?
I know so!
Then let's go…

V.

Rowing as in Rimbaud

The wind drops its gentle pretensions in the fall - it rips the leaves from the trees - they flutter at first - then spiral downward - on their way to death and decay - a fortunate few land on the water - to float for awhile, edges upturned, like tiny Chinese junks...but then a wave comes - washes over them - and they sink- without stopping - to the bottom boys! - to lie there - at peace -

There is nothing the least bit to regret about the fall (my father reasoned)...because it brings out the best in winter...when you can hear music better...

On those late fall days I rowed like mad...back and forth across the lake...out in the middle and along the shore...collecting driftwood and dock pieces already shaped to size to fit in the fireplace.

Everything the same color on those overcast days. Muted shades of browns and grays. Up on the shore those shadowy baseball-capped figures, rakes in hand, standing by their smoldering piles, bare branches above them locking the sky up into little pieces.

One afternoon I rowed all the way down the lake to Terrace Park, and walked up to Lenz's produce stand on the highway to buy potatoes and squash and onions and beets, which I then ferried back up the lake to combine (except for the beats) with some bluegill into a great chowder. It was subsistence living…at its finest…

But there were other times when I rowed just for the sake of rowing.

I rowed just to be out on the water.

I rowed just to feel the jostle of the waves.

I rowed like Rimbaud and Walser had walked, but instead of going from country to country, I traveled from point to point, meeting with my stand up and sit down recollections on each of the points. And I was continuously picking up driftwood, and becoming attached at once to the animal like shapes of it, as well as to its insignificance, and its transitory nature. And always, when I came in to Dixon Beach, I could hear the music…Nancy Wilson…Peggy Lee…Nina Simone…

…but if you want to hear live music these days, my father maintained, then you're forced to buy a ticket and pay a handling fee *and* a convenience charge for a formalized ritual of enforced passivity known as *the concert experience*. You've got to get dressed up and you've got to be on time. Often it's in a theater or an auditorium or a hall with no windows whatever. The ushers who guard the doors point to your uncomfortable seat in the middle of a long row. For the next couple of hours you will be compelled to sit in this same seat, squished and squeezed between who knows who. It does nothing…this so-called concert experience…for my claustrophobia…

The first time I lit a fire in the fireplace that fall, there was a horrendous back draft. Cobwebs and chipmunks flew up the chimney. A penetrating damp cold had driven us off the front porch and into the living room. The smoke drove everybody - man and animal - out of the living room and through the kitchen and the back porch - out out *out* into the back yard, where I saw my father in a new light: his rust colored silk shirt shone in the pale milky sun.

Geese were honking down on the beach. Ginsberg took off running after them:

Rhow rhow rhow!

But Gabo stayed put, burrowing in to a pile of leaves...

Don't bother raking until they all fall down, my father said.

But Skylingstad said...

Don't pay any attention to what that nut says! My god!

After he was hit on the head by an acorn, my father went back inside.

Once the fireplace fire was under control, he continued:

So...as I was saying, you sit and wait for the concert to begin. Believe it or not: there are performers who enjoy making their audience wait. And so you wait...and you read...you read the program like a kid at the breakfast table reads the back of a cereal box...although a long time ago you came to the conclusion that you don't need to know any more about the composers or the performers than what is contained in the music itself. So you're reading and you're waiting and you're looking around... but the concert hall itself is very sterile...like an airport...and so you keep on...waiting...you wait for the lights to go down, for the curtain to go up...you wait for the distracting applause...you can anticipate, as you wait, every cough, every snore, every sneeze, every shiver, every shrug of the shoulders...because you're seated in the same row as all the snorers, sneezers, shiverers, and shruggers. But none of that matters once the music starts...

I got up to throw a couple of more pieces of driftwood on the fire... my leg had fallen asleep...it tingled as I limped...

Somewhere between the shore and the fireplace, I became attached to certain pieces and didn't want to burn them after all. The ones that resembled animal or human forms, they became objects of art, or else talismans and fetishes, to me, and I just couldn't bring myself to toss them in the flames. Instead, I thought about taking them back to St. Paul someday - because St. Paul had been on my mind of late - I was yearning once more for a life in the city - I imagined decorating my apartment - this time one overlooking the Mississippi - with *driftwood*, to collect dust and clutter up the place - or arranging them on my balcony, if I had one - in an attempt to take the lake back with me…

…although there were times, my father shouted above *Ruby My Dear*, when I was unfortunate enough to be trapped in the same row, if not sitting right next to, the village heckler, the guy who's shouting *Get down Thelonious* or *Right on Don Cherry!* or some inane thing, as you peer over and around the head of hair in front of you, who listens to the music with her twitching bare shoulders. Sitting beside her is a man who has neglected to take off his hat, so that it's impossible to see the piano, for instance, or the drums…

After I reluctantly threw a knarly piece of driftwood resembling a pocket trumpet on the fire - reluctantly because I'd been collecting driftwood and shells and pieces of flotsom for a collage that I hoped to construct in the garage (so that I had something to give to someone for Christmas) - it glittered and glowed, this lively piece of driftwood, and hissed in protest! Sparks exploded out onto the rug.

Didn't we used to have a fireplace screen?

Having nothing better at hand to use, I stamped them out with *Snow of Despair* - but so many sparks were in the air that I switched to stamping them with the heel of my shoe. The record skipped - and then skipped again -

My father looked irritated as he took another sip. He continued:

You have people who listen to music with their hands and fingers. You have other people who listen with their feet. What at first was a distraction before long becomes an attraction, because the woman next to you has taken her shoes off to reveal long elegant toes which seemingly have the ability to tap singly or in unison.

I'd left the seduction section of *Snow of Despair* wide open on the rug facing the fire while I went out to sample the fish chowder, which was desperately in need of another onion. I dutifully peeled and chopped one until my eyes stung, blindly adding it quickly to the soup before hurrying back out to the living room to discover a little hole ringed in a black burn on the page which describes the maid bursting in, after the checkout time had expired, on their room at the Burton Hotel in Mankato, on the top floor facing west, to discovered the couple in a compromising position, after having breakfasted at the greasy spoon on Front Street, the morning they're to take the bus back to St. Paul. I shut the door on that poor page, and listened instead to my father discussing the intricacies of musical composition with a bemused Fun House Clown…

…try, just try peeling back the layers of a song until you arrive at what it has to say, in a musical sense, in this stifling concert hall atmosphere. You may make your way through the foreground, you may even listen your merry way as far as the middle ground, but you will never ever truly hear the background, or the true birthplace of the song, in that sterile environment, my father said to the Fun House Clown, as he carelessly overfilled his glass.

The unrelenting melancholy embodied within the dense pages of *Snow Of Despair* made it necessary, eventually, that I read it only in the bathtub, in the hottest water possible, and then only by candlelight. I don't recommend that other readers do as I did: read the last pages first, the part where the river freezes over. It wasn't his fault, the anti-hero who jumped from the bridge. After thawing and unthawing for most of the winter, the river had suddenly frozen over for good in the last few pages, and only hours before he jumped. The man on the bridge couldn't possibly have known what awaited him. It was too dark, too foggy. He couldn't see…

Although I have to admit that often I give in to the urge to leave my seat and squeeze past a vast array of knees to go and stand in the aisle up front on the far left, so that I have a better view of the pianist. Or I stand in the aisle on the far right, so that I can watch the drummer and bassist working together. At times I wander up in the balcony, because the sound is always clearest in the far corner of the balcony. Or if I'm suddenly thirsty, I go out in the lobby for a glass of wine. Or if I need to relieve my claustrophobia and get a breath of fresh air, I go outside and stand on the steps and take in the city and all the lights. I must be an extreme example of an ambulatory concert attendee, but I'm having a great time of it, an absolutely fantastic time of it, at least until the chief usher sneaks up behind me in the aisle or up in the balcony or out in the lobby or outside on the steps. He taps me on the shoulder rather brusquely and demands to see my ticket stub. He asks me to leave the fresh air outside and leave my drink in the lobby. And then he leads me back to my row, and I have to squeeze between all the knees once again…my god! *Help me Pops!*

They squeezed them in between the trees, a lot of the boat hoists, instead of putting them up on the bank. Maybe the bank was too steep or there wasn't any room, so they used their barges, the cranes on their barges, and they lifted these heavy iron boat hoists out of the water, and dropped them down where ever, say, for instance, on one of the points, like Ft. Dodge Point or Pillsbury. Branches snapped and the wild roses got crushed, and my response, when I saw all the damage, was to say what my grandmother used to say (Act Two, Scene II), and that was: *Life is a fight, Carl! Life is one long fight!* So yeah, I saw the damage these boat hoists did to the trees and banks and bushes, often to property that was public, so yeah, it was easy to give in to the urge to do a little damage of my own, oh nothing much, disable some of these boat hoists a bit, that's all, so when they put them back in the water they would…it was nothing, you know, hardly worth mentioning, but life is a struggle after all, as that life long battler, my grandmother, always said, and there are times when you have to fight back, if only to make amends, if only for the birds and the animals who have such a hard time of it, especially in the winter. So yeah, it was nothing, I carried a wrench and a hack saw under the bow of my boat, so that if I needed them, you know, they'd be handy…and they were…they *were* handy…

I left a lot of songs behind when I shipped out to the South Pacific, my father said. But I didn't think of them as I'd heard them on the radio or record player or jukebox. I thought of them as I'd heard them up at the Roof Garden. I heard the Roof Garden renditions in my mind as we were coming ashore on the LSM at one of the Marshalls amidst all the shooting and the bombing and the confusion. And I saw the Roof Garden, even way out there in the Pacific, the way it sat at an angle to the lake, and the long row of windows, with the music coming out of each and every one, as you drove up in the boat…

From a grainy picture on page 35 of *White Men Follow After*, you can see what he's talking about. There's a holiday crowd, circa 1940, on the road between the Roof Garden and the lake, and you can see the angle he's speaking of. And maybe, just maybe, I'm thinking, I'm wondering if my father isn't in that crowd, or sitting up in one of the Roof Garden windows. In the days before he went off to the war he just may be with the other revelers in front of or up at the Roof Garden. I get up on my knees to bend over and peer intently at the picture from so many years ago, and another season to boot, while shifting position on the rug, to warm first this side of me, and then that side of me, while occasionally getting up to check on my chowder. How can it be that things change and yet they stay the same at one and the same time? It was and is a mystery to me. And just to the left of the Roof Garden picture there was a picture of a huge burr oak, and I made a mental note, the next time I was over at the amusement park, to see if that tree was still there

...I didn't even know your Mother when I was in the South Pacific, but I imagined dancing with her just the same. The wind from the big fans blowing her dress...the wind from the big storm on the horizon, which we were completely oblivious to because the music had captured us...the wind from somewhere...the night air from another time...

Single notes from a piano being played by Bill Evans falling *Tenderly* and by *Peace Piece* one after another from out of the speakers, orchestrated by my father as the only thing worth tapping his feet to now that fall was well underway and the trees topless and the gulls swooping over a lake turning bluer by the hour and freed finally of its docks and boat hoists, leaving a long stretch of Dixon Beach open to uninterrupted strolling and musing.

Lots of musing going on amidst the melancholy...

Go ahead and ask him...ask him where and when? The place he first heard it. First heard the song. What song? Any song that has meaning for him. Drown yourself in his favorite song again, no matter how blue the refrain, no matter how quiet the accompaniment. The first time he was given the baton, he knew he had what it took to be a great conductor of popular song. His fantastic ear! His ability to get people to do the thing, to play the thing, to sing the thing he wants done played sung. Look at him conduct his orchestra of one...

After the last dance...we noticed the lightning...how it was getting closer and closer. I said: *Let's make a run for it.* I'd been out in the Pacific, for pete's sake, I wasn't afraid of a little lightning. I believed in taking chances then. I threw caution to the wind, as they say. But she was against it. I had to lift her bodily screaming into the boat. I untied the rope. *Nothing*, I thought, nothing compared to the storms I saw in the South Pacific. We took off, I pushed the throttle all the way forward. Fastest boat on the lake remember. Left Mickey in my wake every time remember. Waves over the bow, over the windshield, in my face, in my eyes, blinding me. Nothing but white caps, ocean-like waves, both of us soaked! *Stay away from Pillsbury Point!* That's what your mother shouted. It was the wind! It was the wind that pushed us toward it. She was crying, she was screaming. There was no shore to be seen anywhere. I was drunk. I couldn't see a thing. I didn't see the rock off Pillsbury…we were going straight into the waves…water in my face…couldn't see…hit it hard… oh god!…I can't…you went…that was it…shit…

Unrelenting wind blowing the cold fall whitecaps down the lake. Long stretches of beach all around the lake wide open to walking. Lake a deeper blue than ever you ever remember. Burning leaf piles ring the shoreline. Let ours blow where they may, I'll never rake or burn another. With the leaves down a complete view. Seagulls circling over the only boat on the lake. They're drifting…he's fishing…she's reading…her long hair sticking out from under her hat. Over rocks as big as a house they say. And then the bottomless hole…

It's a mistake to keep coming back to Okoboji. But we can't help it, can we, Carl? It's a mistake, a goof, a crack-up but, we keep coming back anyway because we can't stop ourselves, and actually, we want to come back, because a little voice in our head keeps whispering *Go back*, and so we do. And, after all, we love being back here. This is *the place* to wind up in once again. But maybe someday we'd be better off fixing it in our minds from some faraway place, because once you're back here…the problem, as I see it, Carl, is to find the right distance from Okoboji… out in Maine I felt to far, but here I feel to close…but here we are, and to truly appreciate it, what the hell, let's spend the rest of the year here anyway, Carl. Hell! How would you like to live here all year round?

Lake steaming late at night. Moon shadows against the cottage, branches, tree trunks, almost like they were painted on the siding. One seagull at night, alone on the dock, lost maybe, icicles on his beak. The only dock on the beach still out. Last one in, last one out. Take the last of it out tomorrow maybe. Nothing but smooth sand all the way up to the old hotel. Wind always out of the northwest now. Makes rowing back from the Park almost impossible. Silence from the south. Claire's cottage completely dismantled. Amusement Park fixtures auctioned off. Invading army of bulldozers poised at the gates, like it's the end of Troy. I bent what I could, after dark. Gearshift, clutch, brake. As the half moon hung over the lake, its reflection following me along Dixon Beach, walking in the direction of the hotel bar, which closed the day after Labor Day. Still I walk toward it, hearing the bird-like cry of their valved voices…*chirp chirp…chirp chirp*

I think we've misplaced *Invitation,* Carl. It's around here somewhere, out of its jacket, buried in the pile. Search the stacks! That's an order! First song that I want to play for our end of the fall dinner! Suspended time…suspended in motion. The fervent cry of the wailing sax. Keep all these memories alive, for you and for me, for as long as we can. We'll see just how long, as soon as we find it…

Find what?

Find *Invitation!* Your mother…once she said…one of our dinner parties…I kept playing it over and over…finally she said: *I think we've all been invited enough!* Everyone laughed. I laughed, she laughed, hell, they all laughed…all the guests. Thought it was funny. Have you invited everyone, Carl? From what you've told me about Pesky, we'll have to put him at the opposite end of the table from Jerry, just to avoid any…conflicts. Nutty will have to sit facing the lake, so he can see the sky. I think he'd be comfortable beside Sheri. Don't you? And what's her

name? Clara? Claire? How long will you carry on this ridiculous non-relationship with her? And her lover that runs the roller coaster. What's he do in the off season? If he's a fisherman, tell him to bring some walleye, will you? Now as for the Fun House Clown, he's already here, he's arrived early. The first guest! My god! We'll leave him exactly where he is, propped up in the chair of the past. He can sit beside me at the head of the table. Say, maybe *Invitation* is still on the turntable, buried under a pile of records. Ten minutes and twenty seconds of straight blue jazz. We could always play the Bill Evans version, but it's only half as long, and half as good. No, they've got to be invited by the best, the greatest. Stick with JC. He's around here somewhere. Gotta be. And then everyone will finally and for evermore be once and for all time finally invited. Yeah, that's the plan. Let's stick to it!

I was there in person. I sat between the fire and the conductor. It was a fall like no other. I heard all these groups, listened to all these performers that my father had seen in person. He described them in detail for me - if they turned their backs to the audience when they took a solo - or if they got up and danced around the piano - the way their fingers worked the stand up bass - and it gradually came to pass that it was like they were there in person too. Listening to music like I heard that fall was an intensely ecstatic experience, although I didn't realize it at the time, caught as I was between gathering firewood and cooking chowders and soufflés, puddings and bread, soups and stir fries. But in the end it was a way to bridge the gulf between desire and assuagement. Gathering firewood and listening to music seem to provide the power to chase off any fears that I happened to have of the future...because when I heard music like *Softly, As in a Morning Sunrise* or *Naima* or *After the Rain* or *Crescent* or *Equinox*, it was almost as if I was protecting myself, without even realizing that I was doing it, from being overwhelmed by the terror of whatever was just beyond that pane of glass in back of my father's head.

All that fall this same refrain kept going through my head. I don't know if it was from a song or not, but the words, they went something like this:

We wait
we seek for all
we find we've left
behind

"*Hey! We're being usurped!*"
"*He says we're just typical puppets after all.*"
"*And that we tend to trivialize what we can't understand.*"
"*So now he's going to do this intro.*"
"*Let him! See if he can do any better.*"
"*He doesn't know how to entertain.*"
"*He doesn't know how to play the game.*"
"*Let's sit back and laugh!*"
"*As he makes a fool of himself.*"
"*He thinks he's such a poet.*"
"*He's trying to make us feel that we're witnessing a tragedy.*"
"*His ridiculously long sentences!*"
"*I like movies better than books.*"
"*Me too, 'cause you don't have to think.*"
"*You just have to sit back and open your mouth.*"
"*Let the camera spoon-feed the images into your mind.*"
"*So…he has the floor.*"
"*The stage rather.*"
"*Is the microphone turned on?*"
"*Maybe it will distort his distortions to the point of being unrecognizable.*"
"*We can only hope.*"

VI.

For All That's Out

And what a fall it was,
it was
And what a fall
it was

A good crow bar was critical in helping to dismantle the old cabins, but oh the dust, the dust that flew up with every nail pried off, making me sneeze my socks off, sometimes twice, sometimes thrice, and the wind blowing the leaves, and the money in my pocket every day, and being able to pay back Claire with envelopes of cash left under her door until
there wasn't a door anymore
anymore,
there wasn't a door anymore

And my meetings on the tip of Pillsbury with the retired history teacher, and all those trips I took back and forth across the lake, and the music and chowders and fires at night, hit me again and for all time with that smell of the seaweedy pieces of dock plank burning, I took it in through my nostrils, I drew it deep down into my chest, I held it in my lungs - all of it pitched in and contributed to a fall when a renewed source of energy came at me out of the dead leaves and the acorns and the squirrels scurrying in the branches over the cottage, and some getting run over, the ones that ran out into the lake road behind the cottage without any warning on mornings when the mist from the lake steaming was so thick that it enveloped everything in a shroud of fog, so no wonder they got squished, you can't blame the drivers, you can't blame the squirrels, unless the drivers saw the squirrels, but who's to say, who's to know, all I know is that Okoboji was deserted, there was no denying the deserted aspect of the place, stripped to the bare essentials like it was, and the breeze, now picking up, now dying down, you could never predict it, even if you listened to the weather, which I never did, preferring to be out on the lake instead, because I finally had it to myself, all to my self, I didn't have to be jealous of the boats anymore, because there were no boats, there was only my boat, my old aluminum rowboat with the creaky (for want of oil in the locks) oars rowing across a huge piece of shifting broken wavy glass with the lake always in my eyes, the blue

nothing but blue in my eyes,
in my eyes, nothing but blue
in my eyes.

And then one day I caught a glimpse, but no more than a glimpse, of the fortune teller's assistant, walking along a back street in Arnolds Park, her little dog on a leash out in front of her. I felt for a wink that I was somewhere in the Crimea, say in Yalta, but then she disappeared in a haze of leaf smoke, and I went back down to the beach in front of the amusement park, right to the bend in the seawall, which was forsaken; there was no one, not even Sheri, about. Before I shoved off, I got out the postcard Lou had sent me from Duluth. She was leaving acting to study geology! I was invited me to come up and visit her, and we could climb the tower on the postcard, Enger Tower, it would be just like old times, climbing up those steps behind her, so I stored that little thought in my mind, but meanwhile, one day, one fateful day, the last leaf, which had been hanging on for dear life, finally fell, and this is where (nodding to the puppets) *our story picks up:*

After lunch we went outdoors for fresh air and recess. Emma and I sat on the swings, not swinging but looking at the boys, and then at the pictures she'd taken of her sister Sheri lying on her bed reading some romantic-type book called *Women in Love*. When the bell rang we went directly to humanities class. We were studying some stupid war, and near the end of class, as our teacher was describing the way people flip out when they're fighting, he stopped in the middle of his sentence and went to stand at the window. His eyes opened wide, he was stroking his stubble, and then his face turned so red that it looked like it could burn up. Emma was the only one brave enough to speak up and ask him: *Whatever is the matter, Mr. Kramer?* He didn't say a thing, he just pointed at all the smoke coming from the direction of the amusement park. Then, without turning around to look at us or give us an assignment, he said: *Dismissed!* Odd, we thought, but Emma and I skipped, hopped, and jumped up the stairs to music anyway, and stood at the door to the music room for a minute, listening. We peeked in before we went in. Our music teacher was having her cry too, she'd shut her windows to keep the smoke out, the sky was black with it, billowing clouds of smoke. Pretty soon she put her handkerchief back in her pocket though, and sat down at the piano and played every old song she could think of, non-stop. But then the tears returned, and she laid her head back down on the piano and cried some more for all that's out. Emma and I looked at each other like: *What is going on here?* Emma has green eyes, while mine are nutty brown. We kept staring into each others eyes for the longest time, 'til we went into a kind of a trance. But somebody must have left a window open in another room, 'cause smoke somehow got into the music room and into our eyes, and then we were rubbing our eyes and crying too, but not over some old crummy dance hall, but because of it.

Jerry was out walking his dog, a long walk all around town, out the Dam Road and back past Sheri's house...

Sheri was reading, she read right through her interview at the nursing home, propped up in bed and turning the pages on a beautiful fall day, until she smelled the smoke and got up to look out the window and happened to see Jerry walking his dog, or rather the dog walking him, tugging at the leash. Oh, that was a mean dog. Jerry so gentle and his dog so mean, always ready to attack something or other.

Keep going Jerry!

Jerry kept going, up the back alley and past Clara's Clutter Closet to the top of Old Town, where the sight and smell of the smoke was

so overpowering that he turned away from it, breaking into a run past the Blue Note…

…where upstairs, in the room facing the lake, a live unedited off-camera quiz show moderated by Joe (Gusty) Guston was in progress, the sole contestant being that eternal borrower and delinquent repayer, Pesky Pete, with an audience consisting of a cat in the window, a hip cat by the name of Kerouac:

Pesky Pete! For a can of tomato soup, a box of macaroni and cheese, and a two point two pound slab of yellow (color added) Reagan's cheese, can you tell me: What is a Puritan?

A Puritan? Humorless men in funny hats. They torture witches.

Very good, very good. Your bonus question is: Who wrote **Main Street***?*

Who wrote Main Street*? That's a hard one, Joe, that's a tough one. Give me an easier one. Like who wrote* On the Road. *I read* On the Road *when I was in the Army. I never read* Main Street. *Hey! Look at all that smoke, will ya. That's a lot of smoke. Oh yeah, today's the day they're burning those old buildings in the amusement park. Let's go watch 'em burn! Want to?*

Buzzzz! Time's up!

Jerry walking his dog past Nutty Buddy's mother's yard. Nutty was out raking around the wind gauges and the rain gauges. Jerry waved. Nutty waved back, looked up in the sky, saw smoke where there should have been clouds, shook his head, and kept on rakin'…

And Jerry kept on walkin'…and holding on tight to the dog, a German shepherd by the name of Busker.

Busker! Slow down!

Busker didn't know how to slow up or down. He charged ahead… past the residence of Madame Jessie, who was on the phone to relatives out east. She was filling them in on the news about the situation in the amusement park. Plans were in progress for her assistant and niece to move east, where there was more opportunity:

Yes, her prospects will be much better out East.

Once I was the kid who sat on his father's lap and gripped the wheel of the runabout so tight that his knuckles turned white as we shot past my fort on the tip of Ft. Dodge and out…out to the middle of the bottomless hole spring-fed lake with its splashy waves and the windshield and lights rattling their heads off as my father pointed to the tree all alone all by itself on the end of Manhattan, its bonzai-style branches hanging drooping over the water and arranged so Turner-like against the sky…

Let's stop!

We stopped to swim under those gnarly limbs, letting the Cris Craft float offshore while we waded in, little minnows nibbling at out skin…

Later I grew up and turned into the guy who one day just happened to be rowing up the coast off Echo Bay, with bright red maple leaves clinging and falling from the oars. I was looking for driftwood dock pieces tossed up on the rocks…when I heard the mad whirr…of a chainsaw coming from Manhattan…so I rowed in a hurry across the narrow strait and beached my boat and met and talked to the *tree cutter,* who told me straight away that:

Nothing lasts forever! Buildings, trees, boats or bodies - none of them last forever. *When you see the last leaf / fall off the tree / Willow weep for me* - or something like that, I can't remember how it goes. Things eventually outlive their useful lives and must be cut down or otherwise removed to make way for new things to grow. That's the way I see it anyway. Now, if you'll excuse me, I must sharpen my chainsaw. Every tooth must be pointed. This is gonna be a tough old tree…

As he was sharpening, I asked the tree cutter what he thought would come up in place of this tree that you could see from nearly every point on the lake.

I have no idea, he said. No idea at all. Maybe a fountain, or a monument of some kind. It's in the hands of the developer. All you can be sure of is that the seagulls will find it. Whatever it is, I'm afraid that it won't be any more eternal than this poor old tree which, if you'll pardon me, I'm about to cut down, after I first choke my chainsaw.

He was about to start his chainsaw. I was about to shove off. But then, for some reason, Clare's questions concerning the Human Torch (Act Six, Scene I) came back to me, and I asked the tree cutter quickly: *Say, where are you from, anyway?*

Canada! he shouted across the beach quite shrilly. We have lots of trees up there. I cut them down professionally. They called me up and asked me to come down here and take care of this one. It's a nice old tree, but it means nothing to me. I don't get personally involved with my trees. It would make things too painful if I did.

He yanked the cord, goosed the engine…how it whirred, how it whined…how he angled his cut as close to the sand as possible, narrowing his goggle-less eyes against the spray of shavings as the blade sank deeper and deeper into the wood, the tree man keeping his finger snug on the trigger, cutting most of the way through the tree, a V cut, then dancing to the opposite side, and with a quick cut, finishing the job, pushing the tree over with his index finger, as if he'd chopped it down with a toothbrush.

I was just offshore when I heard the sound of the tree falling. Falling my way, falling toward me with a force, such a force that it touched off a wind, a wind and then a wave, a wave and a wind that pushed my boat with me in it down the lake, past all my little private memories and misconstrued recollections, which had been building up all that fall like ice along the edge of the shore. Frozen memories are quite easily shattered. You throw them up in the air, but instead of breaking up into little pieces - which would have meant that I'd finally lost my bearings - they mingled, my memories, with the smoke in the air, the overhanging pall associated with smoldering piles of leaves and smudge pots, and ballrooms and an old vaudeville halls turned Fun Houses…burning…

Because on this one fall day one particular ballroom built in 1927 was purposely set on fire for a fire drill. They got it going with gasoline, and then they let it burn out of control so that the flames were leaping and lepping and consuming rafters, walls, colors and essences, melting it all into a primordial black.

Past the amorous couple…in my rowboat I'm swept past the pair in their rowboat; they're oblivious to it all; she's kissing him, he's kissing her, most passionately, almost deliriously, they are obviously consumed with a fervor for each other on the bottom of the boat, under a blanket, in a bed of leaves: two mouths, four arms, twenty fingers gripping *the other* for all they're worth.

Past a red beret…I see it…floating over the waves…

Past Lucius Fitch, shampoo magnate with shotgun in hand, on the bank above Metz's, firing three blasts in the air to signal the start of the race to destruction…

Past the man in the cottage at the bend of the bay on Dixon Beach… searching for a song to match the smoky sunset…

Past an old Chris Craft Runabout barreling straight down the lake for the fire…

Past a wild kid running along the beach toward Ft. Dodge Point…

Floating past the girl in the burr oak with her short shorts and her tender ability to kaleidoscope any series of private calamities into one big catastrophe…

And the guy in the tree wrapped for burial in his dance poster memories…

Swept down the lake with a seagull coming along for the ride…sitting on the bow of the boat…

Past the fisherman who is unable to recognize the futility of fishing off the end of the longest dock on the lake, now that it happens to be the last dock on the lake…

As the gulls fly off for Santiago…

Past the stone lions on Des Moines Beach, and Abbie's Pine towering above them, prominent monuments to unrequited love…

Past the Chateau where Claire had peeked in and seen the piano, and asked *if this was the place…*

Past Mrs. Spotts…and where the books fell over the wall humpty dumpty like in front of the O'Farrells sign…and past those two giant cottonwoods, portals to Okoboji…

And then under the Okoboji Bridge and past the store where Larue sat at his card table waving postcards at me, as the Wilson brothers worked at their boat works…and sold their crawdads and minnows and night crawlers…

Which brings us - sadly, unfortunately - to the Queen…

It is inevitable, is it not, that a Queen's reign, whether over a kingdom or a lake, must one day come to an end. And it's a royal coincidence, if ever there was one, that she takes her last ride on the day the last leaf falls. (A trailer fit for a Queen waited on the beach for her reluctant approach). Her prop gets tangled in the thick seaweed of Smith's Bay. A Queen is always the last to admit that she has outlived her useful reign. In the meantime the rain…had turned to flakes of snow, and the few people who had gathered to watch and shout *Goodbye!* wondered: How will she ever fit on the trailer, and how will she ever adapt to the artificial lake that they're sending her to, or will she simply rot away in peace? She'd been *on Okoboji* for so long that when she was finally *off Okoboji* and riding down the highway, seaweed still clinging to her propeller, the cars that pulled over for the wide load, as if for a funeral, had no idea that they were witnessing to a tragic abdication…

A similar refrain was wrapped tightly around the shaky supports of Fisherman's Wharf, because it happened to be in the way of a highway that had to be widened, because ten thousand six hundred and ninety four cars crossed the old bridge in front of it last Fourth of July, and traffic was backed up from the cornfields of the north to the bean fields away down south. *Fisherman's Wharf,* emptied of its ovens and knives and tables and chairs and wine glasses, does not warrant historic preservation any more than a *Queen* or an *Okoboji Store* or a *Crandall's* or a *weeping cottonwood,* and may be dispatched in due haste, whether it's snowing or raining, as long as the last leaf has fallen. After all, there was nothing we could do to prevent *The Fall.* So wrap the old refrain tightly around its' shaky supports. And then *yank it!*

Roll it Pete! A little smoke, a little music…

First the smell, then the sounds…

The burning of the Roof Garden and the Fun House, Take Ten:

All smelled the burning smell:

Claire, MacJames, Jerry, Sheri, Nutty Buddy, Pesky Pete, Joe Guston, Madame Jessie, her assistant, her assistant's dog, the Fun House Clown, my father, Gabo, Ginsberg, the retired history teacher, Emma, Emma's friend, Skylingstad, the tree cutter, Ed and Helen, the squirrels, the seagulls, the leaf rakers…

All stopped what they were doing.

Looked up. Saw the smoke. Shook their heads. Rubbed their eyes.

Tried to go back to what they were doing before they smelled, looked, heard…

There was no going…they could not get back…because it was… gone…

The sounds lingered on…they each heard the music they wanted to hear…as they looked up…

They had not heard some of those songs for years!

The songs were in the smoke, the smoke got in their eyes, they cried and they cried: *For all that's out!*

While the smoke is still visible on the horizon…while the sounds are still echoing through the clouds…tell us again how you led the band… and danced the dance…and drank the drink…and fell for her eyes…

Blow that trumpet and rip that bass and pound those drums and bang that piano and toot that flute and sing that song…*for all that's out!*

And bury yourself in a big pile of burr oak leaves…the year's great crop…they show us how to flutter…and how to expire…every fall…for all that's out…

One…Two…

One-Two-Three-*Four!*

"You're so beautiful But you're gonna die someday."

PART SIX

LETTERS

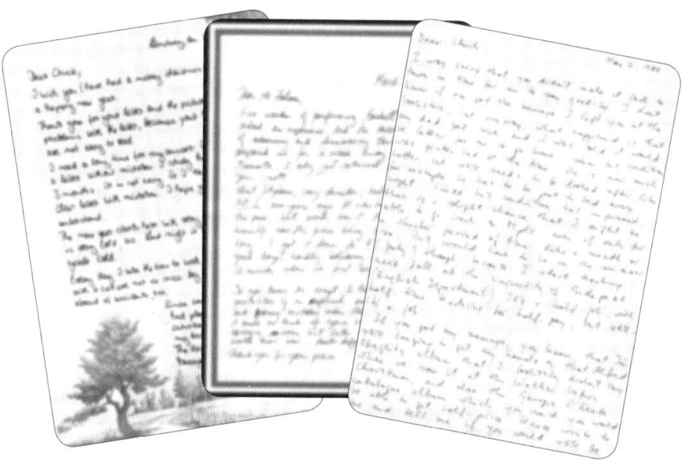

"It's the last act, then?"

"The grand finale, as they say."

"And it's winter…"

"Yes, and an especially cold winter, with lots of snow, heaps of snow, mounds of snow."

"Snow would be so pretty if it weren't so cold."

"It's the longest, coldest, snowiest, darkest winter since…"

"It doesn't matter. All that matters is…we're nearly done…"

"But what if they haven't made it this far…the readers?"

"Then they're going to miss the best part!"

"Perhaps they've been…skipping around…"

"Whatever gets ya through the night, like the old ex-Beatle sang."

"And sang very well, I might add."

"Now, with this act, we're not going to interrupt it, as Carl calls our impervious introductions. We've made an agreement to… we're just going to let it roll. OK?"

"Sounds good to me!"

"Because it all takes place in real – if that's the word – time."

"Let's just say it takes place in the present, and leave it at that."

"But this 'present' was still a few years back."

"Forget it! The reader, if there is such a creature, won't need our help keeping in step with the timeline. That's all that I'm trying to say."

"I got 'cha! Ladies and gentlemen: I present to you: Part Six, unexpurgated and uninterrupted."

I.
The Man with the Sled

So that I used to take my pen and notebook and go sit - in the sun and out of the wind - on the inside of Ft. Dodge Pt. And it was there - wearing sweaters from Scotland, Sweden, and Faribault (at times, all at the same time) - that I made the notes which would eventually coalesce - along with all my other notes made in boats and on points and beaches and, most significantly, in the kitchen, where I stirred the sauces and monitored the chowders and whipped the puddings - into this so-called *paper mache of memory*, with Okoboji serving flawlessly as a backdrop.

Out of the nippy wind then, but under the tepid sun, and on the seaweed encrusted rocks, with the waves raging past the tip of Ft. Dodge Pt., but the water divinely calm and translucently serene in front of where I was sitting.

And as I wrote - as I made my crabbed and nearly illegible but somehow indispensable *notes* - out of the corner of my eye I was watching the ice creeping and sneaking, building up slowly, so that you hardly noticed it, first along the shore, covering the rocks closest to the water, and the long tree branches snapped off and strewn at angles across the rocks, victims of those obtrusive and obnoxious boat hoists that had been so rudely implanted up and down that narrow boulder-lined point. The pieces of dock lumber scattered about the rocks were turning white too, as well as the ripped life preserver washed up on the shore at my feet, and the rusty beer can from Milwaukee, and even my old tennis shoes – *nothing*, as I noted down carefully, with a bare minimum of exaggeration, that was close to Okoboji on December 13th was out of reach and immune from the gathering frost.

Eventually my father ran completely and absolutely out of his beloved French white burgundy, at which point he quit drinking wine, being adverse in his obstinacy to any wine not made in France or in one of its protectorates - of which it had many - *many more than you realize* - he emphasized. His mood immediately improved, and his sense of humor too. He began telling jokes again, long convoluted jokes which often lacked a punch line, but that were still funny anyway, especially the first time through. I tended to daydream my way past any reprises though, as I'd just begun an exciting, but at the same time, *consuming* major restoration project: a repainting of the Fun House Clown's face. I was restoring it to its original brilliance, which meant highlighting his perpetual imperturbability, the same *sangfroid* that my grandfather had always spoken of in awe and admiration. I had the clown propped in the chair of the past, with an old towel covering his shoulders, and I was working on his nose one afternoon, giving special attention to his nostrils, when the color of my father's voice shifted to a more elegiac tone, as he said:

...because you know that we're going to have to sell the cottage, don't you? You knew that, didn't you? I was sure you did. That's why I didn't say anything. That's why I've been having these serious discussions with Skylingstad. What could be more convenient, when you want to sell your house - or in this case *your cottage* - than having a realtor for a next door neighbor? I admit he's a little odd, and that those three doxies really get on my nerves when they bark at the squirrels and Gabo and Ginsberg, but he is an expert at moving lake front property. You must have been gone during my negotiations with him. You must have been out gathering wood or fishing when we were having our little conversations. He sat right over there in the chair of the future, and immediately agreed to be my realtor. Maybe you were out looking for your old girlfriend. The one who left you for somebody else. Someone with better prospects. I'm just guessing. I don't know where you were. Anyway, we're out of money. Unless you have some stashed away...do you have some cash stashed away, Carl? No? I didn't think so. So we have to sell the old place. It's sad, but then lots of things are sad when you think about it. There's some kind of sadness in just about every direction you look these days. All this snow that we just got last night makes me sad. This song that's playing right now - *Theme from Spartacus* - that song makes me sad as hell! I don't know why I keep playing it. Maybe it's because it has such a gorgeous melody. But we're still going to have this damned party. Only now we'll have to call it our *end-of-the-cottage party*. Or something like that…

Behold the snow, I declaim to the animals, standing at an upstairs window facing the lake. No former occupants of this room to hear me, and not a living soul out there. Anywhere. Gabo's on the chair and Ginsberg's on the bed. No tracks of theirs or mine in the yard or on the lake path.

I say it again: *behold the snow*, this time adding a *bright* and a *white* to enhance the rhyme scheme.

By a strange coincidence, in my hand I hold Claire's *Snow of Despair.*

White…white…covered in white…

The lake an ice blue, bluer than any blue I'd ever been hued or glued or subdued by.

Sick as I am, I drink it all in.

Sick as a dog too, my nose running like a river, still I drink it, the brand new frozen soft sight of the white, with the blue between it and the clouds, steel wool-like, scraping the treetops.

It's another season, a new season, one full of hope, one serene with dreams.

A season for visions…

I sit and hallucinate at the upstairs window…

That's me up there behind the glass, my face a foot from the frosty pane, looking out at the lake.

I looked and listened and dreamed and stared and waited to get well again.

Well enough to get out and make some fresh tracks in the new snow.

Make new paths to all the old places to see how they'd survived the first snow.

In winter, I thought, we're always going back to haunts that we left a long warm time ago.

It'll be good to get this cold over with, I wheezed between sneezes, while running a hot bath.

Put this cold behind me and then I'm home safe, I hoped, testing the water with my toes.

Yes, the rest of the winter before me, cold free, more or less.

My father, ensconced in front of the dormant fireplace, shaking and stamping his feet.

Carl! Please go gather more wood for the fire! Pronto!

(As soon as the lake freezes...it'll be easier to gather wood...)

You haven't done a very good job in describing these people that we're inviting for dinner. You've given me their names - and what names! Nutty Buddy! Pesky Pete! My god! That doesn't give me much to go on. It would be nice to know what they look like, for instance. The shapes of their noses, the span of their foreheads. What distinguishes them from other people? *Traits*, in other words. Give me some *characterization,* for pete's sake! Which way do they lean? Does their song match their stride? Otherwise, for all I know, they're just fictitious characters, which is fine if you're writing a book, but we're not writing a book here, we're having a dinner party, we're setting places at a table for concrete people with substantial appetites and irrefutable opinions. Right? Isn't that what we're doing here, Carl? It's kind of like a last supper. But without any prophets, of course. We're all disciples here. Oh no! Lookout! Your crazy cat is about to jump on the turntable. Grab him, Carl! Quick!

It was a dreadfully cold morning. I was on the north side of the house, picking up sticks for the fire, when I noticed how the lake stones were falling away from the foundation. Among the stones I found what

remained of an old rag. Even in its tattered state, I recognized it as one of my window washing rags from those summer days (Act Four, Scene III) when Patience and I had washed windows directly opposite each other, and we'd used the ruse of letting a rag fall purposely to the ground to set up a brief meeting behind the fireplace, where we could not easily be observed by her employers or my grandmother, and where we had just enough time to plan another rendezvous for later on, at the burr oak tree with the bent green ladder on Ft. Dodge Point.

On either side of the lake stone chimney were octagonal stained glass windows. They were like two giant golden eyes for peering inside the cottage. I looked in through the one on the right, still holding the rag, and with the unknown fate of Patience still wringing my mind. I could see in silhouette my father sitting as if etched in front of the fire, a Dutch still life: now a Vermeer, then a Rembrandt, later a Van Gogh. He was leaning toward the heat; he was planning a trip; he was plotting his next move; he was reconstructing his past; he was swimming with the sharks; he was racing across the lake; he was flying toward the ballroom; he was running a restaurant; he was concocting a sauce; he was rotating to the warmth while his mind was in motion; he was absolutely still, as if posing for the artist (except for his right foot, which always had to keep the beat); he was someone from the page of an old newspaper, a distracted Faulkner figure, a *Big Two Hearted River* character out of Hemingway, submersed in the pale yellow aura of an antiquity only as old as the last sunset. With nothing but painted cedar siding and plaster lath separating us, we shared the chilly instant, along with the fading glow.

He turns his head, he's calling out for me, but I'm not in the kitchen or the bathtub or upstairs in my room.

I'm outside. He's inside.

He's hunting…for me…while I'm gathering wood…

Gabo moves toward him, he's rubbing his back against my father's leg.

My father picks up the cat, puts him in his lap, and pets him rather heavy handedly.

The cat raises his head appreciatively. He becomes yet another source of warmth.

It's as if I'm watching a shivering silent movie, because silence has descended upon us, a snow of silence, falling softly on my shoulders, on the tree limbs, on the sticks and branches and leaves…

It had begun to snow once again…

Winter daydreams, in all their cool and incondensable limpidity, accumulated in my mind like the snow on my incorruptible tennis shoes.

I stood on the edge of the bank and looked out on the lake and saw that it was solidifying…freezing over…one bay, one bare shoulder, one waist, one breast, one arm, one point at a time…

(It would freeze…and break up…and refreeze…and break up again, the wind pushing the paper-thin sheets of ice up on the beach in front of the cottage, a cubist pile of ice, like an omen or a sign for me to step on…step through…)

(On Ft. Dodge Point I'd hastily rebuilt my figurative fort…to protect myself against the ravages of all this freezing and breaking up and refreezing.)

And then one morning, after a frigidly still night, I woke up and scraped the ice from a windowpane with my fingernails, and *lo*: the waves: they'd met their Waterloo, their Gettysburg, their Verdun; they'd come to a full and a final halt.

A scant few days after that (I should have noted the date) the lake ice was thick enough to walk out on, but cautiously…gingerly…you wanted to stay close to shore at first, but you couldn't be too afraid, because the ice in its infancy was still forming and therefore constantly *cracking*, which sent your heart *vaulting* each time, no matter how ready for it you imagined you were.

I'd lifted the rusty sled down from the garage rafters, and while I was lacing up my grandfather's old figure skates down on the shore, I began to understand that what I was essentially doing, in addition to double knotting the bow, was transferring my attachment to summer into a devotion to winter…and my passion for unadorned motion into a yearning for unequivocal stillness…and my infatuation with Claire into a longing for Lou…and my love of the cottage into a desire for an apartment some place else…say in St. Paul…or Duluth…and so

on...this change of seasons and speeds and attachments and places being the source of all this inner turmoil...

But then I was suddenly free of agitation and turbulence and riot, because my skates were on and, dull blades or not, I was off skating across the lake...

For some buried reason I was drawn back to...the ashes...

Ashes, ashes, all fall down...

Where the ballroom had been...what was now covered in snow...

I pawed through the snow, Ginsberg was pawing too, we pawed and we pawed 'til we got to the ashes...and those few boards which had escaped the fire drill...red, white, and blue boards...mostly white...I pulled them out of the snow, gathered them into my arms like little lost puppets, and stacked them on my sled carefully, and then put the groceries on top of the boards, and Ginsberg on top of the groceries - just to try and keep the grapes and the lettuce from freezing - and pulled all of it back across the lake, my skates digging into the ice for traction...to tow this heavy load...

I became known as *The man with the sled* - that's what they said anyway, as soon as they saw me, all the unemployed and bored seasonal snockered guys on their way to the bar, Skylingstad the pernicious gossip among them. I think he's the one who came up with this 'the man with the sled' business, scrawling it across one of his damp drink napkins, along with the floor plan of the Dixon Beach cottage...

To play the part to the best of my ability, I stopped shaving and let my beard grow. Outside in the wind my face became an icicle gatherer. I continued to skate back and forth across the lake, realizing that a heavy snow would mean the end of skating. I tried not to fall, but sometimes I fell anyway. The thing to avoid was hitting your head, so I wore multiple stocking hats. I was the man of many hats on skates with a sled.

As soon as I got home I always ran a hot bath. Down I sank, down in to the warmth. I read some more of *Snow Of Despair* down there…I was skipping and skating around in it now…the hero always seemed to be trudging through the snow of St. Paul…seeking warmth…sipping free coffee in the Hill Library…sitting in those comfortable leather chairs… where there was nothing for him to read but books on business…a beautiful library thick with dreary statistics…I skipped around some more… and read the part again…where he calls his former girlfriend, and she invites him to come out and see her in Woodbury, because her father is gone for the evening. So he rides the bus all the way out there, and has to jump over a fence and run across the freeway…I-94 at rush hour, imagine that!…and then jump over another fence…(I could hear the trees creaking…creaking in the cold as I read in the tub)…so then he…what happens?…oh yeah, he knocks on the door of her apartment, and she lets him in, wearing his father's bathrobe, which he'd only *loaned*, and not *given*, to her…she's been reading *The Diary Of A Seducer*…in fact, she's holding it in her hand when she opens the door…She places it on the couch between them…as if the book is to serve as a buffer…She's reading it as an assignment for a class, while drinking a glass of Chilean red. She has to read the whole book that night, and then write an *essay* on it. She gives him some soup, they listen to a few library records over dinner - Irish music of course - she continues her reading – and she's writing her paper propped up in bed with him beside her when her father suddenly calls…he's coming home, it seems, after all…yup, he's had another fight with his girlfriend, and he's on his way home…he'll be there in a few minutes! So he has to get up, the so-called main character has to get up and get dressed and jump back over that freeway fence…and dash across the freeway and up over the other fence…the buses have quit running by then, so he has to walk…all the way back to his little room across the alley from *This Side of Paradise*…he takes a shortcut across a frozen lake (this is all too familiar to me) and then he stops at a bar…but he doesn't have quite enough money for a beer…so the magisterial bartender gives him a beer anyway…he drinks it and dreams…and then he resumes his walk...on and on...walking toward the lights of downtown...steam coming out of the First National Bank building...the BIG RED ONE in all its glory...like so many characters in so many stories, he walks...on and on...and after a while, the reluctant bathtub reader, my skin wrinkling self, glasses fogging over, I walk along with him...he's a little like me and I'm (Claire was right) somewhat like him...and we're both in St. Paul, which is a lonely old town, especially in winter...we could both use a little company, and he could use a warmer coat, and so could I... we walk and we talk, but we mostly walk...*trudge on brother!*...until I get sleepy with all this walking and talking...just the sheer unrelenting description of it all, the block after block of endless narration, down wind swept snow blown streets, past architecture old and new...the original and the unoriginal and the half baked in between...the combination of the reading and the hot water is enough to make you sleepy...yawning drowsy weary sleepy...until the book falls in the water...and the author's signature, which meant everything to Claire...but nothing to me...dissolves...

II.

Snow World

In the frigid depth of winter he bundles himself up to the point of being *unrecognizable,* in order to foolishly attempt a daredevil return to the dizzying heights of summer.

Because he's always going back to places that he'd left long – or not so long - ago.

That's just the way *it* is…and *he* is…

The lake is never more all his than when it's frozen and he can walk away from the cottage in the morning with the fire in the fireplace shooting smoke through the chimney behind him.

In what appears to be a last ditch effort to squeeze the last degree of heat from some buried hot August trinket or fading memory or historic (to his mind) location associated (in his consciousness) with *warmth* and *the summer…*

And at the same time an opportunity to hand out handwritten envelope sealed invitations to *the end of the cottage and the winter dinner…*

He leaves a cottage where chowder simmers and the driftwood spits and the records spin and the wind tries to…come in…

Again and again he appeals to the wind:

No, no, after you!

As he graciously accepts the supreme gift of winter:

Its oragami-like wrapped-in-white type of *clarity.*

To get around in the deep snow - because every day after the first snow it snows and snows again - he takes advantage of the snow-less circles ringing at the base of every burr oak, to go hop-scotching from tree to tree.

An inner voice cautions:

Watch out for those slippery steps!

Beware of that ice that's under the snow!

But still he falls, and falls once more…

He takes great care to avoid bumping his head on those vacant piles of boat hoist iron which litter the shores and dig their webbed feet into the banks and points with little or no regard for the consequences of progressive irreversable erosion.

The sheets of ice overhanging the beach are jagged and brittle, and conceal carnivorous - and *cavernous* – little caves.

The same kind wind which opens the door for him stings his cheeks sharply if he's foolish enough to face it scarf-less.

Following the path of least resistance, he lets the wind take him in its feathery grasp and whisk him down the lake or waft him across a field or drive him up an airstrip or push him across a godforsaken golf course…

Do with me what you will! he shouts.

What is it about winter, he wonders, which encourages this continuous visiting and revisiting of the summer's hot spots, which the snow has buried to a depth that…

To the unfathomable depth of…

Out on the edge of the bank in front of the cottage, for instance:

He has to jack up his double stacked stocking caps above his red ears and listen extremely closely before he can hear Claire telling him once again:

If for some reason I am unable to continue…

He walks, skates, shuffles, and strides, revisiting one little scene of past passion after another, always taking his camera and his dog along with him.

A sympathetic sense of non-friction comes over him as he takes a picture of the little roller coaster in the amusement park, with Pillsbury Pt. in the distance, cut up through the crosspieces of the big coaster, with the snow on the red railing and the little seats and the long handle

which keeps the kids locked in, and all of it *motionless*: the waves, the Ferris wheel, the ghost riders, as if waiting expectantly for the shrieks and screams, the whoops and hollers, to resume. Only *he* is in motion now. The rest is still, the rest is resting, the rest is frozen.

He makes fists with his fingers in his gloves, and he celebrates this stillness by breathing visually.

He sees pictures everywhere, he can't stop taking pictures, it all becomes a pictorial subject, the visualized present, he wants to capture it, its fleeting nature, he aims his foggy lens…but …he's out of film…

Then out of the blowing drifting snow those familiar figures begin to appear, approaching him in laughter muffled behind their scarves… or bearing down on him on snowmobiles…waving as they fly past…

He wastes no time in trying to hand out handwritten invitations to them…

But who among them has half a chance of recognizing him, the way the scarf shields his eyes and the stocking cap covers his head, as the wool sweater irritates his skin, and the moth eaten ankle length herring bone scrapes the snow in front of his tennis shoes?

Tennis shoes?

The winter sun is a low dog that hides behind water towers and scribbles its pen name, and the names of every single one of its muses, on the sides of the water tower that it hides behind all day, all winter long.

As he plows through drifts that are up to his waist, and his shoes fill with snow because his pant legs have hiked themselves up, he runs and sings good non-Sousa marching song like:

He's a real…nowhere man…

Out on the lake, alone amidst the whiteness…

But up on the shore - *look* - squirrels are out and about, and they're digging…they're digging in the snow too…

Shriveled hardened rose hips set against the white on Ft. Dodge Pt. He picks a few to drop in his tea later…to soak and bloat and eventually point the way to…

The way forward…the way north…to Duluth!

Back once again to the bend in the seawall, sheets of ice pushed up in front of it, rearranging the sand and the piles of pebbles and chert. Sound of the ice shifting, and the wind through the bare trees, as he remembers how his grandfather had praised winter to the skies at the height of summer, and how that had made him *shiver,* even way back when…

Then another time the wind blows him up the lake, over shifting checkerboard patterns of snow and ice…

When he's out in the middle of it, there's no apparent end to it.

A tottering stack of frozen summers condenses into one proto-photo-moment, as seen on a slippery trespassing climb to the top of the Tipsy:

- a flaming Human Torch on his way to a splash crash in a hog trough filled with snow…
- as Darlene of the daring seals combs her hair in the frost infested Shell Shack window…
- while Jerry yells at the Sons of Silence to quit banging on the Auto Race machine with their mittens…
- as Nutty Buddy trips over a red spinning stool in his haste to turn up the weather report predicting a long string of below zero evenings…
- while Sheri twirls another apple through caramel colored ice and snow, and Edith sweeps the icy cobwebs off the Fun House Clown, whose frown remains fixed and frozen, as the prodigal sunbather on the end of the pier flips over to brown the back of her snowmobile suit, while three seagulls are frozen in flight above her…
- and MacJames, reporting for duty at the roller coaster, shouts *Goin' up to Barrow!* instead of *Goin' back to Jackson!*

- while under the coaster, Helen and Leo are setting traps for the raccoons...and muskrats...
- and over at the bend in the seawall, Carl's digging down through layer after layer of lost and forgotten snows, digging with frozen frost bitten fingers, Ginsberg digging too, looking for something lost in the heat of summer (a toy soldier or a fine toothed comb) when everything was so effervescent below the surface of the lake, and love was just a matter of slapping a mosquito on a bright red sunburned shoulder, or pulling a tick from a sting weed irritated leg...
- but then Claire turns, doesn't she, to look off toward Ft. Dodge Pt....hoping to see *him* making...his turn...
- or maybe it was one of Tennessee's rhyming lines that comes back to Lou, and she yanks her playbook out of her back pocket to make sure she has the right words in the right order, and the appropriate grimace where she's supposed to frown...down...right down to the last frozen syllable...

To extract the last bit of intimacy out of a red magic marker dropped into space from the top of the water tower...or from the raspberry container that Lou threw under the picnic table on the day she left...a blue bunny cottage cheese carton ringed with red raspberry stains...in the snow drift in front of the picnic table behind the actor's lair...he digs and the dog digs and neither one of them gives up until one of them - the dog - finds it, still intact, still stained, right where she'd tossed it.

Inside: there's snow on the table, snow on the chairs, snow in the wide open oven, snow on the floor of the sleeping room, snow on Lou's little bed. The wind has shoved the door open and invited every snowflake to *please come in.* He's followed the illusion of Lou across the fields, across the slew where she'd buried her eggs. He's found a loose window and climbed in and seated himself in the last row of the theater, watching her mirage strut across the stage, a performance alive as any production. *Lisen to her voice ring out!* But the vacantly smiling gaze from the movie star's poster in the actor's lair is not what he left the fireplace in the first place for. He wants to fall in Lou's eyes again, but she's not there, it would be like falling through a hole in the ice. She hadn't been at Fisherman's Wharf either - so was she simply an apparition, one that he'd followed across fields and up water towers? Was she another actress up on the stage? The hallucination which vanishes once the curtain is lowered? She must have left something of herself behind, and he finds it eventually. It wasn't warm, but it contains the perfect stain of her method - acting, personality, and he takes it back with him across the fields...

Hey! You wanna climb the water tower again?
Ice on the rungs; icicles hanging from the iron railings...
Let's keep this revisiting obsession in perspective, shall we?

But not to see anyone he knows or thinks he might know for days (except for his father), and then to look up from his fishing hole at sunset with the sky a flaming red and imagine that he sees Claire skating across the wind blown ice toward him, visibly pregnant, with her long black coat dusting the snow ahead of her thin black figure skates...

Excuse me but...did you get your invitation to *the end of the winter and the cottage dinner?*

(He tries to look right in their eyes, just to be sure that it really is Madame Jessie's assistant...that there could be no doubt whatsoever that the person in front of him is indeed Nutty Buddy...but then they vanish before he can determine...for certain...if they are who...he thinks they are...)

One day he crosses the seam running from Ft. Dodge to Pillsbury, and he follows that seam toward Pillsbury, and then back toward Ft. Dodge, until the tracks of his comings and goings gradually interweave and interlock with each other...until the wind...obscures them...

A winter with an impressive and perhaps unsurpassed range of low temperatures...

A man with a sled who to the outside world appears to be but a distant...figure in a landscape...

At the end of the day, as the dying sun flings glittering but speculative spangles against the windows of the cottage on Dixon Beach (sitting in the snow as if it had fallen there like a prebuilt cedar siding snowflake) he trudges toward those glassed in flames, that dimming fire, their simmering soup, the hungry cat, his full tilt music, those twice told tales... abandoning himself, as he draws closer, to a wistfulness unique to this lake...and its environs...

III.

And I Wish You Were Here

The holidays arrived, with tension hanging in the air like an angry ornament, as my father insisted:

All that I want from you for Christmas, Carl, is an idea: a firm fixed solid rooted immovable substantial idea of what you are going to do with the rest of your life. Just give me something that gives me hope...

But rather than go out in the cold and dig through the snow in the front yard or the back yard or down on the beach for an h - shaped symbol-of-hope *stick*, I hitchhiked to Spirit Lake to buy my father a bottle of French white burgundy. But it didn't seem quite enough - one bottle - so I grabbed an expensive pouilly fusse. Two bottles, both by Louis Jadot...

Then I went to see my friend, Steve, at the drug store, and he helped me pick a fast quick pen for myself, and a notebook and some paperclips, and rubber-bands and a tube of glue. I filled him in on my *project*, and he gave me all sorts of encouragement. He encouraged me to keep on with it, and that's about the best thing that a person can do for you, and for that one act of support and reassurance I am eternally grateful to him.

I continued to work on my collage construction, in secret, up in my room. I'd intended to give it to Claire for Christmas, but then Christmas passed, and in the meantime another postcard from Lou in Duluth arrived - this one a picture of the lift bridge - saying how much she missed me. So then I began to construct my collage especially for her - she became my muse - which altered my conception of it. Progress remained slow, and I kept finding more things to add to it, such as the raspberry carton, and the marker that Lu had thrown from the watertower. It was a work in progress...a true *WiP*...

My father and I had a little party on New Year's Eve...we drank the wine and played song after song...alternating between Monk and Bill Evans...*Mysterioso* and *Stella By Starlight*...*April in Paris* and *Blue Monk*...the battle of the marvelous melancholiacs, played out against the sunset across the lake...and then the darkness...and the lights across the lake...as we dug up the old days again, and my father told me one hilarious restaurant story after another, and everything was light and easy once more, except for that ugly **For Sale** sign in the front yard.

After the first of the year, the bitter cold set in again. Whenever I went outside for any length of time - whether it was to gather wood or to feed the squirrels peanut butter sandwiches - I was never quite warm enough. But one overcast afternoon I discovered, in the racks of Clara's Clutter Closet, the coat of my dreams. It was a well worn deep blue Navy pea coat with the name *V. W. Goettsch* marked on the lapel. This coat looked and felt as if it had sailed in and out of many a port of call. I put it on and it fit beautifully. I loved the anchors away buttons, and the collar that hugged my neck like sailor's knot. It had a red tag, it was on sale, and it came with a few old love letters secured in a secret inside pocket. It was interesting that the stamps had all been snipped off, but the passionate phrases and endearing expressions remained intact. To say that I immediately fell in love with this coat is no exaggeration.

On that same afternoon I found an old pair of Army boots with the name *M.J. Fritz* inscribed on the tongue. These scuffed-up boots were a little large, but with a couple of pairs of socks, they'd fit ok. And like the coat, they looked as if they'd tramped the world, from Okinawa to Ozette. So I had my Navy pea coat, my Army boots, and a Russian hat, and gloves from the Pine Ridge, and a long soft red scarf emblazoned with colorful little moths.

Before I paid, I thought I better take a look at the bookshelves in the rear of the store. And who was back there but Sheri!

Winter is the best time for reading, isn't it? she commented offhandedly, not for a second taking her eyes off the books on the shelves.

I couldn't have agreed more. I thought of recommending *Snow of Despair* to her, but her arms were already full of books. A few of them looked familiar. I asked if I could see one, and turning to the copyright page, I saw Claire's name carefully written at the bottom, exactly where she always signed her books. I made a mental note to skim some money from my next trip to the store, so that I could save some of these books for her. She must have been in dire need - otherwise she would never have considered selling them…

Out on the sidewalk, I asked Sheri if she'd like to go for a walk out on the ice, but she declined.

Maybe another time, she said absentmindedly, her bag full of Claire's old books.

I'd said goodbye, and crossed the street, but then I turned around and ran down the sidewalk until I caught up with her, giving her a fright, as she had already started to read one of her books as she walked.

I wanted to give you an invitation to our party! I said.

She put it in her coat pocket, and said that she wouldn't miss it, not for anything.

Is there something I can bring?

Oh, some *black walnut fudge* maybe, and some *salt water taffy* if you have any, and a few *caramel apples* would be good too. And maybe some of that *white fudge with pecan*s too.

I'll see what I can do, she said. *I'll have to see what I can do.*

I knew that she'd be there, and that she'd bring something with her. She had that Midwestern dependableness about her. And she could *read* and *walk* on a slippery sidewalk.

Down on the ice in front of where the bathhouse used to be, it remained a frigid world, compared to the cocoon like atmosphere in Clara's Clutter Closet. But I was ready for any kind of weather now, after I'd donned and buttoned and pulled on and laced up my new used government-issue gear.

Those overcast winter days were short and sweet, although long and arduous from a wood gathering point of view. The light was Bosch-like, and not only at twilight, but all day long. The snowbirds had long since abandoned their lakefront roosts for their condos in Florida or Arizona, and so the only light along the shore was the reflected glare of the sun off the plate glass windows. And that was only if the sun happened to be out that day at sunset. And if the sun was out, I was out. And if I was out, so was Ginsberg. But Ginsberg and I were usually out anyway, during the day, whether or not the sun was out.

Out on the ice at twilight - to ward off the snowmobiles that always seemed to be bearing down on me like a pack of wolves whining a horrible noise - I lit a rusty kerosene lantern and hung it from a pole that I'd fashioned for my sled. I'd survived the boats of summer only

to be hunted and nearly run down in my tracks by the snowmobiles of winter. I skirted the ice shacks for safety. One late afternoon, outside of one shack which had a fish painted on the outside, I saw a beautiful perch lying stiffly on the ice.

Quite gradually, and almost supernaturally, while cleaning out the cottage to get it ready to be sold, all of Claire's letters that I'd neglected to mail, as well as the postcards picturing Duluth that I'd been getting from Lou - all of these letters and postcards ended up in the pockets of my pea coat which had once belonged to the sailor. And these letters and postcards mingled with those love letters that were already in the coat when I bought it. So all the letters and postcards were stuffed in my pockets to serve as padding and insulation, and in carrying them with me on my long treks back and forth across the ice, I used to bury my cold wet icy fingers among them for warmth, with the result that they not only mingled, but began to get mangled as well.

There was an endless supply of wood in the piles of dock lumber which dotted the shore. And if most of the dock pieces were too long, I always had my crosscut saw along to cut them down to fireplace size. And if some of the cottage owners discovered the following spring that their docks were not as long as they'd previously been, due to some *missing planks and posts*, they might not have minded so much if they'd known that this stolen lumber had served the noble purpose of keeping a father and son and cat and dog warm in winter. Because I only took a post here, and a plank there, spreading it out so that nobody would end up too short. Most of the docks didn't need or have to be that long anyway...

Those were the days that I was constantly combing the rip-rapped iced over snow covered shoreline of Lake Okoboji to scavenge for wood, because my father and I kept a blazing blaze going in the fireplace all day and all of the night. And many is the time, and oft were the moments that I would call a *halt*, and Ginsberg would jump off the sled and sniff his way up the bank, while I would sit on a boulder warmed by the sun and out of the wind, and quite randomly remove a letter or a postcard - or what remained of a letter or a postcard - from my pea coat pocket, as if I were drawing the winning prize in a contest. These letters and postcards warmed not only my pockets and my fingers, but also my blood and my heart and even, I suppose, my soul - if it's true, as they say, that I have one - simply by the poetry of their heartfelt emotions:

I miss you so much! I keep hoping you'll appear like a vision at the foot of my bed, playing your hurdy-gurdy to take away my loneliness...I'm dreaming of you so hard the bed is squeaking, and my books are falling on the floor to make room for you and your hurdy-gurdy. I'm curling up on my side til you arrive...be soft with me...be soft...

The cottage was still for sale...

There was a sign in the snow on the edge of the bank in the front yard.

I scraped the ice from the windowpane with my fingernails and looked down on it...with disgust...and sadness...

Later in the day I would make that sign go away...

Put that sign on my sled and go stick it in front of somebody else's cottage. But then Skylingstad would come by and tap another one into the snow.

At the end of every day, for want of shear warmth, I had to go back to the pea coat letters and postcards:

...and I'm sad you're not here to help me eat all these raspberries, and then we could walk or row over to the amusement park and see the lake from Pillsbury...It's too bad you missed the bus to Okoboji, and got on the one for Chicago instead. Was there someone waiting for you at the station in Chicago? I sat in Fisherman's Wharf long after your bus had left...

I'd intended to mail all those letters that Claire had asked me to mail. I'd taken them to the post office…I'd just never put them in the slot marked **Outgoing**. I didn't take that last crucial step, and now I had all these letters in my pea coat, and when I pulled one out and read it, it was like the summer itself had reappeared:

…after you come, after you finally get here, first I'll take you up to Omaha Pt., which is a beautiful place where the steamboats used to land. Wait to you see how the lake washes around it, and how steep and deep it goes down, and the mound of little pebbles and pieces of chert and shell and probably arrowheads and other artifacts pushed up into a high bank that you can lie against with you eyes closed and listen to the wind through the cottonwood leaves until one of the people who lives in one of the big houses in back of the beach comes all the way down to the beach in his or her bathrobe to yell at us to leave or he or she will call the police at which point we'll probably just have to get back in the boat and row off for another point, there's lots of them, you can just go from one to another all day long…

*…and I'm sad you're not here…*she wrote that over and over like an echoing refrain, until I read it and understood it as addressed to me, though the seasons and many other reasons had in the meantime come between us, still, she had the strength and the skill, through her literary ability, to transport us back to the previous summer:

…and I wish you were here, she wrote to me by way of her hurdy-gurdy guy, *to walk down to the amusement park with me, late on a Sunday afternoon, after most of the tourists have left, to watch the Empress come in and the Queen go out, though you should know how much I hate the Empress, because of what they say she's going to do to the Queen, sell her down the river to Des Moines like that…*

There was something invigorating and inspiring about being with her again…her handwriting alone made me feel like I was parting the curtains to feel the steamy air of summer…in one of those old cabins with the crazy names above the doors…with their canvas covers rolled to the top…and their porch sitting people rocking and fanning themselves and each other…

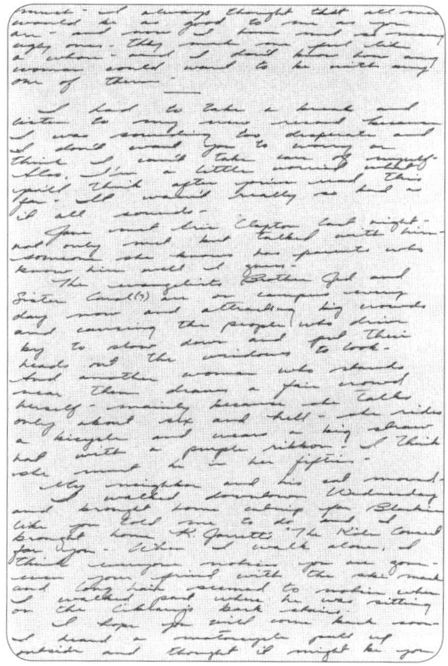

It wouldn't be winter again until I put the letter back in a pea coat pocket…and looked around…and saw the whiteness…and felt the biting cold…and pulled out another letter, as quick as I could:

…til we come around the curve by the roller coaster and the breeze off the lake hits us full in the face and you smell and taste the air and say there's nothing to compare to this…nothing to compare…

I tucked the letter away with the others, and went back inside to build up the fire…but then a few hours later I go back outside to raid another dock pile down the beach…and after I saw a few sixteen foot two by twelve inch planks into two or three foot fireplace pieces, I sit down on the dock pile and take off my gloves and remove at random a letter from a pea coat pocket. In taking the letter from the envelope, I first unfold it carefully, and then I read it out loud to Ginsberg, his nose covered in snow:

Take me to have a nutty buddy bar! Twirl me around and around on the red stools til I stop and point to…the Roof Garden! Or the Fun House! Or Laugh in the Dark! …and that's where we'll go…twirl me faster if the fortune teller walks past, carrying her crystal ball in her cupped hands …

take me to meet the famous daredevil who stood up past the Point Of No Return…I want to see exactly where he landed…and don't forget to bring your hurdy-gurdy so we can have some music…

This hurdy-gurdy guy she kept talking about, I remembered him, I remembered him quite well, in fact. He was much taller than I, much taller. I was jealous of his altitude, as well as his facile ability with his hurdy-gurdy. Claire had a thing for musicians, that much was obvious. But she needn't have reminded him to bring his instrument, because this guy never went anywhere without his hurdy-gurdy. He took his hurdy-gurdy to Chicago, I'm sure of it. He was very tall and very thin. His pants were never quite long enough for him. In the winter he wore a long coat that he tripped over and stepped on until the seams were ripped. His name was Horner. Or Korner He used to play around the folk clubs of St. Paul…

I hardly ever made it to the post office anymore. It was much too slippery to ride the bike. There'd been another increase in the postage rate, but mailing a letter was still a bargain. Occasionally I wrote to Lou in Duluth. I kept her postcard of the ship on Lake Superior in the right vest pocket of my pea coat. There was ice on the steps and snow on the road…

In the winter it's as if some omnipresent artist has taken the time to outline everything with a dark pencil.

In the winter I find that my mind is clearer.

My fingers were cold, though, from making snowballs.

I enjoyed practicing my pitching if it was warm enough. A tree became the strike zone. An imaginary crowd yelling behind an imaginary umpire bent over an imaginary catcher crouched behind an imaginary batter…but no smell of popcorn…and nobody shouting in a Boston accent: *Cold beer!*

Again and again my fingers sought the warmth of the letters and postcards…which soon dampened and began to crumble.

The frosty branches were in sharp outline against the sky.

They grabbed at the sky, they clutched at the clouds.

I could smell the burning dock lumber from down on the beach.

I gripped the wet letters in my pockets so tight that I could feel them falling to pieces.

Later, if my father had fallen asleep on the couch, I tried to dry them in front of the fire.

In piecing them back together, I came up with weird combinations like: *I wish you gurdy that time Queen came in to nutty Enger Tower.*

My father made me jump when he talked in his sleep.

One time he said: *They think they can destroy history…*

I threw the man-shaped piece of driftwood into the fire without thinking that it might possibly have a purpose other than keeping us warm…

IV.

Dinner Preparations

the fish *the fish* *the fish*

I threw the chopped shallots into the shallow pan and stirred them into the sizzling butter before I scurried back out to the living room.

My father had not taken his eyes off the marinating bluegill in the glass baking dish atop the pan full of snow on the low bamboo table beside the couch which had become his bed before the flushed fire.

He'd insisted that the fish heads and the fish tails marinade together with the fillets. Left to right then, he had his heads, followed by his fillets - placed carefully atop the spines - and then his tails. It was an arrangement which appeared to please him…for he nodded in approval…and sipped from the water in his wine glass…holding each cool sip pumped from deep off the old hotel high in his cheeks…his fingers entwined around the sinewy glass stem…until a thought came to him…and he swallowed…and set down his wine glass…on the bamboo table beside the bluegill…to instruct:

Will you please sprinkle a bit more of the French seasoning on that one in the middle.

This one?

Yes. *That one.*

A sprinkle fell into a wide open fish eye, but it didn't blink - none of them blinked, all their eyes remained wide open, as only a bluegill that's been caught through the ice in front of where the Roof Garden used to be on a cold day with the wind out of the –

How many more bluegills do we have in the freezer?

the guests   *the guests*   *the guests*

How many are coming? Do we have any idea how many are coming? Say we have twelve. Just say we have twelve. And then someone else shows up unexpectedly. Is there anyone that you know of…are any of these *mystery guests* of yours superstitious enough that they won't sit down at a table where twelve people are already sitting? You haven't done a very good job of bringing these people into focus for me. I feel like I hardly know them, other than their names. If I'm going to be heating plates in the oven for these people, I'd like to at least have a feeling of what…what they're passionate about? It affects everything, not the least of which is the seating arrangement. You've said that each guest is an expert on at least one thing, but you have yet to tell me what that *one thing* is, with the exception of Sheri - who loves to read and will have to have light - and Nutty Buddy - who tracks the clouds, and will have to sit where he can see the sky. Now the Fun House Clown - he's easy! – because he's already here, and I feel like I'm getting to know him. We'll just prop him up in the chair of the past, and he can sit right beside me at the head of the table. And from the little you've told me about Pesky, he has to be seated at the opposite end of the table from Jerry, just to lessen any conflict over who owes who money. Would Sheri be comfortable sitting between Madame Jessie and Jerry? I woke up in the middle of the night trying to imagine if that seating arrangement would work. But do we even know for certain if Madame Jessie is coming? No matter who comes, it's going to be a late dinner, I can see that now. But they've all got to - and this is something that I *insist on* - they've all got to sit down while the food and the plates are hot. I hate cold food on cold plates. Nothing is more distasteful to me! *Nothing!*

As the guests begin to arrive, tell them to throw all their coats and hats on the bed.

Whose bed?

Your bed, my bed, *any bed!*

We'll need candles, of course. Sheri will probably need two or three just to read by. I can't believe that she reads at the table while she's eating. My mother would never have allowed that. Maybe you can find some candles at that second hand store you're so crazy about in Arnolds Park. Flowers would be nice too. *Real* flowers!

We've got to keep the conversation flowing! A good dictionary, an impeccable almanac, and an up-to-date atlas should be strategically placed at potential flash points around the table to settle any disputes concerning words or facts or boundaries…just in case they should arise…

What else do we need? *Let's make a list!*

We're not inviting the Skylingstads, are we?

No. But hopefully we'll get some earnest money to help pay for the wine and flowers and candles and…

Now, if we seat Jerry between the retired history teacher and the fortune teller's assistant, and put Nutty Buddy straight across the table from Jerry, with Pete on his left, and you on his right…Would that work? That would mean that you, Carl…you'd be sitting directly across the table from the fortune teller's assistant. She's not planning on bringing her little dog, is she? Tell her to please leave her dog at home…

Tell them all to bring wine!

What kind?

Any kind! And then we'll see what *kind of wine* we end up with.

the sauce *the sauce* *the sauce*

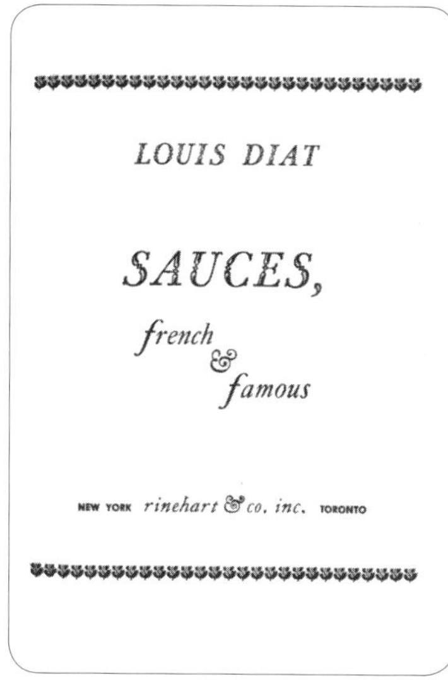
LOUIS DIAT

SAUCES,

french & famous

NEW YORK rinehart & co. inc. TORONTO

I scuttled back to the kitchen to *correct the seasoning*! Winter does wonders for your enthusiasm. I threw in thyme, salt, bay leaf, lemon pepper, garlic, frozen mushroom peelings.... and then watched in amazement as the seasonings simmered in harmony, to eventually blend, simmer, and stand corrected! I'd carefully chosen a sauce from the little green book propped open on the counter: *Diat's Sauces, french* and *famous*. I trusted in Monsieur Diat completely. He had never let me down. When he told me to wave my hand over the pan until I can smell the aroma arising, I did so, and the aromas which wafted into my nostrils did not disappoint, no, they inspired, and I dashed back out of the kitchen, waving my arms...

the song *the song* *the song*

Each time I hear this song, my father said, his eyes fixed on the marinating bluegill, I think of the first time that I ever heard this song, which was in the winter, a winter like this one, but with not quite so much snow...

In the winter - I think you've figured this out by now, Carl – in the winter, music comes to us unadorned...direct...unfettered...*you can hear it!* At times it's like you're hearing it for the first time...this song, for instance...this song that's playing right now...*Once Upon A Time*...once you started to cry just as this song came on...it was when you were very little...I got up to turn it down...and you suddenly...disappeared...you ran out the back door...and you ran away...I couldn't hear the song anymore...I got in the Chris Craft and cruised up and down the shore looking for you...all along Dixon Beach...shouting: *Carl! Carl!*...I asked everyone I saw if they'd seen you...finally I found you...on Ft. Dodge Point...out on the tip...hiding in your fort, of course...

I listen to music, Carl...to chase off any fears...that I have of the future...

I listen to music (I said to myself) to protect myself against being overwhelmed by whatever lies in wait just beyond...that **FOR SALE** sign in the front yard...

...because I sought out and sat in the front row and heard and saw these groups...these virtuoso performers...so that when I hear them *again*, on record, it's like I'm seeing them again...except for Bill...

Bill?

Bill Evans! *The Paris Concert.* Edition Two, side one, first cut. *Re: Person I Knew.* It's a live record, but even the applause is good...French applause is always very tasteful...I had a chance to see Bill Evans once... but I blew it! He came to Hammond...Hammond, Louisiana, where he went to school...and I was in New Orleans...and *all I had to do* was take the train or bus or drive up there to see him...but for some reason...I didn't...one of my biggest misses...maybe my biggest...he was playing at his old school...and then a few months later...he was dead...but his music defies death...and this song...This song is perfection, isn't it?...It mirrors my mood...and the mood of my world...as seen from a cottage on the east shore of Okoboji...in winter...Oh god, Carl!...Please play it again, Carl...We've got to hear *that one* again!...Don't we?...Oh, look!... Look at it snow!

le pudding *le pudding* *le pudding*

Ok!...now...this is tricky. If I were you, Carl, I'd approach the oven on tiptoes and holding my breath. Then I'd open the oven door very very slowly. What ever you do, don't let the pudding think that you're peeking in at it. Yorkshires are tremulously shy when they're rising. And they're unforgiving when they're scared. We must do our best to try and avoid a tragic collapse of the Yorkshire pudding, because it's going to serve as the centerpiece of this dinner that we're having.

the winter *the winter* *the winter*

When you were a child…you jumped in every pile of snow that I ever shoveled…and then you'd build a fort out of it…I shoveled snow so that you could build forts…to protect yourself…but from what?

From bullies maybe?

Your mother used to wear thick sweaters instead of winter coats. Her sweaters always had big pockets that she used to fill with pieces of chert from the beach. The one winter we spent here - the winter I kept Fisherman's Wharf open, or tried to keep it open - she used to walk up and down the beach, filling her pockets with these pieces of chert. All shapes and sizes of chert. Several times I asked her what on earth she was going to do with all that chert. *I don't know*, she said. She just didn't know…

(shadows on the bright snow…and on the house next door…the light, how it changes from one minute to the next…snow covers a tuft of dead grass in the lee of a tree…then the wind comes and takes it away…the petrified interlocking branches of the oak trees against the backdrop of a grey sky…a small herd of deer cut across the yard…icicles hanging down in front of the front porch windows…he's staring at them…)

Would you like me to knock those icicles down? I ask.

No…no, leave them there…because I like the way they look through the light…

But would you scrape the inside of the windows for me.

(Every time I scrape a pane with my fingernails and look out it seems that there's another ice shack that's appeared…)

the chowder *the chowder* *the chowder*

I hope we're not overdoing the bluegill. I mean, we've got bluegill in the chowder…and then we're going to have bluegill baking in the oven. It's too bad that you can't catch anything but bluegill. No walleye, no northern, no perch. *Just bluegill!* We'll probably turn into bluegill before this winter is over. My god! When I was you're age…when I was you're age I caught them all!

the knock *the knock* *the knock*

Who could that be? Knocking on our door this time of day!
Go see what they want, will you please…

the popovers *the popovers* *the popovers*

Do we serve the popovers with your raspberry jam? Or apple butter?

Hodlers *Hodlers* *Hodlers*

Your mother loved art…She was never happier than when she was in a gallery or a museum…Whenever we traveled, we always visited every city's art museum…She never felt claustrophobic in an art gallery or a museum…

I'll never forget the last winter we spent here. She hadn't seen a painting in months. But one day she said, out of the blue, completely out of the blue: *Today I'm seeing Hodlers.* She was standing at the window and looking out at the lake. Then she said that Hodler would have done wonders with Okoboji. Hodler evidently had his Lake Geneva, and he had his Lake Thun, but he never saw Okoboji…in the winter…in the sun and the snow…

Hollandaise *Hollandaise* *Hollandaise*

Don't worry about it! It's easy! Believe me, it's not going to curdle if you take the proper precautions. First, use a double broiler. You know what a double broiler is, right? Now, be sure and add a splash or two of cold water every so often to keep the temperature just under the boiling point. Are you following me? Ok. Add the butter a little at a time. Make sure that it's fully incorporated before you add the next bit. Now, most important…are you listening? You look like you're drifting away…ok, you've got to stir the sauce every second of the time until it's finished. Got it? Now…listen to me…if it does curdle, you can bring it back by putting a fresh egg yolk in another pan and gradually whipping in the curdled mixture. Ok! *Go to it!*

the accident *the accident* *the accident*

…it was a wide open pitch black lake in the rain…we were flying, I was steering with my foot, my arms were around your mother, the bow was raised up in the air so high that we couldn't see what was in front of us, the windshield and the lights rattling with each wave we hit…we'd just left the Roof Garden, but the band's last encore was still ringing in our ears…and then her hat flew off, as I told her it would if she didn't hold on to it, and her long hair of the most striking brown flew in front of my face…so I was blinded…by her hair and the lightning and the raised bow…I could not see that partially submerged rock off the pointed rock on Pillsbury…its always been there…it never goes anywhere…now I can see it, years later, where the propeller hit it, scratched it…I can see it now…I don't even have to look…

the doilies *the doilies* *the doilies*

We can't forget to iron the doilies and...what else? Oh yes. Polish the silverware! And the seating cards! An original design on each card would be nice...it would become...something of a keepsake...for the guests...

the war *the war* *the war*

When I heard the sirens I jumped off my bunk and ran to my station up on deck. A kamikaze had hit the destroyer off our bow...none of you people...the crowd coming to our dinner...none of you ever went through anything like that...

the future *the future* *the future*

But what's to become of us?

What's to become of you, Carl, after the cottage is sold?

If I were you, why...I'd...be worried to death...

I hope you haven't burned all your bridges back to St. Paul. That seems to be the only city you have a chance of making it in.

How long will you carry on this ridiculous non-relationship with what's-her-name?

the sunset *the sunset* *the sunset*

From the curved couch with the deep blue cushions...dressed in all blues...before the fireplace...blue slacks...under a lap blanket...beneath a portrait of his father and mother...a blue silk shirt with tiny white specks sprinkled like snow on it...the window frosted completely over...

I had to scrape it so that he could see the thin band of light across the ice…coming right at him!…he was wearing a thin blue necktie…and reflecting…but only to himself…as the thin band retreated, shriveled, and vanished…the sun long departed…to leave behind…a sky streaked with burnt umber…

Look at that sky!

Freeze that sunset right where it is! he commands, as if you can congeal a moment of time right before someone's eyes…from where he crouches on the edge of the sofa…

V.

Strong Song

Early in the morning, and he's convinced that he's alone on the ice, because not one fish shack has a truck parked beside it. He alters his course for a more direct route, one that has him coming ashore at the Villa. But then off Abbie's pine he perceives a bundled up little person coming toward him, followed at a distance by a dog, a woolly collie. When the little person stops and turns around to shout, his words freeze a few feet from his mouth, and the dog halts. The boy (his voice gives him away) resumes his slide by running over the snow drifts and sliding across the ice, his dog slipping and sliding after him. Just as these two distinct routes are about to collide directly in front of the Chateau, the kid loses his cap to the wind. It flits across the ice, and would keep on flitting, right out of the picture and into a snow bank, if not for the dashing diving scrambling dog, who snags it and then returns it eagerly to the boy, who pets him and puts his cap back on.

Ginsberg growls…

I'm going to be late for school, he says.

What a novel way to get to school, the man with the sled enthuses. Across the ice, and followed by a collie.

She follows me every day. There's nothing I can do to discourage her. I don't want to leave her tied up all day. My mother won't let me leave her in the house. She has to go to work early. My dog waits all day for me to get out of school so she can follow me home. Sometimes she stands on her hind legs and looks into the window of my French class.

French class? *Comment tallez vous?*

Tres bien, merci. Et vous?

I think I've seen your dog before...

Ginsberg growls again...

Was it by Fisherman's Wharf? the boy asks, pulling a biscuit from his pocket. That used to be her second home. They fed her scraps out the back door. But now that it's been torn down...

She'll have to find another restaurant, I guess.

Yeah. Her best friend at school is the janitor - his name is Hugo - he lets her warm up in the boiler room if it's really cold, like today. He feeds her too.

The boiler room, the boiler room...the man with the sled pictures the dog and the janitor together in the boiler room: the old dog, grey around the edges; the ancient Kewanee boiler, knocking and sputtering; the portly janitor, wiping the dust off the gauges in the warm cave of a furnace room.

What's your dog's name?

Lassie.

Of course. Lassie.

Lassie lying on the frayed oval rug in front of the boiler, looking up at Hugo with endearing watery runny eyes...the man with the sled could have stayed down there with them until the ice melted, reading and re-reading the manufacturer's name and city on the chipped raised surface of the boiler plate, if the boy had not interrupted his daydream to ask: Say, if you'd hold my dog for me until I get to the bank, maybe she'll turn around and go home.

He slides off, and he's left holding the dog by the collar. The dog pulls, but gently...gently...Ginsberg jumps off the sled. The dogs sniff each other. Their ears are straight up, they're listening to the shifting plates of ice beneath them. The collie's friend and hero has gradually slipped away from her...until he's out of sight...and saying hello to the janitor, shoveling snow in his shirt sleeves...and opening the door to the school...and in the third period: the cover of his history book. His history teacher appears to the boy as heroic a figure as the ones he is so fond of describing in such great detail. Tired and thin, the history teacher keeps threatening to retire, while never actually retiring. He'll illuminate the pages at least one more time for the boy who walks to school across the ice. Most of the other children silently question the usefulness of this information. There are those *great pauses* for them to puzzle over and try to comprehend...these come when the history teacher breaks off his story to stare out the window. Maybe he thinks he sees Abbie and Inkpaduta - captive and captor - setting off across the ice from Pillsbury Point, walking north and west, into a snow that stings if you look straight into it. They're walking toward another kind of freedom, one waiting for them on the tip of Manhattan Point, so they keep walking, their tracks zig-zaging across the ice. They disappear gradually, out of sight and into the history book to which the teacher refers to on occasion, disdainfully, in a distinctive voice, his very own cigarette stained voice. *Into the frozen horizon*, he mutters, still staring out the window...

The man with the sled eventually has to let the dog go, and off she bolts in the direction of the school's smoking smokestack. Another day maybe he'll follow her and lift up the window to hear a bit of the lecture. There's nothing like a good lecture to stimulate...but here he comes across that rarest of holes, an open one. He sits down on his sled, baits his hook, lowers his line all the way to the bottom, and then raises it a few feet. And he sits. And he waits. A bite will be along directly. He was on his way to the store before he stumbled upon this warm hole in front of the Villa. While he's waiting for that first bite -there's no better bite to wait for - he looks across the shore to the vacant space where the Roof Garden used to be. But if he quickly looks away, then in his mind anyway the Roof Garden is restored again to its rightful place, that weird angle at which it

faced the lake. The shutters are open once more, and he's standing beside Gusty at bottom of the steps, watching the singers mount each one in their high heels, one step at a time, while their back-up band whales away, and Patience, who ha*s his* ticket, is helping Freeman take tickets. Once you've heard the music played live, it's always there for you: it lifts you up and takes you along in its high heeled arms, all the way to the top of the stairs. That's been the goal all along, from Part One on: to make it in one piece to the top of the stairs. The front stairs with the double landing that will lead you up to the Roof Garden. Count 'em sometime when you've got a few seconds. They're in the air now - those stairs - the air that always sticks around, the old air that never abandons the place, the air of the old days that hits you every time you open a stuffy moth ball closet door and come upon a puppet show of memory or a postcard from the past hiding in the pockets of the faded polka-dot outfit that the Fun House Clown wore to the Count Basie dance. And Freeman, he's pressed the stamp on the pad, and the back of your hand is ready to receive his damp and easily transferable stamp, and as you lean toward him he has to shout in your ear 'cause the band is playing so loud, he has to *yell* to tell you what *tense* you're supposed to be in, because you've lost track *again* – it always happens in the pandemonium - just as you feel a tug on the line that sends your balled up fingers shooting back into their glove fingers...

And there he goes again, *the man with the sled*, shuffling across the ice, following the summertime route of the seagulls, a list of ingredients folded with a little cash in his left shirt pocket. And the wind...the ever present wind is like a rapacious baby with strong fingers who pinches cheeks and throws a plastic cup of water in your eyes and then *laughs*... laughs out loud and clear about that feeling of freedom which always accompanies a trip across the frozen lake...along with the cracks and the echoes...the patterns and the seams...

But the wind's a bully, so he turns his back to it and contemplates the water tower wrapped in cold clouds, and after making a quick casting call for warmth, Lou reads for the part in her brightest wide-eyed voice:

Can you believe that we once crawled up there and wrote our names and that they're still side by side facing south?

Then taking his tight fisted fingers out of their gloves, he places them unhesitatingly, as if it's a radiator, on the memory of her sun-burned shoulders, as he falls once more into those warm eyes, like they're little fish holes drilled in the ice. But she flew north against the geese, and her shoulder, where he touched it, has faded to its natural color, and if she happens to be writing a postcard to him at this moment, it's to inform him that no one talks to anyone on the ride down Superior Street on the bus…

Who?

Who thinks the ice shifts only at night?

Who?

Who thinks the owl hoots every time he hears the ice grind against the pointed rock?

The brief life of an eternal winter afternoon at Okoboji…

Like a snow ring around a tree, a fleeting sunset encircles the house.

His glasses fog over as he gently closes the door, and a common sound greets him: the measured amplified skip of a needle that has reached the final groove.

His father is asleep on the couch, covered by a Welsh blanket. He arranges the pieces of dock plank in the fireplace. The boards hiss…in all this skipping and snoring and hissing, he hears quite distinctly the tyranny of the family…

He sits on the piano stool - hero and villain, knight and fool - watching and warming to the fire. Gradually he rotates until he faces the piano, and the carved vines of its front piece once again lift him to the waves breaking on the rocks in his great grandmother's painting. Each hears and smells and sees what he or she was and is and will be. His grandmother (once upon a time) had opened the songbook to a song unlike any other song - *My favorite song!* She'd flattened the spine and smoothed it open against the carved vines. And then she'd said: *Let's see if you can play this one!* How clear he remembers the tone of her voice. The notes flooded for him like Hokusai's *Great Wave*, his feet reached for the pedals but fell far short, Mt. Fuji was off in the distance, yet another wave was on its way to engulf his grandmother, so he crossed his thumb and played dumb and watched his fingers freeze...

What he could not play he simply listened to...in silence...

The guts of the piano at least were completely in the dark in regard to his poor finger coordination. His grandmother had thrown up her hands and left for the liquor cabinet, and its array of colorful bottles, long ago. The golden age of the piano, when all the faculties cooperate in unison, had passed him by, leaving him stuck in the shade, a lonely little edible forest mushroom in the Age of Cage. His fingers nevertheless were poised to play a little easy listening dissonance, when his father startles him by coming out of hibernation on the couch to shout:

I can smell the Roof Garden burning!

He's thrown his Welsh blanket off and is sitting as straight as a smokestack, completely dressed in black and belching a torrent of recollections:

After I read about the tornado that blew the old roof off the Roof Garden, and after I'd learned of Darlowe's death in a plane crash, and especially after I'd heard Coltrane play *Equinox* at the Village Vanguard, I knew there was no hope for the Roof Garden, that it would be burned down or torn down. It's the spirit of the times that we happen to live in. But I have to wonder about the misguided man who lit the match...was he even from around here? Had he ever danced up at the Roof Garden on a hot summer night when the windows were wide open and the fans were whirling and the glass balls were sprinkling their lights across the floor? Let's hear *Softly, As in a Morning Sunrise*, Carl, because that's the only song that can comfort us now. How about Abby Lincoln's version first, and then Coltrane's…leave the arm to the side, why don't you, so we can hear it as many times as we need to…

On the warmer winter days they flung open the French doors to the front porch and removed themselves out there to sit in the sun in the old chairs and listen to tunes like *The Days of Wine and Roses* and *Tenderly* and *Nature Boy*…Nat Cole seemed to rule the atmosphere as they watched the wind swirl the snow past the fish houses, while the records got separated from their sleeves and jackets: the stacks of records here (the sun shining on them), the mess of sleeves and jackets on the table there (Gabo serving as an anchor). And outside the frosty window behind the cat's head, a squirrel, digging a hole in the snow, looking for…acorns…

His father reached out with his right hand to retrieve another thought, but he only grabbed a little part of it: *because once you're back here…*before it got away from him, and he puckered his lips and turned to look out the window.

The first time that I was handed the baton at the Roof Garden…you know, I don't think I ever gave that baton back, did I?

Gradually…over the years…he has assumed most of the attributes of the dictatorial conductor. He has taken the Roof Garden baton with him wherever he's gone, and increasingly…by degrees…he has acquired the fame and the acclaim and the know-how of a celebrated orchestrator. He snaps his fingers, he paces the rugs and the carpets, he looks out at the lake, he pauses to carefully reconsider a musical phrase…

(But if there's a fire in the orchestra pit, a great conductor is often the last one to find out about it.)

Woe unto him who brought up the subject of the Roof Garden…or the Fun House…because he'd seen the smoke that day, but he hadn't said a word about it…

He'd only nodded…

A great conductor is above all a great *nodder*. Because the great conductor knows that the slightest nod can prick the orchestra to perform in a frenzy. The great conductor has developed a fantastic ear, and perfect pitch to boot. He *heard* the Roof Garden burning, he *listened* to those sounds going up in smoke, when his son brought back the blue, white, and red boards, and burned them in the fireplace. Live music was finished for him after that. No more concerts, no more dances – because the *concert hall* and the *dance hall* had all been burned to the ground.

For a fire drill! Don't forget! **For a fire drill!**

A great conductor has the ability to get his players to do what he wants simply by a wave of his wineglass.

His first violin (his son) understood the wineglass motion for:

Fold in the hollandaise!

But: Poach the grapes! was a little more complicated.

Where was he to find juicy green grapes this time of year?

It became more and more evident that the man with the sled must make yet another trip across the ice…to the store…

If there's a knock on the door, a great conductor is usually the last one to hear it, so wrapped up is he in his Dizzy and Charlie, his Thelonious and Miles. He doesn't hear it even in the pauses between songs. The knock gets louder and louder. I run out from the kitchen to answer it. It's the real estate agent, with snow on his cap, on his nose, on his horn rimmed glasses. He's shivering, his words are like icicles hanging from the gutter, he's trying to say that he thinks he's found a buyer for the cottage - *They'll be flying in next week from La Jolla to look at it!* – and would I shovel the snow from the road to the back door? The potential buyer might forget his boots. There's no such thing as snow in La Jolla. Quite a winter we're having isn't it? Worst one in years! Do you need a shovel? I can bring a shovel by for you. See you next week!

My father's face *stands out*, as if it's been painted by an artist who only bothered to briefly sketch in the rest of him.

And beyond him? What's past my father? Outside: the lake, its cracks, its shifting eerie noises day and night. A picture of all this I keep

locked up inside of me. I speak and think only of winter now. Winter is all that matters…all that there is…

The grapes had frozen on my trip home across the ice, the lemons as well, but the wine was merely well chilled, and I poured a glass for my father, and one for myself, while butter sizzled with crushed garlic in the skillet…

Outside the kitchen window a rabbit was eating the bread I'd left in the lee of a tree…

What is it that simmers here, that twitches there, where one song passes into another with barely a break? Each hears what he hears; years of intense listening have brought the mind into a harmony with the music. Once there was a song strong enough to pick you up with one arm, and lift you high enough to see and smell and hear what you are…what you were…

The past and present are sitting on either side of him out in the living room. They meet in the carpet patterns, in the melodies, in the frost on the inside of the windowpanes.

Can you turn up the volume for me, Carl? Loud enough so that I can hear the stand up bass! All I'm hearing now is the heels and the toes shuffling across Roof Garden's dance floor…and its walnut booths and mirrored pillars…and the bandstand and the beams…creaking and crackling. When I hear music like Ellington's and Gershwin's and Kern's, I feel like I'm on a long trip…looking out the window of a train at a wide river…I never get tired of it, no matter how many times I hear it…there's always something new in it for me, something I haven't heard before…it frees me from my confinement in this body…this house…this season…this moment…*this tragedy…or comedy*…it lets me experience time unfettered…what I'm trying to say is…it breaks down all the barriers for me…so that there is no past or present or future…only rhythm and tones and melody…rehearing these songs is like revisiting a place on a lake… or going into a museum to see one favorite painting…you think you've committed the song or the painting or the place to memory, and yet it always surprises you…no two songs are alike, just as no two waves are alike…what I feel inside of me…what I can't seem to put into words… and what I see of the world around me…what it was and what it is… these two worlds meet in this music that we're listening to…and then, when you throw in a little wine…it goes to my head, but it also goes to my feet…so that sometimes…sometimes I just have to get up and…and dance…

He knocked over his glass as he jumped up. It rolled under the bamboo table, but he didn't miss a beat, quickstepping as usual into a slow counter clockwise spin, rising and falling on his toes, often appearing about to fall, before catching himself and dancing on…either the song would end or he would collapse…

I thought I was hearing a drumstick tapping on the side of the snare in a song…but I kept hearing them – ever louder, harder, longer taps - even after the song had ended and my father had sat back down, picked up his glass from underneath the bamboo table, poured himself another, and then left for the bathroom upstairs, *to indulge myself in a long hot bath…*

The real estate agent was at the front door. I let him in, followed by a man and a woman in leather coats. What did they want? They wanted to see the *inside* of the cottage…to see if there was anything *worth saving* when they bought it, because they planned on *tearing it down* and building a new *summer house*. Would my father care to *sign the contract* the real estate agent had drawn up in advance? The buyers were from *California* - they were only here for a few hours - they were in *a hurry* - they would like to know that the deal was closed before they left town - they were offering more than your father asked for – they were in love with the property - it had a beautiful *view* of the lake - they had two or three *plans* in mind for their new summer house - their architect was from *Santa Monica* – a *world famous* architect – *Frank* something or other - he usually only designed *art museums*...and *concert halls*...but because he was their *buddy*...

The prospective buyers spoke of saving the stones in the fireplace...to make *a California style patio*...The man was tall - even taller than Dr. Seashore - he bumped his head a couple of times on the low wooden beams in the living room. I tried to explain to him that people were shorter in the days when the cottage had been built by the trapper Dixon.

The trapper Dixon? he asked excitedly. You mean the beach is named after the man who built this cottage? Then we'll save these beams too, when we tear it all down.

Yes, his wife said, they'll tie in nicely with the fireplace stones.

This place has a lot of character, you know, she said to me. It's quaint, she added, but it's just not big enough for all of our grandchildren...and all of our friends. Although we're only going to be here a few months out of the year, right dear? *July* and *August*. How can you stand this weather? We could never live anywhere but Southern California, could we dear? Most of our time will be taken up in La Jolla: *the jewel of the Pacific!*

And Cabo, dear. Don't forget Christmas in Cabo San Lucas!

Oh yes, oh sure, how could I forget Christmas at our condo in Cabo?

I finally herded them back to the front porch, where they stood shivering on the rattan rug.

Where's your father? the real estate agent asked.

I said my father was sick. *Sick with a highly contagious illness.*

The real estate agent handed me the contract, and a pen with his name on it. He said he would return tomorrow to collect it.

Your father wanted to sell the old place, and now he has, Skylingstad said. I knew your grandmother and grandfather...and your great grandfather and your great grandmother...*Eccentrics!*...Every one of them... *Eccentrics*!

I watched him pluck the For Sale sign out of the snow, and take it with him, a smug look on his gossipy face...

I quickly deposited the contract in the fire. The buoyancy of those ashes…pursued by those flames…

Who was that? my father asked.

Somebody wanting to shovel the snow…I said no…I can shovel our own snow…

And I wish you would, before the party…

You know, Carl, I was thinking…while I was taking my bath…I was thinking that we should have bought *Crandalls*…and that we should have bought the *Okoboji Store*…and *Vern and Coilas* too, when we had the chance. But that would have meant that we would have had to live here all year 'round.

Year after year. All year 'round…

How would you like to live at Okoboji all year 'round, Carl?

. . . .

Somebody's skating…

Doing figure eights in the places where the wind has blown the snow away. Her long hair is sticking out in back of her cap, trailing along behind…and her stomach…big and round…

She's skating on one leg, one arm straight out ahead of her, the other one straight out behind…

But then she suddenly falls, her skate must have caught in a crack, she crumples to the ice and lies there, on her back, just lies there, not moving, just looking up…at the sky…

I saw it all through my father's well worn World War Two cracked and chipped Theatre of the Pacific binoculars…

VI.

Fog

Unless you've spent a winter at Okoboji - *an entire winter* - you would have no idea - how could you? - what it's like to live on an island in an ocean of snow. Because snow, in the end, is all there was - and is - and unless you've lived right by that lake all year round, you just don't know - given the paucity of words in our language that have come down to us to describe it - *snow.*

Oh, but it was cold...much too cool for profundities, unless you happened to be a *Symbolist* from St. Pete on the Neva...

My dangling fleshy lobes might have been tingling to the point of freezing, but the venerable hammer, anvil, and stirrup were in good working condition, so I still had an ear for the shifting ice cap that I pulled my sled across on the way to the store to load up on provisions for *the end of the cottage and winter dinner.* My left shirt pocket was bulging with earnest money, because another contract had been drawn up and the cottage had been sold to the couple from La Jolla, and at the very first hint of spring - whether it was a robin returning or an icicle leaving an eve - they were going to *rip it down* - Skylingstad knew a few good demolishers - and then the architect would fly in and get things mov-

ing on the new house which would *dwarf* all the other houses around it. Yes, it was all arranged, it was all 'just around the corner', I mean the tearing down and the building up, and another summer and skimpy clothes and *You Don't Know What Love Is* and MacJames shouting above the noise of the coaster climbing the hill to the Point Of No Return: *Gonna take ya back to Jackson!* and the prodigal girl in a two piece on the end of the pier…it was all about to come around once again…so I went without hesitation to seek counsel and prophecy (having spent my whole life *avoiding* counsel and prophecy) on a snow covered bench in front of a blue clapboard building underneath the roller coaster, where Madame Jessie had once dispensed her prophecies for a crisp ten spot.

My shirt pocket stayed stuffed with earnest money because Madame Jessie was not only not prophesying on that snowy day, but she would never - as I'm sure she realized - be gazing into the future from that sacred spot ever again. But I still came away from that icy slat bench with something beyond a wet behind, although what it was is hard to say, given the fleeting nature of the spirit world in general, and my rapturous love of the past in particular. Eventually I trudged on, though, like a plow horse through the snow, up the hill, still on my way to the store of course, for it was the day of the party after all - March 8 - and the anniversary as well of the battle at the Gardner Cabin.

And if I could not pass by Clara's Clutter Closet without going in, who's to say if it had anything at all to do with prophecy or profundity, or massacres or juke box tunes? I wasn't planning on buying anything, even though I could feel that big wad of money pressing against my left breast. No, I just wanted to warm up in Clara's cozy cluttered nest, amongst all those used clothes and chattering customers. Gradually the feeling in my toes returned…

Among the myriad books for sale in Clara's, which I surveyed and perused as if I had all the time in the world, there were some *familiar ones,* books that I'd given to Claire, feeding off of and at the same time indulging myself in her passion for the Russians. They were scattered throughout the shelves in no particular order, and I ignored my inclination to arrange them, maveling instead at the *odd pairings.* Mandelstom, for instance, was sandwiched in between Smiley and Steele, while Tsetevera lay at the bottom of a stack of Louis L'Amour. On and on, these incongruent conjunctions: Pasternak with Patterson; Chekhov with Clancy; until I took pity on the poor Russians, and began extracting them, one by one, from their predicament: here's Blok, and here's Olesha! (I was shouting out their names by now). And here's Bakhtin and Brodsky and Akmantova and Khlebnikov, which, along with Tsetevera and Mandelstam and Chekhov and Pasternak - plus the two volumes of Flaubert's letters that I'd given Claire on April Fools - made twelve, as in the twelve apostles. Why must everything in the end have a religious connotation? Is there no escape from it? *And what did Flaubert think he was doing amongst all these Russians?* I wondered at the time (being unaware, at the time, of Flaubert's friendship with Turgenev) as I carried them all - a tall towering stack - up to the counter to pay for, and therefore, reclaim them.

The woman who brought these books in will be very pleased to have sold them, the clerk told me. *She's going to have a baby,* and I know she needs the money for clothes and diapers and...

As she was computing my total on a scratch pad, I happened to overhear a conversation about a family...a family, from just down the street, that was on the verge of breaking up because they didn't have enough money to go on...they had simply *run out of money*...for whatever reason...there was no money for food or clothes or rent or anything...the parents had lost their jobs, and the kids...and the kids were crying and... the parents were just about to go crazy and...

I paid for the books, and then I went over to the women who were talking about this family...they were standing in front of the shoes... and I reached in my shirt pocket and took out the wad of bills...several hundred dollars…and I gave it to the woman…*the kind one*…the concerned one who'd been telling the other woman about this family…I knew that she would know what to do with it…she gasped…she looked at the money…then she looked at me…and gave me a huge hug…and started crying…and then the clerk and a few other women came over to see what had happened…that's when I got out of there…made my get-a-way like I was a Robin Hood in army boots and a Navy pea coat…

Claire's beloved Russians, and her muse Flaubert, the whole crowd of which she'd taken on the bus, along with her equally adored Irish and French and South American and Chinese and African and Icelandic authors, all the livelong way from St. Paul, through Mankato and Sleepy Eye, to the isthmus of the Okobojis, and which I'd carried in boxes from Fisherman's Wharf to the Dixon Beach cottage…and then MacJames had rowed them across the lake…and then Claire had trundled them - reluctantly I'm sure - to Clara's Clutter Closet…now I was about to pull all these books back across the ice to the cottage on Dixon Beach - which in the meantime had been sold to the couple from California - for safekeeping. *For safekeeping?* Maybe buying back Claire's books was a way to make it right with her, I reasoned. And a way as well to preserve them until Claire's daughter or son was ready to take on the Russians and Flaubert. Because otherwise, Claire - when the day comes that her child is ready to hear Khlebnikov's *Incantation by Laughter* - would feel the sharp pain of the bibliophile who searches her shelves for a book that she's forgotten she's sold. And so I would spare her those pangs of regret…

There was no point in going to the store anymore…

I started back across the ice, but a wall of fog - rising up, tsunami-like, from out of the Dakotas - had come in thick and heavy during my time in the Clutter Closet, and I quickly became disoriented. Nevertheless, I kept going, believing I could find my way by instinct alone, like a dog, like Ginsberg, who was perched on top of the box of books. I followed tracks that I hoped were mine, but as it turned out there was nothing of me in them; the boot prints were much larger, I discovered, when I finally paused to compare them.

I walked on and on through the fog, in a line which wasn't straight at all, I noticed, looking back into the dim recesses. A *series of curves*, and nothing more.

In my blindness I imagined that I was heading for Fort Dodge Pt., pulling my sled with the books and the dog across a patchwork quilt of dark and light ice. My moves were jerky, very here and there, like someone lost upon a chess board. And in fact I hadn't felt so disoriented since the Fourth of July evening out on the lake, when I'd had to abandon my boat to land in what at first had seemed like the Black Sea to me. But now, on the ice and in the fog, it seemed more like the Chuckchi Sea.

All white, nothing but white, with not a landmark in sight to sight in on. Abbie's pine...and the pointed rock...where had they gone off to? I felt that I was surrounded by vestiges - both real and imagined - but I was unable to see any of them.

I started to question the very nature of this thick fog. Was it inside my head as well as in front of my eyes? Because at times a few of the old landmarks came popping back up in front of me from out of the fog...as if they'd become part of the fog...Vern and Coilas and the Manhattan Beach Hotel and Fisherman's Wharf and even Red's...buildings that I knew were not there anymore. (This curious attachment to old buildings that I have, and which follows me everywhere, even out on the ice in a fog: where on earth does it come from?) The pre-tornado Roof Garden suddenly reappeared, in all its architectural splendor...in the fog...out on the ice. And then people started popping up...like Inkpaduta and Abbie...and LaRue and Mrs. Spotts...and the Human Torch and Darlene the seal lady...only to disappear again...before I could invite them to the party...

I can't even say if the red beret that I found - or believed that I'd found - out on the ice...I can even say if that red beret was *real* or not... and if it was real, do I still have it? And if I still have it, *where is it?*

You can see what tricks the fog plays with your sense of past and present...and with all of your other senses too...because strange sounds came to me out there on the ice...as they always did...this time it was someone somewhere who sounded like they were playing a toy piano... one like you hear in John Cage...as a solitary goose from Canada flew low, just over my head, honking as if sounding the hour...as I came to a seam, a big seam, and I promised myself that I was going to follow that seam for as far as it went...thinking that in the end it was bound to take me to one of the points...Atwell...or Pikes maybe...I'd given up on finding Ft. Dodge...I could find something to do on any or all of them...I mean a way to survive...

It was not entirely unpleasant being vanquished by the fog. It turned out to be not that much different from my usual state. Because what passes for normal to one person is absurd to another...and so on...

Occasionally I would hear the sound of a distant truck...

And then there were the echoes of ice shifting...beneath my feet...

Let me say again that it was not an altogether disagreeable feeling to be *lost on the ice*, pulling a sled full of books anchored by a dog, and thinking that you're hearing a suite for toy pianos. I suppose it goes back to my feeling at the sink (Act Four, Scene III) as I was doing the dishes: my awareness of an innate happiness whenever I am over or on or in or near *water*, no matter what its state.

So that it was almost rude of the fog to lift without warning, to be deposited back in the world of winter, and to find myself just off a familiar point thick with trees. It was like...it was like coming out of the water after holding your breath for an abnormally long time. Then again it was similar to waking up suddenly from a long involved dream.

A ray of light at the surface...which I swam for...to find myself...

At Gull!

The wind had fanned most of the snow off the south facing beach, so I set up camp there, out near the tip, under a cottonwood and away from the wind.

And because I was on Gull Point, I imagined I saw a seagull sitting on a snow covered rock on the tip of the point…

But there was no seagull - all the seagulls were in Chile - or on Russian country estates - and that imaginary seagull, like so much of life, was simply an illusion. There were no birds or animals…other than Ginsberg…there were no people on Gull Point…beside myself…and best of all, there were no boats pulled up on Gull…just one sled…

I tried to build a fire out of the little driftwood that I could find. One of the pieces seemed to be anchored to the sand - it was a cottonwood root, and it made me feel balmy yanking on it. I remembered Claire tugging on this same root…and then writing about it in her journal…a humorous entry which I'd read and reread…

It took a good while and a lot of tending to get this fire going. I had to sacrifice some of the letters in my pea coat. Don't ask which ones! I have no idea. All that lovely handwriting…up in smoke! I'm afraid I almost completely emptied my pea coat pockets of letters and postcards before that fire finally took off. I only kept the one postcard from Lou which said: *You should come to Duluth. You really should.*

Then I began to arrange the Russians and Flaubert in order of warmth. Chekhov, as it turned out, came in first, dashing, despite his poor health, over the finish line by a hair, simply because of the ending to his marvelous *Gusev.* Odd how art keeps us occupied even in the direst of circumstances, for darkness was falling, and the temperature dropping.

The ray of light I'd seen had all but shivered away. The only light that was left was the flame of my little fire burning on the beach near the scene of my conception. What a symmetrical correspondence there is to this world, which only becomes evident when the all enveloping fog begins to lift.

The ascension of the fog can be a transcendent thing when it takes place at sunset. The sun came out just in time to burn a hole in the haze, and set the glass of a window ablaze in a cottage across the lake, which I assumed to be my grandparent's old cottage on Dixon Beach. In that glaring reflection, which only lasted a second or two, I felt some added degrees of warmth, in addition to the books and the fire.

The fire!

I needed more wood…

A few young oak trees were lying askance across the snow. The chewed chips, left by the beavers, lay scattered about. I threw the ends of the oaks in the fire, but they burned slowly.

By that dim firelight I discovered that Flaubert the Norman had been a prolific letter writer. But then there was more *time* to write letters and postcards in the nineteenth century.

I had a letter or postcard of my own that I wanted to write.

I imagined writing this postcard or letter, and receiving an answer.

It was to be a love letter…a passionate postcard…

Is there any other kind?

Flaubert's letters had done their job on me and my sensibility…

I began to compose this passionate postcard/love letter to a lake early on the evening of March 8 on the end of Gull Point in the winter of 19__ in near darkness…in my head, you understand…

In my mind

To a lake…

You think it's a snap to write a letter, and a pinch to scribble a postcard, until you try to transmit and transcribe your thoughts and feelings to words and sentences in the cold and the dark. I watched idea after idea vanish right before my eyes.

I looked to the Russians on the sled at my side for encouragement and inspiration. There was Alexandre Blok. He wrote some poems addressed to a beautiful woman, even as he was nailed to the bar with liquor.

The fire created shadowy dark dancing figures from the spines of the trees…they reminded me of the painting, in the Gardner Cabin, of the Maddock cabin on fire, which used to give me such nightmares (Act Six, Scene V) as a child. But these same trees that tried to scare me also sheltered me, anchored me, and I chained myself to them, in a matter of speaking, in the cold, in the dark, so far from anything and from anyone. They had become my new home since reemerging from the fog.

If I were you I'd…why I'd be scared to death…

Claire's line, which my father had echoed, came back to try to haunt me that night, but I wasn't scared, I wasn't scared at all, I sailed right past their predilections of fright, as if I were on a great voyage, the captain of my own ship, sailing through the night on the bow of Gull Point…

And now, retrospectively speaking, as I stare into the memory of that little fire, it seems inevitable that Claire would carry her treasured Russians - *I can't live without them!* - to Okoboji in the spring, only to offer them for sale in the dead of winter at Clara's Clutter Closet. And that I in turn would buy them with the earnest money my father had given to me to buy the final supplies, and especially the drinking supplies, for our end-of-the-cottage-and-the-winter-dinner party, and tow them across the ice - not to the Dixon Beach cottage, where they would be safe and warm until we received our final notice to vacate, and where even now the music, loud music, so loud I thought I could hear it, was playing - but to Gull Point, under the frozen cottonwood of my conception, where I would arrange the volumes, as if I were a librarian, in order of their warmth.

Images seem to fade like the setting sun, but words inscribe themselves on the sympathetic mind…

Our teachers foolishly imagine that by simply dropping us off at some *spectacular vista* - such as the one that I found myself out on - we can easily find our way back home by the same old road…

Claire, for one, would have no use for my letter or postcard to the lake. I could hear her ask incredulously: *A letter to a lake? You've got to be kidding me!*

Nothing of this had been planned out in advance.

And yet, once I was there, and had settled in with my fire and my books and my letter/postcard composition, I was almost comfortable.

Because Gull Point in the winter has two advantages over Gull Point in the summer:

1. There are no biting horseflies, deerflies, sandflies, noseeums, ticks, mosquitoes, or any kind of bugs or spiders.
2. There are no boats pulled up on the beach, with their waist-high ropes and belchingbeer cans to step over, and unbearably loud and headache inciting noise to shut out.

I must tell Claire, when I see her again - and she was supposed to be at the party - I must tell her that she should consider spending some time on Gull Point in the winter. She could dig a hole in the sand, and lean back against a cottonwood, and give a new name to everything, in the light *or* in the dark. She should know that the conspiracy of boats and flies which kept her from working in the summer has all but evaporated in winter's fading light.

To think that I used to live only for the summer, simply so that I could dive below the surface and then burst back up out of the water, to see my grandmother telling stories on the beach, and my grandfather banging on the piano, and the elephants in the amusement park dancing to *Petrouchka*.

First locate the North Star, then you can always find your way home, my father said, handing me his compass from the Pacific Theatre, for the first and the last time.

Now I can see that we go through life pulling our collected works on a sled behind us. The sled becomes progressively heavier as we add to it, and the snow - at first dry, then wet - piles on top, and the drifts form in front of us and in back of us, and the wind, like it or not, is seldom at our back,usually in our face…but at least we can still feel it…

All this is more than obvious to anyone who has ever been marooned on the tip of Gull Point…in winter…

I have located it again: that light in the window of the cottage across the lake. The candle and the lamp illumine…

So…the table is set, and the place cards have been filled out in the form of riddles: you have only to solve one to see where you sit. My father has pried and wrenched his chair of reflection up to the head of the table. His back will be feeling the heat from the fireplace, where the last of the boards from the Roof Garden are hissing and crackling away in 4/4 time.

While the guests have been getting settled, my father's been playing and replaying his many and various recorded renditions of *Invitation.* By now, everyone that was invited has arrived, but they're still being formally *invited* and *reinvited* by this one particular ballad,

which they're hearing, in its various guises, over and over again. I know from experience exactly what they're being forced to endure.

But now they're all sitting in their places, and a few of them are even sitting on their hands, for warmth maybe. At the head of the table is The Fun House Clown. His hands are on the table. He's obviously been chewing his fingernails. But he is also listening. He listens closely, and he listens carefully. I imagine him to be the only one who is enjoying these seemingly endless reprises of the same song. I see MacJames acting very impatient. But the Clown is carried back to his glory days, when the crowds that gathered to watch him play were *second to none*. It's a little late for an encore, but my father keeps playing encores, and his love for this song does not embarrass me in the least.

Yes, the *farewell to winter and the cottage dinner* is finally about to begin…and I, for one, hadn't realized how hungry I was. Of course there'll be complaints about the boney bluegill, especially from MacJames, but in filleting them I believe I got rid of most of the bones, except for that big bone of *regret* that becomes permanently lodged in the craw. There will be disappointment over the collapse of the Yorkshire pudding, but you know folks, *there was nothing I could do about it*, given the temperamental nature of Yorkshire puddings…

I've got bone to pick with you! I could hear Claire saying to me from across the table.

Try some of my homemade bread first, I suggest, but she goes on to list my many quirks and traits that bother her: I'm an exaggerator *extraordinaire;* I'm losing my hair; I don't have a job; I talk to paintings; I can't play the piano; I sing worse than you-know-who, and I haven't paid her a *penny of interest* on the money I'd borrowed from her!

I knew I had a few faults, but when confronted by such a long list, I stare and take comfort once again in my plate's cracked designs. (Act Three, Scene IV)

The sound of a spoon tapping on a wine glass carries across the lake!

My father is signaling that the dinner is about to begin!

But first, in lieu of a prayer, he wants to say a few words before we eat.

I'm hungry, but like everyone else, I have to wait, only at a much greater distance than the others…

His remarks stretch on and on…

He begins with a history of the cottage…and then moves on to a chronicle of his Chris Craft runabout…and then to his time in the South Pacific…as we watch…all of us watch the steam rising from the platters of fried bluegill and baked potatoes and green beans and the shrunken sculptural Yorkshire pudding and the tureen of chowder…everything is gradually losing its heat and heading for room temperature…as my father continues on about coming home from the war with all his booty of tapestries and teapots, and then how he met my mother and they danced up at the Roof Garden and the bandleader – the one they called *Pops* - handed him the baton 'cause he was the best dancer so he got to lead the band for just one song and now he was going to play that song for all of us…after which…we could eat…

But first he had to *find* the song, which was out of its jacket and away from its sleeve…stacked on the floor somewhere…or leaning against the wall…it would just take a minute to find this record…and then we could all eat…

Hold on…be patient…patience is a virtue you know…patience…is a…that song has got to be…around here…somewhere…

Under the table, someone's toes intertwine with mine (which are so cold that they feel like they're about to break off) and together they become like the roots of a tree which is dying of thirst and going down deep in search of refreshment…

I think I know who these other toes belong to…

But I didn't want to know…

I didn't really *want to know,* because I was afraid of what it could lead to; I saw the situation being played out to its conclusion - her fate decided, mine up there in the air somewhere - and so I kept my eyes on my plate, and tried to crawl in between the cracks.

It was going to be a delicious dinner; you could tell from the stimulating smells which washed over us in wave after wave of delectable expectation.

We all sensed – with the possible exception of Claire and MacJames - that this dinner would be *one to remember.*

There's nothing that beats entertaining!

Although then you have the clean up…

For the first and last and only time, I summoned the strength, not to mention the courage, to look up and straight across the table and deep into the eyes of the person whose toes have joined with mine.

The fortune teller's assistant…minus her little dog…

So this was *her* version of things, *her* idea of life, *her* dream and *her* awakening…

Her puppet show of memory…*her* postcard, song, letter to a lake…

I can authenticate that being lost in the fog on the ice is nothing compared to what goes on inside the eyes of the fortune teller's assistant.

First I saw the Black Sea, which I had always wanted to see. And it didn't disappoint me - no, not a bit, it was everything that the sick doctor from Tanganrog had said it was in his *The Lady with the Dog* - especially the waves…they really were black…

But then I was surprised to see the Caspian Sea, and the Sea of Azov, and the Ural Sea, and the Saltan Sea, and the Chuckchi Sea too.

And the Mediterranean and the South China and the North Sea as well.

All these seas that I was finally seeing…replete with waves…frozen in the case of the Chuckchi…

And then, to my fascination and amusement, my delight and my pleasure, I saw my adored, my pet, my intimate, my favored…

My venerated, my revered, my treasured, my prized…

My constant, my companion, my friend, my lover…

I saw:

Okoboji

Epilogue

Well, that all came together rather nicely, don't you think?

I really do, although it was perhaps a shade willy nilly, with him out on the ice in the dark, walking toward the cottage, following the music…

And then the party…

Yes, and then the party!

A nice touch that, to end with a party.

And *what* a party it was, wasn't it?

I loved it, how all the guests appeared at once, entering the living room from the kitchen and the dining room and the front porch, as if on cue.

And leaving narry a trace of a footprint in the snow, not a one, did you take note? How did they pull that one off?

And the way they'd moved the dining room table into the living room and in front of the fire.

Yes, it was quite chilly in the wings where we were hanging, but I believe most of the guests were warm.

I observed that a few of the guests, the ones farthest away from the fire, like Nutty Buddy and what's her name…Sheri…left their coats on.

Did you notice Sheri's sweater?

I did. It was beautiful, wasn't it? A deep red wool sweater from one of those Scottish islands, I imagine.

And did you see how she read throughout much of the dinner?

One time I saw her, without ever lifting her eyes from her novel, reach for a piece of bluegill and put it in her mouth and pull out a bone and turn a page.

Magnificent! What was she reading that engrossed her so?

Something called *The Years.*

The Years? Interesting. She didn't say much, did she?

Hardly a word. But the person on her right, he had a lot to say, didn't he.

That was Pesky. He got wound up on the wine, didn't he? He and MacJames were arguing about something to do with *cyclones.* Is that a sports team or what? They lost me there. I don't follow sports.

And of course Nutty Buddy, going on and on about the weather.

He's certainly a weather expert, isn't he? But I liked the conversation between Jerry and Madame Jessie concerning the amusement park, its future, its past.

I was trying to listen in on that, but Carl's father, great an entertainer as he is, made it hard for me to follow that particular conversation because of the loudness that he insisted on playing that song he kept reprising over and over and over.

That was irritating, but at the same time I found it humorous, if not endearing - his attachment to that song, I mean.

Wasn't it funny, though, when the cat jumped up on the turntable, and his song screeched to a halt?

That was priceless! One of the highpoints!

The Fun House Clown...do you think he had a good time?

Wasn't he distinguished looking? He lent an air of formality to the entire proceedings, don't you think?

I do. He shed his pokka dots for the occasion, didn't he? I loved his cape and his hobnail boots and his granny glasses, and especially his wide brimmed black Stetson. He was eye catching, and at the same time thought provoking, how he always tried to steer the conversation back to music. I don't know how many times I heard him shout that same identical question across the table to someone: *And who's your favorite piano player?* And every time, after they answered - if they answered - he would always say: *Well, mine is Glenn of course. I mean, who else but Glenn?*

That was fascinating. He and Carl's father were head to head at one point. They both appeared to be actually enjoying themselves.

And then the recurring ongoing refrain of *Where's Carl? Where's Carl?*

Remember when they went around the table, everyone giving their answer to: *Where's Carl?*

What were some of those?

Oh, let's see…Pesky said he was probably in the Blue Note, and Sheri thought he might have fallen asleep in Clara's Clutter Closet.

That's right. And Nutty Buddy said he was probably up in the clouds - I believe he was speaking figuratively - and Jerry thought he might be out on Pillsbury, and Claire…Claire didn't care where he was, did she?

No, she seemed bored by the whole thing, and in kind of a bad mood too. After a while she went over and laid down on the couch.

That's right. Madame Jessie was the only one who seemed certain of where Carl was.

Yup. When it was her turn, she didn't hesitate. She said: *He's out there!* And then she pointed dramatically toward the lake. Her arm was covered with bracelets, and they made the most beautiful jingling sound when she pointed.

That was a moving moment, wasn't it?

A climatic moment, a Chekhovian moment, if you will, until Carl himself burst in through the front porch door with his dog.

His dog! I'd forgotten all about his dog. What was its name?

Ginsberg.

Of course. Ginsberg! Because he loves to howl his head off.

Yes, and everyone shouted, *Where've you been, Carl? Where've you been, Ginsberg?*

They looked frozen, didn't they?

Boy, you can say that again. They were *cold.* I didn't think that either one of them would ever thaw out!

But then they seemed to warm up quickly, after they'd sat in front of the fire for a while.

And after Carl had dipped a few fried bluegill in that awful looking sauce.

Yes, he rebounded quickly, and then he made a big show, didn't he, of presenting all those books of Claire's back to her.

Oh, that was touching, wasn't it? She was resting on the couch, very pregnant, her eyes closed, and Carl stacks her books on the bamboo table in front of her, and she wakes up and sees them all there and starts to cry.

She *loves* her books!

What a great mother she's going to make, reading to her child every night at bedtime, reading in that sing-song voice of hers, *A Child's Garden Of Verses* and *Songs Of Innocence And Experience* and *Alice In Wonderland* and *Huckleberry Finn* and…

Wait a minute! You think she should read an innocent child a story like *Huckleberry Finn?*

Oh sure…because, I mean, it's a book about freedom, and floating down the river, and…

That's what I mean. What if the child takes that book to heart, and one day takes off floating down the river?

Like all the way to *New Orleans?*

All the way, baby. *All the way!* When do we leave? This endless wintertime is getting' to me! I can smell the magnolia! I can smell the chicory coffee! I can smell the beignets with the powdered sugar on top! I can smell the crawfish Etouffée and the gumbo and the shrimp creole and the…

Hold on, hold on. Not so fast. We've got to wrap things up at Okoboji first.

Why'd you have to mention New Orleans? You know how I get when I even hear the name *New Orleans*. It does something to me. I just…

Don't worry, don't worry. We'll be back on the *Panama Limited* and heading for you-know-where before you know it. But 'in the meantime', did you notice that no developers were invited?

No developers, and no real estate agents either.

I believe the idea was to keep the unimaginative ones away. Far away!

Not a bad idea really…but what about that wad of earnest money that Carl disposed of at Clara's Clutter Closet?

Well…Carl and his father will just have to work that one out when the dust clears…

It was a fun party though, wasn't it? It just kept rolling along…

Wasn't it interesting that the high school history teacher and the janitor showed up.

Yes, and they really seemed to enjoy themselves, and the bluegill.

I suppose bluegill will be all the rage now.

And remember that character - what did they call him - Gusty?

Yeah, Lusty Gusty. He tried to swing the talk in a political direction, didn't he, by opening that big book he brought along, *The Story Of America*, and going around the table asking everyone what the American dream means to them.

Jerry's answer was good. *It means step on your brother for the buck!* he said.

Pesky Pete had a good one too: *We're all gonna die waiting to get rich!*

And Sheri weighed in, poetically as usual: *Outside these windows and on our TVs and in our minds and on our laps the story of America continues and will continue to unfold, with its endless accounts of who got the head start and the big jump and mowed down everyone in their path to finish first, with the dates forever fixed on some tablet outside some courthouse, lest we all blissfully lose track, and forget.*

And then that cat that had already jumped on the record player once had to jump on it *again*. And then it yawned and closed its eyes. Remember?

That would have been a perfect end to the party right there.

It would have. And everyone looked tired too. That miniature of Napoleon in the center of the table - his head was under Marengo. A beautiful last shot if there ever was one. Zoom in and fade out. And then the credits over *Invitation*...

But Carl had to drag things out by saying: There's one thing that's always bothered me. What exactly does the word *Okoboji* mean?

That opened a whole new can of worms, didn't it?

Yeah, everyone had to put in their two cents worth on that one. The history teacher, the janitor, Carl's father...

The history teacher said *bullrushes!*

And the janitor said *broomsticks!*

And Carl's father said that to him it means: *Do you see her anywhere out there?*

And then Carl had to say: *To me it means that I'm moving to Duluth.*

Duluth! Of all the places in the world to move to!

We're going the opposite way, aren't we, puppet pal of mine?

We sure are! I'm going to miss this old cottage, its low beam ceilings and the view of the lake, but it's high time we got back to the Crescent City.

Yeah, we've been up north a long ol' time.

Too long, way too long! What do they always say? You can take the puppet out of the South...

But you can't take the South out of the puppet!

It's a little sad to end this on a cliche but...

We're done up north!

We've finished our job!

I can hear the conductor shouting *All aboard!*

How are we going to get to Chicago to catch the *Chicken Bone* for the Crescent City?

I don't know. We'll think of something...catch a bus maybe...or hitchhike!

I am not hitchhiking! It's too cold up here to hitchhike! Too cold, in every sense of the word *cold.*

But still, the winter has its charm, doesn't it. The stillness…the silence…

Yeah…if you say so…I might miss it…but not for long!

Well then, what are we waiting for?

Are you ready?

Sure am!

Then let's go!

Wait!

What is it now? I had one foot out the door!

I've got…one more question…

Only one?

Just one. But it's a big one.

Hit me with it!

What was *this* about?

What was *what* about?

This whole 'puppet show of memory' and 'postcards, songs, and letters to a lake' thing that we've just gone through. Because I'm thinking that once I'm back in New Orleans, see, and I'm going down Canal, say, and maybe at the corner of Canal and Royal, or Canal and Decatur, I bump into somebody like Charles Neville…

Charles Neville! Of the Neville Brothers? You know him?

Oh, I've seen him play many times. But I still can't say that I actually *know* him. I'm just saying that maybe I bump into him or somebody like him…

Somebody *like* him?

A man of the world, you know. A man of intelligence. A man with charm. A man like Carl's father, as much at home in Barcelona or Istanbul as he is in Minneapolis or New Orleans. A man at home with himself in the world, no matter where he is. A man who's always ready to duck if he has to. A man who always has a book in his hand. You can see somebody like that coming from a mile away, unless they're hidden by a hill or a building. They walk with a particular gait. They notice things as they stroll along. They don't miss a thing, really, because they're alive to the situation which surrounds them, unless, god forbid, they should happen to have a hangover.

I've forgotten where we're going with this. I had one foot *out* the door, but my other foot seems to have gotten stuck *in* the door.

So I run into this man, who I know vaguely from the old days, and he asks me what I've been doing, 'cause he hasn't seen me around for a while, and I'm trying to tell him about the *puppet show* and all the *postcards*, but it's hot on the pavement, and I've only got a few minutes before *he* continues on his way and *me* on mine, so, what do I tell him, what do I say, what was all this about?

Well…that's not hard…in fact, that's pretty easy…just tell him…just tell him that it was about…about how life once was…around this magical lake scooped out by the Wisconsin Glacier…maybe you should say *enchanting* instead of magical…you could say mystic lake, but not mystic in an occult sense.

(They hurry around the room gathering books in their arms: *White Men Follow After, Okoboji: Puppet Show of Memory, Snow of Despair, The Sailor from Gibraltar, Flowers of Evil*)

Anyway, depending on how much time you have, tell him about the pointed rock and the canoe at the bottom of the lake. And tell him about Abbie and Inkpaduta. And the Roof Garden and Fisherman's Wharf. You better mention Carl's grandparents. You better say something about Claire and all her books. And the music! Maybe if you don't have much time, you should just say that it's about the music. Tell him that the author was *like a piano player in that he knew how to build a line.* That should interest him, especially if it's someone like Charles Neville.

So…it's about how to build a line…and about how life once was…at one time?

And about how it may be again…very soon.

How soon?

Sooner than you think…

They go dangling off

SWAN SONG

Was it because
At Okoboji
There was always
Light and darkness
Shallows and depth
Music and silence
Moon and sun
Love and absence of love
Trees thick with leaves
And trees bare of leaves
Beautiful rippling sparkling waves
And waves stiff
Frozen
Sculpted

INDEX

A

B

C

D

E

F

H

I

J

K

L

M

N

O

P

Q

R

S

T

U

V

W

X

Y

Z

The good doctor from Taganrog.

APPRECIATIONS

Sally Parks, the author's mother, who answered the question: "How would you like to live at Okoboji all year round?" by sticking it through fifty and counting winters on Des Moines Beach, Dixon Beach, and Echo Bay, maintaining homes to which the author returned to constantly for inspiration.

Ryan Lamb, the author's wife, who once said: "I just know that I'm going to have to raise them all (Alonso, Sebastien, Dominic) by myself!" before going off to work to support the family so that the author, being out of a job, could sit and write.

Mike Koppert of Arnolds Park, a close and dear friend, whose artistic talent and sensibility in many mediums grace the cover and many of the pages of this novel.

Helen Roth, the one and only, also of Arnolds Park, who provided, among many other things, comfortable accommodations in the form her fabled "woo-woo" cabins.

Ron Robinson, who wrote so eloquently in regard to the author's first book, and adapted sections of *Okoboji: Puppet Show of Memory* in to a 'play of voices', a few of which he and his wife Margaret (Madame Jessie) made their own.

Pine Hill Press, including owner Joe Mierau, printer Gerald Watson, folder and binder Sheldon Davis, and especially Jennifer Walker, whose diligent attention to text and picture contributed greatly to the look of this book.

ABOUT THE AUTHOR

C.E. Holmes grew up in Okoboji, Iowa, and attended universities in New Mexico, Iowa and Minnesota. He has published one previous novel – *Okoboji: Puppet Show of Memory*. His play, *Like a River in Spring*, was performed in Sioux Falls, South Dakota in 2006. His plays, *On de Battlefront* and *The Tear*, were included in short play labs of the Great Plains Theatre Conference in 2007 and 2008. His stories, essays and poems have appeared in the *Vermillion Literary Project*, the *Tempest*, the *Sioux Falls Argus Leader* and the *Aberdeen American*. His story, *Toward the Blue Peninsula*, won "best story" award in the Vermillion literary Project's writing contest in 2007.

C.E. Holmes and his wife and their sons divide their time between an old house on the Big Sioux River in Dell Rapids, South Dakota, and a tent with a broken zipper on the shore of Lake Superior.

Holmes addresses a diminutive audience in Winona, Minnesota, circa 1989. The subject was Robert Musil.